AF098775

RONALD, THE RONIN

A SERVANT'S CREED
BOOK I

CURTIS A. DEETER

Ronald, the Ronin
©2026 Curtis A. Deeter

Curtis A. Deeter asserts the moral rights to be identified as the author of this book.

This book is protected under the copyright laws of the United States of America. No part of this publication may be reproduced, stored in a retrieval system, or transmitted in any form or by any means, without the prior permission in writing of the publisher. Nor may it be otherwise circulated in any form of binding or cover other than that in which it is published and without a similar condition including this condition being imposed on the subsequent purchaser. Any reproduction or unauthorized use of the material or artwork contained herein is prohibited without the express written permission of the author and publisher.

The scanning, uploading, and distribution of this book without permission is a theft of the author's intellectual property. If you would like to use material from the book (other than for review purposes), please contact queries@riverfolkbooks.com for assistance.

Print and eBook formatting by Emily McCosh. Artwork by Emily McCosh.
First published in 2026 by Riverfolk Books.

Riverfolk Books
riverfolkbooks.com

This novel is a work of fiction. The names, characters and incidents portrayed in it are the work of the author's imagination. Any resemblance to actual events, locations, or persons, living or dead is purely coincidental.

For my stunning wife, Danielle, and her frequent reminders that she's (im)patiently waiting—thank you very much—for my writing career to take off so she can retire early. Here's to this next step towards our dream, Babe.

CONTENTS

Prologue: Before 1
Chapter One 11
Chapter Two 29
Chapter Three 34
Chapter Four 45
Chapter Five 56
Interlude One: Before 67
Chapter Six 70
Chapter Seven 78
Chapter Eight 89
Chapter Nine 98
Interlude Two: Before 109
Chapter Ten 114
Chapter Eleven 128
Chapter Twelve 138
Chapter Thirteen 147
Interlude Three: Before 158
Chapter Fourteen 164

Chapter Fifteen	170
Chapter Sixteen	182
Chapter Seventeen	199
Chapter Eighteen	206
Interlude Four: Before	215
Chapter Nineteen	220
Chapter Twenty	227
Chapter Twenty-One	234
Chapter Twenty-Two	246
Chapter Twenty-Three	256
Interlude Five: Before	264
Chapter Twenty-Four	270
Chapter Twenty-Five	277
Chapter Twenty-Six	285
Chapter Twenty-Seven	292
Chapter Twenty-Eight	302
Chapter Twenty-Nine	310
Epilogue: After	323
About Curtis	327
Acknowledgments	329

PROLOGUE: BEFORE

Flames rose from the hillside like cherry blossoms erupting in spring. Smoke plumed, choking the emerald forest in puddles of rolling black. Akuma Araki breathed deep, her lungs raspy and strained. She could not understand why she was choking just like the trees. All she understood was the smoke and the heat and the violence.

She had never been so afraid in her life. Before today, fear wasn't an emotion she had ever contended with. Hunger. Loneliness. Wonder. Never fear—not like this.

When *they* came, whoever *they* were, life as she knew it came crashing down. One moment, she was comfortably asleep, dreaming of fox whiskers and steaming gyoza, clutching the bamboo doll her obachan had made to her chest. The next, Father was shaking her awake, and fire was spreading throughout the village, engulfing everything within its reach. The flames were so hot she could feel them on her cheeks and nose. He jostled her from the safety and warmth of her bedroll into the front room, sweat and ash already stinging her bleary eyes.

Father ignored her questions, offered no explanations. He squeezed her tight, ordered Mother to gather only what was important, and yelled when she hesitated at the threshold of the life they'd built together.

"There is no time." He grabbed her by the arm. "You must do as I say."

Tears streamed down Mother's cheeks, drawing squiggly lines in the soot caked below her bloodshot eyes. She tried to yank herself free from Father's grasp, who despite his roughness seemed to only want to keep her safe, keep his whole family safe.

"My jewelry box—"

Just then, the beam supporting their house cracked and crashed to the floor, reduced to no more than splinters. Dust and smoke filled the air. Fire spread in all directions, and Mother slipped from Father's grip. She tumbled to the floor, crying out in pain. Had she not fallen, Akuma was sure Father might have struck her.

She knew Father as a man of little emotion, a patient and quiet man. Akuma had only seen him lose his temper once before, after a threshing incident that had taken one of her brothers' arms at the elbow. Benjiro and Itsuki thought a fake duel like the samurai of legend would be a clever way to pass time. It ended in blood, and Father beat Benjiro black and blue as the village ichiko tended to Itsuki's wound.

With Akuma still clinging to him, Father helped Mother to her feet, an unfamiliar wetness glinting in his eyes. "Ren," he barked. "And nothing else."

Ren! How could Akuma have forgotten her sweet, baby sister, left all alone crying behind the cherry blossom shoji at the back of their hut? By the way her mother's eyes widened and her mouth dropped, Mother had forgotten, too. It was a look Akuma would remember forever. One of horror, of vulnerability. One last glimpse at Mother's tear-dropped cheeks before Father wrenched her outside into Hell to face the gold devils who had come with fire and steel to burn everything in her world to ash, and she never saw her mother or sister again. Had she known, she would have grabbed them, held them tight, told them one last time how much they meant to her.

And where had Benjiro and Itsuki gone? Fighting, surely. A farmer's boys, skilled with hoe and sickle, giving their lives to protect the village. A waste, like the rest of the village's forfeited lives.

Now that Akuma was alone with the cold, choking on the dark, billowing smoke that was the simmering remains of everything she had ever known, these questions and more raced through her mind. For the first time that night, she cried for her family, for her village, for all those who died so needlessly, so suddenly. So violently.

Rain trickled from the branches above, dripping cold on her exposed neck and shoulders. Besides the added chill, she hardly noticed the wet tickle down her back. What was a little rain when she was already covered in blood and soot and sweat?

There is nothing left. No one.

Mother. Father. Ren. Benjiro and Itsuki. They were all dead.

Keiji and Rose down the hill, their family's terraced rice paddies stomped into an unrecognizable mash of mud and broken stalks, the once clear water stained rust-red. Everyone Akuma had ever known... Dead.

Why? She could not make sense of it. What had her people

done to those devils? They did not deserve to die; they never hurt anyone.

Akuma had witnessed Father's death, as she had been clinging to his shoulders, and even in her innocence, she knew the horrific image would be burned into her mind forever.

His eyes bulged, the steel tip of a katana bursting from the back of his head. Then, he tripped, dropping her onto the dirt, knocking the wind from her chest. There was yelling all around. Villagers or devils, people begging for their lives. Boots trampled suffocating dust around her. One slammed into her ribs. Another stomped her thigh. Before she could reach out for him, Father was lost in a storm of dust and noise and chaos.

She had experienced blood before, of course. On scraped knees. From the chickens when she helped her mother prepare festival feasts. When her brother lost his arm. She shuddered. The image of Itsuki's wound flashed in her mind until she was sick on a pile of rotten leaves.

Tears continued to stream. Rain continued to pour. Memories continued to ache like fresh wounds, festering as she rocked back and forth for what little comfort the motion offered.

They are all dead, she reminded herself. But why was she alive? How had she alone survived the attack and made it out of the village? Such a small, insignificant girl... What plans did Fate have in store for Akuma Araki?

A stick cracked in the forest. Akuma shrieked and scrambled away on all fours. She rolled over a log, pressing her back against it and trying to make herself as small as possible, will herself far, far away from this horrible place. Would death hurt? Or would it be fast and painless like with the chickens? Just *snap*. Done. No more pain. No more struggle. No more anything.

A millipede crawled out from the log, slithered between her shoulders. She could feel its tiny claws on her chest as it wound its way across her body. She stifled a squeal and clenched her muscles to remain still despite the nasty creature and its prodding antennae.

When the purple devil stepped out of the forest, a bow slung over its shoulder and a long sword fastened to its waist, she screamed and crawled away backwards on all fours. She begged the devil not to hurt her, to leave her alone, but the devil continued its approach as if it could not hear her. Or did not care even if it could. Like one of her nightmares, no matter how fast she tried to escape, the devil seemed to draw closer and closer, its fang-masked face twisting into a scarier and scarier grimace.

Then, the devil stopped and brought its hands to the back of its head to remove its face. She screamed again in anticipation of the horrors trapped within. Instead of blood and bone or something equally grotesque, the devil revealed a soft face of dark skin, an almost kind smile of fangless teeth, and sunken, tired eyes.

"It's okay," the devil said, its voice like sweet rice syrup. "I'm not going to hurt you."

"Leave me alone!" Akuma answered, throwing a fistful of mud and twigs.

"I won't hurt you," the devil repeated. "I didn't know what they were going to do. I came with them, but I didn't... I couldn't stand the things they were doing. I'm... I'm so sorry." The devil knelt beside Akuma, placed an armored hand on her shoulder. "My name's Che. Are you hurt?"

Akuma sniffled and shook her head. Her insides hurt: Her heart, her mind. But physically, besides the biting cold and her bruised thigh, she was unharmed.

"Why?" she mustered, wiping her face on her sleeve.

The purple devil named Che cast her eyes to her feet. "We came because of a prophecy."

"A... what?"

"Behold, a child born of Struggle and Strife," the devil recited as lightning crackled behind her. "Beware, a child born of Shima Gōdatsusha, tempered by the fires of Her trials. Sower of Chaos where there was once Order. Uprooter of the ancient Bonsai, awash in golden waves of destruction, reborn anew under a crimson dawn."

Akuma drew her eyebrows together. Why should she care about some stupid prophecy, anyway?

"Here." The devil handed her a bundle wrapped in dried maple leaves. She peeled back a corner to reveal seaweed rolls and rice balls. "I have a child around your age." The devil's features softened, and she placed a gentle palm on her armor near where reed met iron at the waist. "And another on the way."

Akuma felt a deep sadness from the devil, an almost human emotion filled with equal parts regret and dread. She almost pitied this horrid creature named Che and her spawn. *Almost.* But devils could not feel, and she could not afford to feel anything for them. Devils were devils, and that was all they would ever be.

Then, the devil made a noise like heavy breathing and looked out over Akuma's burning village. "There's nothing left down there. But you're not alone. There are other clans that might take you in. People like you, who survived. They're hiding, but if you look hard enough, you might just find them.

"I... I tried to stop this. Really, I did." Was that a tear? Could devils cry? "I'm so, so sorry. I wasn't strong enough..."

There came a distant shriek, like an eagle's cry but louder. Akuma covered her ears and whimpered. The devil put her face back on in a hurry.

"I must go. Survive, child. Never forget what happened here." The devil rested her hand on Akuma's dirty cheek. "As I will never forget about you."

The devil dipped back into the forest, disappearing among the trees. That was when Akuma first saw it, a monster worse than her worst nightmares:

Slim, golden, majestic as it wound its way through the clouds, a plume of gray spikes set upon its head like a crown of iron. She had never seen a dragon before, but everyone had heard the stories. Great beasts of scale and fang. This one shimmered in the sun's returning light, rainwater glistening on its scales. After a series of graceful dives and twirls, it too disappeared over the edge of the horizon, leaving her alone with the mud and the fresh memories and the tears that continued to slide down her cheeks.

She waited three dawns, hiding in the hollow of a fallen tree trunk and eating the devil's food sparingly. When she could no longer see smoke besides in scant tongues and the only sounds were the breeze and the eagles, she stepped carefully from the hillside, towards the village. All the while, she surveyed the horizon. Would the golden dragon return to finish what it started? Was it just now watching from the clouds?

The dozen or so huts of her childhood were little more than ash. Soot covered every inch of the village until nothing was recognizable. She could not even tell which rubble pile had once been her home or which formless heaps might have once been her family and friends.

She found her father's corpse, picked at by crows and stinking worse than anything she had smelled before. Like the village elders when the sickness struck, she gathered sticks from around the village to build a rudimentary pyre around him. She unburied some flint from ash and lit the sticks, but she did not watch as her father's body forever burned away from their island.

The devil had told her there were other people like her. Clans, it had called them. It made sense. Theirs was a big island, but Akuma had never heard of any Others. Could it be true? Was there actually a chance that she was not alone? Could she hope to find them? She had no idea where to start. She had never traveled more than half a day's walk from the village, and even that had been through thick, ever-twilight forest.

First, she walked the span of a white sandy beach abutting the diamond-studded ocean. Besides crabs and gulls, she found no sign of Others. When the sun dropped low in the sky, she gathered driftwood and built a fire that offered little warmth. Still, she was able to cook a crab and listened with her mind closed to the gentle lapping of water just out of sight until it lulled her into a blissful, almost peaceful stupor.

Next, she scoured the forest. She climbed high trees, whistled, and listened for no answer. She trekked on long after darkness fell. Through the treetops, moonlight was little different than sunlight. She saw with hope rather than sight, and if she could not find these Others soon, she was afraid she would die alone and become one with the trees. Though she could imagine a worse fate than a lonely death, she was not ready to give up.

Finally, she came to the base of a great mountain. There, she rested for two days, finishing off the last of her food. She climbed and climbed and climbed. At the snowy top, it was colder than expected and her ragged clothes did little to protect her from the persistent sideways wind. It blew in gusts so strong she could barely see her frost reddened fingers in front of her face through the white fog of snow and ice.

So, she accepted that she would die, hungry and cold. She supposed she should not be surprised that a devil had lied to her. Devils could not be trusted. They fed on souls and played wicked games with the living.

But she was not destined to die on the mountain. Mid-way down the opposite slope, she saw faint wisps of smoke venting from within the mountain itself. Cooking smoke, not the suffocating black that had almost overwhelmed her on the hillside. That meant people, that she had not been lied to, and that she was not alone after all.

By dusk, Akuma stumbled into this new village, which was two or three times the size of her own, stretched across a series of caverns that cut deep into the mountain. A tall man with long, windswept hair dropped his pick and ran to catch her as she fell into his arms. He called out to others for help, but he spoke a harsh, unfamiliar dialect. Everything was hazy, far away. They were like ghosts, carrying her into the afterlife. She was taken deeper inside, stripped of her tatters and redressed, piled high with blankets and fed hot soup. She was so grateful for their mere presence, she allowed herself to forget the horrors she endured a few short days ago.

When the villagers finally left her, she slept. For the first time in uncountable days, she did not dream about the night the dragon came or of the devils. In fact, Akuma Araki hardly dreamed at all.

RONALD, THE RONIN

She slept knowing she would survive.

She slept, and she remembered. When the dreams came, she dreamed of one thing and one thing only:

Revenge.

CHAPTER ONE

The basement was a hazy blue-gray, and the two samurai looked like ghosts as they approached their family shrine. In their matching black and purple do and as-of-yet unadorned kabuto, the warriors were nearly indistinguishable from one another. One stood several inches higher and walked with the gait of experience, but their path to Hachiman, Shinto God of War and their family's chosen patron deity, was coldly coordinated, flawlessly executed, as if they were one body and mind. It was all part of the ritual, taught to them over long years of training through blood, sweat, and failure, all leading to this very moment.

After today, they would no longer be among the uninitiated. After today, they would become true samurai, and a world of Order secrets would be opened unto them.

If they succeeded, at least. If they failed, shame and death could be the only outcomes.

An old man with a thin mustache and pointy beard watched

from the bottom of the stairs, arms folded across his chest, sallow eyes squinted. He was wearing simple robes and sandals, but tight muscles and thick scars visible from beneath the loose fabric showed him to be no stranger to the warrior's path. He had been here before, taking these same first steps, and come out triumphant. He expected the same from his sons. No less than perfection would satisfy the elder samurai.

The two younger samurai-in-training, Jiro and Ronald Hashimoto by age, stopped before the shrine, bowed their heads in reverence to Hachiman, and kneeled, hands on their knees. A warm draft wafted through the basement, kicking up dust and old memories, scattering the cherry blossom leaves sprinkled across the floor in a swirl of pink and white. The old man stifled a cough, but his sons remained statue-still, their dual swords—one long, one short—resting upon their laps as they listened for the whispers of their ancestors to guide their path.

The older boy leaned forwards, raised to half-height, and plucked an ornamented tanto from Hachiman's outstretched hands. It was an unwieldy, overly showy artifact, not suited for any other purpose than ceremony. The samurai slipped their hands free and took turns drawing the blade across their palms. Blood trickled onto the floor, mixing with dirt, spreading to the base of the shrine, encircling it in a rusty, crimson ring. It flowed like rainwater in a stream, drawing an intricate, circular pattern in the dirt: their family crest.

The samurai replaced the dagger, and Hachiman accepted its return with silent gratitude before the entire shrine began to fold in on itself. All around them, floorboards peeled apart. A deep rumbling pulsed through the house's foundation, and a stairway swiveled open beneath the shrine, a waft of stale, musty air filling the room. A torrent of suffocating air swirled through the basement, and they bowed to Hachiman once more before descending into the dark opening.

The shorter boy hesitated, risked a single glance back at the old samurai impatiently watching, and took a deep breath. The other turned, rested a reassuring hand on his shoulder, and they both disappeared beneath the shrine.

The old man watched intently, showing no emotion on his stoic face. This was the way of things. This was their destiny, and he had long since done his part to ensure their success. It was up to them now. His sons were bound for greatness, if only they were willing to accept their fate.

The floorboards slid back into place. The shrine rematerialized one plank at a time, and Hachiman stood as staunch and silent as ever. One last pink swirl of leaves blew past before the basement fell into utter stillness once more.

The haze cleared and light burst forth from the shrine. A school of translucent, glowing carp appeared from Hachiman's chest, swimming lazy laps around the basement. They bounced from workbench to storage shelf, wriggled beneath the furnace and around a stack of dusty, rotted boxes, casting shimmering reflections upon the wall along their path. Another flash of light and a dragon unwound its slender, scaly, luminescent body and let out a roar of bright light. A vixen stepped forth next, followed by a trail of wide-eyed, bushy tailed kits. The ethereal beasts swam and swooped and frolicked, filling the basement with the radiant warmth of their magic.

Then, when they had their fill of their games, and it was

time for them to head back home, they returned to Hachiman, disappearing back to wherever they had come from, sucked through the eyes of their Master. The blue glow in Hachiman's eyes was a sure sign the two samurai had made it through to the other side of the Out Beyond, to Shima Gōdatsusha, the Island of Usurpers. What happened next, however, depended entirely on their ability to utilize everything he had taught them over their hard years of study and training.

Stars and night: a whole galaxy of possibilities, stretched across a place in between islands. A place called Out Beyond where time moved too fast to truly appreciate the spectacle. At its heart, one star shined the brightest. A beacon. A dread—a place wholly detached from the samurai's own island of existence but impossibly interwoven with its fate:

Shima Gōdatsusha. the Island of Usurpers.

Ronald blinked away the brightness seared into his vision from that star. Vertigo threatened, and his reality ebbed around him. He felt almost as if he were a newborn again, breaking from an egg, and dripping through the cracks between his world and the other.

Then, as the swift soaring through the clouds, he saw Shima Gōdatsusha in all its verdant splendor, and it stole his breath from his lungs.

From such a great height, the island was a crescent moon swallowing the emerald disk of the sun. It was surrounded as far as the eagle's eyes could see with peaceful, crystal-clear waves that flowed from high tide to low through its epicenter: a smoldering volcano that reached for the stars. Ho-Musubi made rock and ash. Sharp, jagged, alive with roiling fire and black ash.

Ronald dove, as the swift breaking for a swarm of insects, and Shima Gōdatsusha's inner workings became clearer. Its emerald forests; its spine of white-capped mountains; its smatterings of cherry trees, falls of blue water and white spray, and plains of wheat and rice.

It was resplendent, an endless and otherworldly bountiful place unlike any he could have ever imagined. It was a natural wonder keeping Earth—as it had become to be known by the short-lived denizens of the mortal island—on the brink of utter and unrelenting destruction.

Closer still, Ronald could see himself, crouched side-by-side with his brother, Jiro. They were clad in full samurai armor and hiding precariously behind a fallen black pine. Behind, the forest's thickness choked the sun, its ancient shadows stretching down the hillside like grasping fingers. In front, gray smoke curled from hundreds of campfires, banners fluttered in the cool breeze, and the forest wept where it had succumbed to axe and saw. Compared to the rest of the island, the crescent's northernmost tip was reduced to a desolate waste where hordes of soldiers—human and otherwise—leeched what little life remained.

Ronald collided with his body, and his breath was sucked from his lungs and spilled upon the dirt and rocks. He sucked in deeply, and all within sight was pulled towards him for an instant before snapping back into place like a rubber band released from tension.

"Have you ever seen such destruction?"

"Huh?"

The words sounded distant, booming. Ronald blinked away his

blurred vision and met his brother's eyes.

"Have you ever seen such destruction?" Jiro repeated.

Unable to find a worthy response, Ronald shook his head and tightened his grip around his longsword. He couldn't understand how his brother was so composed after embarking on such a jarring transition between islands. It was both their first times, and it had nearly stripped Ronald of his sanity. Yet there Jiro was, poised and stoic as always, his eyes on the horizon.

"Easy, brother." Jiro placed a reassuring hand on Ronald's shoulder. "We are here as scouts only. There will come a time when we bring Akuma Araki to justice, and I plan to be there with you by my side for her execution, but today we seek information. Tomorrow, retribution."

Far to the east, Shima Gōdatsusha's crimson sun began its final rotation beyond the horizon. A pale, pink light spread across the sprawling camp. As the sun crested, light gray fell over the world. Then, blackness, save the twinkle of a million, billion distant stars. A reflection of the Out Beyond, projected on the sky as far as the eye could see.

"It seems Tsukuyomi has abandoned this place," Ronald observed, gazing up into the moonless night sky. He nodded towards the empty place where the moon should have been.

Jiro grunted in agreement. "He is repulsed by Akuma Araki's transgressions." Then, he indicated to the mass of war tents stretched out before them. "It's time. Follow close and stay alert. Her warriors have had their fill of sake and more tonight, but we must remain vigilant. We cannot allow them knowledge of our presence. There's more at stake on this mission than our official induction into the Order."

"I understand."

"Good. Akuma Araki stands among her soldiers on feast nights. Her tent should be empty. Do you remember your role?"

Ronald nodded. "Stand watch while you look for anything useful. Ledgers, maps, troop counts, official decrees."

"Aye. Anything with Akuma's seal to provide the Order insight into her plans." Jiro extended his arm and Ronald grabbed his wrist. "May the wind be at your back."

"And your sword at your front," Ronald said, reciting the second part of one of the Order's customary battle mantras.

Their initiation rite was simple: infiltrate Akuma Araki's war camp, acquire proof of her plans to traverse between islands and invade Earth, and escape without being seen. If they could accomplish those three things, they would be official members of their father's lifelong clan, the Order of the Golden Bonsai, a mysterious and secretive group of samurai sworn to protect humanity from the countless dangers found on other islands.

They moved like shadows through the camp, stepping carefully and silently around sleeping bodies, staying away from dying embers despite the night's bitter cold nagging at their bones. Jiro navigated the haphazard, labyrinthine camp as if he'd been there before, and Ronald struggled to keep pace with his brother.

Jiro raised his fist and came to an abrupt stop. They slipped into cover behind a tent. Two guards, tall men with wobbling gates and nasty body odors, staggered past. They were talking among themselves about women and conquest as if they were far across the camp from one another. Jiro stared into Ronald's eyes, fist still raised, never blinking once. He stood like a statue until the drunken guards were beyond earshot. With a subtle nod, they headed deeper in the camp towards their target: Akuma Araki's generals' circle.

They came to her tent. It was four times the size of the others, reinforced with sturdy rods of reed and adorned with decorative symbols representing the various armies and races pledged to her cause. A makeshift path lined with torches and flags led from a clearing to her tent's entrance flap. Without a word, Jiro ducked inside. Ronald hid in a darkened corner where he could safely watch for approaching enemies.

The night was so quiet Ronald could hear crickets chirping, the gentle breeze rustling fabric, and countless logs crackling in countless fires. The camp's song lulled him into a false sense of security, and his mind drifted to better places, warmer places.

He saw the warrior's dancing shadow first, stretching and reaching towards Ronald as he appeared from the opposite side of the tent.

Ronald, as the swift warning of the kestrel's approach, whistled into the night, but his warning came too little, too late as the barrel-chested, unarmored man twice Ronald's size turned the corner, nearly crashing into him.

"Huh?" Drunk and stupid, the man froze with a perplexed look on his face. He managed to recover his senses just as Ronald buried his short sword into his gut. "What the—"

The man gurgled a wet plea as he grabbed the handle of Ronald's wakizashi, but he had no strength left to push against it as it slipped deeper into his body.

"I'm so sorry..." Ronald whispered, hands trembling. "I... I..."

Their eyes locked, the man's bloodshot and bulging. His was the first life Ronald had taken, and even in that briefest of moments, Ronald realized the imprint of his dying, slack face would forever be ingrained in his memory. A scar ran the length of the man's chin. His blue, beady eyes were lost in a spider web of veins. His nose, with its slight bend to the left, flared and ran red with blood.

A horn sounded nearby, drowning out the dying man's final desperate words, and Ronald cringed as his limp body slid to the dirt. All around Akuma's circle, men and women were grumbling and rising groggily from their sleep. Another horn sounded, further off. Then another and another. In a short time, the entire camp was alerted to the intruders' presence.

Ronald called out to Jiro again as he wiped his sword clean on the grass. "Psst," he hissed, "it's time to go."

There was rustling inside the tent, and Jiro poked through its flaps, a bundle of scrolls fastened to his belt opposite his swords.

"What did you do?" He noticed the body and clicked his teeth. "Oh… I see."

"The whole camp's waking up. We have to go. Now!"

Jiro slid his long sword smoothly from its sheath and gripped it firmly in both hands. To Ronald, Jiro never looked more like a warrior than in that moment. And he never felt less like one…

"We move fast, stick to the shadows."

"Right. Shadows."

"Avoid direct fights. If you find yourself in an unavoidable confrontation…" Jiro paused, glanced at the corpse again, and shook his head, a cheeky smile threatening at the corner of his lip. "Well, you know what to do."

Strike first. Strike fast. Never let an opponent take your measure. If possible, don't even allow them to draw their sword.

An early lesson from Daichi, learned the hard way with plenty of flat side-shaped welts and minor flesh wounds. A lesson taught again and again until both boys would never forget. A hard, often brutal reminder to Ronald that their father cared more about their training—and their so-called greater purpose—than their own personal health and well-being.

They wove between tents and campfires, latrines and sleep sacks, careful to choose separate paths without losing track of each other's whereabouts. If the soldiers hadn't been drink-weary and feast-full from earlier in the evening, Ronald and Jiro would have been in quite the impossible predicament. As it was, most of the soldiers were still groggy enough to sneak past with little trouble.

One, however, clad in thick hide and wielding an axe the size of a small child, moved to intercept Jiro. He swung the axe in a lazy arc at an angle that would surely cleave the young samurai in two, but Jiro reacted too fast for the warrior's half-hearted attempt. Midstride, he pivoted and twisted his body to one side, and Ronald watched, breath held, as the axe stuck harmlessly in the dirt behind his brother.

When the tide of battle shifts, seize the advantage. In a duel, mercy is for the dead.

Ronald pictured Daichi's grim face leering over him, felt the broken wrist he'd been dealt by his father, and heard the blood pumping behind his ears as he struggled to regain his wits. All the while, the old man laughed as if taking immense pleasure in beating his boys.

Jiro ducked as the soldier ripped the axe free, and its sharp edge flew over his head. He snapped upward like a spring, landing face to face with the attacker, shoulders heaving from exertion, but beyond a few heavy breaths, he stood tall, a stoic visage of honed battle prowess. The axe dropped from the soldier's clutches with a thud, and he dropped to his knees, a red gash forming from his temple to the top of his ribs.

As far as Ronald knew, that had also been Jiro's first time taking a life. He wondered how his brother handled death, about what was going through his head as he processed his kill. Would the soldier's face forever haunt Jiro, too?

But he didn't have long to wonder. A volley of arrows whistled by, planting feathers in the dirt at his feet. One nicked his shoulder piece. Another ricocheted off his facemask, breaking it near his jawline. Sharp ceramic bit into his skin, and the taste of fresh blood filled his mouth.

He found Jiro, who was using the dead man as a pin cushion and nodded towards the dark hillside. "Let's go," he mouthed, stripping off pieces of his broken mask.

They didn't get far before two demonic-looking monstrosities tore through a cluster of tents to block their escape. Oni, by the look of them. Ugly S.O.B.s with reddish skin, twisted horns, and sharp teeth like bent rebar. Their smell was part sulfur, part bleach. One wielded a club bigger than Ronald and studded with rusty spikes. The other brandished a katana twice as long as Ronald's own, its blade jagged with deep nicks from countless places where steel met steel.

Ronald gulped. His heart drummed in his chest, palms sweaty, and muscles aching. He'd never been more afraid in his life, other than maybe the first time he managed to disappoint Daichi.

But then there was Jiro, standing tall, sword tip pointed directly at the oni, knees bent slightly. Always ready. Always confident. Everything Ronald only wished he could be...

"Which one do ya want?" Jiro asked.

"I... I'll take..." Ronald stuttered. He didn't want either of them. He wanted to be far away from this awful place, from these giant demons intent on taking his life. He exhaled and fought against a wave of nausea threatening to overtake him. "I'll take Clubs, I guess."

By the way his eyes lit up, Jiro was grinning. *Actually* smiling. "They're faster than they look. Weak at their heels."

"Uh huh. Fast. Got it. Heels, no problem."

"Go for the tendons. Never move in the same direction. We'll be okay. *You'll* be okay."

Jiro charged. Ronald followed closely behind. He feinted to the oni's right, and the demon raised its club to smash him to pulp before the fight could even start. As the club fell towards him, Ronald dug his left foot into the dirt and propelled himself in the opposite direction. The oni watched helplessly as its club slammed into nothing. The ground shook like an earthquake, nearly knocking the young samurai off balance.

Ronald's momentum took him too far beneath the demon's wide stance to strike effectively with his longsword. So close, he could see the monster's bulging muscles, throbbing veins, smell its awful sulfur and bleach stench. He twisted at the hips, reached for his wakizashi with his off hand, and uncoiled like a viper, slicing a deep gash into the underside of the oni's leg.

It let out a terrible roar and staggered, crashing into the other. Ronald winced as he watched Jiro squeeze free from between the two hulking bodies as they slammed together with an audible *thud*.

With the oni still off balance, Ronald and Jiro pressed their attacks. Their strikes and slashes were coordinated, a display that would have made their father proud, and before the demons had a chance to recover and mount a proper defense, they were splayed on top of one another in a heap of shredded red flesh.

Ronald and Jiro shuffled their feet for a moment and laughed nervously. Ronald couldn't quite convince himself that the fight had actually been so easy. But it had. They'd done it. They'd won. They'd survived.

"Are they... dead? Like for real?"

Jiro kicked the sole of the closest oni's foot. No reaction. "They, uh, seem to be. Yeah." He kicked it again for good measure. "Dead as dead, at least."

Ronald laughed louder now, almost delirious, and didn't stop until he started coughing. Jiro joined in too.

"Shit," Ronald said. "We just killed demons. Actual. Freaking. Monsters."

"Yeah." This time it was Jiro who seemed to be at a loss for words. "We sure did, didn't we? Ha!"

The brothers embraced, patting each other on the back, and then held each other at arm's length.

"I'm proud of you, Ronald. For real, man. I wasn't sure you had it in you, but you just slayed a real-life frikkin' oni. Absolutely legendary."

Ronald was about to return the compliment when his attention was severed by an explosive *thwang*, louder than if Ho-Musubi itself had just erupted. His ears rang, and all the commotion of the stirring camp sounded like distant, muffled echoes. Dizziness threatened to overtake him, and suddenly everything around him became distant, hollow. Ronald forgot where he was, what was at stake, who his own brother was. Nothing made sense, and time oozed to a complete stop as he numbly fumbled for some semblance of sanity.

Jiro's eyes widened, bulging almost like the man whom Ronald had killed. His grip on Ronald's arm was vice-like, and his lips quivered.

"Jiro? What's wrong?" Ronald asked, but he couldn't hear his brother's response—if there had been a response—over the screaming within his head.

He looked down and saw the arrow, its shaft as thick as his wrist, its tip barbed and wicked sharp. It had pierced clean through Jiro's back, splitting his ribs above his sternum. Jiro reached for the barb, but he couldn't muster enough strength to wrap his fingers around it.

Over his shoulder, Akuma Araki stood over eight feet tall, holding an elegant yumi nearly the same size. A horde of samurai clad in lords' armor flanked her, each wielding a long, cruel-looking tachi. The general's facemask resembled a twisted, grotesque demon that made the oni look almost handsome. Her samurai wore similar faces, each unique, each leaving a lasting, nightmarish impression on him.

Jiro fell forward, his dead weight bringing Ronald to his knees. Ronald cradled his brother, tears streaking down his cheeks behind what was left of his mask.

"Take these." Blood spurted out of Jiro's mouth as he untied the scrolls from his belt. "Get them. Back. Home..." He coughed until he choked.

"But I can't leave you."

"Go." Jiro grasped Ronald's collar. "Now. I... I love you, Ronald..." Little did Ronald know, that would be the last time anyone told him that for a long, long time.

Ronald dropped his brother's body and turned to run. What happened next was a blur of motion and sound and confusion.

His brother's final words... *I love you...* followed by a war cry of a dozen overlapping voices. Samurai charging. Akuma standing with her bow resting before her. Calm. Patient. Assured.

He snagged his foot on a sleeping sack. He tripped over a horse trough. He grappled with a man not much older than himself, stabbing over and over with his short sword, scrambling up a hill. The hill they came down from originally, he hoped. *Together.* Two Hashimoto sons.

There was another *thwang,* less explosive but equally threatening. An arrow lodged in a rocky outcrop some fifty feet above him, dislodging fist- and skull-sized rocks that cascaded on him. He covered his head and neck with one arm, clung to whatever brush he could without the other, and dug at the soil with fast-pumping feet. Rocks pummeled him from every angle, denting his armor's plates and splitting its wrappings.

As he desperately clawed through the rockslide, Daichi's words came unabated once more.

When facing overwhelming odds or challenging an opponent who far outclasses you, do not run. Running is a coward's game. Instead, smile at Death and invite her for tea. Treat her with the respect you would offer an honored guest.

The old man's words had been almost funny at the time. The closest thing to a joke Ronald's father ever told. Now, with rocks raining down on him, arrows the size of saplings aimed at him, and his brother still down there, lost to the mortal world forever, there was nothing funny about them. Death was suddenly far too real and far too close.

And Ronald was a coward. He was not ready to die yet. He'd met Death, just moments before as she twice stared him in the face, and he wasn't ready to invite her over for a third visit.

A large rock, a boulder really, slammed into his shoulder—the same shoulder the arrow had weakened before. The plate shattered, and his arm went numb. In the short seconds he lost his grip strength, the scrolls fell loose, skittering out of sight down the hillside.

He cursed his ill fortune, but only for a moment. Compared to Jiro's death, the loss of some stupid scrolls seemed insignificant. Why should he care anyway? The moment his brother died, he had already decided never to return to this terrible place, to leave all the violence behind, to forget the Order ever existed.

A third arrow sunk to its feathers beside him, not six inches from his face. He summoned what little strength he had left and continued his scramble upward, a task made much easier now that he had to free hands to use.

As he stumbled his way into the forest, distant shouts became quiet whispers. Then, there was silence. Loud, oppressive silence. He dropped to his knees, tore off his helmet, and screamed. The canopy swirled around him faster and faster until he was too dizzy to stand upright.

He fell to the dirt, and everything went black.

Minutes later, or what could have been hours, Hachiman's glowing blue eyes turned red. A crackling of powerful energy exploded from the shrine, sending a scattering of ethereal creatures to every corner of the basement and knocking the old man against the wall, nearly sending him down the stairs. Heat followed in waves. The shrine's once reassuring warmth burned hotter than embers, and when the stairway reopened, his worst fear was confirmed.

One stoop-shouldered samurai emerged, armor disheveled, helmet cracked across its faceplate. There was a nasty gash across his face from jaw to upper lip, and what little intact armor he had left was caked in mud and chunks of grass.

Ronald stumbled into the basement, falling to the floor as the shrine began to close behind him.

"Father, I..."

The old man frowned and shook his head. A twitch of emotion crossed his face. Sorrow? Disappointment? Anger?

Ronald scampered through the dirt and threw his arms around the older man's legs. The man growled, kicked his legs free from the warrior's embrace, and planted one sandaled foot firmly between his eyes, sending him tumbling backward in a heap.

"Otousan..."

The old man took each sure-footed step towards the fallen samurai slowly. His shadow hovered over the limp warrior, a specter come to take the samurai away, and the old man leaned towards him and snatched the family crest dangling beneath his chest plate: the onaga-domoe, three swirling tails with sharp, blending points at their ends.

"Papa... please..."

"You are no son of mine," the old man said before disappearing upstairs. The crest clattered across the basement floor, a trail of dust following in its wake.

Ronald, left with the solitude of his thoughts, slumped against the wall. The shrine flickered red once more, and the basement fell silent, dark, save the would-be warrior's deep breaths and fast-beating heart. He stared at the crest lying in the dirt until everything else around him faded to blurry oblivion. The silhouette of Jiro's dying face was the last image Ronald saw before slipping into unconsciousness.

CHAPTER TWO

He was running out of time, and way faster than he wanted to admit.

But there wasn't a lot of regular high school stuff that Ronald Hashimoto looked forward to. He didn't like Friday night lights or Saturday night parties. He didn't care which company was the latest to drop Kanye, which billionaire tech-boy was revolutionizing the industry, or how many NBA all-stars the eldest Kardashian had hooked up with.

Blah, blah, de-blah... BLAH!

He didn't follow Tik Tok trends or give two craps about the so-called influencers behind them. What was the point, anyway? None of it was real. None of it mattered.

But what he *really* didn't like was his new school. For all he could tell, Normal Community High School lived up to its name. Another suburban cookie-cut, built to replace fallow cornfields before real estate prices sky-rocketed. Down to the angsty, middle-class teenagers that filled its halls, kids plucked straight out of every early 2000s sitcom, Normal Community oozed Midwest aspiration. Every house looked the same, every family behaved like their neighbor, and nothing real ever seemed to happen. At least nothing of significance if you didn't count overblown family drama and idle gossip.

In short, it was *boring*. Sterile. Homogenous to the point of offensive. But they were the nicest people in the world, these safe and secure white folks from Normal, and they were always *so* quick to remind you, too.

Besides their kids, of course. Their kids were the absolute *worst*. Most of them, at least.

But it was safe, he supposed. And it was separate. Living in Normal, he could pretend the events of his past were nothing but bitter ghosts, haunting him for the man he was supposed to be. That wasn't Ronald Hashimoto. This was. Passionate musician, regular teenage boy.

Normal was nothing like New Province, though. When he lived in the city, Ronald could hop out his front door, shoelaces tied tight, and walk for miles while listening to "Black on Both Sides" in its entirety without seeing the same thing twice. In the city, *real* was alive and well. And in all its ugliness and beauty, *life* happened every damn day. It was the life he always envisioned for himself.

A grating voice echoed in the back of his mind: *You must accept everything just the way it is, and do not waste your energies fretting over that which you cannot control.* Daichi's voice. His father's voice...

Ronald's eyelids twitched, and he scratched the back of his neck as he refocused on the melody. One hand pressed against the left side of his headphones, the other working his mouse, he tweaked and adjusted, trimmed and cut until the sound was perfect. He'd pirated a new drum kit off some third-party torrent-sharing forum and an anonymous SoundCloud fan sent him the koto sample. Since then, he'd done little else besides mix and repeat, mix and repeat.

The beat was *almost* done. He was so, so close to finishing the masterpiece of his young career...

...when suddenly the music stopped. A ringing silence filled his ears, and his eyes shot open to a blank computer screen. Reflected in it, he couldn't help but notice his dark bags and droopy cheeks—the inevitable side effect of his pursuit of greatness—before he saw a blur behind him: Ronald's dear ole dad had barged into his room slash studio with an aluminum baseball bat in one hand, an unplugged power cord in the other, violent intent palpable between his scrunched, beady eyes.

"Dad!" he yelled. "What the hell do you think you're doing?"

Ronald ducked as the bat arced towards him and smashed into the center of his monitor. The glass shattered, spreading cobwebs to the edges of its screen, and the bat stuck, jutting at an awkward angle. Daichi stumbled forward to yank it free, nearly knocking Ronald's entire rig off his desk. It was all he could do to secure his PC and MIDI board before they too fell victim to Daichi Hashimoto's drunken rage.

On his back, Ronald's father cursed and flailed. When he finally managed to get to his feet, he reached for the bat once more, but Ronald stepped between him and his computer.

"What is wrong with you?"

"You're late, boy. Always with this playing, never tending your garden to grow what's important in life. We came here for you to learn, to be a normal boy, not to waste away on that damn computer of yours."

"At least I'm not a worthless drunk…" Ronald mumbled his retort so quiet there was no way the old man should have heard.

But his words had been loud enough, or maybe the tone had been just right to set Daichi into another outburst. The old man grappled Ronald, holding him in place with two powerful, battle-experienced hands, before tossing him onto his bed. Ronald rolled across, toppling over the opposite edge, and his father took the opportunity to reach for the bat once more.

Daichi wrenched the bat free from the broken monitor and swung it over and over, smashing every piece of tech Ronald had into tiny plastic and metal fragments. Ronald held back tears as he watched from beside his bed with equal parts shock and horror. When Daichi was satisfied, he cracked his neck and tossed the bat aside. It clanged across the wood floor before rolling into the baseboard, chipping faded white paint and wood filler.

"I can't drive you." He glared at Ronald from the corner of his eyes, swaying gently. "You'll have to walk. If you leave now, you might still make it before your first class is over. Maybe your teachers will have more patience for your insolence. Or maybe not, but what do I care?"

I hate you, Ronald wanted to scream. *You're a bastard, and I hate you, hate you, hate you!*

Daichi had ruined his life well before they moved, and he somehow continued to make every subsequent day worse. Now, he had destroyed Ronald's last will to live and taken away the most important aspect of his new life: his music.

When the old man staggered out of his room, Ronald scrambled to his desk. He sifted through the broken parts, hoping to find something he could salvage, but he soon realized it was a hopeless endeavor. There was no way he could fix his computer or replace his lost work. It was done. His life was officially over, thanks to a man who was too drunk to realize the damage his belligerent rage had caused.

The front door slammed, and Ronald collapsed on his bed and cried. When his phone started to ring, he wiped snot on his sleeve and took a deep, less-than-calming breath. It was that kid, DJ, who kept trying to force them to be friends, calling to check on him no doubt. The fact a near stranger cared more about his well-being than his own father made matters even worse.

Ronald silenced his phone, rummaged for his backpack beneath his messy sheets, and sighed. He took one last look at the wreckage that used to be his last lifeline and headed downstairs for another "wonderful" day at Normal Community High School.

CHAPTER THREE

Ronald jerked awake with a sharp inhale of breath, slurped a line of drool from the top of his hand, and popped up from his desk, a sharpened pencil gripped firmly in his fist. He blinked away the heavy feeling of falling, falling, falling, his heart racing, pounding behind his temples, and his palms were clammy and hot. He was ready for a fight, his muscles tense, eyes alert and active.

His fellow sophomores in Bio gawped. The sudden silence in the classroom was palpable, until a few in the back began to whisper and giggle.

"Oh my gawd," one of them was saying, "was he *actually* drooling."

"Gross!"

"What's he about to do? Shank the final bell?"

The bell! He'd slept through the entire lecture, and it was only the bell.

Ronald relaxed and slipped the pencil into his pocket as

nonchalantly as he could manage. He wiped the sweat off his brow. It was only the bell, the end of ninth period and time to pack his bag and go home. He repeated it over and over until his heart finally stopped racing and the reddish-amber fight-or-flight outlines dulled from his vision.

It was only the bell...

Ronald gathered his books as he waited for the rest of the class to shove their way out of the classroom. Desk legs skidded across linoleum. Zippers zipped. Phones came out, fingers working deftly across their screens. Someone—most likely Skylar Waugh from the overpowering reek of Axe Phoenix body spray—shouldered past him. The impact nearly knocked Ronald off his feet and sent his haphazard stack of books sliding across the floor.

"Watch it, *nerd*," Skylar spat.

Ronald glared and twitched for the pencil in his pocket, but he managed to hold himself in check. Skylar wasn't worth it. None of these inconsequential kids were.

After a brief struggle, Ronald got his books in order and stuffed them into his backpack where he found his headphones. They were of the "old school" variety, meaning bulky and encumbering, with an aux cord and all, but he loved them for two reasons:

Number one, they canceled out all the noise around him—including noise from mouth holes as big and loud as Skylar's—and there seemed to be a *lot* of noise lately. From what Ronald could tell, that's what high school was at the end of the day. Noise.

Number two, he could afford them. That was the important part. What little money he stumbled upon went to his computer, his recording gear, and all the accessories and software he used to produce his music.

RONALD, THE RONIN

But that's all over now, isn't it? Ronald's face flushed with a sudden wave of anger, and his eyes burned with the image of Daichi swinging his bat. He flipped his hood to conceal what would inevitably end with him on the wrong side of Skylar's bullying again—*crying in school, of all things. Can you even imagine?*—and left the empty classroom behind.

In the hall, kids slammed lockers shut and exchanged elaborate handshakes. A freshman Ronald vaguely recognized rolled by on a pair of Heelys, throwing him double sideways deuces. A tall girl shouldered past, her nose in a book. Football players ran routes with less than a little awareness of others, and a kid with a fake neck tattoo drummed on every passing surface with well-worn sticks. He wasn't in a band, for all Ronald knew, and it felt like an elaborate choreographed lie. *High School Musical* without any music.

A group of cheerleaders huddled around a single locker were practicing their routines, and DJ "Danger John" Terri—the simp of all simps according to popular opinion, and one of the only people remotely resembling a friend to Ronald—was busy filming their every move with Jess Avery's sparkly-pink iPhone.

DJ was a gangly kid, a year younger than Ronald. A freshman. He wore too-baggy jeans that flared at his ankles, oversized sweatshirts that he seemed to hide in, and was more legs than anything else. As soon as you saw past his mop of shaggy, golden hair, his freckles stood out as his most noticeable feature.

DJ noticed Ronald, and he tossed the phone in Jess's general direction. She yelped in high-pitched cheerleader, barely caught the spiraling device, and yelled something nonsensical at DJ, but he was already shoving through the crowd towards Ronald, Jess and the other cheerleaders forgotten for the moment.

DJ's lips started to move, but Ronald hadn't thought to remove his headphones. He gestured that he couldn't hear as he fumbled for the volume. DJ reached in and yanked the headphones clear of their port.

"Sup, man? Lost in Bieber city again?" They exchanged an awkward fist bump, and Ronald clicked his tongue on his teeth. "Comin' to the game tonight?"

"Nah, probably not."

Even on the rare occasions when Ronald found common ground with his fellow teenagers—a love for hip-hop in DJ's case—they were still worlds apart. After everything he'd been through, everything he'd seen, he had a hard time seeing eye-to-eye with them or finding anything below surface level to connect with.

"How 'bout you?" he asked out of a sense of obligation rather than genuine interest.

A goofy grin stretched across DJ's face, accentuating his freckles, and he nodded his head with so much enthusiasm he looked like a Johnny Loughran bobblehead. "Jess asked me. *Me.* Can you believe it?"

He peered at her over his shoulder, but she was too lost in conversation to notice. To a girl like Jess Avery, guys like DJ were usually ghosts by the time they left their immediate vicinity and treated the same as pesky fruit flies when they insisted on hanging around.

"You should come, man," DJ continued. "Be my wingman. Have a little fun for once in your pathetic life."

Ronald snorted. "That's okay. Not exactly my idea of fun, and you wouldn't want me as a wingman, anyway. Thanks for the invite, though."

RONALD, THE RONIN

Ronald turned to leave, headphones halfway plugged back in, when DJ grabbed his arm.

"How's that track coming along? Almost ready to let me peep it?"

Daichi's cruel face came to mind, and Ronald had to rub his eyes to keep them from watering again. He forced a smile and merely shook his head.

"It's going to be epic." Ronald's voice cracked, but he gulped down the lump forming in his throat. "Just you wait."

Ronald couldn't bring himself to verbally relive the morning's fight with Daichi. He liked DJ well enough, but they weren't close buddies or anything. At least not of the variety who shared personal problems with each other. It was easier to pretend everything was okay and feed his friend vague BS instead—nothing any more vulnerable than surface level banter.

"Aight, then," DJ said. "I guess I'll have to take your word for it. Hey, take it easy, man. I mean it. You're lookin' haggard, today."

"Thanks, man. You too." He cursed himself for his slip of tongue. "Well, I mean, you look fine, but you know what I'm saying."

"Oh, you think I'm fine, huh?" DJ blew him a kiss.

Ronald blushed. He stammered but was too embarrassed to form a complete sentence. DJ saved him with a wink and a playful slap on the shoulder. They exchanged another fist bump before DJ ran off to join the crowd of cheerleaders disappearing down the hall.

Haggard? Ronald snorted again. *Ha!* DJ didn't know half of it, but that was okay. It wasn't DJ's problem. It was Ronald's—and Ronald's alone—to deal with.

A trio of teachers moved through the crowd. If it wasn't for their name badges, they would be young enough to blend in with the students. To restore some semblance of order, they yelled at kids to slow down, grabbed backpacks to yank lovers apart, and whistled to grab the attention of some of the rowdier students. Football players, mostly. It was football Friday, after all, and they were antsy to "get out on the field and hit somebody." There was banging on lockers, loud chanting, foot stomping, and arrhythmic clapping. The entire student body seemed to be stirring itself into a frenzy. The war cry-inspired commotion brought Ronald back to a place he never wanted to revisit, and suddenly, he couldn't get out of there fast enough.

He scrolled through his YouTube likes until he found just the right walk-out track and pulled his hoodie tight around himself. As soon as hi-hats started *chicking* and bass started bumping, his head began to bob and nothing else mattered. Under the music's influence, he was drunk on contentment. People streaked by him in inconsequential blurs, becoming swirls of color, a current of silent motion, ebbing to the rhythm of Hip-Hop. Life was no longer a complicated mess, and that was exactly how Ronald Hashimoto liked it.

There it was, the bright, orange sun at the end of his long week: Normal Community's exit sign, right above the threshold between a dark place and an even darker one: home. The sign was close, though it seemed to draw further away with every step. It blinked in sporadic intervals, mocking him. Slowly but surely, he would pass underneath it, only to return three short days later, but at least he had his music.

Distracted by his own thoughts, Ronald all but ran over Aubrey

Page. His instincts took over, and his arms shot out like striking vipers to catch her around her waist. He held her there, half falling to the floor with her, and lost himself in her large, round, hazel eyes. Thick black hair fell over her shoulders like cascading willow branches, and he fought his would-be romantic impulse to move a messy clump off her pale face.

Aubrey's lips were moving, he realized. Puckered even. Did she expect him to kiss her? He was basically dipping her, and that's what they always did in those rom-coms he sometimes tolerated as background noise. It was a classic move, and he wouldn't have thought himself capable of such suavity under normal circumstances. Here they were, undeniably sharing a moment, but Aubrey Page wasn't interested in him like that. She couldn't be. There was no way... Was there?

She reached for his cheek, and he closed his eyes in anticipation, lips quivering...

Was this actually happening? Like, for real?

His headphones slid off his ears and the all-too-familiar noise exploded around him. He whimpered and jerked back.

"Hi there," Aubrey said. "You can let go of me, now."

Ronald's gut churned, and he all but dropped her. He stepped away from her, ears ringing as if a bomb had just gone off beside him, feeling as if he might pass out, as if he wanted to die. At the very least, he should run. Fast, for the exit, never to return.

Idiot. How could he be so stupid? What would Daichi say if he knew Ronald had allowed himself to be entrapped by such a mind-numbingly idiotic snafu?

Do not let yourself be guided by lust or love. These are ephemeral, meant only to trick the weak of mind.

Yet here he was, letting a girl catch him off guard and make a bumbling fool out of him.

Then, she smiled. A couple of her friends giggled, but her ease in return set him at ease. A little, and that was a good enough start to bring him back to his senses.

"Ronald, right? You moved here a few months ago." He nodded, mouth slightly ajar. "Must have been hard, starting over mid-year and everything. My dad's military. We move all the time, so I get it, the whole feeling like an outsider thing."

His mouth was dry, and he couldn't swallow. He stammered, but if he could've found the right words to respond, he probably would've choked on them. His whole body was hot. His skin tingled, and a wave of dizziness threatened.

Aubrey Page! *Talking to me...*

She wasn't exactly popular—not like Jess Avery and her crew—but Ronald had developed fast feelings for Aubrey the moment he laid eyes on her. She was short, wore thick-framed glasses and clothes to match her hair. Yet there was more to her than the darkness, than the tinge of hot girl nerdiness she portrayed. Those big eyes were intelligent, observant. He wondered what secrets they held. She was different from other girls, and Ronald didn't have to "man up" and actually talk to her to recognize the truth behind how she carried herself. Like him, she'd been through some things. Well, maybe not exactly like him, but *real* things, nonetheless.

"Here you go." Aubrey handed him his headphones. "Whatchya listening to, anyway?"

Ronald was thankful she didn't mention the whole puckered lips fiasco. Maybe she hadn't noticed, he tried unsuccessfully to convince himself. He shook some sense back into his brain and, hands sweating and slightly shaky, pulled his phone out of his hoodie pocket. Once he remembered how to read, he glanced at its display, cleared his throat, and slid it back into concealment.

"You, uh, probably never heard this one."

"Try me."

He scratched the back of his neck and looked at his feet. It was a great track. Blew all the other modern stuff off the tables. Why did he suddenly have this sinking terror screaming he was a weirdo and Aubrey was about to laugh at him for his horrible taste in music?

"Alright," she said, rolling her eyes. "If you insist on doing this the hard way."

Aubrey moved so suddenly she caught him off guard. She reached both hands into his hoodie pocket from either direction, and he immediately started to squirm. Ronald tried to block her, but she caught him so unaware all he could do was twist away. He was too late, though. She already had his phone, the headphones attached sliding out with it.

"RZA, huh?" She nodded her approval, brows raised in surprise, almost as if impressed. "Some of his new jams, too. Got some backlash over this album. Came way outta left field, but I love it. Most diehard fans do, especially if you like a little fusion with your jams."

She started humming the tune—*everywhere I go, Lord knows*—as she swiped away his lock screen, flipping his phone to capture his face, and opened his contacts. Her fingers slid swiftly across his keypad, and then she handed it back as if she'd done nothing extraordinary. Ronald's jaw dropped, and he was lucky drool didn't drop with it. Wouldn't that have been perfect? Trouble was always finding him, so he wouldn't have been surprised.

No matter how many times he read the digits, he couldn't believe the trick his eyes were playing on him. Aubrey Page had given him her number, with a little black heart by her name of all things.

"Whenever you decide you're ready to talk, give me a call." She closed his jaw with a single soft finger to his chin. "I'd love to show you my record collection sometime." Finally, he managed to look up from his phone and she winked again. "See you soon, Ronny Boy." She peered over her glasses. "I hope."

At that, Aubrey and her friends disappeared into the ever-dispersing crowd. Not even one of them pulled off the goth look like she did, though. On them, it was forced, like they'd stumbled into a Hot Topic with daddy's credit card. On her, it just worked.

He watched Aubrey go until he could no longer make out her form from the rest of the student body, going over all the things he could have, should have, would have said and done over and over again in his head. To say he felt like a dweeb was the understatement of the 21st Century.

If he wasn't a total loser yet, a sudden shove in the back by Skylar sealed the deal. The side of Ronald's face slammed into a locker, and the wind was knocked out of his chest. Skylar and his pathetic retinue—*Chad and Eli*, Ronald thought with a grunt of loathing—laughed and made obscene gestures and fart noises as they left him behind, alone with his misery. It took all of Ronald's self-discipline not to go after the bully. Doubly so when he noticed all the eyes on him. Triply when he scooped his smashed headphones from the floor, and they hung limp and lifeless in his fist.

"Dammit!" He punched a dent into the nearest locker, immediately regretting his knee-jerk reaction as pain shot up his wrist, and then tossed the useless plastic mess in Skylar's direction. "What. An. Asshole."

A kid he recognized from one of his classes bent over and picked his headphones off the ground. He was a tank, more muscle than teenager, and Ronald wasn't sure if he'd ever heard him speak. When he did, his voice was low and booming, a Gen-Z Conway Twitty. See, Ronald knew more than just rappers.

"Here you go, man." He shrugged. "Might be able to fix 'em. Who knows?"

Reluctantly, Ronald took them and folded them into his pocket. "Er, thanks?"

Deadpan, the kid shrugged again. "Don't even sweat it."

"Excuse me?"

"Skylar. The other two. They're nothin' compared to you."

Ronald was suddenly exhausted. "I'm sorry, man, but who the hell are you?"

"Robert. We have Geometry together."

"Right. Well, Robert, thanks for the weird, stalkery compliment, but I... uh... I gotta go, okay?"

"K. See ya."

Ronald flipped his hood and shuffled through the exit, never happier to be leaving Normal Community behind for a little while. Until he remembered what awaited him at Daichi's, of course. Between the two, he wasn't sure which hell was worse, but he figured it didn't really matter at this point. On the off chance he'd ever be brave enough to text her so she could actually call, he set Aubrey's ringer to *Trouble Shooting* by RZA and hit the kind streets of Normal, miserable yet resigned to any new form of BS he might encounter on his way home.

CHAPTER FOUR

Ronald was surprised to find he'd already made it home. He'd been in a fugue state, trying his best to silence the whirlwind of thoughts in his head, when he stumbled up his front steps. One of the foldable porch chairs was in the bushes, and the small glass table was covered in smashed cigarette butts and surrounded by discarded beer cans. He stretched over the bushes to grab the chair, dusted it clean of pollen and twigs, and set it alongside the others. The chair tilted to one side, but its awkward disrepair complimented the house's picturesque façade of missing siding and moss-filled gutters.

The front door was wide open, and Ronald took a deep breath, closed his eyes, and prepared himself for the worst. He could already hear the argument, devolving quickly into Daichi and him yelling over each other. He could feel the back of Daichi's hand throbbing on his cheek, but that wasn't even what would hurt the most. It would be his father's utter lack of empathy. Daichi didn't care that Ronald was doing all he knew how to keep their little family of two together.

The old man didn't—couldn't—understand how hard life was for him right now. He needed a friend, a parent to hug him and tell him everything was going to be okay. Short of one, he'd settle for a single moment of peace or even just an illusion of safety and security in his own home. Gut-wrenching nerves every time he walked through the door were starting to feel cliché and played out.

Instead, he got a drunk, passed out in a Lay-Z-Boy with an open bottle of sake dripping on the carpet. Instead, he got a worthless excuse for a father who smelled worse than he looked. Less than a shell of a man, and someone he could only depend on for physical and emotional abuse.

"Jesus, Dad," he mumbled. "Pull yourself together." *I need you, old man. More than ever,* he wanted to say. *If you ever plan on showing up for me, today's the day.*

Accepting reality, Ronald grudgingly worked his way around the living room. Someone had to clean Daichi's messes before the house started to reek like stale tobacco and spoiled yeast, before the mice and cockroaches moved in, and it sure as heck wasn't going to be Daichi. He huffed and groaned as he cleaned, fully aware no one cared about his woes, but the exaggerated show of teenage angst made the job almost tolerable. It helped to blow off steam, at least.

Once the house was back in something resembling order, Ronald crept to the basket where his father kept his car keys and wallet. He slipped the faded black billfold free from the clutter and sifted through corner store receipts until he found a wad of cash.

He side-eyed Daichi, who snored loudly and shifted in his chair, before stuffing the wad into his hoodie pocket.

For a moment, as his fingers toyed with the edges of the money, he was overcome with guilt. Then, he remembered the wreckage of his computer upstairs, his broken headphones, and the fact that if he didn't have money for, say, groceries, he and Daichi would both starve. The guilt of a few hundred dollars was a small price for the old man to pay. His father never mentioned the missing cash, and he always seemed to have plenty more the next time Ronald snooped. He wondered where it all came from, but he'd learned early not to ask questions he wasn't prepared to hear the answers to.

Bottom line, he needed the money more. Without his music, he would die. Without his booze, Daichi would just hit Ronald a little harder next time. Life was all about tradeoffs, and this one was a no-brainer.

Ronald plopped onto the couch with a heavy sigh, dug out the remote from in between the cushions, and risked a glance in Daichi's direction. *Out cold.* The old man was sawing logs loud enough to wake up the entire cul-de-sac. A black and white samurai flick—maybe *Throne of Blood* or *Samurai Assassin* by the camera work and cinematic style—played on TV. In Ronald's current state of mind, it was hard to focus on what was happening on screen, and he didn't normally watch TV, but he was ready to mindlessly flip through channels until his brain slid out of his ears.

As soon as the channel changed, Daichi stirred. "Don't touch that remote, boy." The ole drunk gazed around, a pale caricature of a man. He might as well have been a ghost in the television's dim light. "I was watching that, you ungrateful little..."

Ronald rolled his eyes. "Whatever."

He tossed the remote onto Daichi's lap without bothering to be gentle and stormed off towards his bedroom. A big part of him wanted nothing more than to slam the door, to knock a crooked picture or two off the hallway wall, to stomp his feet and pout, but with his father downstairs, dead-to-the-world drunk, it wouldn't have had the desired effect. Besides, he was better than that, wasn't he? He was a warrior, not a baby. Still, he gave the edge of his bed a strong kicking before dropping face down into his pillows.

Smothered in down feathers, Ronald pictured the wreckage of his personal studio in his mind's eye. Every attempt to bring his focus to something else—anything else—failed. It had taken him years and innumerable odd jobs for less-than-savory characters to piece together all that hardware and software. Computers weren't cheap. Nor were licenses.

But that was the least of his concerns. His latest project, hours of work over many sleepless nights, was gone forever. It was his own fault, really. He'd gotten lost in the music, forgot to save. If he dared dream of ever pulling together a second rig, he supposed he could try to recreate it, but it was damn near impossible to replicate such divine inspiration, especially without the terabytes worth of drum kits, samples, and vocal recordings he'd accumulated and tweaked over the years.

No, without his rig—or his headphones as a distant second-place alternative—Ronald had nothing to look forward to. No outlet to distract his restless mind.

He tossed and flailed in bed. No matter what position he tried, he couldn't get comfortable. His bones ached as if he were getting sick, but he knew better. This was a different kind of ache. It was the stress getting to him, tearing him apart nerve by fried nerve. It was the effort of fighting off his mental demons, a war in a constant state of stalemate in his mind. He couldn't escape those demons, no matter how much time or space he put between himself and last summer.

Ronald dug for his phone, desperate to find anything to distract him from his own thoughts, even stupid videos about people he'd never meet and whose lives he cared little about.

He swiped to his contacts, found himself staring wide-mouthed at the first name on the list. A new name. One that brought both eager anticipation and giddy fear. His thumbs twitched. A tight knot twisted in his stomach. He tapped the screen, displaying ten as-of-yet unfamiliar digits. Then, he immediately closed out and buried his phone underneath his pillow.

Come on, Ronald. Why are you like this, man?

He snatched his phone off his bed and mindlessly opened and closed apps before tossing it away again in frustration.

What could he even say to someone like Aubrey Page?

Hey, it's Ronald. I grabbed you super awkwardly by your waist earlier today and didn't let go. No, no, no. I'm not a creep. I just almost kissed you for no reason at all. Want to try it again?

Sup? Ronald. WYD? He snorted. He wasn't half as smooth enough to pull off a line like that. It would come off as super disingenuous, in the least. But Aubrey wouldn't know, would she? What if he played the part for so long she just learned to think he was cool? An easy enough proposal, it could work. Acting on it was a whole different story, though yet alone maintaining the persona.

I think I might love you. Too forward. Too *desperate*.

Want to come over, sit on my bed and stare at the wall while my drunk of a father sleeps it off downstairs? Yeah, that was it. That was how he'd win her heart. It was practically the beginning of a fairy tale.

Ronald buried his head in his pillows and screamed into the void. The more he waffled over whether or not to text her, and what he'd say when he finally did, the hotter his inner rage burned, self-loathing and frustration fueling the flames.

He couldn't understand why he got this way sometimes. When it started, there seemed to be no stopping it. One minute, he was perfectly fine. Well, as fine as possible given his circumstances. The next minute, he'd be on the verge of exploding for no discernible reason. At least tonight it sort of made sense. Tonight, Ronald Hashimoto had plenty to be angry about.

He closed his eyes, drummed his fingers on his knees, and hummed an old West Coast melody. It didn't quite have the same effect, but the disembodied silken voice of Nate Dogg running through his head certainly helped.

"Nobody," he sang, more than a little off-key, "does it better..."

The only difference was that Ronald wasn't close at all. He was as far away from where he wanted to be as possible.

He looked to his pantheon of heroes for answers, posters taped across nearly every surface of his wall. They looked back, neither in judgment nor scorn, but they didn't give him any answers. They just *were*, and maybe there was a certain wisdom he could follow in their simple existence.

Meth and Red, clad in matching yellow and red tights respectively. Out to save the world one bar at a time.

The RZA—whom he couldn't help but relish Aubrey had instantly recognized—two fingers across his illuminati eye, a splash of green paint across his face.

J Cole, thick locks framing a pensive, genius yet humble face.

MF Doom, rest in peace to a legend, an unseen spotlight glinting off the temple of his namesake mask, a microphone in hand.

Slug with his stupid, glorious soul patch and sideways grin. The glint of pain in his eyes.

Future, rocking a fedora, fingers to the sky.

OGs, Herc and Rock, because Ronald was the type of fanboy who appreciated all eras and complexities of instrumental arrangement and storytelling delivery.

All these brilliant creators, all their masterworks. They were lyrical masterminds, gurus of rhythm and melody. What they collectively accomplished—of what Ronald could only dream of contributing to in any significant way—was more than music. It was a movement. Religion. Their collective works a life-saving holy book upon a pedestal higher than all the others. Beyond music, it was Hip-Hop, with two capital Hs. It was culture.

Ronald chastised himself. Did these incredible emcees and producers tangle with such emotional turmoil? Did they run home and cry every time things got tough? What would Pac or Biggie think if they caught him wallowing in self-pity?

"Shit," Ronald said. *I really need to get over myself. And a new pair of headphones.*

When he ran out of heroes to admire, and there were a lot of them on his walls, Ronald's gaze inevitably rested on the broken wreckage of his computer. There it was, in exactly the same condition he'd left it that morning. A perfect reflection of how he felt in the moment: broken beyond repair.

Then, there were the two swords hanging over his bed. A

katana and wakizashi. *His* katana and *his* wakizashi, with their matching gold, hand-wrapped tsukas. The swords were deadly, least of all because of their sharp killing edges. He wanted to forget about them forever, but for some reason, he hadn't been able to shut them away yet. Was it because completely turning his back on them would be like turning his back on *him?*

"I'm sorry, Jiro. Man, you must be so, stupid proud of your younger brother right now, huh? Doing so well without you…"

Downstairs, he heard a glass break and Daichi swear, followed by a loud sound like one immovable body slamming against another. Heat welled behind his eyes, but he blinked it away before the tears came.

"That's it," he said, launching himself off his bed.

It was time to get out of the house. Take a walk, clear his head. Maybe hop a bus to New Province and hit up Che's Shogunate Records, his favorite music shop of all time and a damn good refuge too, for some new headphones, maybe a secondhand album or two. He wasn't about to show his face at any football game, especially not Normal Community's where someone he didn't want to talk to might recognize him, and a trip back home might be exactly what he needed to keep the demons at bay.

But Daichi met Ronald at his door. By the stern look on Daichi's face and the stone-cold clarity in his eyes, Ronald already knew this conversation wasn't going to end well. A sinking feeling in his gut made him wonder if the old man knew about the cash, but that was the least of Ronald's concerns.

"When are you going to finish your initiation?"

"I'm not having this conversation again."

Ronald tried to squeeze past, but Daichi side-stepped to

intercept him. "We will have this conversation when I say so, and you will give me the respect I deserve as your father. As your *master*."

"Dad, I don't wanna talk about it. We've gone through this so many times and rehashing the same thing over and over ain't gonna change a thing."

"I wish Jiro were still here. He would never dare disappoint me or treat me the way you do."

"Yeah, well, I wish he was here, too. At least he gave a damn about my life." Daichi opened his mouth to speak, but Ronald cut him off. "And I wish Mom was here, but because of you, they're both gone, aren't they?"

"Excuse me? How dare you speak—"

"You heard me. It's all your fault. It always is. If it wasn't for you, Jiro would still be alive, Mom wouldn't have left us, and I'd still have my freaking computer. And you expect me to respect you, after everything you've done? I'm not going to let you manipulate me like you manipulated them. Now, get the hell out of my way. I'm leaving."

Daichi slammed a fist into the door frame. "You will go nowhere, you insufferable child. Why do you put me through such agony? Why do you insist on bringing shame to our family? Have I not taught you better? I was wrong about you. I guess not everyone can be like Jiro."

"You know, I'm trying my best. I really am. I just can't do what you're asking or be who you want. I just... I'm not him."

"You're not trying hard enough."

"It's never enough, no matter what I do. Even if I go through initiation, even if I fulfill our family's destiny or whatever other bull crap you spew, it still won't meet your standards. I'll never replace your favorite son, so why should I bother trying?"

Daichi didn't look angry anymore. He looked sad. A glint of tears threatened, but he wiped them away in a huff.

"You should bother because it's your duty. Because it's honorable. I did not bring you into this world to sit around on the computer, wasting your life away. A nobody. A coward who hides from his own shadow."

"I'm afraid of my own shadow, huh? What about you, old man? All the beer... the sake. What's that if not hiding?"

Daichi smacked Ronald so hard his ears rang. "Even if you won't admit it, you have Hashimoto blood coursing through your veins. The blood of great men, bound for greater purposes. You are a warrior, Ronald. Not some geek who can sit out life's precious moments behind a screen. Our family has a sacred duty, bigger than you or me, or even Jiro's sacrifice. Your mother couldn't see it, and now neither can you."

"Whatever. I don't have time for this. Now, get out of my way." *Or else,* he was too afraid to add.

Daichi looked Ronald in the eyes in an almost playful manner and beckoned with two outstretched fingers. "Why don't you try to make me, son."

Ronald didn't have the energy to fight. "I don't know if you noticed, but it's been a really awesome day—no thanks to you—and I'd hate to ruin it by embarrassing you in your own house."

Daichi grinned a devious grin and grumbled something unintelligible, making himself big enough to cover most of the doorframe. Ronald ran his fingers through his hair, sighed, and admitted to himself that this confrontation could no longer end peacefully.

"Please." Ronald's voice cracked. It came out almost as a pathetic plea. "Just let me go," he whispered.

Daichi poked Ronald's shoulder with two firm fingers, who in return slid towards a small gap between his father and a peaceful end to the argument. Daichi moved to block his escape, but Ronald was too fast, and the old man was too booze-addled to react as swiftly as he might have in his prime.

Years of early mornings and long, hard days came flooding back in a flash of sharply honed instinctual motion. Ronald positioned his front foot, his foundation foot, between his father's legs, just behind his heel, and slammed Daichi in the gut with the palm of his hand. The strike spanned no further than an inch or two, but it held all of Ronald's latent strength behind it, all his pent-up resentment towards his father.

He had never thought to strike back, never stood up to Daichi with anything other than a grapple and a shove. It felt good. Too good.

Daichi stumbled backward, off balance, and tripped over his own feet, slamming the back of his head against drywall with a resounding thud. Ronald scampered past, hardly looking twice, and skipped down the stairs three at a time.

No, a few hundred dollars wasn't much at all. It was a small price for the old man to pay.

The least he could pay for everything he put Ronald through…

CHAPTER FIVE

The bus lurched with a *hiss* and a black puff of exhaust, and Ronald followed a stinky, piss-stained homeless man out onto the streets. Hood up, he skipped onto the sidewalk, shoved his hands into his pockets, and walked. Just walked. No music. No thoughts about his father or school or Jiro. No memories screaming back in searing red flashes, in vivid, violent detail. It was Ronald and the city, the place he had called home most of his life.

On the list of things he liked, New Province was close to number one. He didn't mind the suffocating smell of emissions, the lingering ammonia aroma you could taste around every corner, or even the thick, ripe wafting of last week's garbage. He barely noticed the gunshots in the distance or the constantly blaring car horns of angry commuters. These were simply the byproducts of a living, breathing steel and concrete organism. One of humankind's greatest achievements: civilization, in all its glory and ill repute.

There was rhythm to these streets. A type of melody, often

reflected in the music that would have otherwise been streaming through his aux cord at too-high decibels. The checkered cabs thrummed and pulsed to the beat, halos of gold like the sun. The indecipherable chatter, a wall of noise at first listen, became the background singers of a song that never slept. It sang about opportunity, about progress, about the hustle and bustle of the fast-paced modern world. When needed, it sang about community, kinship, and love.

And, yes, sometimes it sang about death too. And pain, because without pain all the other stuff couldn't be written into song to begin with. Without pain, it was just noise.

Maybe that was why Ronald liked the city so much. It put things into perspective for him. It reminded him that some of what he was dealing with was simply part of life, to do what he could in the moment to ensure his pain wasn't in vain, to accept his circumstances for what they were and to simply be happy to be alive. Not everyone was so lucky.

Homeboy Sandman, who put it into words where Ronald couldn't, said it best. He spoke on the innate juxtaposition of the city, of the neighborhood, of this modern-day organism.

When I walk around my hood, I see smiles, different styles...

When I walk around my hood, I see broken hopes, smoking dope, eyes looking comatose...

In the city, you couldn't have one without the other. It was a perfect reflection of the human condition, projected into a tight, overcrowded space. It was a petri dish for humanity to grow, evolve, and thrive.

For the first time that day, Ronald smiled. It was a slight, half-hearted gesture that made him feel suddenly light on his feet. He found himself dancing to the rhythm, enjoying the city's company, and forgetting everything else for a moment. Sometimes, all you needed was that single moment.

Ronald stumbled over an uneven sidewalk crack, and someone snorted from a nearby stoop.

"Smooth, kid. Real smooth."

The speaker wore loose-fitted pants in the traditional hakama style and a golden-lined haori, not entirely unusual in the city but rare. He had gaunt cheeks, a thin mustache, twirled at the ends, and long hair tied in a messy bun.

Ronald's cheeks flushed. He wondered if this stranger had seen him dancing too. *How embarrassing.* He wanted to bury his face in his palms, hide from the world within the safety of his shell like a frightened turtle.

"Don't worry." The man stood, holding his back as if in pain, hunching slightly, and raised his arms in the air as if to say it was no big deal, that he didn't mean any offense. "I didn't see a thing, kid. Not. A. Damn. Thing."

He hobbled off in the opposite direction, hand resting on the small of his back, steps tentative yet steady. Ronald watched him, dumbfounded, until the stranger disappeared into an alleyway further down the block. He shook his head and tried to laugh off the odd encounter, but after his conversation with his father about finishing his initiation, he had a sneaking suspicion that there was more to the stranger than a playful jab about Ronald's awkwardness. He shrugged. He was too tired to overthink such an absurd notion.

But he'd lost his rhythm. The city no longer moved as it had when he first stepped off the bus. There was a sluggishness to it, a mundanity of spirit. It was just buildings, after all. Tall stacks of glass and steel, concrete and wires, filled with people going about their average day-to-day lives. How was this place any different than Normal? How was this urban monstrosity any better than the burbs? Stripped to its bare components, New Province wasn't anything special to dance about.

Shit, Ronald thought, kicking a rock into a gutter. There came the demons, back for another round of tormenting him.

He found one of his old favorite spots: a small, unmarked, unnamed sushi restaurant owned by a nice first-generation Chinese family, believe it or not. They greeted every customer with a smile and rolled the best ebi he'd ever tasted. Tonight was no exception. And, despite the language barrier, he was welcomed like a long-lost relative.

Mrs. Ling, who seemed to be the only one ever there and who looked exactly the same every time he saw her, grabbed him by the arm and ushered him to the nearest booth. Before he could look at a menu, she had an ice-cold pitcher of water, a bowl of steaming miso soup, and a small plate of gyoza on his table. It was all perfect, and his sushi was just as good as he remembered.

When he finished, he thanked her with a slight bow, and Mrs. Ling offered him a neatly wrapped to-go box. He tilted his head and began to protest, but she cut him off with a sharp, grandmotherly sigh.

"For you to take home. Or for your okaasan, maybe." She smiled, her eyes bright and wide. "Help put some meat on your bones."

Ronald forced a smile in return—there was no way the plump woman could have known the reality of his situation—then waved her off. "I'm fine. Thank you, though. I really appreciate it."

She shoved the box into his hands, scowled and tapped her foot on the dirty burgundy carpet. "You take. No choice."

He laughed and accepted the box. "What is it?"

She tapped her temple as if whatever she had handed him had been her very own stroke of genius. "Ah, secret family recipe. Moon cake, very delicious. You like, you come see us again."

"I always come to see you."

"But not for a very long time. Too long. We were thinking you forgot about us. We are like family, you know?"

She leaned in for a tight hug, and Ronald realized it was the first time he'd been hugged in as long as he could remember. He tensed, tried to wriggle free, but then the warmth of her embrace won him over. He wrapped one arm around her and rested his cheek on her shoulder. After what could have been a second or five minutes, Mrs. Ling kissed him on the forehead and patted his head, her lingering scent of fryer oil welcome and oddly comforting.

"I will." And he meant it at the time, but his life didn't always go as he planned. It had a nasty tendency to go the exact opposite, in fact. He had a sneaking suspicion that, yes, he would be back soon, but under very different circumstances.

Outside, he heard a crash of aluminum on pavement in the alleyway behind the restaurant, followed by muffled grunts and shouts. He crept around to peer into the alleyway. Three people: a woman struggling against two tattered, menacing looking men. One had her purse by a strap and was attempting to yank it loose from her grasp. The other brandished a cruel-looking knife, like something that might be used to skin a deer.

"Aye, lady, just give him the purse. It'll make this a lot easier for you," the thug with the knife was saying. "Hand it over, and we can all go home."

"Screw you!"

She gave one last push against them, but they were too strong for her. The purse tore from her fingers, and she fell forward onto her hands and knees, skirt getting bunched messily underneath her thighs.

"Oh, a show too."

"Very nice."

Knives reached for her face, but she slapped his hand away. He rubbed at his jaw and grimaced.

Two guys in suits saw the exchange from across the street and ran in front of traffic. A taxi driver laid on his horn and yelled an obscenity in Greek out his open window. The business guy slapped the hood of his cab and flipped him off.

"What's going on here?" the other asked.

The two thugs risked one last leer at the lady before darting out of the alley and down the block, suit guys close in toe. They had made off with her purse, but she was fortunate that that had been the worst of the whole ordeal. A few scrapes and bruises, nothing lasting. No deep scars of either the physical or psychological variety.

Disheveled, and more than a little shaken, she picked herself up off the grimy concrete and wiped snot from above her lip. She held her skirt tight against her hips as she limped out of the alley, stopping to glare at Ronald.

"Thanks for the help back there."

Ronald gulped. "I... I..."

"Don't worry about it." She sucked air through her teeth. "Not everyone can be a hero."

Not everyone can be a hero, he repeated to himself as she disappeared.

Not everyone can be like Jiro...

Ronald slumped against the building's brick façade, slid his knees against his chest, and wrapped his arms around them. She was right, of course. Not everyone could be a hero. The words echoed what Daichi had said to him earlier that day and rang too true, cut too deep. She was the one who had been mugged, yet here he was, trying to convince himself that he was the victim.

He wished that just one time in his life he could do something right. Anything. Was that too much to ask? To not be a total loser *all* the time?

What were you going to do anyway? A familiar yet unexpected voice in his head asked. A voice he'd longed to hear again for the past year plus.

"I should have helped her."

How? They were armed. Twice your size, and two of them. A warrior must choose his battles, lest an inconsequential encounter becomes his last.

"Inconsequential? She was—"

She remains unscathed. Breathing. She lives to see another sunrise, and so do you, brother.

"But—"

But nothing. Another sunrise is another opportunity to improve yourself. You cannot be better tomorrow if you are dead today.

Ronald sighed and shook his head. He refused to believe he'd done the right thing by doing nothing. He should have helped, and nobody could convince him otherwise. Could two thugs in an alley really have presented him with more than he could handle? He laughed to himself. What would Daichi think, knowing his only remaining son had cowered in the face of danger? Oh, he would have swelled with pride.

Ronald couldn't say how long he sat there. Long enough for the sun to fully descend. Long enough for the city's daytime people to pull their shutters and its nighttime denizens to slink onto the streets. At night, the city became a wild, free place. A place of celebration and dancing and artificial light. A dark place, with both opportunity and trouble lurking around every corner.

Get up, Ronald. Dust yourself off and get up. It's not too late to try again.

This time, Ronald listened. He needed to do better. To be better. And it wasn't too late unless he stopped trying. It wasn't too late until it was over.

Besides, he needed to get those new headphones. Eazy-E was calling his name.

Shogunate Records's door was propped open, allowing music to spill into the night, a steady two-way flow of customers passing through it. Che Perkins, the shop's owner, was behind the counter, pointing out where requests could be found, ringing orders, collecting cash, and barking directions to her small retinue of part-time employees.

It was controlled chaos, but it was a kind of chaos that Ronald could vibe with, centered around his absolute favorite thing in the world, his lifeline: music.

He squeezed through the throng, and Che waved with both hands as soon as she noticed him. She hopped the counter, squeezed through a group of teenagers, and made her way towards him. Before she could close the distance, the group of people closed around her.

"Hey, Ronald!" she called over the din, standing on her tip-toes and hopping up and down. "Long time no see, man. Let me know if you need anything, okay?"

Damn, but she knows how to make a kid feel special. "Thanks, Che! Good to be seen."

Che was in her late thirties, early forties maybe, light-skinned with dreadlocks down to her knees. She wore the latest Nineties folk-rock fashion, played a mean mandolin set every third Thursday at a dive bar a few blocks down, and had the raspy pipes of an angel. In short, she was a black queen, and after all those warm afternoons that bled into late nights of talking, the closest thing to a mom Ronald was ever going to have.

He waved his gratitude for her offer, but he knew exactly where he was going. Near the back of the shop, he found his stacks: two lopsided thrift shop bookcases bursting at their cheap corkboard seams with used CDs. He'd spent hours here and had dug out innumerable treasures. It was funny, he didn't even have a Discman anymore (yes, Ronald knew what that was, but he probably wouldn't be admitting it to his peers anytime soon), but there was something about holding a physical album in your hands. iTunes, YouTube, Spotify, and the like were nice enough, but they were second fiddle to plastic and paper.

On occasion, he uncovered missed posters buried inside their 4.7 by 4.7 coffins. They practically covered the walls in his room, but he always had enough space left for one or two more.

Ronald was starting on the Es when he saw someone who sent his gut through the floor. He squeaked audibly, crouched as low as his knees would allow, and hurried to the meager cover of a nearby promo cutout.

He peered around T-Swift's hips, careful not to reveal too much of his face, and snapped back into concealment, a scared turtle hiding in its shell from a predator. Who he just verified he'd seen was ten times scarier than any number of armed alleyway thugs.

She was alone, sifting through vinyl. The crowd seemed to part around her, as if they were worried that if they got too close, they might somehow catch a bad case of her cool. She didn't seem to notice them, or care. She was intent on the task at hand, so focused on the matte black discs, so determined to find whatever it was she was looking for. Ronald wondered what record she was hunting for, wished desperately he could pluck it out of thin air and present it to her.

But was she crying? From a distance, he could swear her mascara was smeared, eyes bloodshot. Whatever or whomever had hurt her, he thought for a fleeting moment, would meet the sharp edge of his blade one day.

Then, he found himself a little annoyed, wondering what in the world Aubrey Page was doing in *his* record shop. This visit was supposed to be an escape from Normal, and it had somehow found its way here anyway. The absolute best part of Normal, sure, but Normal nonetheless.

Aubrey turned towards him, and he nearly toppled the cutout trying to scamper away. He felt like Neo in the Matrix as he maneuvered crab-like through the rows of merchandise, crouched and constantly checking over his shoulder. He bumped into a woman in a tight trench coat. She yelped, dropped a stack of records, and swore at him.

"What the hell?" She looked sternly down at him, a wicked smile on her face.

Ronald backed away, hands raised in front of him. "I'm so sorry. I was just…"

She kept grinning her evil-looking grin, and Ronald couldn't help but notice the tree-like tattoo branching out near her collarbone. He stared at it, still in full reverse. She sneered, and he nearly fell over backwards.

"Ronald?" Aubrey appeared at the far end of the aisle. "Is that you?"

"Do you know this *creep?*"

"Um... er..."

He looked at the woman then to Aubrey. At that moment, neither of them seemed like friendly options. Then, he bumped into a display, knocking it over and falling on his back in a heap of earbuds, chargers, and Bluetooth speakers.

"Shit," he said, scrambling free and running for the door. "I, uh, gotta go." *Shit, shit, shit.*

He tore out into the street and didn't look back until Che's record shop, and the embarrassing disaster that was his latest encounter with Aubrey was half a dozen blocks behind him. Only then did he realize he'd forgotten to grab headphones, and he was no longer sure what part of his most recent debacle was worse.

INTERLUDE ONE: BEFORE

Rain pelted her exposed skin. Cold. Sharp. Relentless. But it reminded her she was alive, which was more than could be said for the others, and that life was a gift she was not ready to part with.

She could still hear their screams, their desperate pleas repeating again and again in her mind. Her screaming, she reminded herself. That awful, shrill sound had been her own weak, pitiful response to the actions of a weaker, more pitiful man.

The worst part? It brought to mind *their* screaming. And she saw her father's face in his. Those dead eyes, quivering lips. She already relived the massacre night and night again in her nightmares; she did not need to relive it during her waking hours, too, but it all seemed to blend whenever her adoptive father struck her.

Her wrists throbbed from where he had grabbed her. The torn skin on her knees and thighs stung every time a raindrop fell.

She had told him "No" as he pulled her from their makeshift shelter, a home that had been opened to her when she had needed a home more than anything.

"And don't forget my kindness," he had said as he dragged her across cave's stone floor by her hair. No amount of kicking and screaming was going to stop him from making an example out of poor, defenseless Akuma. Not after she had disrespected him in front of his *real* children.

She should be grateful, no matter the circumstances, no matter how hard he made her work, no matter how many times he hit her.

Anything less was a disgraceful disrespect of their family name. It was for her own good, really. If she wanted to be part of the family, to find her place among the villagers, she had to earn that right through blood, sweat, and tears.

And, Amaterasu Ōmikami forbid, what were Nobu and Touji to make of such insubordination? He could not abide her *wild* nature to influence his perfectly well-behaved and tame children, now, could he?

Akuma could not go back. She could not show her face within those caverns again. Not after they had all witnessed her so... frail, so at *his* mercy. So weak.

She had not felt so much pain since she watched the golden dragon flee from her own village, its gray head spikes hackled, its massive wings blotting out the sky. Her family, her friends, everything they had worked so hard to build was destroyed by fire and steel in a matter of mere moments. What did she fear more, a dragon and its armored devils or a man and his fists? No matter how hard she fought against it, the answer was inarguably the man and his fists and all the awful violence he would continue to do to her if nothing changed—if *she* did not make it change.

Lightning struck, flashing bright blue across the black sky. Akuma jumped and shrieked. Her heart raced, and her wounds began to throb anew. She found herself weeping once more and hating herself for her lack of emotional control

Akuma Araki, the Girl Who Wept. Was this to be her destiny? Had she survived horror and death to hide beneath a tree and cry herself dry?

Sniffling, she straightened her shoulders and wiped her nose. *No.* No she had not. Since no one was coming to save her, she was going to have to save herself. She set off into the rainy night, back towards the caves—*her caves*—and brought the image of his wretched face to the forefront of her mind. His ugly sneer fueled her inner rage, and Akuma Araki was resolute, ready to do what must be done.

CHAPTER SIX

Ronald couldn't decide if it was the fight with Daichi, the unexpected encounter with Aubrey, or the CVS's blinding white commercial lighting, but his head *ached*. On the bright side, he managed to find a cheap pair of earbuds to use until he built enough courage to show his face at Che's again.

Up went his hood, and up went the volume. With one small gesture, life was okay. His contentment probably wouldn't last long, but he sank into the music of the moment.

I walk a thin line... Denaun Porter sang. *Among the masses, all alone.*

Normal was a good six or seven miles from the New Province, but it was a calm, crisp September night, and a long walk was exactly what Ronald needed to clear his head. There were a lot of competing thoughts bouncing around in there at the moment, and it was probably going to take more than one night to unpack it all, but he finally had his music back. That alone was worth the extra effort.

Pharoahe Monch rounded off the last verse. *For peace of mind, install an external drive, so I'd be more driven internally to survive...*

Even though he was lost in the music, Ronald noticed them almost right away. For the most part, people ignored him, but not these people. These people watched him like a kitsune watched her kits, their eyes leering from seemingly every nook and cranny.

Girls, at first. No older than in their early twenties, keeping to the dark shadows of the city. Dead spots behind streetlights, the entrances to alleyways, overhangs in front of closed bodegas. They stared as he passed, and each intense new gaze set him walking faster until he was all but running down the sidewalk, panting with the effort of exertion.

He glanced over his shoulder at one in particular who stood out from the rest. A skinny, pencil-thin woman with a mop of reddish-blonde hair. She had tattoos for sleeves and more metal in her face than all the members of a punk rock band combined, and as she leered, she licked her tongue across her teeth and shot him with coy finger guns. This brought cyberpunk visions to mind, not all of which were entirely unpleasant.

His heart raced, and he picked up his pace, running full force into another girl as he turned around, nearly knocking her onto the sidewalk.

"What the hell do you people want?" He shoved her arms away as she reached to steady him. "Leave me alone."

Prostitutes were regular enough in the city. He'd noticed them on occasion—maybe stereotyping a few for something they weren't—but he wasn't anywhere near where they normally hung out. And it had never been him alone, surrounded on all sides, so there had never been any real potential for danger.

RONALD, THE RONIN

Were they actually following him? Or was he paranoid?

Ronald risked another glance back and saw shadows, blending in and out of the city's dark places, drawing nearer to him. He was sweating, out of breath, and kicking himself for not taking the bus. But how could he have known something like this would happen? It was like a scene from a bad sci-fi horror movie. One with cheesy CGI, worse acting, and a budget less than what he had in his pocket—and he was the reluctant, underpaid star of the show. The problem? He wasn't nearly handsome enough for the role.

He cut a corner, hoping to lose them in the maze of tight city blocks, and found himself surrounded. Not by whores, but by stern men clad in golden robes and armed to the teeth. They stood in formation around one man he knew too well, who wasn't dressed in the loose-fitting cloth of his Order but covered head to toe in golden armor. Iron plates corded together, overlapping in all the right places to provide extra protection. It was ornamented by swatches of golden fabric, and he wore an impressive, intimidating kabuto with a hand-carved golden fox curled upon its crest. In the center of his chest plate, he displayed the seal of the Order of the Golden Bonsai. Daichi's Order, a specter Ronald had hidden from for the last year or so.

Ronald fought two simultaneous instinctual urges: to bow or keep running. In the end, he did neither. Instead, he just stood there, petrified.

"Ah, Ronald? The youngest Hashimoto, I presume?" Oda Musashi circled Ronald, who couldn't read the master's expression through his mask. His skin flushed anyway. His ghostly eyes never once left Ronald's. "Oh, how glad I was when Tomo brought word of your return. And to notice you by happenstance, after all these years? Remarkable."

"Tomo?"

Master Oda ignored his question. "Where have you and old Daichi been hiding? One might take offense at such a sudden disappearance of two revered friends of the Order." He said *friends* with venomous intent.

Ronald gulped. "The suburbs. We're living in the suburbs now. I'm going to school, like a normal teenager." *And Daichi is hiding at the bottom of every bottle he can find,* Ronald almost added, but he made the wise, ever-the-loyal-son decision to keep that part to himself.

The girls who had been following him began to appear from every shadow. He recognized the pencil-thin woman, and there was the woman from the record shop who had set his whole gaff into motion, the one wearing a trench coat, a bonsai tree tattoo branching from her chest. What was she doing there in the first place? Had she purposefully incited his ridiculous retreat at Che's? To test his mettle, perhaps? Or set him off his guard for this ambush?

"So, I see you have met my kitsune already."

Yokai? Ronald couldn't believe what he was hearing. *Fighting alongside the Order?*

He knew very little about the Order itself. Daichi had allowed him to read a few chosen history texts, which he skimmed for the most part, but his training consisted almost entirely of combat skills and physical endurance. From what he did know, it was unheard of for Master Oda's people to throw in with yokai—supernatural beings from other islands of existence—and kitsune and samurai didn't usually play well with one another. Honorable warriors didn't appreciate the all-to-often mean-hearted tricks foxes played, and foxes didn't jive well with being expected to take life so seriously.

"Mhm," he said. "I may have bumped into them." Literally, in both cases. "But we haven't been formally introduced."

"Hikari," Master Oda said, gesturing towards the kitsune with facial piercings. He turned towards the woman in the trench coat. "And Sakiko. Ladies, this is Ronald Hashimoto, my greatest disciple's second born son. Ronald, these are my *daughters*." The last word hissed through his lips with more than a hint of disdain.

Hikari half-saluted. Sakiko dipped and bowed. Ronald scratched the back of his neck and waved to them. They were both beautiful in their own way—now that they were face to face and he wasn't rushing to escape gross ridicule—and he suddenly found himself at a loss for words. He still couldn't believe it. *Kitsune.* Employed by the Order? It just didn't make sense. And Master Oda had called them his daughters. How had Ronald never heard about this before? He hadn't heard about a lot, but this seemed a pretty major detail for Daichi to have excluded from their training.

"We have been looking for you, Ronald." Master Oda unclipped his facemask. He looked older. Tired. "You and your father have been greatly missed. How fairs old Daichi? I cannot imagine he's adjusting well to life outside the Order. Battle is in his blood. And in yours, if you're anything like your dear old otousan."

Ronald found a sliver of courage and said, "Not anymore." His voice cracked, and the gathered crowd shared a laugh at his expense.

"Things are not going well, Ronald. Akuma Araki's hold on

Shima Gōdatsusha tightens daily. Her army swells with ronin and oni alike. Soon, I am afraid, the Order will not have the strength to push her back."

Ronald shrugged. "It's not my fight anymore."

He just wanted to be a kid, for once. He had almost fooled himself that he could just be a kid again, and here he was, yet again letting himself down.

"Ah, but what of your brother's swords? Are those of no consequence either? Does your blood's honor mean nothing to you?"

"It's. Not. My. Fight," Ronald repeated, struggling to keep his mounting frustration to himself. He cast his eyes to the ground, focusing on a smashed, circular piece of gum. "I'm sorry..."

"You say that as if you have a choice. You are chosen. You are Hashimoto and have danced among the reeds of twilight. Even if I were to agree to let you go, you are marked. There is no outpacing who you are, Ronald. There is no hiding from your destiny."

Ronald sniffled. Jiro's last expression, one of fear and pain, came back, and he blinked it away. "I can't... I can't go back there. After what happened... I'm sorry, but I'm not who you thought I was."

Oda Musashi growled, low and deep, full of disapproval. "You do not wear your swords." Ronald reached for his waist but grabbed only air as he knew he would. "Have you so easily abandoned who you trained so hard to become?"

"I won't fight your battles." *I have my own to contend with.*

"Hmm. I see." A wave of mumbling spread between the samurai and kitsune. They whispered, no doubt, because of their own anxiousness about the master's next move. "Is that your final word,

Ronald Hashimoto? Are you truly disavowing your birthright, casting the Order aside, and abandoning your sacred duty? Is this the kind of man you choose to be?"

Ronald stood straight, though he felt as if he might pass out, and nodded. "Yeah, I suppose it is."

The master clicked his teeth and shook his head. Someone behind Ronald whistled, and he caught a glimpse of Hikari nodding her head, lips pursed in a frown.

"If that is so, you have made your decision. Out of respect for Daichi, we will allow you to return home tonight, to make peace with whomever and whatever you choose. Next time we meet, young Hashimoto, will be our last."

Ronald understood what leaving the Order meant. It wasn't something you walked away from like a soccer club or quit like a bad habit. It was a bond for life, one strengthened through blood, sweat, and sacrifice. While his father had made his choice for him, he was in nonetheless. He just wasn't strong enough to do the things they wanted him to do. Not after Jiro's death… not alone.

Master Oda clipped his mask on and turned his back to Ronald, a flowing gray cape extending behind him like a great wing caught in an updraft. His samurai followed. Only Hikari and Sakiko stayed behind.

"It's a shame," Hikari said. "I've heard great things about your potential."

Sakiko lightly caressed the underside of his chin with her finger to bring his gaze to hers. "A real shame. You look like him. Jiro, I mean."

"You knew Jiro?" Ronald's eyes widened.

Hikari snorted. "Knew him? You could say that. Jiro and Sakiko were—"

Sakiko growled, cutting off the other kitsune, then smiled sweetly. "We were close, yes. He cared a great deal for you and your father." She rolled her eyes and sighed as if slighted by Jiro's love for his family. "You two were the only people who mattered to him. I guess this is goodbye, Ronald Hashimoto. When you see him in the next life, tell Jiro I say, 'Osu!'"

When everyone was gone, leaving Ronald alone once more, he swore and kicked a nearby street sign. It wobbled in the air from the force of his kick. By the time it came to a rest, Ronald was long gone too. He couldn't get home fast enough, and he found himself lost in regretful remembrance. To those ends, he forgot to check to ensure he wasn't being followed.

CHAPTER SEVEN

Shima Gōdatsusha. the Island of Usurpers.
Jiro's tomb, and Ronald's worst nightmare.

It was a dream he'd had over and over again since his confrontation with the Order of the Golden Bonsai and their kitsune lackeys. It happened a lifetime ago, when Ronald was a different version of Ronald. Someone whom he'd just managed to let go of before Master Oda resurrected him from the dead. It was a dream he'd lost no small amount of sleep over in the months following his not-so-welcome reunion with the Order. Every time he had it, it felt more and more real, as if he could almost reach out and touch his brother, grab him, and bring him back from his grave. Do it all over. Better this time.

He awoke in a cold sweat, his sheets soaked through, hands clammy and hot. He shot up, threw off his oppressive covers, and panted loudly, unable to catch his breath. There was the vague impression of *her* devil's face emblazoned on the back of his eyelids, but he blinked it away and spots came rushing to cloud his vision.

"Shit!" He slammed his mattress with an open palm. "Come on, man!"

You are in your room, he told himself. *Safe, among your heroes.*

You are Ronald Hashimoto, a regular sixteen-year-old boy, and it is the first day of your junior year at Normal Community High School. It's going to be your best year yet.

Everything is okay.

You're fine, Ronald. You have nothing to be afraid of. They can't hurt you here.

It was a mantra he told himself when the noise got too loud, and it seemed to help. Little reassurances, positive self-talk. But, damn, he wished he would stop having that dream. He'd lived the ordeal once already, he didn't need to relive it in vivid, real-time detail every night... for ten freakin' months straight...

On a positive note, it'd been ten months since he'd heard anything from the Order. He hadn't as much as caught them lurking in dark places, suburban or otherwise. And every other aspect of his life had improved tremendously. There was something to say about confronting your past, about finding closure. Telling the Order off and officially severing ties with them had changed everything.

It was his junior year, and Ronald Hashimoto had been reborn, a new man with a second chance, and he was ready to take on all of life's challenges, mundane and otherwise.

Like what to wear, for example. It was a new year, after all, and he could be whomever he wanted. After flicking through his closet for way longer than he'd care to admit, Ronald picked out a vintage MF Doom tee and a pair of worn jeans. More holes than denim, and no, he hadn't bought them like that. For good measure, he threw a black overstretched beanie over his ever-growing nest of thick hair. He stopped to check himself out in the hallway mirror and realized for the first time in as long as he could remember he didn't feel sick to his stomach thinking about school.

The prospect of friends, of his Hip-Hop club, of regular, plain ole normality made him almost giddy. What once seemed boring was now liberating, and he embraced the days to come with a smile on his face. A *real* smile.

Ronald was throwing together a quick lunch of yesterday's cold pizza, hostess snack cakes, and baby carrots when he heard the first horn. He fumbled through the cupboards until he found a sleeve of Pop-Tarts and all but leapt over the kitchen island, grabbing the strap of his shoulder bag with deft hands as he slid by. The second his feet hit the floor he was on the move.

Daichi, sleeping restlessly in his armchair, grumbled and rolled to the opposite side. Infomercials were playing on TV, something about a set of knives that Ronald couldn't live another day without. He scoffed and grabbed a blanket from the floor and, careful not to knock over any of the half-empty beer cans, draped it over his father's prone body. He almost tucked him in, like he always wished Daichi would have done for him, but he shook his head. He didn't want to wake the old man. Instead, he leaned over him, grabbed the bottle of sake from Daichi's loose grip, and sighed.

"Sleep tight, old man."

The second honk sounded as Ronald was searching for his key and school ID. *Beep-beep, beeeeeep.*

"Yeah, yeah. I'm coming."

He took one last look into the living room, pushed through the front door, and skipped over the puddle at the bottom of the porch steps. A black Saturn Ion idled in the driveway, a familiar and reassuring face behind its wheel.

Shoving his bag between his legs, Ronald said, "Jeeze, where's the fire?"

Aubrey put the car in reverse and rolled her eyes. "Good morning to you too, Ronny Boy."

"God, I wish you wouldn't call me that."

"Sounds like a *you* problem, *Ronny Boy*." She shrugged, pouting. "Maybe if you'd stop crying about it, I wouldn't give you so much grief."

"Whatever. Hey, we're gonna be late. Can't this thing go any faster?"

She shoved him on his shoulder and clicked her teeth. "Oh, it's my car's fault now, is it? Maybe if you hadn't kept me waiting for so long while you put your make-up on."

"You have to admit it's a hunk of junk, though. And I look *damn* good."

Aubrey scowled and stuck out her tongue. "*You're* a hunk of junk."

Ronald let his gaze fall to his feet. He stuck his lip out and periodically glanced at Aubrey until she was forced to notice him.

"Oh, come on! Seriously?" He nodded. "Fine. I'm sorry."

"Thank you," he said, nudging her with his shoulder.

"I'm sorry you're a piece of junk."

After sharing a laugh that almost had him snorting, Ronald found himself staring at her. They'd spent a lot of time together over the summer—at Che's shop, eating sushi, and trading music recommendations—but he hadn't seen much of her the last few weeks. It was a relief to be able to look into those deep, dark eyes again, and he couldn't help but fall back into the old feelings trap he'd fallen into when they first met.

A stupid grin stretched across his face. "It's good to see you, Aubrey."

She glanced at him, cheeks flushed, then right back at the road. Her grip on the wheel tightened, but she managed to smirk.

"It's good to be seen, Ronny Boy. More than you know. Got ya an iced coffee, by the way." She sloshed the ice around in his face. "Extra sugary, just how you like it."

"My hero." He snatched the Tim Horton's cup from her and slurped extra loud, batting his eyes as obnoxiously as he could. Aubrey shoved him again, and they both laughed.

It was a short drive to the school, mostly spent waiting in bumper-to-bumper traffic. Sixteen- and seventeen-year-old kids, blaring their horns, hanging their heads out of windows, creeping up to within inches of rear-ending each other. Ronald shook his head. These kids were living their lives the best ways they knew how and finding little stupid pleasures to make their short time as teenagers as enjoyable as possible. It was admirable, in a way, but he was still annoyed when Skylar swerved into the turn lane to pass everyone, slowing by Aubrey's car for one of his minions—Eli, maybe, but it was hard to tell from his current viewpoint—to press his pale butt cheeks against the window.

"Get bent!" Aubrey yelled out the closed window.

Ronald snorted coffee. "Get bent? What is this, 1976?"

"Shut up, man. It just kind of came out."

Up ahead, right before the parking lot's bus entrance, Skylar's Camaro skidded its tires, hopped the curb, and nearly plowed into the school's brand-new signage. The friend whose butt they'd just had the pleasure of viewing got out, flipped off Skylar, and ran towards the building, still adjusting his jeans. Skylar peeled away, cutting off a bus, and shouted something indistinguishable out his window.

"What an asshole," Ronald said.

"No kidding. He's going to kill somebody one of these days."

The hallway noise didn't sound so oppressive this year. Ronald didn't feel the inescapable urge to tune it all out, to run in the opposite direction and hide his life away, either. Not with Aubrey by his side. Not with his friends, DJ and Robert, waiting like goobers by his locker.

"Sup, nerds!"

He gave DJ and Robert "bro hugs"—half handshake, half awkward but pseudo-manly back pats—and stood aside as they both hugged Aubrey. She tensed, held her arms at her sides, and chuckled nervously as Robert lingered a bit too long.

"Alright, alright," Ronald said, "let the girl breathe."

Aubrey gasped, as if she'd resurfaced just in time, and then laughed it off. "Did you guys enjoy your summers?"

"I don't know" A sly look crept slowly across DJ's face until his pearly white teeth all but glinted under the school's extra-bright lights. He cleared his throat, fake coughed. "Ask Jess Avery."

"Whaaaaaaaaa," Robert said, grabbing DJ's outstretched hand and practically shaking him to death. "You're a dog, Terri. A filthy, dangerous freakin' animal."

"You didn't," Ronald said. DJ nodded, one eyebrow raised. "Hey, I'm happy for you, man. Congrats, I guess, and please pass on my sincere condolences to Jess."

"Finally wore her down?" Aubrey asked.

DJ frowned at the slight. "Hey, I'll have you know *she* asked me out. I almost turned her down, too."

"You what!?" Robert was in disbelief. He feigned a heart attack and bumped into an innocent freshman fighting with the locker beside him. The kid went flying back, nearly tripping over his own feet. "Sorry, kid." The kid groaned before shuffling away. "What? I said I was sorry."

"Weird," Ronald said, "you barely touched him."

Robert's cheeks turned red, and he switched his phone on, losing himself in one of his games without further comment.

"I just... I wasn't ready to be tied down, you know?" DJ continued. Aubrey snorted, her outburst getting caught in her throat. "Nothing funny about it. Danger John turns sixteen in a couple weeks. Once I'm behind the wheel, I'm going to be a hot commodity around here."

"Happy for ya," Aubrey said. They all glared at her. "What? Really, I am. I shipped you two from the start. No cap."

Sensing the conversation was shifting towards overly awkward territory, Ronald turned to Robert. "What about you, man? What'd you do all summer?"

Robert looked up at the ceiling, curled his lips as if the act of thinking might explode his brain. Then he snapped and tapped his temple. "That's right," he said. "Absolutely. Freakin'. Nothing."

"You should have come by the record shop. We were there basically all summer."

"Yeah, man, "DJ added, "Ronald's *mom*, Che, is super cool. She pretty much let us have the run of the place."

"She's *not* my mom."

"Dude," Aubrey said, gathering her things, "you guys even have the same nose. If she's not your mom, it's like one of those dog situations. You know, when they start to look and act exactly like their owner because they spend so much time together?"

"Psh, whatever. Don't you all have class soon?" He turned to Robert. "But for real, you should come out to the city with us some time."

Robert shrugged. "Eh, I'm okay with nothing. Besides, I put about two hundred hours into Elders Scrolls. Hit a couple PRs along the way." He popped his pecs up and down. "Time well spent, if you ask me, and plenty of work left to do."

The first bell went off. Class started in five minutes.

"Alright," Ronald said, "I've got Bio first thing. I'll catch you guys later."

The boys exchanged hugs again, and Ronald stood awkwardly by Aubrey. They each moved one way, then the other as if dancing around each other—dancing around their feelings—and nearly bumped heads. In the end, Ronald grabbed her hand and shook it with a wet-noodle grip.

"Oh brother." Robert blew air out of his cheeks. "Sexual tension much?"

"Shut up, *Robert*." Aubrey's cheeks went blood red, and she looked away, scratching the back of her neck.

"Yeah," Ronald said, "You wouldn't know sexual tension if it flashed its tits. Alright, peace out y'all."

He was several strides down the hall when DJ called out. "Hey, I bumped into Mendez at Kroger the other week."

"Oh yeah?"

"I told him about our club idea. He's in as Faculty Sponsor. We might actually make it happen this year."

"That's great news! We'll talk more in study hall. Fifth period, right?"

"Fifth period," DJ agreed, but Ronald was already disappearing down the hall and turning towards the stairwell.

It took every ounce of self-control for Ronald not to look back, to check to see if Aubrey was watching him go. He could feel her eyes on him. Or, at least, he hoped he could.

Halfway up the dingy stairwell, he stooped suddenly. A heaviness spread through his chest, to his hands and feet, settling behind his eyes. He felt flush, distant from himself as if he might melt into the dirty tiles beneath his Adidas. His mind screamed, and Ronald didn't have enough energy to scream back. The darkness overtook him, the bad thoughts barraging his senses until he felt as if he might explode.

He slid down the wall, below the barred windows, and buried his face in his hands. He sobbed until it hurt even though he couldn't come up with any rational explanation for the outburst. The second bell rang, but he hardly noticed. He didn't stop crying until a voice brought him back to reality.

"You're late." Mr. Mendez, Ronald's Bio teacher, sat beside him, their knees close but not touching.

Ronald sniffled and wiped his nose on his sleeve. "So are you."

"I'm the teacher. What are you going to do, write me up?"

Ronald laughed at his teacher's attempted joke, and it wasn't forced either. The moment had passed as if it had never come in the first place.

"You okay, man?" Mendez put a firm, reassuring hand on his back. "Wanna talk about it, or would you rather I pretend I never saw you here?"

"No, I'm good. Can you just give me a sec?"

"Sure." Mr. Mendez stood up and gathered his bags. "Don't take too long, or I'll have to make an example out of you, yeah?"

Ronald rolled his eyes. "Whatever, Mr. M. I'll be your martyr if I have to."

"Sooooo dramatic. I mean it, though. Get it together and get to class. We're hittin' it right from the jump today, and I have high hopes for my budding Hip-Hop guru."

Mr. Mendez was most of the way up the stairs when Ronald stopped him. "Thanks for sponsoring our club."

"Word." Mr. Mendez flashed the hang loose sign. "As you kids say, 'It's going to be *dope*.'"

"Nobody says *that,* Mr. M. Not anymore, at least."

"Get to class, Ronald."

Ronald took a few deep breaths, adjusted his beanie, and rubbed his eyes until they no longer burned. He wasn't sure if he was "composed," but he felt like a human again, and some days, that was the best you could hope for.

He repeated his mantra: *Everything is okay. You're fine, Ronald. You have nothing to be afraid of. They can't hurt you here.* But if it was true, why did he keep feeling this way? Why couldn't he be better? Maybe, just maybe if he repeated it enough, he might start to believe in his own affirmations. Safe was safe, and that should have been enough.

Ronald peeked out the window, down at the full student parking lot, and shielded his eyes to the sun. For the briefest moment, he could have sworn he saw the coattail of a gold-lined haori disappearing behind a Jeep, but that was crazy. There was nothing out there besides hand-me-down cars and fresh asphalt, and Linda, Normal's head nurse, smoking one of her Marlboro

Reds behind the dumpsters.

He took one last deep breath. "It's all in your head, Ronny Boy. It's all in your head..." *Now, get yourself to class, and stop being so... you.*

CHAPTER EIGHT

Ronald hesitated at the door. His first day of junior year in the books, he was feeling a little better, but he never knew what to expect whenever he entered his own home. What version of Daichi would he get? How long would he have to spend cleaning the old man's mess?

He pushed in, and it was worse than expected. Much, much worse...

"What the... What did you do this time?" Ronald surveyed the foyer and living room in disbelief. "And what did this poor furniture ever do to you?"

The coffee table was split down the middle, splinters of wood scattered about, and the screen of Daichi's beloved TV was smashed to pieces. Glass lay in shards on the floor. There were large, fist-sized holes in the drywall behind the TV and trailing between the living room and kitchen, with a smattering of smaller, nail-sized holes in a streaking pattern directly across from the front door. There were beer cans everywhere, smashed and spilled, carpets soaked and smelly, and a broken bottle near where Daichi lay prone on the floor, his arm and head sticky with blood, face scrunched awkwardly against the stained carpet.

Ronald tiptoed to his father's side and mustered all his strength to pick him up and drag him to his chair. The old man grumbled something incoherent, but he was less conscious than usual, as if that was even possible.

He checked Daichi's wounds, glass cuts on his arm, most likely, and figured he had hit his head falling over the table. It was hard to tell, but whatever had happened, he was in bad shape. Ronald propped him up and grabbed a wet rag, some rubbing alcohol, and bandages from the kitchen. He cleaned the drying blood as best he could, disinfected the wounds, and wrapped his arms. All the while, Daichi moaned and smacked his lips, but he never fully woke up enough to appreciate his son taking care of him, let alone thank him for his efforts.

"Don't mind me," Ronald mumbled. "Just saving your life. Again."

Oh well, he thought. *He may never know what I do to take care of him, but no matter how much of a prick he is, he is my dad.* Besides, Ronald was convinced that if he stopped, Daichi would wither and die.

"You're a bastard, you know it?" He envisioned punching the old man square in his disfigured face, took a deep breath, and abandoned the notion to better thinking. "You're a bastard, but for whatever reason, I love ya anyway. Sleep sweet."

Daichi shifted in his chair and choked on his spit until his eyes opened halfway. He looked at Ronald, or rather through him, and said, "Jiro. Get Jiro."

Now, the anger threatened. Ronald was so damn tired of hearing about how he wasn't Jiro. He clenched his fists until his knuckles turned white, and his neck muscles twitched.

"Jiro's not here, and you know that," Ronald said. "It's just me, Ronald. The son you wish you never had. Your prodigal failure, in the living, breathing flesh."

"Jiro..." Daichi repeated, his eyes blinking open and shut, open and shut until they slowly closed tight. He let out a single loud snore and rolled over again. "We need... Jiro. He'd know... what to do."

Daichi choked again. This time, blood splattered across the carpet. Ronald's stomach dropped, and he rushed to his father's side. He'd been so busy being annoyed about the cuts on the old man's arms, assuming this was just another one of his drunken escapades, that he'd missed what had been so glaringly obvious all along: a puncture wound in Daichi's side, blood seeping through his clothes, saturating his chair's cushion.

He reacted on instinct, pulling Daichi towards him, off the chair, tying his wound as tight as possible, and sprinting off towards the stairs. He had to get to his room, grab his swords. Whoever was here, whoever the Order had finally sent, couldn't have gone far, not with how fresh his father's wound was, and if they caught Ronald unarmed, he'd be worse off than Daichi soon.

Ronald took the stairs three at a time, barely stopping to cut the corner towards his room. A thick chain flew over his head, and a small, curved blade at its end cut a huge gash into the wall beside him. He ducked as it snapped back, narrowly avoiding a clean decapitation. Before he could process what was happening, the chain flew towards him again, rattling in the otherwise silent house, and he rolled to avoid this second strike. The blade lodged in the corner of the wall by the railing, and Ronald had enough sense to grasp it in both hands and yank it towards him with all his strength.

Ronald's quick reaction caught his attacker off guard, and the would-be assassin came stumbling out from the shadows. Ronald recognized him immediately as the man from the stoop, wearing hakama pants and a gold-lined haori, his stupid mustache twitching below his pointy nose.

"Oh, it's you again..."

The man cried out and dropped his modified kusarigama, a long chain weighted on one end with a sickle-like kama on the other. It fell clattering to the floor, but he was already drawing a new set of weapons: two gleaming sais, their handles wrapped in fine, golden velvet. They had nasty, sharp tips stained rust-red and a series of tiny barbs along their bladed edges. Ronald gulped. There would be no recovering from a clean stab with one of those nasty boys.

"Yup. Me." The assassin circled Ronald, stepping one foot over another, careful to keep their bodies squared. He sneered, bared his teeth, and spun his sais artfully around his hands. He raised his shoulders and pouted his lower lip. "Aren't you happy to see me?"

Ronald circled to match his steps, keeping his distance and mentally weighing his chances of survival. They weren't great. He watched his attacker carefully. Any slight muscle twitch and this deadly man could get the upper hand, especially considering Ronald was unarmed and unprepared.

"You're Tomo." It was more a statement than a question.

He remembered back to nearly a year ago, when he'd met the Order of the Golden Bonsai in New Province. *Met* may have been a stretch. They'd stalked him with hired kitsune until he was practically crapping his pants and then surrounded him on a side street, giving him no choice but to listen to what they had to say. The Order's master, Oda Musashi, had given him an ultimatum: Complete his initiation, retrieve his brother's swords, and fulfill his destiny, or face the blade. Oda had mentioned a man named Tomo in passing, after an unsettling encounter with a stranger on a stoop. Ronald should have put two and two together, and he should have known that sooner or later Fate would catch up to him.

"So, the Order finally sent you." Ronald slid one foot behind him, preparing for his next move. "You gonna kill an unarmed man? That's savage. Thought for sure you people had more honor"

Tomo laughed through his nose. "Honor? I'm a killer, kid. I don't give two shits about honor"

The assassin lunged, stabbing with his sais. He was proficient, like an angry wasp, and his fury of attacks drove Ronald back, back, back towards the open bathroom door.

Ronald bobbed and weaved from side to side, careful to angle his dodges just right so the barbed edges of the weapons didn't catch hold of his skin. He dodged to the left, then to the right, then left again. He allowed his years of training to show him where the assassin would strike next. He leaped over a low flourish, nearly slamming into the ceiling, and maneuvered around the assassin. Tomo was ready, and he swung his elbow outward, catching Ronald on the jaw.

Senses wobbling, Ronald staggered out of reach. Tomo taunted him, but he wasn't about to spring into another trap. Despite his lack of recent practice, his carefully honed discipline had taught him better. Daichi had forged him into a weapon, no matter how much he longed for it not to be true.

"Would have thought a slayer of oni would put up a better fight." Tomo folded his arms over his chest, sai blades pointed toward the floor, and chuckled. "How disappointing."

Ronald massaged his throbbing face. He didn't have long to reorient himself, because Tomo dashed forward, sais at the ready. Again, Ronald scrambled to avoid getting poked. Back pressed against the wall, he dodged the best he could. Tomo jabbed holes in the drywall, the barbs on his weapons pulling a shower of dust every time he retracted them.

He anticipated the next strike late, and Tomo dealt him a shallow cut across the cheek. It stung and sent tingly needles through his neck and down his spine, causing his muscles to spasm.

The assassin didn't even seem tired, so Ronald had to act fast, and he was starting to get desperate.

The moment Tomo retracted another strike from the wall, Ronald knelt as his wobbly knees allowed. He concentrated all his energy into his legs and propelled himself upward, throwing his shoulder into the assassin's chest. Together, they nearly tumbled down the stairs in their struggle for advantage. One of Tomo's sais was knocked loose, but he continued to work at Ronald with the remaining weapon. Ronald managed to hold it at bay, keeping the numerous wounds superficial at worst. Still, his ribs burned, and the same tingling feeling began to crawl throughout his body.

He jammed his knee into Tomo's groin. The assassin snarled, but Ronald didn't relent. He tried to jam his thumb into the man's eye, something he'd seen in movies, but Tomo launched him into the wall. His body left a Ronald-sized indentation, but the damage had been done. He had the assassin reeling.

Tomo hunched over, holding his lower abdomen, and coughed until red-tinged spittle sprayed out of his mouth. "Christ, kid. *That* was savage."

Ronald stood over him, gasping from exertion. He felt his ribs where Tomo had punctured his torso, and his hand came up bright red. He limped towards his closed bedroom door—towards his swords—careful to keep an eye on the assassin. When he reached for the handle, a series of shuriken slapped into the door, the last one ricocheting centimeters from Ronald's bloody hand.

"Ninja stars? You brought friggin' ninja stars? How cliché."

Tomo sighed as he wobbled to his feet. He held another round of shuriken off to one side, murderous intent in his eyes. "Hey, one of these bad boys will kill you just the same as my blades. Faster even."

Tomo began to throw but Ronald moved faster. He threw himself once more at the assassin, slamming into him with all his weight. Intertwined, they toppled as they fell down the stairs, each taking turns hitting the steps one by one. Ronald saw stars when his head cracked into the banister, and he fought against the fringe of black choking his vision.

As soon as they came to a stop, Ronald punched Tomo in the throat as hard as he could. The assassin wheezed, hands immediately moving to protect his windpipes. Ronald kneed him in the groin a few more times for good measure and crawled away, careful not to stand up too fast. The last thing he needed was to pass out mid-fight.

Voice strained, Tomo growled, "Oh, you bastard. That hurt."

Ronald spat blood. "Next time I won't go so easy on you. Next time, it'll be the last time." *Because I won't survive another fight like this*, Ronald thought, but he was caught in a moment of supreme awesomeness and wasn't about to let this unexpected "hard-ass" mask slip.

Tomo attempted to stand, but he slumped in a heap. His back heaved as he fought to catch his breath, and it almost sounded as if he were laughing.

Ronald's skin crawled. He couldn't imagine what could be funny. All he could think about was getting out of there before the assassin regained his strength. Despite having the upper hand, he knew he was outmatched. In this fight, he'd gotten lucky and almost knocked himself out in the process. In another fight, things wouldn't go his way.

Daichi growled, and Ronald turned to him.

"Dad!"

The old man grumbled something unintelligible. His eyes were still mostly closed, but he was up, swaying gently and bracing himself on the arm of his chair.

"Come, Ronald," Daichi managed. "It doesn't take long."

Ronald bit his lip, tasted blood in his mouth. *What doesn't take long, old man? Talk sense for once in your life.*

"But—"

"The assassin's poison... I know where we can go. Where we can..." Daichi trailed off and stumbled forward into Ronald's outstretched arms. He was a slight man, but his weight was almost enough to bring them both down.

"Dad?" Ronald helped Daichi back to his feet and maneuvered his father's arm over his shoulder so he could support his meager weight. Tomo was starting to stir. "I got you, old man. I'll trust you this time." *Like I have a better choice.* "Where to?"

A sudden rush of dizziness struck. His whole body tensed, cold and rigid, the slice on his cheek and wound down his torso throbbing.

He heard Tomo laughing hysterically, maniacally. "It's as Master Daichi said. 'It doesn't take long.'"

So, they went, leaving the barely conscious assassin behind. For the first time in as long as he could remember, Ronald placed his trust entirely in his father. *I'm screwed,* he thought. *I'm screwed. I'm screwed. I'm sca-a-rewed.*

But what other choice did he have?

CHAPTER NINE

Dunes as far as the eye can see. Swirling sand, the color of rust. Ronald holds his arms in front of his face, against the wind's constant, shrieking howl, and doesn't recognize his own hands.

Ahead, beneath the black sun, he sees shadows moving about. He hears hammer striking stake, bachi striking drum. A savory, smoky meat smell fills his dry mouth with saliva.

At the chaotic camp's apex, the shadowy figures stop and stare. They each wear a unique kabuto: stag, bull, fox, dragon. Demon. Their faces are covered by menacing mempo. But one stands out from all the rest: it's Akuma Araki's. Jiro is tied to a spit, rotating slowly around an open fire. Suddenly, Ronald's very, very sick to his stomach.

"You shouldn't have come," Akuma says. "You are not welcome here."

Ronald draws his swords. They feel heavy in his fists, like strangers.

Akuma and her samurai's tanuki-like cackles echo in the black night. Their laughter fills the desolation, stirs the sand itself into a frenzy.

"Come, then," she says. "Take what is yours."

Ronald dashes forward, his swords once again extensions of his hands. He slices, slashes, parries. He rolls beneath the legs of an oni, crossing a gash in the shape of an X that brings the demon to its knees.

In ones and twos they come, an endless horde of samurai. In ones and twos, they fall until their blood flows in rivers through the sand, caking and clumping beneath his feet. Ronald is a tornado of death, but they keep on coming. On and on, and on.

Then, it is just them: Ronald and Akuma, Jiro stuck fast to the spit. The fire rises higher, closer, hotter. Burns brighter, deeper.

"I am glad, Ronald Hashimoto, that it shall be you who strikes me down. I have waited a long time for this day, and I feared it would never come."

Ronald cuts a downward slash, expecting resistance, hoping for a real fight, but Akuma drops her arms to her sides and accepts the deathblow. Blood splatters from the wound, sizzling on the flames, drawing dots like constellations in the untarnished sand at her feet.

Jiro cries out, but Ronald is transfixed by the fallen general. With slow, tentative steps, he approaches her corpse. With the crimson tip of his katana, he lifts away her facemask. Beneath it, she's smiling. Beneath it, she's Aubrey Page, and Ronald can no longer hold back from getting sick.

On his hands and knees, he crawls away from body to body. He lifts the samurai's helmets to reveal all the people he loves and idolizes: Che Perkins, DJ, Robert, and Daichi. Rakim, Aesop Rock, Sa-Roc, and Common. One by one, they crumble to sand, mixing with the endless, rusty dunes. The wind carries them away, out of reach. Far, far away, where Ronald has no hope of ever finding them again.

Jiro screams. Ronald whips around to see a wall of flame. It *explodes all around him, and all that's left is fire. Fire, and that awful, awful screaming.*

Ronald gasped as he awoke, his first few breaths burning in his throat. He sat up, chest heaving, and hyperventilated until he was able to catch his breath.

A nearby gurgling sound caught his attention. Pipes, he realized, behind brick-bare walls and exposed ductwork. Steel beams intersected on the high ceiling, with two large metal columns clinging from their center to the smooth, polished concrete floor.

Where the hell am I? Ronald thought. *How did I get here?*

It took his eyes several long moments to adjust. When they did, he saw his surroundings for what they were: an old warehouse converted into an apartment. The only light to see by came from slatted mini blinds over the room's single rounded window.

A pipe popped nearby, and Ronald nearly jumped out of his skin. Stars raced across his vision and nausea threatened until he had no choice but to close his eyes and lay his head back down. Even so, he was sure he would pass out. Or vomit.

He was drenched in sweat from head to toe. A cold, evil tingling sensation crept across his skin, but it was the worst around his ribs and the left side of his face, where he couldn't feel his jaw or cheeks as he opened and closed his mouth several times. He tasted rust and swallowing brought fresh waves of pain to the entire midsection of his torso.

What... what happened to me? Fuzzy flashes of motion and violence came to mind, but nothing tangible, nothing to ground him to his current state of reality.

Each new question brought a dozen more. His memory of the last few days was foggy at best, and he almost laughed wondering if maybe this was how Curtis Jackson felt waking up after leaving his grandma's house in Queens. Nine kinds of in pain, disoriented, and more pissed off than he'd ever been in his entire life. But Ronald didn't even know who he needed to be pissed off at. Himself? Daichi? Whoever put him into his predicament, whatever it was? Who could he blame?

He attempted to sit up again, but pain exploded from his ribs. He winced, groaned, and punched the thin mattress he was lying on. Not even a mattress, really. A metal cot with musty blankets piled on top of it.

Ronald flexed his throbbing fingers and rolled his eyes. *Great. Now my fist hurts too.* He swore at his knee jerk reaction and forced his legs off the side of the cot. They were heavy and sluggish, but it felt reassuring to feel the pressure of his soles against the floor.

From there, Ronald could see the rest of the apartment. It was small, no bigger than his bedroom, and sparse. It had a kitchen with an oven, stove top, microwave, and sink. Pots and pans and other various cooking utensils hung from the wall, were shoved into any possible empty space, and strewn across every surface. An accordion wall divided the kitchen from an alcove with a toilet. He was sitting on the apartment's only "bed," but there were two piles of sheets with pillows nearby, as far from one another as possible. Which, he was moderately amused to admit, wasn't far at all. One pile was stained blood-brown. A fresh wave of nausea threatened as the possible origins of that awful hue ran wild in his mind.

Ronald steadied himself and forced his way to his feet. Getting out of bed was a simple task, something he'd taken for granted as he strained under the immense effort. The exertion made him dizzy, but as a sheer act of defiance, he tried to walk. He stumbled over his own feet, vertigo bringing him crashing down into the kitchen. Pots and pans clattered all around him. He grabbed for the counter to balance himself, but he only managed to knock a pile of plates onto the floor. They shattered, and the clamor of metal on concrete and breaking ceramics sent rings of searing white light from his eyes to the back of his head. It was so loud he couldn't hear the door as it creaked open.

"Jesus Christ! Are you trying to kill yourself?"

A strong, soft arm lifted him off the floor, held him upright, and for a moment, Ronald was no longer in the strange apartment. There was music, a hint of vinyl and home. He smiled at the smell of shea butter and beeswax and let his body go limp. Whoever was holding him stumbled but managed to get him back to the cot. The metal springs complained as it grudgingly accepted their weight.

Ronald heard another set of footsteps approaching and then a familiar voice asked, "Is he awake?"

"Nearly gave himself a concussion, too. Stubborn kid, just like his father."

Daichi groaned like he always groaned—an unmistakable sound that grated through Ronald's tremendous pains—and Ronald tried to turn towards his father and the mystery woman, but he couldn't muster enough energy. He found his eyes refused to open, and a sudden relaxing, pulsing sensation massaged his body until he was nearly asleep. It was like how he felt sometimes when he closed his eyes while listening to a viscerally moving song. He sunk into himself, plummeted into a moment where nothing else mattered. In this case, nothing else but drifting off into a deep... long... uninterrupted...

"And resilient," he heard a distant Daichi say as he slipped back into sleep. "Just like his mother."

"You don't have to do this, Daichi. You can still make things better."

Ronald strained through his waning consciousness to hear what came next. There was an air of importance to Che's words, a sad familiarity between the two. What came next might mean something, if only he could stay awake long enough to hear it.

"I have to. I've failed my boys so completely at this point, there is no other way out."

"Bullshit!"

Ronald tried to blink, to keep himself from slipping away, but the last words he heard his father speak were distant, muffled, almost as if spoken in a different language. Yet, they were among the most "Daichi" words ever spoken.

"Honor demands it."

For Ronald, his body demanded sleep, and he couldn't fight it any longer.

Ronald wasn't sure how long he'd been unconscious. When he woke up again, he was still in tremendous pain, more so after the lingering effects of whatever he'd been dosed with had worn off, but he was at least able to sit up without immediately blacking out. There was more sunlight in the apartment now, and the mess in the kitchen had been cleaned up, replaced by the sweet applewood scent of crisping bacon and the last person he expected to see.

"Hey, man. Don't get up." Che slapped something onto a griddle that sizzled, adding the aroma of sweet cinnamon to the mix. "How ya' feelin'?"

"Che? Is that really you?"

She opened one of the only cupboards, which turned out to be a mini fridge, and pulled out a glass jar of milk.

"She's the only person I've ever been. As far as I'm aware." She winked at him over her shoulder. "How do you like your eggs?"

Eggs? *Eggs!?* Ronald was on the verge of a complete mental breakdown, and she was asking him about eggs? He glared, and his lips parted slightly. If angst had a poster child, Ronald was it in that moment.

Che frowned. "So, no eggs?"

At that, Ronald exploded. He didn't mean to, and he immediately knew he'd regret it after he finally shut up, but he couldn't hold his frustrations back anymore.

"Che, what the hell am I doing here? Last thing I remember, I was coming home from school, Daichi was passed out drunk, and then, I don't know. Then, I wake up God knows where. I think my old man was here, I don't know. I've been having these godawful dreams all the time, it's hard to know what's really happening anymore, what's now and what was then, what's just my imagination trying to drive me absolutely nuts, but Daichi—that's my dad, I guess I forgot to say—was talking. And you were there, I think. And now you're here, asking me about eggs. And I still don't even know where here is. And—*arrrgh...*"

Ronald's abdomen cramped, and he grabbed his side, slamming down onto the cot. He gritted his teeth against the pain and fought the urge to cry, but he couldn't help it. It was just too much to bear.

The cot creaked and sagged: Che, sitting beside him, her hand resting on his chest.

"You need to take it easy. I'm shocked you're already up and moving around after two doses. The first time I was in your position, I stayed in bed for almost a week. I couldn't even hold a damn spoon for three or four days."

Again, more questions. Ronald's head throbbed.

"Doses? Of what?"

Che snapped, as if remembering something important, and hustled back to the kitchen. She worked a few different pans as she tried to explain.

"Our assassin friend—" A corner of Ronald's lip rose and his forehead furrowed. "Right. So, your memory still ain't back. You said you remember coming home from school. Anything after that?" Ronald shook his head. "Daichi told me the gist. It seems an old friend of ours, Tomo Nakajima, paid the Hashimoto household a visit. You're lucky to be alive, man. Truly, you are. Warriors much older and more skilled than yourself have fallen victim to his many dirty tricks, strychnos-blended poison being one of his favorites."

Ronald accepted the plate she handed him. It was piled high with overcooked eggs, rubbery bacon, and golden-black pancakes. He hadn't realized how hungry he was, and the culinary disaster looked like it just might be the best meal he'd ever tasted. As he ate, the chaotic duel at his house replayed in hazy snapshots.

With his mouth full, he asked, "Tomo Nakajima. You said he's an assassin. But whose?"

"The Order's."

"The Order?"

Che rolled her eyes. "Look, man, if I have to keep repeating myself, this is going to be a long explanation. Longer than it's already going to be. The Order of the Golden Bonsai, of course. Who else?"

It made sense. *Of course,* like Che had said. But why had they waited so long to come for him? Ronald choked on an overly large bite, and eggs shot out of his nose.

Che didn't seem to mind. She handed him a glass of milk and gently patted his back as she spoke. "Daichi... he told me that they came to you. He said they gave you another chance. An ultimatum. I'm proud of you. You're an idiot, but I'm proud of you, nonetheless."

It dawned on him like a rising sun at midnight.

"How do you know about the Order? And why are you involved with all of this? And how do you know Daichi!? My father..."

Che looked suddenly downcast. Her eyes glistened, and she scooted away from him.

"Yeah, that makes sense. Yup, yup, yup. You would want to know, and I knew we'd get there eventually. I just didn't think it would come up so soon."

She took a deep breath and held it. Ronald was surprised her cheeks didn't go rosy, but she finally let it out in a short sigh. Then, she stood up and started shaking her arms and hopping from one foot to another as if she were preparing for a sparring match.

"Ahhhh!" she yelled, sounding as if she might cry. "You can do this Che. You've been working through this conversation in your head for years. You got this, girl." She slapped her arms and cracked her neck to each side. "You got this!"

Ronald took another bite, but it fell back onto his plate as Che smacked herself upside the head. "Uh, everything okay?"

She stopped at the sound of his voice. It was as if she disappeared and reappeared at the foot of the cot. One second, she wasn't there. The next, she was, and Ronald nearly fell off the bed in surprise.

"Ronald," she said, leaning towards him. Then, she stood and started pacing. "Sorry, I didn't think it was going to be this hard. Well, I did, but I thought I was ready."

"That's okay," he said. "Nothing's been easy lately. I get it."

She sat cross-legged beside him, elbows on the edge of the cot, her chin resting on her fists. He'd never seen her this close, or this vulnerable. It was sort of terrifying, but it was also comforting. If someone as cool as Che Perkins could be so human, so relatable and imperfect, maybe his flaws and mental health issues weren't so abnormal after all. Maybe he was just... normal. Or as normal as anyone ever got, at least.

"I'm your mother." Che blurted it like it was nothing, and Ronald dropped his plate. It shattered on the concrete, spilling badly cooked breakfast foods all over the floor. "I'm sorry I waited so long to tell you. Every time you came into the shop, I wanted to. I really, *really* wanted to. But the Order... They wouldn't allow me to be part of your life. They said I could... that I could taint you, lead you astray from your destiny, or whatever the hell it is they're calling it nowadays. Ronald, I'm so, so sorry."

Ronald stared off into space, mouth wide open. He swallowed hard. A million competing thoughts swirled around his poison- and shock-addled brain, none of them coherent, none of them worth expressing, none of them came close to explaining the emotional whirlwind he was experiencing in that moment.

"Please," Che said, grabbing his hands in hers, "say something. Anything."

A chill crawled down his spine, and he shivered. But it wasn't a chill that forced its way back up. "I think I'm going to be sick," Ronald said. He leaned to one side and got sick all over Che Perkin's—his mother's—floor.

When at last he thought he was done, it all started over again. The nausea, the dizziness, the questions and self-doubt. The inexplicable rage that swelled within him until he could hardly breathe. Any progress he'd made over the last few months was erased by those words.

"I'm your mother," she had just told him.

You're my what!? He swallowed a lump and whimpered. Had she really said that?

Back to square-friggin'-one, he thought, on the verge of collapse. And where the hell was he supposed to go from there?

INTERLUDE TWO: BEFORE

Akuma Araki killed for the first time on a calm, sunny day. A gentle breeze was blowing in from the west, sending her long, black hair in waves over her dirty face, and cherry blossom petals were beginning to settle in bunches on every surface of the countryside, giving the valley its rare ruby glint for the season.

Much of what her people had clung to in order to keep living had long since spilled from the caves, and they had grown confident in their safety from destruction. There had been no appearances by the dragon or its devils for months, and they dared to hope for better days ahead. She alone remained cautious, wary, and the rift between her and the others grew larger each day. They wished to return to their old, pastural lives, forget about the people they had lost, and start fresh. She, on the other hand, could not forget. She could not move on, pretending a plague of death and violence hadn't swept their lands.

Her morning's work was typical: tending the rice paddies,

feeding the chickens, gathering water from the well outside the caves. Hard work. Honest work. Most importantly, it allowed her enough space between herself and the other villagers to find something almost resembling peace.

The night before, it rained, and her feet were soaked through to the bone as she slogged her way back, two full, sloshing buckets balanced across her shoulders. Far off, gray clouds were rolling in, a sure sign of another wet, cold afternoon. She relished the opportunity to enjoy the sun's kiss on her dried skin before the world darkened once more. It was one of those small pleasures that made life worth living—some of those pleasures were just easier to recognize and appreciate than others.

A group of older boys—Hifumi, Arata, and Ritsu if memory served—were playing beigoma outside the elders' hut. Even from a distance, the boys looked like devils. No different than the devils who came to her village so many lifetimes ago. Twisted, jagged teeth. Grins like specters. Eyes that watched her every move. Hungry, stupid eyes. Blank eyes filled with devious schemes and violent intentions. They were only missing the armor, replaced instead by their drab peasant's rags.

She lowered her head, picked up the pace despite the heaviness of all the wet and mud in her boots, and prayed for the impossible. If she passed quickly enough, maybe they wouldn't notice her. Twice so far this week, she found herself in this predicament. Twice so far, she had been left with painful wounds, both physical and emotional, and the prospect of another scar sent needles of ice across her clenched shoulder blades.

Ritsu's head shot up, his gaze fixated in her direction. Even though she had been watching them closely and was careful to avoid direct eye contact, she knew it was already too late. She was the boys' new target, a different game for them to play. Suddenly, the rusty hand sickle tied to her waist felt heavy and hot. While she never used it outside the rice paddies—and never gave the elders a reason to mistrust her with such a potentially deadly tool—she had imagined using it in other ways often enough that the prospect of blade against flesh was as familiar as the constant cold rains.

"Kangei sa Renai!" Ritsu called, rising to his feet. *The Unwelcome*, better than most of the foul names they hurled at Akuma Araki, but her least favorite of them all. She did not want to be there as much as they did not want her there. But what other choice did she have? Where else could she go?

"It would be a shame if you spilled those buckets and had to travel back to the well. Storm's coming. Maybe you get struck by lightning. Maybe you drown in the mud." Ritsu shrugged, nonchalant. "It's dangerous beyond the village, when the storms come."

The other boys were up too, and people were beginning to emerge from their huts, gathering around Ritsu to hear what insightful insults he had for the unwelcome orphan girl today. Even one of the younger girls, a cousin of Ritsu, Minata, Akuma thought her name might be, emerged from behind a clothes line, careful to keep to the shadows as she watched the drama unfold.

"We all must drink," she began to say, but someone hurled a stone. Nobu, maybe—one of her own adoptive brothers. It struck her in the temple, and she blinked away the blinding pain, water spilling onto the dirt beneath her feet.

The boys of the village began chanting, stones in hand.

"Kangei sa Renai! Kangei sa Renai!"

"Little orphan bitch."

They chanted their insults and hurled their stones. They laughed and howled when they struck true and chided each other for close misses. Their cruelty was matched tenfold by Akuma's rising anger.

"Lost with no home to call her own."

"Kangei sa Renai!"

Another stone skimmed Akuma's cheek, just below her left eye, and finally she let her buckets drop to the ground. What happened next happened beyond consciousness. She watched, powerless, smiling deep within her soul at the actions of a strong, fearless woman—the woman she had only been in her daydreams up until that moment—as they unfolded before her eyes.

Ritsu approached with his fists clenched, the others a few strides behind, always quick to follow their leader but hesitant to take any kind of lead. They were leering shadows, giants with crooked teeth, sharp claws, and sharper tongues. This time, she refused to back down. This time, Akuma Araki was not going to let devils get the best of her.

The boy moved to shove her, but her hand flashed to her hip. She felt a warm spray across her face. Ritsu staggered backward into the unsuspecting arms of his friends, fingers clenched to his throat. They let him drop between them, mouths agape in horror. He tried to speak, to insult her one last time, but it came out in a gurgle. He groped at the wound, but it was far too deep, and he was far too late to staunch his life from bleeding out onto the soil.

After a brief, convulsive struggle with Death, Ritsu flopped hard to one side, forever still. Someone in the crowd screamed, shrill and elongated. It was a cry that seemed to last forever.

But Akuma Araki hardly heard it. She stood tall, as steady as a stream, with an ear-to-ear grin of self-satisfaction. Her life in Shima Gōdatsusha was forever changed in that single moment of bloody contentment, and she could not help but wonder why she had not taken control of her own destiny much, much sooner.

CHAPTER TEN

Che rushed over and snatched the box of vinyl—Snoop's latest—out of Ronald's arms. He began to protest, but she hip-checked him to the side with an exaggerated eye roll and stuck out her tongue.

"Just because you miraculously recovered doesn't mean I'm going to let you lift heavy boxes. If you want to make yourself useful, grab that label maker over there, by the computer, and get to labeling."

Ronald hobbled through the cluttered shelves. "Are you really my mom?"

Che dropped the box on the nearest clear surface and wiped her dusty hands on her jeans. "What, you didn't think you got your impeccable rhythm and glorious locks from Daichi, did you?"

Ronald snorted, then he scrunched his nose in disgust. "That means you and Daichi—"

"Ew, no." Che cut him off. "No, Ronald. That's gross. We may have become pretty good friends over the last few years, but I've been your mother *much* longer. We are *not* going there. Nuh uh. No way, man"

Ronald forced a half-smile and shuffled his feet. He felt flushed, a pit of nerves dropping in his stomach, but he had to know. If he didn't ask now, he would probably talk himself out of it forever.

"What happened? Between the two of you... Why did you leave? I could have used a mom, you know? But all I got was... a Daichi."

Che sighed. "Yeah, I can only imagine. Look, I'm sorry. I don't know where to begin."

"From the beginning works. Help me understand."

"It's complicated, man. It's messy. Really. Frickin'. Messy."

"Bullshit!" Ronald slapped his palm against a box. "Bullshit. Don't tell me, 'It's complicated. It's messy.' If you want to hear complicated and messy, I'll tell you literally about my entire childhood. Maybe I'll start with how Daichi worked us so hard our bones broke. Or how we sat at home alone while he disappeared for days on end. How Jiro had to beg on the streets for money to buy us food while he was gone. Or steal during some of Daichi's frequent longer absences from our lives.

"And when our old man bothered to grace us with his presence, he talked to us in riddles and fortune cookie proverbs, insulted us for things that didn't even make sense. That got pretty complicated, let me tell you. Can you imagine, second-guessing every little thought that crosses your mind? Never knowing if what you're thinking about a given situation is right or wrong in your tyrant of a father's eyes?

"Oh, oh, oh, maybe I should tell you about how he sent us into

Shima Gōdatsusha the day of my fifteenth birthday. There, we infiltrated a camp of thousands of, I don't know, demon warriors? Other planar samurai? I'm honestly still a little murky on the details, seeing as Daichi told us literally jack all while he pushed us to our breaking points, 'Preparing us to embrace our destinies,' or whatever. I killed an oni there, you know? I didn't even think they were real, and I killed it with swords. Crazy, right?"

Ronald stopped to catch his breath. Rage swelled, and he tightened his fists until his fingernails drew blood from his palms.

"Then, seconds after my big triumphant moment—what Daichi had been pushing me towards my entire life—I watched my own brother die. An arrow split his chest open, right in front of my eyes. Guess what I did?" Che began to open her mouth, but Ronald kept going. "I left him there to die. I abandoned Jiro and ran like the coward I am. Is that messy enough for you, yet? If not, I could tell you all about how Daichi became a filthy, worthless drunk and all but abandoned me to fend for myself. Except when he needed to ridicule me, of course. Or hit me. But, hey, any parental bonding is better than nothing, amirite? Good thing my love language is physical touch…"

Che moved to embrace him, but Ronald shrugged her off. Cheeks moist, she pursed her lips. "Look, man, I get it. I do. Leaving you and your brother was—"

"*Abandoning*," Ronald corrected." Abandoning me and my brother."

"Right, well, it was the hardest thing I've ever had to do. I don't expect you to understand, and I've got a shop to open, but will you stick around for a while? Give me half a chance to explain myself…"

His instincts told him to run, to return to Normal, grab his swords, and never look back. If he kept moving, none of them would be able to find him. Not Daichi. Not the assassin, Tomo. Not Che—who he found he loved dearly but loving her only made the pain she'd caused hurt so much worse. He'd leave them all behind, live off small jobs and begging, like he and Jiro once had, and make his way to the other side of the world. Then, he'd travel farther still until even he couldn't find himself.

Ronald whimpered, and his legs no longer wanted to support his weight. Che rushed to his side, helped him over to a folding chair in a dusty, seldom-used corner of the shop's storeroom. The metal was cold, and the chair squeaked as it accepted the burden of his wounded form.

She kissed his forehead and said, "I'll close up early tonight. We'll grab sushi across the street, you and I, and I'll explain everything, okay?"

Ronald mouthed "Okay," but his voice cracked, and he managed less than a wheeze.

The rest of the day passed in a blur. He didn't move from his spot on the chair. He couldn't. Several times, a record shop employee, or Che herself, came into the storeroom, struggled with a box or with a ladder, and he wanted to get up and help. He urged his legs into action, but he just sat there, numb.

One employee, a girl wearing all black who he'd seen before while perusing the back shelves for new old music, nearly knocked over an entire stack of precariously sorted records. She swore and cried, but Ronald didn't move. Not. An. Inch. He just watched her struggle in his peripheral vision and sulked, bringing to mind the woman in the alley.

He was a statue. Frozen in place. But by what? Fear? Anger?

Anxiety? The lingering effects of Tomo's poison?

The shop sounds were a distant echo, Che's yelling to customers from behind the register reduced to mere whispering. The clamor of the streets—horns blaring, engines sputtering, and music bumping—were all a distorted and dissonant chord.

Che's Shogunate was his sanctuary, a place where he could dance to the music of life without feeling judged. Now, it felt more like a prison, New Province as scary a place as the suburbs. Just like that, he'd lost his safe place to the oblivion of reality. He couldn't go home. He couldn't show his face at school because he didn't have a clue how long he'd been gone or what his friends could possibly be thinking about his unexplained disappearance. Would they forgive him for ghosting them? And he certainly couldn't hide in the back of Che's record shop, crying about his bad luck and turning to stone.

What do I do now? he wondered, but he realized there was nothing he could do. Soon, the Order would find him again, and it would all be over anyway. He had no hope of beating Tomo in one-on-one combat if it came down to it a second time.

He couldn't help but wonder where Daichi was when he needed him. The old man had saved his life when Tomo attacked, brought him here to his mother, only to disappear. It didn't make sense. Wouldn't his own father want to make sure he was okay? Didn't Daichi care even a sliver about his well-being? Of course he didn't. Nobody did. Ronald was as alone as he'd always been... since Jiro died, at least.

"Hey, man." Che's voice startled Ronald, and he snapped back to reality. "How ya' doin'?"

His body ached, both from the attack and from sitting all day.

Getting up from the chair was going to be an act of sheer resolute will, but suddenly, with Che there by his side once more, he felt somehow lighter and relieved, because he now knew exactly where he stood with his father.

"I'm okay," he said, unable to look her in the eyes.

"Hungry?" He shrugged. "Good, because I am. Let's go across the street. Mrs. Ling's pot stickers are callin' my name." She cupped her hand over her ear and leaned in the restaurant's general direction. "You hear that? 'Che, oh Che. Come eat us. All of us. And bring that handsome boy of yours, too.'"

It was hard for Ronald not to laugh, but he refused to give her the satisfaction of bringing a smile to his face. He may have had plenty of time to accept things as they were, but he didn't have to forgive her. Not yet. Not ever, if he decided he didn't want to, but the lightness he felt around her told him a forever-grudge against her was pretty unlikely.

His stomach grumbled, and he realized he couldn't remember the last time he ate anything besides Che's less-than-stellar cooking. Or the last time he'd seen anything outside her apartment or the record shop. Days, for sure. Maybe weeks. He'd been too tired and hurting in too many places to worry about meaningless days ticking off the calendar.

Reluctantly, he forced himself up and followed her through the maze-like storeroom. The shop's lights were off, with only the dim, orange glow of a single security light, but he'd been in Che's Shogunate so many times he didn't need light to guide his way. He could walk the shop blindfolded if it came down to it, and all he had to do was trust in his mother's guidance to lead the way.

***

RONALD, THE RONIN

A lukewarm bowl of miso soup and a ceramic kettle of green tea made everything better. Not much, but at this point, a little was all Ronald could hope for, and an inch felt like a mile.

Che slurped and smacked her lips. "I've always loved this place. It helps that it's right across the street, but the Lings sure know how to navigate their way around vaguely related Asian line of cuisine. There's something about sesame chicken, bao bun, coconut curry, and California roll that just works, don't you think?"

Ronald shrugged, focusing on the lonely bay leaf floating on the surface of his soup.

Che continued unabated. "And Mrs. Ling is so welcoming. From the first time I stopped in, she made me feel like family. That's so important in mom-and-pop places like this. You come for a good meal and stay for a home away from home."

Right on cue, Mrs. Ling pushed through the kitchen's swinging doors, a cheek-to-cheek smile on her face, half a dozen plates balanced on her thick forearms. She crossed the dining room remarkably quick considering her stubby legs and short steps, and the plates slid off one by one into perfect tasting formation on the table. Ronald's mouth watered with every new dish.

Mrs. Ling produced napkins and chopsticks out of thin air and regarded Ronald. "Did he bring you those mooncakes like I asked?"

Che smiled a sad smile. "He did. Thank you."

At first, Ronald couldn't figure out why she lied. Then, he decided Mrs. Ling must've known all along. Is that why she had treated him like a son, because Che was already like a daughter to her?

After Mrs. Ling left them to their spread of earthly delights, and had enthusiastically kissed Ronald on both cheeks, Che cleared her throat. "So, should we dive right in?"

"I think I'll go for the sashimi first. Maybe the salmon." She slid the plate away as he reached for it. "Hey, what gives?"

"I've been thinking about this morning's conversation all day." *Good for you,* Ronald thought. He nearly rolled his eyes, but he shoved a California roll into his mouth instead. "I don't know how to make it right, but an explanation, with nothing held back, might at least be a good place to start. Will you hear me out? I probably don't deserve it, and I understand if you'd rather just eat and leave. Either way, I'm here for you, Ronald. From here on out. Whatever you need."

He could think of a hundred things he needed without as much as straining a single brain cell, but he couldn't trust her enough, yet. Not when she'd been lying to him for so many years.

Ronald nodded across the table. "Just the salmon, please. And more wasabi."

Che obliged without complaint, but he could tell she was getting annoyed. *Good,* he thought. *You're starting to feel a fraction of the frustration I've felt my whole life. A little more, and maybe you'll understand.*

"Your dad and I, we were fated. According to Oda, who raised me like his own daughter, we were destined to inherit the Order. All its duties and responsibilities, blah, blah, blah. All its burdens, more like, and neither Daichi nor I had any interest in fate or destiny. When we were your age, the Order and all its talk of demons and dangers, all the impending doom creeping from the other islands, none of that mattered. We were young and in love. Two sword-crossed samurai, ready to take on the entire world with nothing but our burning passion for each other.

"I see your face, and believe me, Daichi is nowhere near the man he used to be. The man I remember... Well, he wasn't a useless drunk when I knew him. Not even close. He was handsome, smooth-talking, and the greatest swordsman I'd ever seen. Better than me. *Far* better. And better even than Master Oda himself. There wasn't a single samurai in the Order, or elsewhere, skilled enough to beat your father."

Che held her chopsticks deftly between two fingers and watched Ronald, as if waiting for his reaction. He glared at her for a moment, then reached for a tuna roll. She snatched it as fast as a lightning strike, and before he knew what happened, she was chewing greedily with full cheeks and a shit-eating grin on her face.

"Delicious," she said. "You really oughta try one."

He reached for another, and she snatched it away from him again. This time, she nearly lost her cool from laughing, her cheeks overstuffed to the point of bursting.

"Hey! I would if you'd let me have one."

"Sorry, I couldn't resist. I wanted to see if I still had it." Mrs. Ling appeared to clear some plates, and Che bowed to the older woman before turning back to Ronald. "I've been away from the Order for a long time," she continued. "Running a record shop doesn't exactly keep the blade sharp, so to speak."

Ronald leaned close and whispered, "Should we be discussing the, erm, this stuff around her?" He gestured towards Mrs. Ling in a not-so-subtle way, who all but squeaked and winked conspiratorially at him.

"Mrs. Ling?" Che asked. "Ha! What do you think about that, Mrs. Ling?"

The woman merely shrugged and winked at Ronald. "I just

cook the dumplings and serve the rolls. Nothing more."

Che took a sip of tea and folded her arms across her chest. "She's a gatekeeper. One of the last in this city."

"A gatekeeper?"

"Christ, did Daichi tell you nothing?"

"Other than telling me about how useless I am, no. Not really. Whenever he says anything else, it's always so slurred and cryptic I usually just ignore him. Makes life easier that way."

Mrs. Ling managed a sweet frown, if such an expression was possible. "I keep the peace, honey. Nothing more. Peace and dumplings." And off she went, disappearing back into the kitchen.

"Speaking of cryptic..."

"She keeps portals. Between this island and the others."

"Like Shima Gōdatsusha?"

There was sadness in her eyes again. Che was almost too cool to actually be sad, but there was an undeniable hint in the way they glistened.

"No, not like Shima Gōdatsusha. Nothing is like Shima Gōdatsusha. But that portal is safely tucked away and well-guarded. No, there are places much worse, and others that are better, beyond your wildest dreams. Mrs. Ling is the gatekeeper for a fraction of them, and she is indeed a force to be reckoned with."

"She makes a mean moon cake, too."

"She makes a mean moon cake, too. You're right about that."

Mrs. Ling poked her head out of the kitchen to flex her muscles. Ronald nearly blew food out of his nose.

"Well," he said, "I see we're in good hands."

"The best."

Even though their brief conversation left a lot unsaid, they finished their meal in silence. Ronald was carrying a heavy load, and he was unpacking it pretty slowly. For now, that was the way of things, and he needed to learn patience, to give himself grace as he picked and rifled through his ever-growing problems.

After Mrs. Ling brought the bill—which Che insisted on paying—and forced more moon cakes on Ronald, they meandered a few blocks. The early evening passed in tense silence, neither ready to dive back into the deep stuff, but the streets had a rhythm to them again. There was music to be heard in New Province's comings and goings, and Ronald was all about its vibe.

As Che's shop came back into view, she grabbed him by the shoulders and knelt before him. "I had to leave, Ronald. After the fun stopped, and your father got serious about Order business, I couldn't stay anymore. Jiro was just a baby, and you were on your way. I thought I could get both of you out, before your lives became forfeit to their agenda. Before you were forced to spill blood, before your very own was spilled to further the Order's cause.

"They came for me. For us. The only way to save you was to let you go. I couldn't let you pay for my mistake. I couldn't let you take the fall for me abandoning my duties. So, I promised. They made me promise, Ronald." She cast her eyes to the pavement. "I could never see you again. I couldn't be your mom or watch you grow up. They'd kill me. And you. Somehow, despite it all, I had convinced myself that one day I would come back from you boys, that I would rescue you from growing up to be like your father.

"The first time you entered my shop, so grown up, so handsome as the young man you'd become, they almost did kill me. They've been watching ever since, but I don't care anymore. Not after they came for you anyway. Please, you have to believe me. I never wanted to let you boys go. It broke me, and I deserve every second of my misery, but I won't stop trying to make things right, to be a better mom. The mom you deserve."

Ronald found himself on the verge of tears. Che's confession was so raw, so unexpected, and he honestly wasn't sure if he'd ever witnessed such honest emotion—beyond Daichi's drunken outbursts, of course. Those were always honest enough, he supposed.

"They sent Daichi. The love of my life. The father of my children. He couldn't do it, of course. But he came close."

"You and my dad *fought*? Like with swords?" Ronald had a hard time picturing Daichi going head-to-head with anyone, yet alone his favorite record shop owner.

She laughed through her nose. "We both have scars to prove it, too."

"But you won."

"Neither of us won, Ronald. We nearly killed each other. You and Jiro, I think, were the only reason he held back. I don't know how he got the Order to leave me alone after that, but I finally stopped seeing them over my shoulder everywhere I looked. That's when I fooled myself into thinking it was over. Ha! Can you believe that idiot, bringing you back to my doorstep? Things are going to get... interesting now, Ronald. As just another customer, we were safe. But the Order never forgets. We're all back in this. One hundred percent."

"So, they'll come for me? Will they come for you, too?"

Che sighed and her lower lip quivered. "They will. It's only a matter of time."

Ronald wondered if Tomo was watching as they spoke. Careful

not to arouse suspicion, he glanced all around. People going about their business. Street performers amusing the masses. Taxis and buses creeping along to earn hard dollars. Men and women, any of whom could have been with the Order, lurking in the shadows, peering out windows, lighting cigarettes. It was all the city's normal music, of course, but there was a new dissonance to it that Ronald could only explain through the anxiety of not knowing what came next.

His executioner was coming. Che's too. The question was when and where, ninja assassin or kitsune? More questions Ronald needed answered, but he'd had enough answers for one night. Almost.

"What now?" he asked.

"You go home. Daichi's been on high alert ever since Tomo's attack. He might be a bastard, but while he's still breathing, he won't let them hurt you." It sounded as if she were trying to convince herself more than anything else. "He tried to save you, Ronald. Both of you. And soon, it might be your turn to save him."

"Will you come too? Stay with us for a while until we figure everything out?"

There was that sadness again, and Ronald already knew he was going to be disappointed.

"I've got something for you," Che said, her face suddenly lighting up. "I almost forgot. It's not a bribe, I swear, but you're going to love it. Come on, check it out. Help me load it in the van, and I'll drive you back to the burbs."

Ronald didn't bother to ask what she could possibly be so excited about. Everything seemed about as bad as it could get, but he didn't have the energy to argue. He followed Che back into the shop, through the twist of loaded shelves in the storeroom, to a small nook serving as Che's office. She slid a stack of boxes out of the way, threw a pile of paper over her shoulder, and opened a locked metal utility cabinet. When Ronald saw what was inside, he nearly squealed.

"Shut up." He picked his jaw off the floor. "You're kidding me."

Grinning, Che shook her head enthusiastically. "It's all yours. Daichi told me what happened, and it's the least I could do."

Ronald moved to embrace her, but at the last second, he remembered he was still supposed to be mad at her. Instead, he let his creative mind run wild. If Ronald Hashimoto was going to be assassinated soon, he'd at least get one last chance to do something he loved. He wouldn't tell her, but this was the best gift a mother could possibly give her son: an opportunity to spread his wings and fly, to be his genuine self once more.

A brand-new computer! He could almost die from excitement. Nobody had ever tried to buy his love before, and gawping at the super-taped, unopened box, he couldn't help but think it was something he could get used to.

CHAPTER ELEVEN

Ronald felt like a ghost as he floated to his locker. All around him, nothing had changed. There was the same ole noise, the same scummy teenagers thinking they were way too cool for school, having the same meaningless conversations. But it was worse than that. After everything that had happened, and fearing the inevitable, Normal seemed even more mundane and pointless than it had before.

Inside his locker, Ronald's black queens greeted him. Most boys taped up sexy pics or slapped 59/50 stickers on the insides of their lockers, but not Ronald. At home, he had his pantheon. At school, he had his queens:

Nikki Jean, sitting sukasana, with nothing but her hair to cover herself, body *and* soul.

Sa-Roc, sitting upon a throne of gold, *shinin' on 'em* because by his estimation she was and always would be a star.

Lauryn Hill, smiling with her Grammy, somehow managing to

look fierce AF and humble at the same time.

There were countless others there too. Women who changed the face of hip-hop: Missy Elliot, Queen Latifah, Salt-N-Pepa, Lil' Kim, Erykah Badu, Mumu Fresh. There were also the guilty pleasures of a seventeen-year-old hip-hop aficionado. Women whose contributions blended genres, transformed expectations like Braxton, Cole, and Giddens. He'd run out of room, or he would have included more. Not for their looks—though each was gorgeous in her own irreplaceable way—but for their sound, for their contribution to the culture, for the ever-lasting impression they left on music as a whole.

And then there was his picture of Che—his mother—from when she was younger. He couldn't remember where he'd found it. Before she started the Shogunate, Che sang at clubs, seamlessly blending acoustic folk and hip-hop. After a rabbit-hole deep-dive down the strange and uncharted territories of YouTube, he'd caught a few of her live shows. Her raspy voice, practiced finger picking, and quick transitions between belting soul-bearing alto and spitting staccato bars of truth were more than enough to hook him from his first listen.

When he found out she was opening a record shop across town, he had to check it out. A chance to meet somebody so talented? He'd have kicked himself if he hadn't found a way to make the grand opening. Luckily, bus fare was cheap, and passion was free. They hit it off immediately—almost too well come to think—and the rest was, as they say, history.

Until it wasn't. Until it became the front row, center, and all-encompassing present.

"Shit," he said to the poorly printed cutouts. "What are we going to do?"

Two weeks. It had been two whole weeks since the attack, and it seemed like he'd blinked and missed out on everything while nothing around him had changed. Part of him was grateful for that, but his gratitude wouldn't last long. Nothing ever did for Ronald Hashimoto.

"Ronald!" The shout came so unexpectedly that he jumped and slammed his locker shut. DJ looked perplexed. "What's good, man? Everything okay?"

When Ronald caught his breath, he tried unconvincingly to laugh it off. It had been two weeks since he'd last seen DJ and Robert. He thought he'd be a little bit more excited for their grand reunion, but instead he just felt hollow.

"Yeah, sorry." *Just trying to simultaneously figure out how to keep myself alive and from going absolutely, bat-guano crazy is all.* Ronald started to open his locker again. He'd left his Biology books in there, but it would've been weird after slamming it, so he made the decision to just deal with the consequences of his jumpiness. "It's been a minute. How's Jess?" He glanced over at Robert, whose thumbs were busy on his phone. Some game, Ronald figured from what little he could see on the screen. "And whatever it is you're doing, Robert."

DJ began to make an obscene gesture, but Aubrey appeared from the crowd of students. He cleared his throat and tried to act the gentleman, but it was already too late.

She gave him a gentle shove into a locker. "Don't be so gross, DJ. We all know you haven't even come close with Jess. Hey, Ronny Boy. Where've you been? Mr. Mendez told us you were out sick, but two whole weeks, dude? Milkin' it much?"

Out sick, Ronald mused. *If only.*

What could he say? Could he tell them a ninja assassin from an ancient protectorate attacked him on his landing? That he survived the attack but was dosed with a poison that kept him bedridden for literal days? Then, when he woke up, he saw his mom for the first time since he was still shitting his diaper, too little to even remember her. Ha! They would think he was crazy, playing for attention, or both more likely.

"Yeah." He shrugged. "Something like that."

The vein on Aubrey's neck pulsed, and she clenched her teeth. Ronald had a good idea what came next, and he tried to push through his friends as they crowded him, to walk away before it was too late to avoid the inevitable confrontation.

She grabbed him by the collar of his shirt and turned him to face her. "*Two weeks,* Ronald. Not so much as a call or text. I thought you were dead." *Not too far from the truth.* "I thought you'd said, 'screw this place and these people,' and left us without saying goodbye. I thought you of all people would understand how much I hate that. Why didn't you just tell me what was going on? And I'd finally started trusting you, too."

She sniffled and wiped tears off her cheek. DJ looked around, doing everything he could to pretend he wasn't part of their increasingly awkward exchange. Robert kept playing his game, oblivious to the rising conflict. Or pretending to be, at least.

Ronald clenched his fists. Aubrey's sudden outburst grated at the back of his skull. Who was *she* to yell at *him*? How were her trust issues suddenly his problem? Didn't she realize there was a lot more at stake than him not texting her? After everything he'd been through, the last thing he expected was a reprimand and a guilt trip.

While Ronald's rage simmered, DJ cleared his throat. "We, uh, started the club without you. The deadline was last Friday, and we didn't know if you were coming back so..."

"...So, Mendez sponsored us," Robert added without missing a beat on his game. "Like he said he would. There're a few others who joined, not many. Skylar, actually. Believe it or not. Aubs is president. DJ vice. You can still be Treasurer if you want. I don't mind."

"You don't mind?" Ronald was practically trembling at this point. "You don't *mind*?"

Before he could stop himself, his hand shot out and slapped Robert's phone. It flew over Robert's head, landing on the hard tiled floor, its screen shattering beyond repair. Robert looked up slowly, dumbfounded, his hands and fingers frozen in place, twitching almost imperceptibly as if his phone were still there.

"Jesus, Ronald," Aubrey said. "What the hell is wrong with you?"

"Not cool, man." DJ shook his head, disappointment clear in the way he glared at Ronald. "Not cool at all."

Robert looked as if he might be on the verge of crying when Ronald finally exploded.

"The hip-hop club was my idea. *Mine*. None of you would have even wanted to be in one had I not come up with it in the first place. And you went and started it without me? And invited Skylar, of all people? How could you do that to me? If you knew only half of what I've been through the last few weeks, you'd realize how stupid you all sound. You don't mind? I can be Treasurer? The hell I can. Who are you to tell me what I can and can't do?"

Stop, Ronald. Stop it right now. But the floodgates were already open, and even though every part of him wanted to leave it at that, he couldn't seem to stop his mouth from flapping.

"A girl like Jess Avery is NEVER going to sleep with you, DJ. I'm honestly in shock that she's seeing you, if she even is. I won't be at all surprised if you're just making it all up. Or if she's doing some kind of elaborate dare. Why would she want to date a loser like you? Why would anyone!?

"And, Aubrey, you're upset I didn't text you? I almost died. I was almost killed, for God's sake. Like not a bad case of the sniffles killed but stabbed-in-my-freakin'-face killed." He moved his hair out of the way to show the nasty, partially healed wound. "Look, I get it. You've got some weird little personal issues you won't share with any of us, and you expect everyone to pander to your little sensitivities, but there are bigger problems in the world than you feeling abandoned because I didn't let you know I was gonna be gone." Ronald said the last part in baby talk, scrunching his face into a cruel, condescending sneer. "To hell with all of you."

He slammed a fist into his locker, angrier with himself than anything, and pushed through them. His cheeks flared with heat, and he was starting to feel dizzy with the flush of emotions swirling through his system. All three of his friends were dumbstruck, Robert still unmoved from his original position, but it was almost as if they weren't even there anymore. That was the only way he could make the whole ordeal feel less real, thus removing the immediate guilt and saving that part for later. Hopefully much, much later...

As he blended in with the moving crowd of students, he could hear Aubrey sobbing. "To hell with you too, Ronald Hashimoto," she yelled. "You're officially uninvited to the club."

The last thing he heard was DJ, probably saying something

snippy to Aubrey, and then they were gone. Ronald was all alone with his thoughts—just him and his misery. He put his head down and pushed through the heavy double doors into the stairwell. He whipped his books against the wall, an explosion of loose-leaf paper floating to the ground. He banged his fists on the windowsill and yelled at the top of his lungs. A couple freshmen were on their way up, and when he turned his gaze to them, they whimpered and stumbled over each other to run in the opposite direction.

Once again, Ronald found himself with his elbows on the ledge, staring out at the student parking lot. He had to laugh to himself. He'd never driven a car before. In fact, he knew less about cars than he did about being a teenager. To Ronald, cars were heaps of painted metal. To Ronald, they were an afterthought in an old, forgotten world of swords, bus stations, and nighttime walks through the city.

But it wasn't the cars that caught his eye. There, leaning against the hood of Aubrey's Saturn, was Tomo, his shirt unbuttoned, hanging loosely at his sides. If Ronald didn't know who he was, he might have mistaken him for just another one of the "cool kids," truant, and far too self-absorbed to bother with anything as lame as class. The assassin was picking at his fingernails with a knife, bobbing his head as if jamming to a catchy tune. Ronald couldn't help but wonder what kind of tunes a trained killer might unwind to after a hard day's killing. Death metal, surely. Or creepy old Fifties music.

Tomo glanced up, and they made direct eye contact. The assassin sneered, baring his teeth, and threw Ronald a finger gun with a wink. Tomo then checked a fake watch on his wrist, nodded his head as if he knew something Ronald didn't know, and shoved his hands into the folds of his pants. He casually walked away, whistling and bobbing his head some more, hands in his pockets, until Ronald lost sight of him within the nearby neighborhood.

Ronald's heart raced. He felt a sickening twist in his gut, and then the rage was gone, replaced by sheer terror. If round two was to happen here and now, Ronald was as good as dead. He was unarmed and, even worse, unprepared.

Shit, he thought, sliding out of view. "Shit, shit, shit!"

"You okay, Ronald?" The small voice caught him off-guard. It was Robert, creeping up the stairs towards him.

Ronald shook his head, buried his face in his palms. "No, man. I'm not."

"I get it," Robert said. "When I'm not playing games or lifting, there are voices in my head. They tell me how worthless I am, how everyone hates me. They tell me I'd be better off dead. It makes me so mad, too, because I know it's all lies. But when you hear it over and over, it's hard not to listen, ya know? When you're in that moment, it's hard to remind yourself that it's all bullshit. Do you want to talk about it?"

Robert's question echoed Mr. Mendez's. Ronald didn't deserve these friends. He didn't deserve a place in the real world. The Order, and Daichi, had taken that privilege away from him a long time ago. When he drove his sword through that soldier's body, he also cut any tethers he had to the mundane. High school? Bah! How could he do high school with the dying image of his brother always in his mind? How could he have a normal conversation with a cute girl he liked when he'd just met his folk singer/ex-samurai mom after she'd mended him back to health after being nearly assassinated?

And here was Robert Polson, someone he hardly thought twice about lately, reaching out to him, checking on him. After he broke his phone, too…

"No," Ronald said. "I… I can't."

"I get it. Hey, man, if you ever need anything…"

"I appreciate that. I wish I could tell you guys, but I can't. Not yet. Not until I fix everything."

"No worries, but you don't have to do everything alone. Not anymore. You were a real dick back there, but if you want to be forgiven, they'll forgive you. In time."

And what about you? Ronald wanted to ask. At an impulse, he'd broken Robert's phone. His lifeline, as it were.

"Can I ask you something?" Robert nodded. "What do you do, when those voices are louder than everything else?"

Robert looked up, as if thinking, and then said, "I tell them to shut the hell up. That's what. If they're still jabberin', I grab something heavy or turn up the difficulty a notch."

Oddly, there was wisdom behind Robert's words. In the short time Ronald had known him, he hadn't said much. He was usually lost in a screen of one sort or another, but his advice resonated with Ronald. Robert had his games. DJ had his sense of humor. Ronald had his music.

But Aubrey was still an enigma. Somewhere behind her tough-girl facade, she had to have her coping mechanism too, right? There had to be something; he just couldn't quite figure her out.

Maybe he was more normal than he thought… just maybe…

Then, he remembered the assassin waiting for him in the parking lot. No, Ronald Hashimoto did not get to experience that kind of life. He couldn't possibly be anything other than a trained killer, now. He might have run from the Order, but he would never get away. Not until he finished what he started. He couldn't afford anyone else getting hurt because of his failures.

"Hey, Robert," he said, gathering his stuff, "I'm sorry about your phone. I have something to do, but I'm gonna' replace it as soon as I can, okay? Tell the others I'm sorry, too?"

Robert nodded again, and that was that. Now, all Ronald had to do was deal with a pesky assassin, appease an order of murderous samurai, return to Shima Gōdatsusha to retrieve Jiro's swords and avenge his death, make amends with his drunkard of a father, find room to let his long-lost mother back into his life, and make up to his other friends for being a supreme dickhead.

Light work.

No big deal.

He took a deep, cleansing breath, and for a moment—albeit a very small moment compared to all the others he'd experienced lately—he saw everything ahead of him with an inexplicable clarity of mind. Yes, he realized, he needed to finish what he inadvertently started that day with Jiro. He needed to tie all those loose ends before he could close that part of his life and start a new chapter with his friends, one where he didn't blow up on them like an insufferable teenager every time things didn't go his way.

But how in Shima Gōdatsusha's moonless sky was he going to do any of that when he could barely keep it together on a normal day?

CHAPTER TWELVE

Ronald paced in front of his locker. He had it closed for the moment, but not locked.

The sound of stomping, clapping, and chanting echoed from the far end of the hallway. The Normal Knights "battled" the Kingsley Cavaliers tonight, and the entire school was worked into a frenzy. School spirit was palpable, as thick as fog, and Ronald was the only one who couldn't care less. He had a more important battle to fight, with much higher stakes. A *real* battle.

At least that's the story he told himself. It had nothing to do with the fact that he wasn't one of them—could never be one of them—and even less to do with the nagging desire tugging him towards those gymnasium doors. Could he open them? Could he cross that threshold and enjoy himself along with the others, just for one afternoon? Pretend he had school spirit rather than chronic anxiety?

The silvery tinkle of a thousand glass shards on linoleum

brought Ronald out from introspection. His rage was properly tempered, and he was as ready for the inevitable fight as he was ever going to be, but the sudden interruption of his thoughts got his heart racing.

As expected, *he* stepped into the hall from the school's side door—the exit teachers used to smoke cigarettes and talk shit about their least favorite students. Tomo entered on silent, deliberate feet. He glanced in the opposite direction, then found Ronald, still pacing. He grinned and held an extra-long yari behind him; its shaft rested on the small of his back and its pronged end pointed slightly downward.

"You look tense, Ron. Who ya waiting for?" Tomo winked and brought the spear around in an impressive yet impractical flourish. "Lil' ole me?"

"Aren't you worried someone might see you here? Officer Pact, for example? Her 9-millimeter might have something to say about that little stick of yours."

"What's a little more bloodshed?"

Ronald cringed. He knew the assassin was serious. Dead serious. Tomo was a merciless killer who thought little about the prospect of innocent bystanders.

"Something's been bothering me," Ronald said, inching ever closer to his locker.

"Oh yeah? Just one thing?"

"Why'd you take so long to come for me? You followed me home that night, right? Or one of those kitsune did. Why wait?"

The question seemed to catch Tomo off guard. He brought his fingers to his chin and scratched at his little beard. Then, he shrugged. "Alright, the truth's better than a clever lie, right? As soon as we got to the burbs, I lost you in your neighborhood. Can you believe it? I've tracked warlords through jungles, chased deserters to the far corners of the world, and I got lost among a bunch of freaking copy-and-paste houses. Had to learn how to use the Googles, as you kids call it. Can you *even* imagine?

"But man, I didn't expect you to put up such a fight. I'm not taking any chances this time." He pointed to his yari and slammed the butt of the spear on the floor a few times, punctuating the muffled chants coming from the gym. "Trust me, I won't be letting my guard down like that again anytime soon. Thanks for teaching this old dog a lesson."

"You're welcome." Ronald relaxed and blinked the impending panic away. The weight of fear held between his shoulders lightened, and he took a deep breath. He opened his eyes, beckoned, and said, "Come on then, *bitch*. Let's get this over with."

Tomo sneered and crouched, ready to spring, but Ronald couldn't help notice the assassin's hesitation. He bet Tomo's groin was first and foremost on his mind in that moment and the image of Tomo keeled over, gasping for breath brought a brief sureness to his step.

Still, Ronald almost didn't react in time as Tomo brought the yari in an upward arc, its vicious, pointed blade detaching from the shaft. Tethered to the spear by a long, thin chain, it flew towards Ronald like an arrow. He threw his locker open at the last second, and the bladed end stuck tight, its tip splitting the flimsy metal and grazing his cheek.

Inside his locker, his katana and wakizashi awaited like two ever-reliable friends. Normal was a safe school with no metal detectors, and he'd been paranoid enough to keep them on him at all times. When the whole week passed with no attack from Tomo, he figured it out. The assassin would wait to get him as alone as possible. What better time than during a school-wide pep rally?

Ronald grabbed his swords, shrugged them loose from their sheaths, and slammed the locker shut on the thin chain. He spun the lock then stabbed his short sword through the link closest to the end, effectively jamming Tomo's weapon in place. The assassin yanked once, twice, but Ronald was fast closing in, his katana poised to strike.

Tomo tossed his yari at Ronald, who took the blow on his shoulder without slowing, and drew his sais. *Are they poisoned again?* Ronald wondered, but he didn't worry about it for long.

They collided in a flash of metal, Ronald pressing the initial attack. He slashed, cut, changed directions and used his sideways momentum to slash again. Tomo's smaller weapons allowed Ronald's blade to pass within a hair of striking true, but he was fast and skilled enough to knock each of Ronald's attacks aside without much trouble.

Ronald overcommitted, exposing too much of his torso to the assassin. Tomo made him pay for the mistake with an elbow to his stomach.

Wind knocked loose, Ronald blocked a few jabs, but he let too much of his focus slip to the pain in his gut. Tomo's foot struck him between the ribs and set him sliding across the school's polished floor. His katana came loose and skittered out of reach.

The gymnasium door creaked open, and Ronald turned to see a wide-eyed DJ.

"I, uh…" DJ stammered and stumbled backwards towards the door. He looked from Ronald to Tomo, then down at the katana resting at his feet. "I, uh, just have to take a dump. I'm sorry, I'll... I don't actually have to go anymore."

The assassin set his eyes on DJ. Tomo had no qualms about harming innocent bystanders, and Ronald knew it was now his responsibility to save his idiot friend's life. It was the least he could do after being such a jerk.

"Kick me the sword, would ya?" Ronald said.

"Wait, what?"

Tomo was in motion, and DJ was playing dumb? Ronald couldn't believe it.

"Kick me the damn sword."

DJ slid his foot clumsily towards Ronald's katana, nearly cutting his own toes off, but he managed to nudge it just far enough to reach. Ronald grabbed his sword's comforting handle, gripped it tight and relieved the pressure before spinning to block a leaping attack.

Tomo's attacks came more aggressively now, with Ronald still on the floor. He was a wasp again, stinging and stinging and stinging. Ronald fought desperately to keep from getting poked, scrambling crablike away with each successive block until his back was pressed against the wall.

Cheers erupted from within the gym. A voice through a megaphone, Skylar's by its undeniable smugness, egged the crowd into a frenzy with one of the worst school chants Ronald had ever heard.

"Beat 'em, beat 'em, fight, fight, fight!"

"Knights charge, Cavaliers flight."

"Beat 'em, beat 'em, fight, fight, fight!"

Tomo chuckled. "That the best you people can come up with?

Psh. Can't blame ya for skippin'."

As Tomo re-engaged, Ronald's katana nearly slipped from his moist grip, but he held on and managed to keep up his defense. But Tomo didn't relent. There weren't any stairs for Ronald to throw them both down this time, and he was starting to get desperate. Was this it? Somehow, he had almost convinced himself this second fight with the assassin would end differently. Why in the world had he thought he could stand up to a seasoned killer? He knew better.

Then, Ronald noticed a dusty roll of silver streamer shoved into the corner. He snatched it and hurled it at Tomo's face. It caught the assassin off guard, and in his temporary confusion, Tomo managed to get silver paper wrapped around his arms and shoulders.

In the assassin's brief, confused struggle, Ronald sprang and disarmed Tomo with two quick flicks of his katana. He held the tip of his blade against the assassin's throat, and Tomo held out two bloody palms in surrender, looking ridiculous covered in shimmering streamer and clumps of floor lint.

"Dammit, you're unpredictable, kid. Mercy, I guess?" He grinned. "Nah, you don't have it in you. Killing an unarmed man in cold blood? That ain't your style."

Ronald's shoulders were heaving from exertion, and he wanted nothing more than to slide the blade forward, yet he hesitated. Was Tomo right? Was he going to fail at this like he failed at everything else?

No. With a flash of his free hand, Ronald drew his short sword. In another flash, he pressed in close to the assassin, the sharp edges of both blades crisscrossed at the assassin's neck. From there, all it would take would be a gentle flick of his wrists and one of his major problems would be solved. His vision blurred as his muscles tensed, and a wall of red closed in around his periphery. He *could* do it. He *would* do it...

But then he heard a familiar voice, and the red wall retreated, better sense rushing back to take its place.

"Ronald!" DJ yelled. "Don't, man. Just... what the actual hell, man?"

Ronald gulped glass and relaxed. What was he doing? He wasn't a freaking cold-blooded murderer like Tomo.

"You're wrong," he said. "I *will* do it."

Tomo snorted. "Cap. Or whatever you kids say nowadays."

"I'm serious." Ronald tossed his swords to the floor. "I'll do it. I'll return to Shima Gōdatsusha, take my brother's swords back, and finish my initiation."

Tomo scoffed. "Now you change your mind?"

"No thanks to you." Ronald snorted. "If I let you live, will you pass the word to the Order?"

"You know what, kid? I'll do you one better. I'll help you."

Ronald couldn't believe what he was hearing. Was the man who had twice tried to kill him offering to help? It didn't make any sense.

"But why?" Ronald asked. "What could you possibly have to gain?"

Inside the gym, the pep rally was starting to wind down and time was running out.

"I like your spunk. My job's to 'take care of you,' but nobody explicitly said I had to kill ya." He shrugged, nonchalant. "Look, we'll talk more later, kid. Your friends are about done in there."

He scooped up his sais, a concerned look on his face. "Should I be worried about him?" He peered over Ronald's shoulder at DJ. "Oda wouldn't be too happy if word got out about—"

"Don't. Touch him. I'll take care of it. Tell the master I'll be back in a week. To finish what I started, with or without his approval."

"Thanks, kid," Tomo said.

"Erm, you're welcome?"

"For sparing me, I mean. I can't say I would've done the same if I were in your position, but despite this cold-blooded exterior"—he indicated to his body with a flourish—"I didn't really feel like dying today."

"You wouldn't have spared me. That's what makes me better than you. One of the things, at least."

Tomo shook his finger at Ronald and clicked his tongue. "Don't get too far ahead of yourself. The Order might not accept your sudden change of heart as readily. There's going to be a price to pay." He circled back to Ronald's locker to unstick his yari. "Why not come with me now, pay what needs to be paid and be done with it?"

Ronald thought about it, but he knew there was a good chance he wouldn't make it back alive. He couldn't do that to Aubrey again. He couldn't leave her wondering, and he couldn't concentrate on the matter at hand while he still carried so much guilt from how he left things off with his friends.

"There's something I need to take care of."

"A girl?" Tomo asked, uncharacteristically soft-hearted. He smirked. "I'm right. It's a girl. Do what ya' gotta do. I'll try to convince Master Oda to accept you back into the Order. If not, well, I think you know what has to happen if he refuses."

"We end this once and for all?"

"Yezzir." Tomo nodded. "We end this. See ya, kid."

"Yeah, see ya."

Then, the assassin disappeared, just in time for the gymnasium's double doors to swing open. A mass of hyped students poured into the hall, and Ronald barely got his swords stashed away in his locker before the crowd engulfed him. Luckily, his classmates were all too amped up for their big sports game to notice all the damage Ronald and Tomo had caused in the hallway.

CHAPTER THIRTEEN

Ronald used his sleeve to wipe the blood off his cheek. He scanned the crowd, eyes frantic, until he found Aubrey. When he grabbed her, she cocked her arm, ready to strike, but stopped as soon as she realized it was him.

"Jesus, Ronald. I almost throat-punched you."

"I'm sorry. I had to talk to you."

Aubrey sighed. "You're an asshole, though. Not sure I wanna talk. What the hell happened to you, anyway? You look worse than awful."

He grabbed her arm and began to pull her towards the gym but caught himself and loosened his grip. She looked affronted, and the last thing he wanted to do was push her away with unwanted and unwarranted physicality. He held out his hands in surrender

"Sorry. It's a long story. Please, just give me a few minutes. My life has gotten... complicated. If I explain, it might help you to understand that, sure, I *am* a huge asshole but for good reasons. Er, good-ish reasons."

She folded her arms over her chest and leaned her weight onto one foot, tapping the other. Her lips played back and forth, as if considering whether to allow Ronald his few minutes or just throat-punch him. He'd accept either response if she'd only stop glaring into his soul.

"Fine, sure. Whatever." Aubrey indicated towards the rapidly emptying gym. "You got five minutes." She grabbed his wrist to hold up his hand. "And Ronny Boy? If you *ever* grab me like that again, I'll break this. Are we clear?"

Ronald's eyes grew to twice their regular size as he nodded furiously. "Yes, ma'am. Crystal."

In the gym, Ronald started pacing again, his arms clasped behind his back. He paced and Aubrey waited, until the door clicked shut and a heavy silence fell over them. He'd been nervous before fighting Tomo, of course, but this was somehow way, way worse.

"Settle down. You're starting to stress *me* out." Leaned against the bleachers, Aubrey raised an eyebrow. "Your face is bleeding, by the way."

Ronald wiped his cheek again and said, "I'm trying to figure out the best way to tell you this."

"Maybe just try telling me, then?"

He stopped and held her hands in his. She recoiled at first, but he gave them a reassuring squeeze and dropped the Hashimoto family crest into her open palms.

"Here, I want you to have this." Aubrey appraised the medallion for a moment before Ronald closed her fingers around it. "It's been in my family a long time. Ten generations, at least. Longer, probably. We are..." He gulped and could feel the sweat pooling underneath his arms. "We are samurai."

He expected her to laugh in his face. It sounded absurd coming out of his mouth, considering where they were, the bleachers filled with candy wrappers, empty tubes of face paint, left-behind pom-poms, and streamers. *So, so many steamers.*

Instead, Aubrey relaxed and brought the medallion to her chest. "Samurai, huh? And that cut? The gash beneath your hairline?"

Ronald brought two fingers to his cheek. It was still sticky with blood, and it suddenly dawned on him that Tomo's yari could have been poisoned, too. Had he not been in the middle of the biggest confession of his entire life, he might have panicked.

"Would you believe me if I told you I was fighting a ninja assassin in the hallway while you were in here 'cheerin' on the Knights?' Rah, rah, sis-boom-bah, and all of that."

Now, Aubrey laughed in his face. "I happened to be in here, Ronny Boy, because it was a mandatory school assembly. Something that clearly doesn't apply to you. I couldn't care less about the Knights. You should know that by now."

"So, you believe me?"

She shook her head. "Not even a little, but suppose for a second I did. Why are you giving me this necklace?"

"It's a medallion." He immediately felt stupid correcting her. "It's important to my family, and you're important to me. There's something I have to do, related to why I disappeared before, and it's likely I won't survive."

She raised another eyebrow at him, and the Tech N9ne jam featuring Dwayne Johnson started playing in his mind. *Put in the work, put in the hours,* and he realized that's exactly what he had to do if he ever wanted to live a normal life. Maybe even a life with Aubrey at his side. He had to earn it. He had to work on his relationships, face off with the demons that haunted him daily, and confront all the things he was too afraid to deal with.

"If you're a samurai, where are your swords? Two, right? One long, one short?"

Ronald didn't skip a beat. "In my locker."

If Aubrey had been drinking something, it would have sprayed out of her nose. "You're joking, right? Either that, or you're an absolute psycho."

"I have a week, maybe less. After that, if I come back, will you consider forgiving me? I'd like a chance to start fresh, show you who I really am, but I have to take care of this first. I understand if you think I'm just nuts and never want to see me again. If that's the case, I'll honor your choice and leave you alone. Forever."

Aubrey moved in for an unexpected hug and held him tight. He froze, arms at his side like an awkward penguin. The longer she held him, the more he relaxed until he finally wrapped his arms around her too.

"If you don't come back," she whispered in his ear, "I'm going to kick your ass. Then, I'm going to pawn this little *necklace* of yours and buy myself something nice."

"That's fair," Ronald said. He pulled away, and Aubrey brought a cold hand to his cheek, a concerned look on her face. "Don't worry, it doesn't hurt that bad."

"I wasn't." She winked before surprising him yet again with a long kiss—his first ever.

Ronald watched as DJ tramped up the stairs behind him, awkward and goofy looking in his too-long hoodie that hid practically his entire body. This was the first time had had anyone over, and he hadn't bothered to warn his friend about Daichi, who was characteristically passed out on his chair.

"What's so urgent that I had to ditch Jess?" DJ asked, out of breath as he flopped onto Ronald's messy bed.

"I finished it."

Ronald plopped into his computer chair and swiveled to his new rig, a gift from Che. It wasn't as powerful as his old machine, but it came loaded with a lot of good DAW software and more than enough drum kits and sample packs for him to get jiggy with.

"Finished what, man?" DJ was busy scanning Ronald's walls. "No Em? No Drake or Kanye?"

Ronald blew a raspberry. "Overrated." The word stung coming out. Sure, they weren't his bag, but he couldn't deny their raw talent or how many people connected with their music. There just wasn't enough room on his wall. "But anyway, I finished my song."

"The one you've been talking about for, like, ever?"

"That's the song."

"No shit? Finally, man. Took you long enough."

Ronald remembered the fight with Daichi, how he'd felt completely destroyed as the old man took a baseball bat to his computer until there was nothing left but scattered pieces. It sent a chill down his spine, but he shrugged it off.

"There were complications. Check it out." He slid towards DJ and handed him his brand-new headphones: Pioneers.

"What, like being a full-ass samurai warrior and stuff? Yeah, I can see how that could get in the way."

"Whatever. Look, just listen. Let me know what you think."

Ronald leaned back and watched as DJ slipped the headphones on. He hit play, turned up the volume. For good measure, he turned it up a little more. His stomach churned, and to calm his nerves, he followed the gentle peaks and valleys of the two-dozen-plus color-coded waves. There, the hats came in. Then, the subtle violin sample he'd added to undertone the song with a hint of sorrow. Vocals he'd pulled from an old Fifties track. Finally, a low, quiet bassline to bring it all together.

He'd listened to the song so many times, in so many different iterations that he knew exactly which part DJ was hearing for the very first time. Eyes closed, mind opened, he pictured his friend's face, his emotions as the journey unfolded.

But DJ's face quickly disappeared, and Ronald was on a journey of his own. He was in the Shima Gōdatsusha mountains, clad in his family's armor. He was face to face with a dozen of Akuma Araki's most skilled samurai, devils in human form. They came at him in a flurry of action, their mempo masks mocking, but he brushed them aside with ease. They came in pairs, in threes, but not a man, woman, or monster among them could stand against Ronald Hashimoto. Not after what they did to Jiro... When they fell, they dissolved into cherry blossom petals, blown across the ever-swaying countryside.

By the end of the song, Ronald's black and purple armor was stained red with their blood. His swords dripped crimson onto the ice caps beneath his feet. Akuma Araki awaited, the last obstacle standing between him and redemption.

DJ's slow clapping brought Ronald out of his stupor. "Bravo, man. Bravo. That is some heavy, haunting shit right there. Well worth the wait."

Ronald felt himself blushing. "You really like it?"

"Hell yeah. Can you run it back?"

So, Ronald played it again. This time he watched the changes in DJ's facial expressions. He grimaced at all the right times, pursed his lips in the middle of the drops, and never once stopped bobbing his head. When the song finished for the second time, he tossed the headphones onto the bed.

"Love it, Ronald. You've outdone yourself. Hey, do you know who could spit some serious bars to this track?"

Ronald's eyes lit up. "Who?"

"You ain't gonna like it, but Skylar. He freestyles a bit, and his material is pretty dark. I don't know, but if you give him a shot, you might like it."

Ronald clicked his teeth and snatched the headphones. "Skylar's a prick."

"No doubt. I can't argue with that. You're kinda a prick too, though."

Can't argue with that either, Ronald thought. But he planned to change all of that. Once he tied up all his loose ends, he was going to be the friend DJ deserved. And, almost as importantly, he was going to produce some kickass music and maybe even—*sigh*—give Skylar a chance to audition some vocals.

That's when Ronald noticed the faded white lines sneaking out from DJ's long sleeves. He grabbed his friend by the wrist, forced his sleeve back to his elbow, and all but growled in disgust.

"What the hell is this?"

DJ snapped his arm back, ripping it free from Ronald's grasp. He stood, hiding it behind his back, cheeks red and lip quivering. His eyes bulged, and there was something in them Ronald recognized all too well. It wasn't embarrassment or shame. Their fire wasn't regret, either. It was anger. It was the look of someone who had just been betrayed and may never forgive their betrayer. What was worse, it was disappointment.

"Aubrey said it right. Screw you, man."

Chastised, Ronald scrunched his forehead and cursed himself for having acted so brashly. DJ was his friend and deserved better than his insensitive, knee jerk reaction.

"Sorry. Really, I am. I just... Why, though? Help me understand."

"We're all fighting battles you'll never see. You're not special, Ronald. You're not the only one with problems."

"I..." Ronald began to defend himself, but he couldn't find the appropriate words. DJ was right, of course. And there was nothing he could say to change the truth. "I didn't know."

"Damn right you didn't. And nobody else does, either. I'd like to keep it that way, if it's alright with you."

"Absolutely."

"Look, you're not special, no one is, but you're not alone, okay? Like it or not, you've got friends now, and we've got your back. Do you have ours?"

Ronald nodded, and DJ nodded back. He'd gotten so caught up in his own deal that he'd forgotten everyone else had lives of their own. It was another mistake he would spend the rest of his high school career trying to amend.

Ronald found Robert in his garage, benching more than Ronald weighed by the looks of it. He had an old radio cranked to max,

Metallica blaring for the whole neighborhood to hear. When he intruded into the garage and flicked off the radio, Robert nearly fell off the bench. His plates slipped off the bar on one side—five, six, seven, even?—and clanged on the concrete before the bar jerked him in the opposite direction.

"What the—" Robert regained his composure and racked the bar. He leaped up, ready for a fight. When he saw Ronald, he relaxed. "That was less than considerate. 'Bout gave me a heart attack."

"Sorry." Ronald walked the perimeter of the garage and rubbed his fingers through the fine layer of dust that covered the workbenches and utility shelves. Then, he examined the massive pile of plates. "That's an absurd amount of weight. Anyway, I brought you something."

Robert tossed a towel over his shoulders and took a long swig out of an off-brand shaker bottle. He spit some onto the concrete at his feet and rolled his arms in circles. Ronald remained silent as Robert picked up the fallen plates and slid a couple back onto the bar, checking to see if Ronald was watching before tucking the rest away beneath a cluttered workbench. He brushed chalk off hands on his too-tight shorts as he took his seat.

"How'd you find where I live?"

Ronald shrugged. "It wasn't hard."

"Well, now you know. Shithole city, eh? Poor white boy living among a bunch of uppity middle-class folk. An imposter, if you will."

"Not as much of an imposter as me, though. Don't you want to know what I brought you?"

Robert finished toweling his forehead and said, "A million

bucks, I'm hoping. Or keys to a new car." He said the last part like he was hosting The Price is Right.

Ronald laughed and tossed him the phone. "It's new. Well, gently used. I loaded it up with some games and tunes and stuff for you. Pokémon GO, CoD Mobile, Apex Legends, Minecraft, and a few others. Wasn't sure what you like, but there's like three bills in the App Store."

Robert's eyes glistened. Then, he sniffed and wiped them dry, clearing his throat and drawing back his shoulders. "Thanks, man. I... Thank you."

"It's on a three-month contract. Hotspot included."

Robert turned the phone over in his hands, one corner of his lips rising into a smile. "You didn't have to do this, man. But I appreciate you. Girls, boys. Sex. All that stuff, ya know? None of it ever made sense to me. Games, though? Working out? Yeah, I get that. That stuff's easier to navigate."

Ronald nodded towards the weights. "How long you been liftin'?"

"I don't know. Maybe like eight years or so. Started pretty young, to escape a bit, I guess. It's the only time I feel like a 'man,' you know? With how my... With how things are sometimes."

Ronald thought about his music, about Daichi. "Yeah, I get that. One hundred. Got a minute to show me how it's done?"

Robert hopped up and slapped the bench. "Climb on, stud. Let's see what ya' got."

By the third set, Ronald was feeling some kind of way and Robert's cheeks were barely even flushed. It was nothing like when Daichi used to make physical exhaustion his constant companion. Those early morning runs, followed by hours and hours of hard training. The sparring with Jiro and the faceless line-up of other Order would-bes. More running. More training, until he couldn't be sure if his own body was his or not, if the pain would end with him broken or dead.

No, this was nothing like that, but his chest muscles twitched, and his forearms burned. The pain reminded him he was alive, that he could always do better, and the realization gave him a deeper appreciation for Robert. Lifting weights made sense when everything else didn't. More than building muscle, it built character, discipline of mind.

Robert smacked him on the back. "You're out of shape, man."

"Not surprised. Hey, thanks for this." The pain of exertion brought him somehow closer to Jiro. Together, they had been forged. This session with Robert was a fair alternative, and he felt a little like maybe the two high schoolers had just forged something special together, too. "I mean it. Thank you."

Robert allowed a rare smile before asking, "So, you're, like, done with school now, or what?"

"Or what. I have something to take care of this weekend, then I'll be back."

"Cool," Robert said. He wiggled back into place beneath the bar and pushed the bar away from his body as if it weighed nothing.

Ronald left Robert to his business without another word. He had an evil warlord to slay and swords to retrieve. Until his mission was done, and now that he'd made something resembling amends with the people he cared about, nothing else mattered. He couldn't afford any more distractions.

INTERLUDE THREE: BEFORE

At first, Akuma Araki had wanted nothing more than to burn her new village to the ground. But unlike *him*—and the gold devils, those short years ago—she was merciful. Besides, if she continued to let her emotions rule her, she would only prove them right. She was better than that, now.

But she could not allow the boys and men who put her through hell to walk free, unpunished. Their sins were unforgivable, and if anything was going to change, a new precedent needed to be set. After Ritsu, it had to be her. They looked up to her, all the scared little girls and voiceless women across the One Hundred Villages. They needed her voice to speak their own thoughts and desires.

Word traveled fast. Hopefuls came from all across the island to meet the woman whose voice boomed through steel and blood. They came with gifts and stories. They came with young ones to be blessed by the presence of Akuma Araki, Just Slayer of the Oppressive, Harbinger of Peace on Shima Gōdatsusha, Bringer of Tomorrow. Most interestingly, they came with oaths of fealty. Akuma Araki, a little orphan girl, Kangei sa Renai, tried to receive these unexpected offerings gracefully, but they made her uneasy. At first. She smiled, returned her gratitude, then sent them away, her life and role among the villages forever altered, spiraling each day further out of her control.

When they kept coming back, often in larger and larger groups, she began to warm to her newfound command over the masses' admiration. Why deny the workings of the gods? If she were meant to rule, a ruler she would become. It seemed fated whether she wanted to wear the jūnihitoe and everything its multiple layers entailed or not.

"Mistress Araki?" The expected call came during the early hours of yet another cold morning, followed by a light *tap, tap* on her door. "It is I, Minata. Please pardon my intrusion, but the people await."

Had she overslept so, dreaming of her own glorious future? They were better than the nightmares, to be sure, but their equal in dooming Akuma to her endless restless nights.

Minata was among the first to gravitate to her. A village girl, niece to her own adoptive father, she was a timid child two years Akuma's junior. The girl had witnessed the death of her cousin from the shadows, yet she held no grudge against Akuma. She offered little to the cause other than being a devout follower and dependable friend. For Akuma, Minata's unwavering kinship was more than enough to earn the girl a close place by her side. Trust was hard to come by on the island, but the two young women developed an unbreakable bond built around trust's illusion.

Akuma splashed water on her face and drew her long hair back into two tight, upward wings. She crossed her sparse sleeping chamber, slid open a bamboo chest, and lifted the sword held within. Her father's sword. A katana passed down from Araki to Araki, salvaged from the wreckage of her home. Plain, unadorned, a perfect reflection of her quaint, lost village upbringing, but with a cutting edge sharp enough to split blades of grass. She had spent many long nights hunched over a whetstone, sharpening, polishing, re-sharpening, until the blade was as honed as her anger and determination.

Today was the day. All her preparation and patience would finally pay off.

Today, the old Akuma Araki—the victim—died.

Today, Akuma Araki—the warlord—would be reborn, baptized in blood.

Minata bowed at her door. "Mistress. Everything has been prepared as you requested. Representatives from each of the One Hundred Villages await your arrival."

"And you've ensured *their* presence?"

Minata bowed lower, her back nearly parallel to the floor. "Yes, mistress. They stand in chains at the front of the crowd."

Before returning to the village, Akuma stopped at her well—the same well she had drawn water from day in and day out. It was bone dry now, but the other villages brought enough food and water to sustain them without the well. Besides, that was not why she had built her home beside it. The well served as her constant reminder of why this movement was so important. Her people deserved a humble leader, and there was nothing more humbling than the roots of a simple peasant girl, of a weak child struggling to make her way in the world.

Never in her lifetime had Akuma seen so many people gathered in one place. She could hardly recognize the village through the sea of bodies. When they saw her, the crowd cheered and applauded. Her skin tingled as they parted to allow her passage. They reached for her, called her name—the name she had killed Ritsu over, though it had become an honorific rather than an insult. She learned to embrace it, to allow it to fuel the fires of her passion.

"Akuma! Araki!"

"Kangei sa Renai!"

And there were Nobu and Touji, just where she wanted them, standing at the front of the crowd near the raised wooden platform. They had not come under their own volition, of course, and their hands were restrained behind their backs by a deadpan Hifumi and Arata. The powerful yet stupid boys had needed someone with vision to guide them after Ritsu's death. For their muscle, Akuma was more than happy to accept that role.

She climbed the platform steps on light, silent feet, her hand gripping the handle of her katana, knuckles white. Atop the platform, a figure with a cloth over his head knelt beside a wide-brimmed basket. He was tied at his ankles and wrists, deep purple gashes throbbing beneath the hempen ropes.

Without ceremony, she drew her sword, its metallic whisper silencing the crowd. She paced the platform as she spoke, her words echoing throughout the crowded streets.

"For too long have we existed in isolation from one another. For too long has Shima Gōdatsusha been an island of want and fear. When the gold devils came to my village, as they came to many of yours before, I watched, helpless, as they stole everything from me, as life as I had once known burned to ash before my very eyes."

She slashed her sword through the air around her. "Never again, I say. Never again! United, we shall bring peace and prosperity to Shima Gōdatsusha. United, we shall stand up to the gold devils when they return, stand up to *any* injustice that may threaten our way of life. Together, we are unbreakable."

Akuma ripped away the cloth covering the man's head to reveal her adoptive father, his bruised and bloodied face hardly recognizable. Nobu and Touji flinched, and a few gasps arose from the crowd, but no one moved to intervene.

"This man represents the hardships we daily endure. As a young girl, this man brought me into his home when I needed a family the most. He brought me into his home and introduced me to violence like I'd never before known and will never again tolerate. He is a devil, wearing our own clothing. He wears lies on his back and carries deceit in his fists. Today, I offer you a promise." She raised the sword high above the back of his neck, its cutting edge glinting in the morning sun. "Today, I offer you a new age. An age of harmony. An age of peace. An age where *all* of Shima Gōdatsusha's voices will be heard, and our bodies will be protected."

She hoped the crowd could not see her arms trembling, and she herself could not decide if it was due to the heft of the blade or the weight of what she was about to do—what she *must* do.

"People of the One Hundred Villages, with this devil's justice, we are one." She brought her sword down swift and hard. "We. Are. Shima Gōdatsusha!"

The village square erupted in deafening cheers that echoed across the entire valley. She wiped her sword clean, sheathed it with unsteady hands, and raised her arms to the sky as the crowd grew louder and louder. Hifumi and Arata held Nobu and Touji's gaze upon their dead father's corpse as the people began chanting her name once more.

"Kangei sa Renai! Kangei sa Renai!"

At a subtle nod from Akuma Araki, her henchmen stuck knives between the brothers' ribcages, shoving them towards the platform so they too could die before the people.

"Akuma! Akuma!"

Among the throng, Minata bowed her head. She did not shed a single tear for the deaths of three men of whom she once called kin.

A wide, cruel smile spread across Akuma's face. Her mind swam with all the possibilities held between this new age's teeth. A new day had dawned, and it belonged to her. From here on out, they would *all* belong to her.

CHAPTER FOURTEEN

Hands in his pockets, mind wandering among the forests of Shima Gōdatsusha, Ronald approached his front porch. His mind was so lost, in fact, that he didn't notice the foxes prowling his lawn or the armored samurai standing guard at the end of his driveway. He didn't notice the hooded monks darting in and out of his house until he very nearly ran into one. Even then, realization only barely dawned.

"Hey," Ronald said. "Watch it!"

He'd made amends with everyone important in his life besides one: Daichi. The entire walk home, he'd thought about what he might say, repeating the script in his head until his mind had little room left for anything else. No matter how many times he practiced what he wanted to say to his father, it never seemed right. The resentment always took over, even when Ronald's intentions were pure, and he was afraid he wouldn't be strong enough to confront Daichi with anything resembling grace.

A strangely familiar fox darted between his legs, nipping at his Adidas. He skipped and hopped to avoid the creature, watching with detachment as it disappeared down the street.

That's when the full picture became clear. Nearly the entirety of the Order of the Golden Bonsai busied themselves around his property. Urgency—and what? Despair?—was palpable among the chaos, and his fear suddenly evolved into dread.

He grabbed a monk by her shoulder, but she shrugged him off, shaking her head before disappearing around back. The next shunned him too. They refused eye-contact, refused to as much as acknowledge his presence. Finally, he saw a familiar and hopefully friendly face through one of the front windows.

"Tomo!" He waved and bounded up the steps. Tomo nodded, but even he looked away as soon as Ronald came close. "Tomo, why's the Order here? What's going on?"

Tomo leaned towards the monk he was talking with, whispered something into the man's ear, and dismissed him with a flick of his wrist. Message received, the monk shoved past Ronald and shuffled across the front yard.

As Ronald burst into the house—his *own* house—the assassin moved between him and the living room, blocking his passage with outstretched arms.

"Hey, hey, hey," Tomo said, an eerie yet calm and reassuring undertone behind his words. "Hey, man. It's all good. Stay with me, Ronald. Everything's gonna be okay."

Ronald knew immediately that nothing was okay. He flushed with hot anger towards Tomo, towards the Order, towards his life and all the bullshit it insisted on shoveling onto him. He reached for his swords, and it was a good thing for Tomo that they were hanging safely on the wall in his room. He couldn't be sure that he'd be able to stay his blade in his current state of mind, whether Tomo claimed to be on his side now or not. Either way, at that moment, the assassin looked more like an intruder than a friend.

"Don't touch me!" Ronald tried to push Tomo away, but the assassin was too strong for him. "Let me go! What the hell are you even doing in my house?"

"Something's happened. Before you see... I need to try to explain—"

"What happened, Tomo? Tell me already."

"Daichi..." Tomo cast his eyes downward. "He made a deal with the Order. To allow you back in. To redeem the Hashimoto family in the eyes of Master Oda and the others. There... there was no other way. I'm so sorry."

Over Tomo's shoulder, all of Ronald's questions were answered. The cypress sanbo, a stand on four legs presented in ceremony to any samurai about to embark on their final journey. The ivory-colored cloth. The tanto laying on the floor, guilt-tipped with crimson blood. The body, covered by a purple and gold sheet. *Daichi's body*, Ronald realized with horror.

"But why..." Ronald choked on any other words that he might have spoken, and the tears came unbidden.

Daichi may have been a bastard of a man and a terrible father, but he had been Ronald's father, Ronald's only family before Che—whom he still had a hard time thinking of as *Mother*. How could he do this? How could he leave Ronald alone in the world? Orphaned.

Tomo handed Ronald a tightly raveled scroll, streaked with fresh ink. "From Daichi," he said. "For your eyes only."

Ronald's hands trembled as he accepted the scroll. Whatever words it might have contained couldn't possibly make the situation better. Part of him wanted nothing more than to drop the scroll in a trash can and set it aflame. Part of him wanted to scream and kick and scratch until every monk, kitsune, and samurai swarming his house felt half the pain he was feeling, until their blood stained his carpet right along with his father's.

But he unraveled the scroll, slowly revealing Daichi's hastily scrawled death note with shaky hands:

My dear Ronald, Hashimoto by Blood and by Deed,

To say I have failed you as a father is an understatement, but I have been redeemed as Teacher. You have chosen to return to the path, to bring honor back to a family name I have tarnished. The cost of which—my life—is a small payment to see your destiny fulfilled. I am proud of the man you have become, and Jiro would be equally proud to know his brother now flies true with the currents of time. You have earned the Hashimoto name, and all the great and burdensome fortune that comes with it.

Trust in Tomo, Ronald Hashimoto. He guided my life in ways I could never repay, and he will do the same for you. Trust in him, and in the Order, and your path will become clear.

Good-bye, my son. Jiro and I will be forever watching you through keen eyes and open hearts, counting the days until Hashimoto is whole once more in the afterlife.

Signed,

Hashimoto Daichi

The scroll slipped from Ronald's fingers, fluttering to the ground between his feet. Tomo reached for it and stopped short, placing his hand instead on Ronald's shoulder.

"Daichi may have been a scumbag, but he was an honorable man. He did right by you in the end."

"Right?" Ronald slapped Tomo's hand away. "He did right!? How? By killing himself? By leaving me all alone?"

Tomo shook his head. "You're not alone, Ronald. You'll never have to be alone again."

"People keep telling me that, but it's not true. It's never been true."

"Ronald..."

"But why did he have to die?"

"It was your life, or his."

"Says who? There's always another way."

"The Order. It's *their* way, and there's no way around it. Through seppuku, Daichi redeemed your family's transgressions, served the death sentences issued on your names. I told you there would be a cost, that coming back into the fold wasn't going to be free."

A cold numbness crawled through Ronald's skin and a sneer snuck across his lips. So much needless death... So much loss. He couldn't bring Aubrey into such a life. He couldn't expose DJ or Robert to his friendship if that meant their lives would be on the line too.

Invite Death into your home and serve her tea, Daichi had once said. But Ronald was Death, it seemed, and soon Akuma Araki and her samurai would let him in, invited or not.

"Let's go, Tomo. If you're still willing to help me, it's time to finish this."

The assassin returned Ronald's sneer, a rejuvenated glint in his eyes. Ronald, on the other hand, wasn't quite as eager, but he didn't have a choice anymore. He couldn't let Daichi's death count for nothing. If he didn't act now, he was afraid he'd spiral into an oblivion he'd never return from. A numb, sedentary place of apathy.

CHAPTER FIFTEEN

New Province, and its seemingly endless procession of lonely suburbs, streaked by in a blur of shingles and slate, brick and steel. Tomo talked the whole ride, waving his arms, slapping the steering wheel, turning to Ronald for validation.

Ronald didn't hear a word the assassin had to say. He didn't notice the subtle shift in scenery as they turned onto one of the city's forgotten streets or feel his feet on pavement as they walked the broken sidewalks towards the house where the memories of the worst day of his life awaited.

At both ends of the block, smoke plumed from various house fires. In neighborhoods like this, a conflagration or two a month wasn't unheard of—be it electrical fire or disgruntled neighbor, fed up with a lack of city intervention—but two in one night, both near the only known shrine into Shima Gōdatsusha, rang all of Ronald's internal alarm bells. Fight or flight took over where self-loathing had once ruled, and with each heavy step he began to lean closer towards flight. Again, he had the desire to run to the opposite end of the earth, but he knew better. Unless he finished what he started, the Order would find him.

He couldn't keep running. He had to face what stalked his nightmares once and for all. He had to break the cycle.

Now that they were there, without the excursion being officially sanctioned by Oda or one of the other masters, he had no choice. He was already breaking one of their so-called laws, implicating Tomo in his mess, nonetheless, and the only way to exonerate himself would be victory.

Ronald pushed through the overgrown hedges, Tomo close in toe. The rusted iron gate groaned open, and a flock of starlings scattered into the pale dusk, causing Ronald to jump. On instinct, his katana slid free from its sheath.

"Easy, kid. We're not there yet."

The walkway was cracked in more places than not, and weeds grew in bunches, strangling the property, creeping up its walls, inhabiting all the empty spaces around it. The grass hadn't been cut since last time he was there, and it was nearly above his shoulders. He could hear critters skittering about—raccoons, rats, maybe some opossum—and the stench of decay was overwhelming.

He covered his mouth and nose. "Why wouldn't the Order take better care of this place?"

Tomo pushed aside some ragweed and coughed. "Needs to blend in. This neighborhood's gone to shit over the last year and a half. Most of these houses are cut off from power, from emergency services. It would look strange if a single house had a manicured lawn and marble dragon statues out front, wouldn't it?"

Tomo was right, of course, but this took incognito a little

too far. The Order should have had eyes on it. As far as he could tell, they were alone. Cut off from civilization. Maybe that was the point. Maybe by abandoning the shrine the Order hoped no one would come sniffing around. Whatever the explanation, the isolation of it gave Ronald the chills.

His foot cracked the rotted front steps, nearly splintering through to his ankle, and a creature underneath growled and hissed. A mangy cat darted from underneath the house, a golden-hued fox close behind. Tomo kicked in the varmints' general direction, but they zagged between his legs and disappeared into the tall grass across the street. Dozens of slit eyes blinked, grass swayed, and the back of Ronald's neck tingled. He lifted his foot slowly, carefully, and skipped the rest of the steps, preferring trash-strewn concrete to rotten wood and rabies.

The front windows were boarded, tagged with so much spray paint it was impossible to tell where one artist's signature ended and the next began. Orange stickers plastered the wall around the door frame. By how many had been slapped on top of each other, the house had been condemned more times than the number of years Ronald had been alive. He couldn't help but wonder who had been inside since his last visit. Vagrants and drug addicts, for sure. But what about city inspectors and health officials? Could someone else have discovered what was below the house's foundation? Would they have suspected anything unusual about the lone Hachiman shrine?

Ronald whistled and clicked his tongue. He kicked a pile of sun-tarnished Old English cans off the edge of the porch, revealing a mound of squirming maggots and discarded syringes.

"Little too convincing, if you ask me."

Tomo hocked a loogie into the bushes. Ronald could tell the assassin was feeling a similar kind of way about the house's condition but more or less keeping it to himself.

"Something's wrong here," Ronald said as he brushed aside a cobweb.

"Yup." Tomo tried the front door. A loose chunk of glass fell off the storm door, shattering at their feet. "Be on your guard. The Order should be here, but I haven't seen any sign of them. There could be anything, or anyone, waiting for us." Ronald began to draw his katana, but Tomo reached over and pushed it back into its sheath. "If we get into trouble inside, your short sword works better up close."

Ronald nodded, fumbling with his belt to find his wakizashi. "Got it. Thanks for the tip."

"Your katana is too long and unwieldy for close corridors. Depending on what we find in there, even a fraction of a second could make all the difference." He drew his sais and grinned. Ronald's skin pricked at their familiar glint. "That's why I love these. Nothin' faster in a pinch."

Tomo threw his shoulder into the door, and it exploded at its hinges, swinging inward at an awkward angle before tearing loose from the frame and crashing into the house. A wall of the foulest stench Ronald had ever had the displeasure of smelling assaulted him like a one-inch punch. He gagged, doubled over. It took all his fortitude not to lose his breakfast and equal determination not to walk away and forget about this whole thing. Even the unflappable assassin covered his nose with his sleeve.

Ronald tip-toed across the threshold, into the foyer. Tomo ducked off to the right, making a quick, quiet sweep of the side rooms, and reappeared further down the hallway from the opposite side. He nodded all clear, and Ronald moved forward, towards the basement.

There wasn't a single surface in the kitchen free of grease or mold. Black, corroded goop seeped down the front of the oven. Rats poked their way through rancid leftovers. The refrigerator hung open, spoiled milk and other condiments congealed and leaking onto the floor. A sleeping bag was rolled up in one corner, hot plates and old needles scattered around it, trash piled in heaps. Flies buzzed around what Ronald kept telling himself wasn't a bone protruding from one of the bags. The more he stood among the smell, the harder it was to believe the lie.

"Lovely," Tomo said. He prodded a drawer with one of his weapons' hafts, and it slid free, cheap silverware clattering on the floor, sending the rats scurrying in every direction. "Safe to say nobody's here, at least."

Ronald sheathed his wakizashi and breathed a sigh of relief that started him gagging and coughing once more. Alone, they could tend to this awful business without worrying about intruders. Alone, there would be no unexpected interruptions, no witnesses whether they succeeded or not. He shuddered, remembering how Tomo regarded witnesses, but at least alone there wasn't any added pressure like there had been when Daichi watched his every move. He could be fully Ronald, without fear of judgment.

"Ready, kid?"

"No, not really." Ronald closed his eyes and breathed in deep once more. This time, he didn't gag. "But let's do this anyway. Follow me. The shrine is downstairs. This way."

The basement hadn't changed much over the last few years.

There was a little more dust, a little more emptiness, but Hachiman's shrine looked as if it hadn't been touched. The master awaited their triumphant return, ever vigilant, his arms outstretched for those worthy enough to receive his embrace.

"Do you remember the ritual?" Tomo asked.

Ronald remained silent as he approached the shrine. He bowed. Once. Twice. Three times. He knelt and rested his hands on his knees. Tomo mirrored him from a safe distance.

He muttered a short prayer. "Master, guide me through the winds between this island and the next. Sharpen my blade when it becomes dull. Temper my armor when it becomes brittle. Take me under thy wing and wash away my greatest fears so that I may be reborn, a warrior worthy of your strength. Allow me to sail with thee to Shima Gōdatsusha and claim what is rightfully mine by birth and by blood. Open thy realm, so we may enter and please thee with steel and with iron."

Ronald grabbed the ceremonial tanto and ran its blade across the palm of his hand. Without breaking eye contact with Hachiman, he handed the dagger to Tomo, who did the same. Their blood intermingled in the dirt, drifted into a swirling pattern, part Hashimoto, part Nakajima—two families worthy of the master's embrace. He replaced the tanto, and the shrine began to fold away until all that was left was a set of stairs, spiraling down, down, ever-down into blackness.

Tomo's hand rested on Ronald's shoulder. "It's going to be okay, kid. I got your back."

Ronald found he was trembling. He hadn't realized how truly terrified he was of returning to that awful place, of confronting the failures of his past.

He's right, you know? The worst that could happen is death. Jiro's voice again, quiet since Ronald had witnessed the mugging and done nothing to help that poor woman.

"I could fail again." Ronald felt tears welling. "That would be worse than death."

In failure, you find improvement. With improvement, you fail harder, at greater tasks. There is nothing wrong with failure, Ronald. Or fear. You are wrong only when you don't act, when you allow your fear to stay your blade in times which necessitate action.

"What do you know, anyway?"

More than you, but nothing at all. I know only one thing for sure.

"And what's that?"

Ronald was getting annoyed. He was already freaking out enough. He didn't need his brother's disembodied voice in his head speaking in riddles, sounding just like their father.

Tomo's face came into view, blurred at first. He smiled and squeezed Ronald's shoulder tighter. "I know you can do this. You're a Hashimoto, and Daichi would be so proud of you. Jiro, too."

Ronald swelled with hot anger at hearing his father's name spoken alongside his brother's. All the years of violence and pressure came rushing back. He clenched his fists, blood seeping between his fingers from where he'd cut his palm with the tanto. The pain invigorated him, steeled him to the task at hand. They were both dead, and he supposed that made them the same. *Hmpf.* Death, the Great Equalizer.

Ronald ignored his fear and plunged into the darkness. Together, he and the assassin descended step after step until there was no way they could possibly descend any further. Then, they continued further down. He blocked out a lot about that tragic day. What he couldn't, came back frequently in vivid nightmares. He didn't, however, remember having to walk down so many damn steps.

When his calves started burning, he felt a sudden atmospheric shift. There came a steady, echoing *drip, drip, drip,* like water trickling from a cave's ceiling. A chill came over him, and in the faint light, he could see his breath every time he exhaled. His teeth chattered, and he brought his arms closer to his sides for warmth.

They were crossing a vast pool of water, but his feet never quite seemed to touch the surface. It was as if he were floating. Each step left glowing blue footprints in his wake. Two perfect tracks, his and Tomo's, led back into the void from which they came.

Then, the stars began to twinkle. Thousands. Millions. All around them. They were walking through space itself, floating from one universe to another. Tomo held out a hand, poked one of the tiny, crystalline-like spheres of light, and it burst in a brilliant flash of a thousand colors.

"Whoops," Tomo said, and it echoed off unseen walls all around them. Sparks rippled from star to star, creating a vortex of flickering light and color. "Where are we?"

Once Tomo's echoing words quieted, Ronald whispered, "Out Beyond."

They left it at that. Ronald, not wanting to disturb the silence. Tomo, too busy poking stars and causing miniature supernovas.

"It's incredible." Tomo gazed upward, mouth open, arms wide as if he were trying to capture all the stars in the Out Beyond. He spun like a child in their first snow until he was laughing in delight.

Ronald remembered his first time. He too had relished existence among the stars. He had felt like a giant, and Jiro had reprimanded him for acting foolish. He didn't have the heart to do the same to Tomo. It wasn't his place. Tomo was his superior, and it wouldn't suit an Uninitiated to reprimand one of the Order's most ruthless assassins.

Instead, he allowed himself a moment of joy, maybe one of his last, and caught a star in his hand. It was warm to the touch and searing for a split second as it silently exploded within his fist. When he released it, a shower of shimmering stardust spread out before him, slowly drifting to darkness.

"We have to keep moving," he said. "I've heard stories of warriors getting lost in the Out Beyond, bewitched by its beauty and magnitude. It's not an evil place, but it's not a good one, either. If we allow it, we'll die here."

"You know a lot about this kind of thing for a kid."

"I've been here before, remember?" Ronald sure did. "It's not a place you soon forget. I'm surprised you've never been. It's how the Order travels from Island to Island. How everyone does, I suppose."

"I'm a killer, kid." Was that a hint of resentment in the assassin's voice? Regret, maybe? "I'm Uninitiated, too. By design. Not regarded much higher than a common thug."

"What do you know about Shima Gōdatsusha?"

The assassin hurried to catch up, a glint of eagerness in his eyes. "Only what I've overheard. The Island of Usurpers, right?"

"Mhm," Ronald said. "Now, it belongs to only one: Akuma Araki. Once, Shima Gōdatsusha was a verdant place, home to gods and mortals alike. It was a paradise, a place of boundless resources and as much opportunity as the mind could imagine. Everything was possible, it just had to be known and brought into existence, and with so much abundance, everyone lived in harmony, side by side, for all eternity. Or so it is said.

"Demons discovered Shima Gōdatsusha. Devils invaded the minds of mortals, who in turn succumbed to the demons' evil machinations. Together, they turned on the gods, drove them from the forests and the beaches. Together, mile by mile, mountain to sea, they killed the gods, or forced them into the dark recesses of the island and took whatever they wanted, whenever they pleased.

"Warlords rose to great power. Half-demon, half-human, and all selfish, bent on destroying the island as it was originally intended and creating it in their own spiteful images. It wasn't long before the warlords' desire for power turned them to violence once more, against each other now that no others stood in their way. They fought, they died, they burned the island until it was a scarred ruin of its former self. Then, they all went into hiding. They were afraid of their own shadows, afraid of each other, and most of all, they were afraid of the potential wrath of the gods they'd driven away.

"The island replenished itself in time. The forests flourished. The oceans that once ran red with blood cleared, whales and dolphins returned. Everything was right with Shima Gōdatsusha once more. Until Akuma Araki was born, that is. By the time she came of age, it was already known that she thirsted for power even more so than the warlords of old. She would stop at nothing until the island was hers and hers alone. She sent assassins far across the land in the dark of night to slit the throats of her imagined competition. As her reputation grew, men and women—and demons—gathered to her army from all corners of the island. But it wasn't enough. For Akuma Araki, nothing will ever be enough, I'm afraid."

Ronald turned to make sure Tomo was still following. The

assassin's uncharacteristic silence gave him the heebie jeebies, but there he was, pale-faced and sullen.

Up ahead, a single star stood out among the countless. So bright, the others around it paled in comparison. They seemed to orbit it, swirling in a formless funnel towards it, drawn by the star's brilliance.

Shima Gōdatsusha.

Ronald tensed. This close, his reservations and doubts came screaming back to the forefront of his mind.

He wasn't strong enough to face Akuma Araki.

He wasn't brave enough to stand against her horde, to face his past mistakes and make things right.

He wasn't Jiro... And he would never be Jiro.

He gulped and swallowed glass. Daichi had been right. Ronald Hashimoto was no son of his and less than nothing. An embarrassing disappointment, and now, he reminded himself, an orphan.

But none of that mattered. He had to try. For Jiro. For Che. For Aubrey and his friends.

"We're here." He stopped a few strides from the bright star. There was no turning back now. "Once I go, you'll have to follow fast. Don't hesitate. Once the portal closes, it will disappear, and there's no telling where it will reappear. Or when."

Tomo nodded his understanding, and Ronald steeled himself against all his doubt and fear.

You can do this, Ronald. It's in your blood. It wasn't Jiro's voice this time. It was Daichi's, and that somehow brought a smile to his face.

He closed his eyes and leaped into the star. The instant his body collided with the astral body, he was sucked in through a pinhole the size of an atom, reduced to particles, and displaced into Shima Gōdatsusha's atmosphere. His stomach churned, like when an elevator drops suddenly or when you are snatched from the teeth of a nightmare.

The forest floor hit him like a hammer strike, knocking the wind out of his lungs. He gasped for air as he helped Tomo to his feet.

"Holy shit." The assassin threw up bile between his shaking legs. "That was intense."

"Yeah," Ronald mumbled, but he had just seen Shima Gōdatsusha for the first time since he lost Jiro, and it was nothing like how he remembered.

It was worse. Way, way worse.

CHAPTER SIXTEEN

Where Shima Gōdatsusha had once been painted with verdant emerald hills and snowy mountain peaks, white beaches and clear oceans, where the fields had been tinged pink by cherry blossoms, it was now a desolate wasteland. Broken trees and scorched grass stretched as far as the eye could see, and smoke billowed, blackening the once-brilliant sky.

Far in the distance, beyond the clear-cut forests, built upon the highest black peaks, stood a great fortress. Spires jutted like a dragon's spine from its base to its tallest tower. Red rivulets of lava ran freely into a lake of fire at its base. Great winged monsters circled the massive structure, their swarming shapes almost indiscernible from one another, like storm clouds clinging to stone. The rocks around the fortress practically seethed with life. Monsters, no doubt. Oni and other demons—Akuma Araki's army.

Ronald gulped. *Way, way worse.*

Unlike most of his manufactured fears, this one was as real

as real could get. It had claws and teeth and would shred him to pieces if he wasn't careful.

"Erm." Tomo cleared his throat. "It's not as, uh, beautiful as in all the stories."

"It's never been beautiful. Not when you looked close. Beyond the beaches and cherry blossoms, Shima Gōdatsusha has always been a place of war and death."

"Shit, kid." Tomo knelt at the edge of the cliff and scanned the horizon. "This place really did a number on you, didn't it?"

Ronald joined the assassin, vertigo threatening as he leaned forward. Even the mountains had shifted drastically since his last visit. Time moved differently between islands, but had it been so long that the earth itself moved? He could have sworn this was the hill where he'd fled Akuma and her minions after watching Jiro die, where he'd left his brother and his swords behind and lost the scrolls—the reason they'd been there in the first place—and where his life had started to go so, so wrong.

"Before we came here, we knew what it was. We grew up with stories of demons, of dead gods. Ghost stories, meant to scare us into training harder. It was always our destiny to come to Shima Gōdatsusha, to set things right between us mortals and the gods.

"Then, we actually came. It was, as you said, beautiful. The part we had to play seemed easy, almost like a child's game. I killed a man, without hesitation. Then an oni. I can do this, I thought. I can actually be a samurai and fulfill my 'greater' purpose. Save this island, and all the others. Side by side, Jiro and I could change the universe with our swords. Make it a better place. When Akuma Araki split my brother's chest open with an arrow, I knew it was a lie. All of it. I knew this place was doomed, no matter what the Order ordained."

A large rock broke free from the mountain, dropping from the base of the fortress. It slammed into the pool of lava with a loud *pop* and squelching sound before sending embers and ash into the air. Ronald shielded his eyes from the sudden flare, and he could swear he felt the sudden surge of heat tickle his exposed cheeks.

"What are you going to do about it?" Tomo asked.

"Excuse me?"

"What are you going to do? Are you gonna sit here and keep feeling sorry for yourself? Or are you going to scale that bastard of a mountain with me, kill this bitch, and get your brother's swords back?"

Ronald watched the thousands of warriors and monsters moving about the fortress—so many he couldn't even begin to estimate their numbers. Where had they all come from? How had the warlord brought them all together, under one banner? Oni were particularly fickle, and they were not easily conquered or tamed. They didn't play nice with each other, either. So having so many in one place, all marching in the same direction, was more than a little unsettling.

Sneaking through the camp with Jiro had been easy. Akuma's warriors had been drunk, half-asleep. They were off their guard and totaled a fraction of their number, yet he'd still managed to screw it up.

Scaling the mountain and infiltrating the fortress was a different story. Ronald could hardly fathom such a feat, but Tomo's confidence instilled in him the assurance that together they could climb any mountain.

"Let's kill this bitch," he said, flashing his teeth to the assassin, "and bring back my brother's swords."

"Atta boy." Tomo scratched the back of his neck. "The only problem is how the hell do we find her?"

Sometimes, one must descend to ascend. Jiro's voice.

Ronald peered down the cliff face, towards the pool of lava below. He squinted, scanned, and finally found what he was looking for. "There," he said, pointing. Tomo followed his gaze and groaned when he realized what Ronald was suggesting.

Ronald in the lead, they made short work of the descent. At the bottom, Ronald led them along a narrow bank—so close to the lava he could feel its heat through his armor. Occasionally, a bubble would surface and explode, sending a fountain of molten rock in unpredictable directions. Once, a volley of lava splattered the cliff in front of them, knocking loose an avalanche of stone. If it hadn't been for Ronald's faceplate, he would have taken a face full of fire from the sudden slide.

Tomo's foot slipped, breaking off chunks of the precarious rock they were using as a path. Ronald grabbed him just in time and managed to help him find his balance.

"Not how I thought I'd go," Tomo said, exasperated. "Not even close."

The bank narrowed. Ronald found he had to slide sideways, one foot in front of the other. He clung to the cliff, fearing that if he let go, he might find himself sucked to the depths of the pool. It wouldn't be how he wanted to go, either. Not. Even. Close.

After what felt like hours, the rock bridge came into view, floating and bobbing from the bank to what appeared to be a cave entrance at the base of the mountain.

Tomo saw it too. "That's what we came down here for?" He covered his face against another lava bubble explosion. "You're insane, kid. We get across this without one or both of us falling in, then what? How do you even know that goes anywhere?"

"I don't." Ronald shot Tomo a grim look. "And you don't have to follow me, but something's telling me that cave is our ticket in. What's it gonna be?"

"I'm here, ain't I?" Tomo bowed and opened his arms wide, indicating the rock bridge. "Why don't you, uh, go first."

Ronald bent his knees and leaped towards the first rock. When he landed, the rock wobbled and disturbed lava squelched around its edges, but it held firm. Steam rose in a ring around him. Sweat poured down his face, stinging his eyes. He took a deep breath, thankful to be alive, and prepared for his next jump.

As his feet lifted, the rock shifted, affecting the trajectory of his jump. For a moment, suspended in mid-air between one precarious rock and another, Ronald knew it was over. He accepted his fate. To die in a pool of lava, his body never recovered. Sure, Tomo might tell stories about Ronald Hashimoto, stories that could become legend, but it was unlikely. They were breaking Order rules, and Tomo wouldn't risk implicating himself to elevate some kid to false glory. No, Ronald would burn to a crisp and be forgotten, like a thousand other would-be samurai who walked the path of destiny before him.

Then, he struck something hard. Prone, he scrambled up the rock, his foot slipping and teasing the lava's surface. It steamed and hissed, but his armor held fast. He lay on his back, huffing and panting, grateful for the second time in only a span of moments to still be alive.

The rest of the trek across the rock bridge went smoothly enough. After Ronald found the strength to stand back up, at least.

Soon, he could see directly into the cave's entrance, and it appeared deep enough to be a promising option after all.

He helped Tomo over a jagged ridge and dropped into the cave's mouth on the other side. The sound of boots on solid ground echoed in the darkness, but it wasn't the only sound. Far ahead, at the end of a winding, upward spiral, he could hear metal striking metal and the indecipherable chatter of countless creatures.

Tomo slid out his sais. Ronald began to unsheathe his katana, stopped halfway, and let it click back into place. He drew his wakizashi instead and grinned at Tomo's approving head nod.

They followed the upward path, taking slow, deliberate steps, ready and alert around every new bend. The air in the cave became stifling as they climbed, the heat almost too hot to bear. Ronald took deep, purposeful breaths and willed away the migraine that threatened. His legs were stiff, his muscles cramped, but he forged on, resolute in what he had to do, no matter what horrors awaited... No matter how hard it was to keep moving forward.

A dull, flickering red light appeared ahead—the light of an open fire. Metal clanged louder now, and he could hear dozens of different voices, speaking in a language he couldn't begin to understand.

The top of the path opened to a low ledge overlooking a massive chamber. Some twenty feet below, built around a smaller pool of lava, were several makeshift forges. Lesser oni and some humans, if you could call them that, toiled away, forging weapons and armor in an endless loop. Two large beasts of burden chained against the opposite wall worked a massive pair of bellows, one for each side of the forge, and the rest moved about in organized chaos, shaping, cooling, shaping, tempering. The completed armaments were then thrown onto a rudimentary lift, no more than planks of wood roped together, and hauled upward into darkness by another set of kaiju-esque monstrosities.

Akuma Araki's blacksmiths were tight-muscled, imposing figures. They themselves must have been forged through pain and punishment, then wielded for this specific purpose. Ronald could tell they took no pleasure in their endless work, but that they wouldn't dare stop for fear of their master's retribution.

A samurai wearing a full set of Akuma's heavy, black and red armor stood atop a sturdily built platform level with the lift. Ronald recognized his facemask as one of the many demons who served the warlord. He had seen a handful of them when Jiro had died, but this one alone was no less intimidating. Behind the samurai, there was an array of weaponry, schematics, and workbenches, along with a smaller forge and anvil. He surveyed the workers, arms folded over his chest, and Ronald and Tomo just managed to fall back into the shadows before his watchful eyes crossed their path.

Ronald peeked out as the lift began another slow ascent, a heap of weapons loaded onto its center. It creaked and groaned as it ascended, and he expected the ropes to snap at any moment, but it held together until it disappeared among the endless dark above.

The samurai had left his watchdog's overlook and was now hunched over a small wooden table, arms splayed across its surface. He appeared to be reading a scroll or map. More importantly, he was no longer watching the chamber.

Ronald and Tomo moved at the same time, both unwilling to let the opportunity pass them by. They dropped silently from their ledge, circled around the busy blacksmiths, careful to keep in the shadows, and stopped below the platform. Tomo moved into position and interlaced his fingers to offer Ronald a boost. As soon as Ronald cleared the wooden railing, now close enough to hear the samurai's breath, he leaned out on his stomach and reached down to help the assassin.

Tomo struck so fast Ronald barely had time to process what was happening. Crouched, the assassin snuck behind the samurai and rose one sai high in the air. He brought it down in a blur. The samurai gurgled and twitched as Tomo eased the body to the floor and slid it into concealment beneath the table.

Ronald wasn't sure he was capable of such merciless violence. He knew it needed to be done, of course, but his stomach churned at the thought of ending someone's life without them even knowing what hit them. Alive one moment, dead the next. No warning. No chance to make peace with whatever god they worshipped. Just… dead. The assassin's methods didn't seem honorable, though they were no doubt efficient, and he wondered why—or if—the Order approved of such crude methods.

Ronald leaned over the rail to see if they'd been noticed. The blacksmiths went about their work, oblivious to the fact a corpse now lay among them. If they happened to come across it, would they fight or would they be relieved? Were Akuma Araki's generals benevolent rulers? Knowing her, it was unlikely, but servants tended to be unpredictable. He wasn't willing to risk losing the element of surprise to test their reaction.

"Psst," Tomo hissed.

Ronald creeped over to the table, where Tomo was hunched over the documents the samurai had been reading.

"Is that…?"

"Order armor? Yeah, it's hard to mistake."

Ronald's gut sank. If the warlord's army was manufacturing Order armor, they had to have gotten a prototype somewhere.

"I left Jiro's armor behind. Do you think... Did I do this? Is this my fault?"

He wasn't going to like what he heard, but Tomo didn't have time to answer. There came a sudden creaking from above and voices drawing down, closer as the lift descended. The assassin tapped Ronald's chest plate and indicated back the way they came. Swift and quiet as cats, they vaulted the railing and slid to the safety of the shadows, disappearing from sight just in time.

Four samurai stepped off the lift and fanned out around the platform, taking position at each corner. Two others, specters clad in black and crimson red—Akuma Araki's elite—followed as soon as the others found their places. The warlord herself walked close behind, shadowed by a black-cloaked figure whose face was indiscernible behind the folds of their hood.

Ronald's heart raced. The cavernous chamber drew tight around him, and he wanted to scream, to leap into action and throw himself at Akuma Araki. His hand moved to his katana. If he was fast enough, he might catch her off guard. If he acted now, he might even live long enough to send a couple of her samurai to hell alongside her.

Tomo grabbed his wrist. They met eyes, and the assassin shook his head and brought one finger to his throat.

They were outnumbered, and while he had never seen one of the warlord's samurai in action, he couldn't imagine she allowed anyone but the deadliest swordsmen to join her retinue. An attack under their current circumstances would be suicide, but part of him didn't care. It seethed within him, longed for vengeance, throbbed with a desire to draw blood in Jiro's honor. Ronald managed to silence that part for the time being, but it was still there, festering, biding its time.

Heavy metal boots clanged across the platform. Something sharp plunged into wood—a knife into a table perhaps—and he could hear muffled breaths. *Her* breaths.

"Remove the body." The heavy footsteps shook dust loose from the rocks above Ronald's head. He held in a cough. "They can't have gone far," Akuma Araki said. "I can feel the other island coursing through my veins, smell their devil scent on the air."

Ronald clutched the handle of his katana as the steps stopped directly above them. Tomo reached to his belt and grabbed his sais. Their blades glinted silver in the dim light of the nearby forge. The assassin mouthed "Wait," but remained poised to strike.

Fingers covered by clawed, black gauntlets wrapped around the railing. Wood strained and cracked under their strength.

Ronald held his breath. Sweat beaded on his forehead, tickling him as it trickled down his cheek to the back of his neck. Violent red threatened the periphery of his vision, and his muscles twitched in readied anticipation.

Tomo's eyes were closed. His lips moved at a rapid pace. *Praying?* Ronald wondered. He hadn't taken the assassin for a man of faith, but nothing surprised him anymore.

The fingers slipped out of sight and the boots drew away from them, back towards the lift. Ronald allowed himself a small breath of relief and wiped his chin on his shoulder.

"Find them. If it's the younger boy returned, bring him to me alive. If it's any of the others, kill them without mercy."

Ronald tensed, his hand coming to his waistline. He adjusted his belt, lifted his armor from around his body to allow himself to breathe, and immediately felt like an idiot. "*Everywhere I go,*" echoed throughout the cavern as loud as a scream. "*Lord knows, trouble's what I find...*"

Aubrey. Ronald's first thoughts were about whether she was okay. Then, the gravity of his situation settled, and the once-exhilarating tune sent grating ripples of pain through his central nervous system. He pawed at his hip until he found the lump that was his phone. He managed to silence it mid-riff, but it was already too late. He'd already inadvertently triggered the song that he'd had on repeat since Aubrey told him she liked it, and there was no fixing it now.

Tomo gave Ronald a look that said "Are you effing kidding me?" Regardless, the assassin's sais were at the ready. So were half a dozen katanas on the platform above them, drawn one after another with the tell-tale metallic whisper of freed blades thirsty for blood.

"Time to go." Tomo nodded toward the hallway from which they entered. Ronald remained stubbornly glued in place. "Kid, we have to go. *Now.*"

"But Jiro's swords... Akuma Araki..."

From the lift, the warlord barked orders, and her samurai snapped into position to surround them.

Tomo gave Ronald a grave frown. "I didn't know how bad this place was or I never would've agreed to come. We need to go to the Order, tell them what we've seen. We need to come back with an army."

The assassin was right. Deep down, Ronald knew anything short of fleeing was suicide, but he couldn't bring himself to run. If he ran with his brother's killer so close, he'd be abandoning Jiro a second time. He wasn't sure he could live with any more shame, but he wasn't quite ready to die, either.

As Akuma Araki continued to order her samurai into formation, Tomo mouthed his own urgent and stern warning. He tugged at Ronald, trying to herd him towards the exit, but Ronald was a statue, his feet melded to the cave's rocky floor. He couldn't hear the warlord's orders or the assassin's desperate pleas. All he could hear was the loud ringing in his ears and the sound of his heart thumping in his chest.

Two shadows emerged, and Tomo broke from cover. They moved in slow motion, blades striking blades, blood splattering, a helmet rolling. Not Tomo's, Ronald reassured himself. It stopped between Ronald's feet, demon visage staring straight up at him. From behind an outcropping of stalagmites, Tomo waved Ronald his way. Ronald glanced above him, to the platform, and finally drew his katana.

The blood curdling sound of the assassin yelling "Nooooo!" broke the ringing in Ronald's ears. One of Akuma's massive arrows skittered across Tomo's scant cover, cracking through the ancient rock, spraying stones in all directions, and Ronald made his decision. He couldn't allow this opportunity to pass him by. He couldn't give Akuma Araki the satisfaction of another uncontested victory.

Ronald hoisted himself over the railing, narrowly avoiding another pull from the warlord's yumi. The arrow splintered the wood beside him and rebounded harmlessly off the wall. He was in motion the second his feet hit the planks, slipping between two incoming samurai. He slashed his katana one way, then the other, and they both fell. A third arrow left her bow with a soft *thwang* and whistled towards him. Ronald slid out of the way, using an anvil for cover and sparks stung his cheek as iron struck iron.

All of a sudden, he was back in time, scrambling up a hill with boulders pelting him and arrows splattering dirt all around him. He was back at Akuma's camp, holding his brother's limp body, warm with Jiro's blood.

Ronald pulled his knees to his chest, screamed and rocked—anything to make himself as small as possible. He closed his eyes tight, the clatter of battle becoming a roar all around him.

Get up, a voice said.

He whimpered and shook his head.

Get up!

"I can't!"

Another arrow snapped and tore through the planks beside him. He flinched and covered his face from the splinters.

Get up, Ronald!

He understood he was dead if he didn't listen, yet he couldn't bring himself to move.

"Ronald!" It was Tomo's voice now. "Get the hell up."

That was all the convincing Ronald needed. He shot from his scant cover and sprinted for the lift. If he was fast enough, if he got enough spring off the railing—if he only wanted it bad enough—he could still make the jump. Akuma Araki wasn't beyond his grasp just yet... He could still win.

Then, he noticed the extra set of swords on her belt. Jiro's swords, and that night at her camp came rushing back again. The warlord's samurai were surrounding him, laughing and mocking his failure as Jiro's body slipped from his grasp, each unmasked face a reflection of Daichi's. Jiro's corpse was laughing too, telling Ronald how pathetic he was, how he would never live up to the Hashimoto name. How, now that his father was dead, their bloodline was doomed to obscurity.

Distracted, Ronald slipped on something wet and sticky and tripped over his own feet. An arrow skittered across the platform, inches from his face. Had he not tumbled, it would have struck true. If he had the free path to his target he wanted, he would have been dead, too, skewered just like his brother.

The lift rose, Akuma's surviving honor guard standing between Ronald and their charge. The black-cloaked figure's eyes began to glow green, and it became encircled by emerald fire. It chanted in a deep, guttural voice, and the cavernous chamber seemed to rumble under the weight of its words.

"Release them, Minata," Akuma Araki shrieked. "Release them now!"

The black-cloaked figure, whose name—Minata—Ronald knew he would never forget, raised her arms to the cavernous walls around them, and a hundred-hundred concentric rings of green light rushed to the ceiling high above. As Ronald collected himself, blood rushed to his cheeks. The air around him cracked and undulated with immense invisible energy. He craned to watch as the warlord and her retinue disappeared into the shadowy upper layers of her fortress. For some reason, he was able to accept jumping from one island of existence to another, but magic? Like actual, D&D, sword and sorcery type magic? His mind just couldn't process that it was real.

Then, thousands of black specks undulated along the cavern walls, moving ever closer towards them. It took him a long time to realize what he was seeing, but as soon as he figured it out, he scrambled to his feet. They had clear forms now: demons come to cleanse the warlord's dominion of intruders—countless insect-like monsters. Their clawed hands and feet acting as climbing spikes, they descended the steep, rocky walls with terrifying ease.

The first wave hit before Ronald could clear the platform. They swarmed, covered every surface of the forge with their flailing, chitinous bodies. Some had four arms, others even more. They brandished crude, cruel weapons fashioned of chiseled rock and sharpened bone. Those too slow among the front lines were trampled and replaced by a dozen more.

One of Akuma Araki's blacksmiths was running frantically from the swarm. The pseudo-human creature tripped, but it kept scrambling, desperate not to be trampled by a thousand prodding appendages. Ronald cursed himself, but he couldn't watch the innocent creature die from the safety of distance. He slid to its side, hoisted it over his shoulder, and hauled it to the relative safety of a nearby alcove. It looked at him with terrified eyes and while Ronald couldn't be sure, the almost pig-like blacksmith seemed to snort a guttural "Thank you."

An insect slammed into Ronald ribs forelimbs first. A sharp pain spread from his side where the creature punctured through to his muscle and left behind a wriggling sensation beneath his skin. It felt as if he'd been stung, the stinger left behind between his ribs. The insect threw its weight against him a second time, and Ronald hit the ground hard, starting his own desperate retreat. Scrambling crablike away, Ronald screamed as another one flew toward him. He didn't even think about raising his katana. He just closed his eyes, covered his face with his arm, and accepted death. There was no point in fighting the inevitable.

A golden streak arced overhead, colliding with the nearest demon. It chittered, fell flat on its back, legs flailing, and a fox the size of a bear bit into its soft underbelly, tearing flesh and shell alike. Two more golden streaks zipped into the fray. Then, a white one. Bug parts flew in every direction, tossed and shredded by sharp teeth and claws, but they kept on coming. The forge shook with the cacophony of snarling and screeching, growling and chirping.

Ronald finally remembered his sword and stood to join the battle, but the nearest fox turned and bared its teeth. He could have sworn it had a nose piercing, but he shook that delusion out of his mind and turned to run.

Tomo met him and yanked him up the ledge. "Come on, you freakin' psychopath. It's seriously time to go. Now!"

Tomo herded him through the corridor with a series of gentle shoves. It wasn't that Ronald was reluctant to leave, just the opposite, in fact, but his legs didn't seem to want to work. He slammed bodily into wall after wall, using his arms and hands to keep upright as the return journey passed in a dizzying blur.

Back at the cave's entrance, Tomo gave him one last shove. Ronald staggered forward, tripped over an uneven segment of rock, and fell onto his hands and knees.

Tomo knelt at his side. "You wouldn't have made it, you know?"

Ronald sniffled and glared. "She was right there. *They* were right there."

"Kid, had you not slipped on that dude's blood, three things for sure would have happened, none of which include your triumphant victory over Akuma Araki. One, you would have taken an arrow to the gut. Two, you would have missed that lift by about six feet. Three, you would have jumped straight into a pit of lava, so at least your onset stomach pain wouldn't have lasted very long.

"Deal with it."

"She was right there," Ronald repeated, quieter this time. He shrugged off the assassin and slumped, his armor falling in an overlapping heap around his hunched figure.

"We got about forty-five seconds before those... whatever the hell they are catch up to us. I'm leaving, and I'm damn tired of dragging you through these tunnels, so you can sit here and die, or you can get up and come with me. What's it gonna be?"

He's right, you know? You can't avenge me, or whatever this is, if you're burned to a crisp or become insect food.

"But the samurai code... We should embrace death."

"To hell with your code. Live to fight another day. That's my code. That's how you get another chance at Akuma Araki."

Tomo offered his hand, and Ronald clasped his wrist. The assassin hoisted him to his feet, and they were off, headed back to the rock bridge.

As they finished their crossing, Ronald glanced up at the ledge, covering his eyes against the setting sun. A man in glinting golden armor watched their progress. Master Oda, no doubt, flanked by the Order's finest. His wrinkled face was hard and stern, his eyes focused on the pair of idiots stumbling across the lava flow.

It was only then that Ronald began to appreciate the trouble he'd stumbled into, but he wouldn't fully understand exactly how much trouble until they were back to their own island.

CHAPTER SEVENTEEN

Ronald tried to ignore the grave faces around him. They were standing guard in every corner, lined up the stairs, waiting in every room of that putrid house. Samurai, clad in Order gold. Kitsune, watching him with slit eyes. All of them were watching *him,* ready to defend their master against any potential last desperate acts of a twice-humbled teenager.

He shuffled through the house, head down, hand grasping his wounded side. Motion in his peripheral vision caught his attention, and despite himself, he couldn't resist being nosey.

There was Hikari, leaned against a mold-ridden couch, hip cocked to one side. Her arm was in a sling, and there was a gash across the side of her face, from the corner of one tired eye down to her jawbone. She locked eyes with Ronald and winked, though the simple motion of turning towards him made her wince.

Sakiko was there, too, pacing around one of the side rooms with several injured kitsune, stuck in a sort of in-between state, half fox, half human, lying prone on cots. When Ronald passed, she scowled and slammed the door.

Would either sister have accompanied them, if they knew they had a chance to avenge Jiro's death? Would the kitsune have fought alongside Ronald inside that volcano, before their fighting came as a last resort to save his sorry butt? Would their speed have made a difference in his foolish—and failed—attempt at Akuma Araki?

A couple gold-hooded monks rushed past, carrying Ronald's armor and swords away. They would take them to the Shogunate, to his only legal guardian, where Che would be forced to put them under lock and key. He knew the drill. Disgraced samurai were not well-loved by the Order, and they didn't give those deemed "criminal" a chance to fight back against their judge, jury, or executioner.

Master Oda was in the front room, flanked by two samurai. He reprimanded Tomo in harsh, terse whispers. The assassin bowed and left in a hurry, head down like a beaten dog. Then, the grim-faced man turned his focus to Ronald.

"Daichi would be disappointed if he knew what you've done today."

"But I was only trying to—"

"Silence!" Master Oda stuck a hand in Ronald's face, and his voice rattled the entire house. "There is no excuse for today's transgressions. There are protocols for this kind of excursion, and good reasons why the uninitiated aren't allowed to traverse islands without supervision. Not only did you use Order property to move between islands without sanction, but you left the portal open for anyone to enter." He indicated to the room with his arms raised high. "Or worse yet, *exit*."

Ronald shuddered at the idea. Should he tell Master Oda that he wasn't even aware someone had to close the portal? Had Jiro done that for them the first time through? Daichi? Either way, it was probably a moot point now, but he hadn't even considered the possibilities. Those insect things, out in the real world? Terrorizing the suburbs? It was a bleak reality for those of Shima Gōdatsusha, but the people of Normal deserved better, and he had very nearly brought a terrible fate into fruition for them, for the innocent people who couldn't begin to know how to defend themselves.

"Good, good," Master Oda observed. "The shame you feel is but a fraction of the justice you have coming. Many kitsune died today. Tomo, one of the Order's greatest assets, could have befallen a similar fate. There will be a tribunal. Your punishment will be decided by a council of masters, and trust me when I say, it will be worse than a swift death. Until the time comes, you will return home, with Tomo to watch your every move. You will resume your life as if none of this ever happened, until we are ready to bring you in for reckoning. Do you understand, Ronald Hashimoto?"

Ronald gulped. He'd heard stories about council tribunals, none of them ending well for the accused, and he would almost prefer death to any number of other potential punishments. Exile to an island worse than Shima Gōdatsusha. Trial by fire, steel, and blood. An order to commit seppuku in front of his friends and family. Yes, a swift decapitation by Master Oda's katana—or Tomo's, more likely—would be a mercy compared to the alternatives.

Unable to look Master Oda in the eyes, Ronald said, "Yes, Master. I understand."

"Very well." The old master bowed slightly, almost downcast. "You are dismissed, young Hashimoto. Go straight home, and save yourself from causing any further trouble."

Despite his determination to do just that, Hikari blocked his exit.

"Sup, kid? Wild times, huh?"

Ronald grumbled. "What do you want?"

"Just checkin' on ya. I imagine Master Oda has made you feel shitty enough about this whole mess already." Ronald rolled his eyes. "Did anyone ever tell you why he's so touchy about Shima Gōdatsusha in particular? I mean, you'd be in deep doo-doo had you trespassed into any of the islands, but why this one? Why such a fuss about a single drop in an ocean of worlds?"

To be honest, Ronald had put very little thought towards any of the other islands. Shima Gōdatsusha, the Island of Usurpers, had occupied so much of his time and energy growing up. Daichi had made it seem like even if it wasn't the only island, it was by far the most important.

Regardless, he took a stab at an acceptable answer. "Akuma Araki is amassing an army. She plans to invade our—"

"Meh." Hikari waved him off. "If I grew a tail every time an up-and-coming general raised a rabble into an army, I'd have more tails than ex-boyfriends. And that's *a lot*, I'm not ashamed to admit. Well, okay. Maybe a little ashamed." Ronald laughed through his nose, and everything felt a little better for a fleeting moment. "No, it's much more than that. It's prophecy, kid. And it has my old man scared senseless."

"You're telling me Akuma Araki is some kind of chosen one? What is this, a cheesy YA?"

Hikari winked and ran her tongue across one of her canines, the titanium stud through its tip clicking on her teeth. "You bet your ass it is."

"This prophecy, what does it say?"

She glanced over her shoulder as if checking to make sure they were alone. They weren't of course, but no one appeared to be listening. Then, she leaned close and spoke in an overly dramatic whisper.

"Behold, a child born of Struggle and Strife. Beware, a child born of Shima Gōdatsusha, tempered by the fires of Her trials. Sower of Chaos where there was once Order. Uprooter of the ancient Bonsai, awash in golden waves of destruction, reborn anew under a crimson dawn."

Hikari lost her composure near the end and snorted. Ronald held back a giggle of his own.

"That's how it goes, more or less," she said. "Don't quote me, but it's got Master Oda's panties in a wad."

She raised her eyebrows, stood on her tiptoes to see Sakiko, nose scrunched and shaking her head, behind Ronald. "Crap. Gotta go, kid. Catch ya later." At that, she was gone, having disappeared into the room of wounded kitsune with her sister.

Beware, a child born of Shima Gōdatsusha, tempered by the fires of Her trials.

From what little he knew of Akuma Araki's past, it fit the bill. Not only was she a threat to Shima Gōdatsusha, but the prophecy seemed to insinuate she was a much greater threat to the universe at large, to Master Oda's Order itself.

...Where there was once Order...

But could she really bring down the Order? It was a lot to unpack, and Ronald repeated the prophecy over and over in his mind. He needed to memorize it, because he had a feeling it wouldn't be the last time it crossed his path.

Outside, the burning houses from earlier in the day were reduced to smoldering ruins. Yet, there were no firetrucks, no EMS responders. Nothing to indicate there was any value left of all these houses—all these forgotten memories—reduced to ash and rubble.

An entire army of Order samurai were posted up and down the street, with Tomo pacing the sidewalk. Ronald approached, began to say something, but Tomo cut him off.

"This is more my fault than yours, but I don't wanna hear it, kid. Not a damn thing."

"I'm sorry..."

"I said I don't wanna hear it. Let's just go home before they change their minds."

"That... thing, beside Akuma Araki. What was that?"

Tomo throat-growled and then shrugged. "Beats me, kid. Ain't ever seen anything like it."

"Was it magic? Like, for real?"

Tomo sighed. "I'm supposed to be mad at you. I ain't got time for any more questions."

He stormed away, Ronald in toe. When they were far enough out of Order earshot, the assassin stopped abruptly, turned on Ronald, and grabbed him by the throat.

"Don't. Ever. Take outside technology to another island again. You're lucky I didn't mention that little snafu to Master Oda. Even luckier that stupid phone of yours didn't end up in Akuma Araki's hands."

Ronald tilted his head, confused by the assassin's outburst.

Tomo sighed and released his grip on Ronald's neck. "You saw what she's been able to forge from your brother's armor, forged by methods outside Shima Gōdatsusha. For someone who claims to know a place so well, you sure know jack shit."

Akuma Araki, wielding the power of endless technology? Ronald forced the terrible snapshots out of his mind and felt more ashamed of himself than ever before. He should have known better. He should have done better, like Jiro had urged after the mugging. But here he was, an utter failure once again. And a moron to boot, according to Tomo and everyone else, including his own incessant internal monologue.

Tomo was almost around the block when Ronald called out. "We need to make a stop, first. Before we go back to Daichi's."

It's not Daichi's house anymore, though, is it? It's no one's home. If it ever was anyone's home to begin with...

The assassin stomped back towards Ronald, and Ronald was sure he was going to hit him. His fists were bunched and everything. Instead, he clenched them and yelled to the sky.

"You're telling me what to do now? Nu uh. No way, kid. That's over. You do what I say from now on." He started to stalk away but turned angrily and sighed. "Where is it you think we need to stop?"

"It's important." Ronald kicked a broken slab of sidewalk into the street, hands shoved into his pockets. "Please..."

Tomo huffed and turned on his heels, towards the nearest bus stop. Ronald followed a few steps behind. One last stop, then it was to be house arrest before any number of unimaginable punishments. If he was going to become a slave to the Order again, he needed to talk to Che. He needed to see his mother one last time, tell her about... Well, to tell her everything.

CHAPTER EIGHTEEN

Ronald's face glowed a blueish white, and his tired eyes darted back and forth across the screen. He hadn't been able to look away from his phone since they got on the bus. In the grand scheme of his current reality, it wasn't important who called. Not really. All that mattered was that he had been stupid enough to not only bring it with him into Shima Gōdatsusha but to forget to silence the damn thing. It had nearly gotten him killed. Tomo, too. Not to mention, he'd accidentally played the one song that reminded him of Aubrey, of the Earth island, and he couldn't afford that kind of distraction. Not when he was so close to finishing the damn thing...

The bus lurched to a stop, and Ronald slid the phone back into his pocket. "This is us."

"Whatever." Worse than a teenager slighted, the assassin made a big ordeal of getting up, exasperated sighs and groans and all. "Better make this quick, kid."

Ronald ignored Tomo's angst and led the way out into the streets. They were a couple blocks from Che's shop, but the night was clear and New Province was alive with familiar music. A street performer, plastered head to toe in neon glow bracelets, flashing LED necklaces, and rainbow-colored blinking lights danced to a steel drum quartet. Vendors pushed their carts of hotdogs, street tacos, frozen lemonade, and more, passersby calling over each other to be the next to get a taste. Late-night traffic crawled along, horns sounding, drivers swearing in a multitude of languages, engines sputtering and brakes squealing. Even the smells, a vague combination of sewage, fried foods, and exhaust, were a comfort after everything he had been through over the last few weeks.

Here, there weren't swarms of insects trying to murder him or evil warlords haunting his nightmares. In the city, things made sense, and even its secrets were honest to a fault.

All the excitement and entertainment seemed to soften the assassin, and that was just as well. Ronald didn't really care about Tomo's grim mood one way or another, but an amiable watch dog was better than an aggravated prison warden. By the time they managed to navigate through the throng of late-night partygoers, Tomo was all smiles and double-fisting walking tacos.

"Want some?" he asked, mouth stuffed and refried beans stuck to his mustache.

Ronald waved him off and picked up his pace. A large crowd was gathered on the sidewalk outside Che's Shogunate Records, including four police cars parked on the curb. Flashing lights reflected off hundreds of windows, creating a prism of red and blue that spanned nearly the entire block.

His heart sank. If something had happened to Che because of

his actions, it would absolutely break him.

She was pacing the sidewalk, talking belligerently with exaggerated arm motions to a flustered cop who looked way past done listening. Che kept going though, undeterred by the cop's eyerolls and neck scratches. Her cheeks were red, and her mascara was smeared black below her eyes, but she didn't look anywhere near running out of steam. More importantly, she didn't seem to be harmed.

Che flung her arms and kicked a piece of trash in the cops' general direction. He began to reach for something on his hip, but a young woman who was presumably his partner grabbed his wrist and shook her head. She mouthed something, and the cop flung his own arms before walking away from the scene.

"Mom!" Ronald called, shoving through the gathered onlookers. "Hey, mom!"

A police officer moved to intercept him, but he dodged nimbly and ducked underneath the yellow tape. Nobody followed him.

"Mom, is everything alright? What happened?"

Che was facing the other way, face in her palm, shoulders heaving slightly as she sobbed. She didn't seem to hear him, but then it dawned on him. She had probably never had anyone call her mom before, and he felt ridiculous for not having realized it sooner.

"Che!"

She turned immediately to him, and her face lit up. "Oh my God, Ronald. Shit, I'm so sorry. I didn't even..." She ran to him and wrapped him in a hug. He didn't resist. "Are you okay?" she asked, checking him over from head to toe.

Ronald tittered, embarrassed, and shoved her hand off his face.

"Mom, stop. I'm fine. I was just asking you the same thing."

Che's face twisted to something between rage and hopelessness. She whipped around and slammed her fists on the nearest surface, which happened to be the Shogunate's brick façade.

"Shit," she swore again, and evidently not because of the pain. "They destroyed everything, man. Everything. I don't think I'll ever get the shop back to where she was before. I don't know how I'd even begin to afford it."

Some of the crowd was beginning to disperse, but the police were sticking around. keeping their distance, yet hesitant to leave.

Che waved in their general direction. "I told them to eff off. There's nothing for them to do here."

"Don't you want to file a police report? Catch the assholes that did, uh, whatever it was that's happened?"

Ronald still wasn't quite sure what was going on, and the all-eyes-on-him sensation was starting to make him sweat, his skin tingle. Suddenly, his cheeks were flushed and for whatever reason, embarrassment was creeping up the back of his neck.

Che must have noticed. "Let's go inside. We can talk with a bit more privacy, though I warn you there ain't anywhere left to sit."

Ronald scanned the crowd for Tomo, but the assassin was nowhere to be seen. Maybe he finally took the hint and decided to give Ronald and Che some space. In the little time Ronald had known the man, he was impressed with how perceptive he was, specifically of Ronald's emotional state.

The Shogunate's interior was worse than he imagined. Its labyrinth of record displays were toppled piles of broken vinyl and twisted metal. The posters that hung on nearly every inch of the shop's walls, ranging from local open mic night announcements to signed, ceiling-height Prince prints were all slashed to ribbons. Che's tapestry, a vivid, hand-stitched masterpiece depicting the pivotal moment in Takiyasha the Witch and the Skeleton Specter, a statement piece that had caught Ronald's eye the first time he'd walked in, was shredded and left draped in tatters over the cash register. It reminded him of in the movies, where warring clans mounted heads along their battlements. This was a warning, a message not to be ignored.

"Holy…" But Ronald couldn't find a four-letter word meaningful enough to describe how he was feeling. In a way, Che's Shogunate Records had become a home away from home for him. Its messy rows of eclectic vinyl, stacks of used CDs, and too-loud indie folk rock had all become as reliable as old friends, always there for him when he needed them the most.

"They came looking for you. After you stayed with me, and we talked about… well, the Order found out somehow."

"The Order did this?" Ronald's fists balled until his knuckles turned white.

Che nodded slightly and kicked her way through the contents of an overturned display. She pulled herself up onto the counter, beside the tapestry.

"I broke our bargain. I was never supposed to reach out to you, and I knew meeting you would only bring trouble, for us both. But when your father brought you to me, I had to do something. I couldn't let you die, and God knows Daichi had no clue how to take care of you. I was going to find them, explain to them what happened, and try to convince them to let you go, too. Like they let me go." She raised her hands above her head and indicated to her wrecked shop. "They found me first, and the conversation clearly went well."

Ronald laughed through his nose and joined Che on the counter. He sat close enough so their shoulders were barely touching. An overwhelming sadness came over him, but he pushed it back down where it belonged. He wasn't quite ready to face that particular problem yet.

Che ran the threads of her torn tapestry through her fingers. She looked as if she might cry, but as soon as she noticed Ronald watching her, she forced a smile.

"Did Daichi ever tell you this story? The story of Princess Takiyasha?"

Ronald shook his head. "He was never one for bedtime stories."

"Well, a great warlord, Taira no Masakado, led an army against Kyoto. After some success, Masakado's cousin, Taira no Sadamori, routed his army and decapitated him. The great warlord's daughter, Princess Takiyasha, took to the dark arts to avenge her father's death. She learned to summon a Gashadokuro out of the bones of Masakado's fallen soldiers to slay her uncle. Two samurai met the princess with swords drawn in the once great palace of Soma, where they eventually managed to slay the terrible yokai and Takiyasha, the Witch."

Ronald almost laughed again. The odd similarities to his own situation weren't lost on him. Here he was, putting together a small "army" against incredible odds, ready to face down an entire nation: the nation of Shima Gōdatsusha. He couldn't hope to win, of course, but he was holding out for now. Would this end with him hiding in a crack house somewhere, learning how to summon spirits to avenge his brother? How about his mother? *If this conversation goes as planned,* he thought, *there's a chance I could lose her too. I could lose everything.* But if he did nothing, he wouldn't have anything to lose much longer anyway.

"What's the moral of the story?" he asked.

"Don't mess with girls?"

Ronald side-eyed her, and they both chuckled.

"I think, for me at least, the story goes to show that you shouldn't mess with family on one side of the coin."

"And the other?"

"Revenge begets revenge? Raising skeletal warriors only leads to tragedy? Hard to say, really, this far removed from that society, but it makes for a cool-ass tapestry."

Ronald swung his legs into Che, and she bumped his shoulder with hers. They smiled awkwardly at each other before he said, "For me, it tells me there should be no bounds to how far I go to make things right, to make those who've done wrong pay justice for their actions."

Che got overly serious, ignoring Ronald's contribution to their conversation. "It's a story, I guess," Che said. "I didn't really tell it that well. I'm sorry."

"No, you did. You told it great." Ronald rested his head gently on her shoulder. "And you'll have to tell me more sometime." *After this is all over.*

For a long time, long enough for the crowd outside to completely disperse and the cops to return to their routine beats, they sat in silence. Ronald bounced his heels on the counter. Che stared at what used to be her life, her livelihood. Neither seemed to know what to say. What could they say that would change anything?

After a while, Ronald noticed Tomo skulking about in the shop's entrance. They made eye contact, Ronald shrugged, and

Tomo nodded his understanding before turning his back.

"They won't let me go, will they?" Ronald asked.

"Nope."

"And I'm assuming they didn't bring my swords with them?"

"Nope again."

They fell back into uncomfortable silence. Tomo stood vigilant, as still as the statue of Hachiman in that house's basement.

Then, Ronald could no longer avoid asking. If there was any chance to still fix things, he had to know. He needed all the help he could get. Ronald cleared his throat. "Do you still have them?" His voice cracked and came out smaller than he'd planned. Che narrowed her eyes. "Your swords, I mean. Can you still fight?"

She swung her legs around, dropped off the counter, and whistled. "What. A. Question. Planning to take on the entire Order? Not gonna happen, man."

"No." Ronald jumped off, landing face to face with his mother. "I'm going to finish what I started." He motioned to Tomo, who still hadn't moved a muscle. "And not completely screw it up this time. This wasn't the Order's fault. It's all Akuma Araki's."

He expected Che to question his last statement, but she just shrugged. When he sighed, she nudged him.

"I know the name. I met her once, I think, but when I met her, she was a frightened, orphaned little girl. She had just lost everything, had just had everything *taken* from her. By the Order. Because of a stupid prophecy, of all things."

"Regardless, she killed Jiro. I have to avenge him."

Che regarded Ronald with more than a little skepticism, and a wave of weariness washed over him. Ronald realized that if she said no, he was going to have to accept whatever fate the tribunal dealt him. He was too drained to try anything else, and without outside help and a damn good plan, he didn't have much hope in convincing Tomo back into his team. But with a legendary samurai on board, maybe two?

"I don't really understand the full extent of what you've gotten yourself into," Che said, resting a hand on the paneled wall where the tapestry once hung. She tapped it a few times, and it sounded hollow. "But I'm your mother, and now that we're back together, I'll do absolutely everything in my power to protect you."

A wicked grin crossed her face, and Che punched through the paneling with zero effort. She peeled it back to reveal a safe. After inputting a short sequence of numbers, it clicked and swung open, revealing two of the most beautiful swords Ronald had ever seen. Famous swords—swords even he recognized in an instant.

In his periphery, Tomo's face was pressed up against the glass, hands cupped to get a better look, mouth wide in a sort of giddy, child-like shock. Ronald realized his mouth was open too, and he snapped it shut, embarrassed. This was his mom, for crying out loud, but he couldn't help a little hero-worship from slipping through.

The rumors were true. Che Perkins was *the* Murasaki no Doragon, The Purple Dragon, and Ronald was low-key on the verge of a total fangirl meltdown.

By the look of Tomo dancing on the balls of his feet, it had already started for the assassin. Ronald waved him in, and the shop's bell rang.

Things were about to get interesting. *Really* interesting.

INTERLUDE FOUR: BEFORE

She left her honor guard outside the city gates. Four village girls, trained in the art of strategy and hardened by grueling physical and mental trials conceived by Akuma Araki herself. Innocent, fragile things tempered to the sharpness of a blade. If she was going to unite Shima Gōdatsusha, she could not afford to maintain a soft spot for the weak and downtrodden. She needed fearless, determined warriors of heart and mettle. She needed the sharpest the island could hone.

And now, faced with a dozen armed and leery merchants, she wished they were by her side.

"Why should we embrace your banner?" a stocky silk seller asked, arms on his hip.

"You are not welcome here," a young fisherman added. "You bring nothing but violence and death."

"We have been fine on our own, long before you arrived." The city's alderman, a tired, older man with busy eyes and a serious face, shoved his way to the front of the crowd. The smell of fish and saltwater clung to him like barnacles to the bottom of his family tsuribune. "What's changed besides you and your thugs roving the hills outside our gate, menacing our farmers, squatting in our villages?"

Akuma sighed. No one understood what she saw so clearly. Not until she showed them the better way, at least. Her means were unavoidable steps towards her ends. She only wished she did not need to show so many with steel. Spilling the blood of her people was never part of the plan, and she was growing all too familiar and comfortable with Death.

Dokuri, Shima Gōdatsusha's largest and oldest settlement, was the last holdout. With the support of the city's robust merchant class, and access to its established trade routes, she would solidify her hold on the island. If only she could convince this rabble to join her without more senseless bloodshed…

She took a moment to collect her thoughts. The situation was delicate, and her typical firm approach would not serve her here. Still, the way they leered, how they looked down upon her simply for being a woman, she could not help but see Ritsu and her adoptive father's faces instead of theirs.

"Gentlemen," she said after allowing the silence to grow tense, "believe me when I tell you I understand your hesitancy. Before the gold devils came, before I saw my village burned to the ground, a united Shima Gōdatsusha never even crossed my mind. We were fine on our own. We had everything we needed. Then, they came, and alone we were not strong enough to stand against them.

"I lost everything that day. All I'm asking is for you to join us, to allow us to ensure this great city never meets a similar fate.

United, we will protect this island against the gold devils, or any other would-be usurpers. United, we are stronger than if we remain separate. So, what do you say, wise men of Dokuri?"

Murmurs traveled through the growing crowd. Distant onlookers joined as Akuma finished her speech. It seemed the entire city was gathered in the plaza, waiting to see what Kangei sa Renai would do next. It was hard to say, but the mumbling consisted of equal parts accord and dissent. A start, to be sure, and better than expected so early in her visit.

But the stubborn alderman refused to budge. If anything, his face was set harder in stone than it had been upon arrival.

"United?" The alderman closed in within a few paces from her. "United!? Don't you mean subservient under Akuma Araki's iron rule? Bah. Take your unity and your false securities and..."

Akuma did not hear whatever he had to say next. Near the back of the crowd, she caught sight of a trio of hooded onlookers, a peek of gold through the shadows enshrouding them. Her hand moved instinctively to the hilt of her sword, and Akuma Araki, the killer, overtook Akuma Araki, the diplomat. She shoved the alderman out of her way, needled through the increasingly restless crowd. The front figure saw her coming and pulled their hood tighter around their face, but it was too late for the trio, who were already backing out of the crowd.

"Gold devils!" she yelled, the steel blade of her katana ringing as she drew it. "Come, face your death."

Three other blades slid free, the morning sun glinting off their sharp edges. Hoods came down, revealing the armor beneath. Two young, baby-cheeked men, hair tied back in tight buns. One older woman, Akuma's age, with distant, darting eyes.

Akuma sidestepped the first's initial strike, a wild, downward cut, and collided with and nearly toppled over the nearest bystander. She gathered herself just in time to dodge a series of left to right slashes and sliced upwards as her attacker shifted from offense to defense. She hardly noticed the warm blood splashing her face as she adjusted her stance and stabbed into the second man's gut. He doubled over, and his sword clattered on the cobbles at his feet. She forced him back, gripping her katana tight between both fists, her teeth grinding between parted lips.

When he fell, the surviving woman also dropped her sword. She raised her hands above her head and staggered away from Akuma. Before she could beg for mercy, Akuma struck her down, regretting the act for only the briefest of moments. She had caught a glimpse of her younger self in the woman's eyes. Scared, naive, lost. Maybe she could have been convinced to abandon her devilish ways, to convert to Akuma's cause. Maybe she would have grown to be one of Akuma's most trusted warriors. But none of that mattered. She was a devil and had to be put down lest her wicked ideals poison the entire population of Dokuri.

Deed done, she turned her scorn to the alderman, who was already attempting an escape from the scene. By these actions, it was all made clear. They had been so adamantly against her offering of peace and unity because Dokuri was already in bed with the gold devils.

Calm, resolved, she followed him on light feet. A smile crossed her face as the crowd parted to allow her passage. He peered over his shoulder, panicked when he saw her approaching, and tripped over his own feet. She flicked blood from the tip of her sword onto the cobbles and slid it silently back into its sheath.

"Please, I had no—"

She shrugged a massive yumi from her shoulders, strung it with deft, patient fingers, and pulled back an eagle-feathered arrow. Her arms were steady as she held him in her sights, allowed him to get far enough away to dare to hope for his life, and let loose. Her aim was true, and Akuma Araki was satisfied that the rest of her negotiations with Dokuri would proceed smoothly. All of Shima Gōdatsusha was hers at last, and it would finally be safe from everything and anyone who might threaten her island.

CHAPTER NINETEEN

Ronald resisted shoving Tomo back into the back seat. Had it been DJ or Robert, he wouldn't have hesitated, but he was still worried about getting on the assassin's bad side again. Two assassination attempts and the scars to prove it would do that to a guy, but every time Tomo bumped his shoulder leaning forward to chat up Che or kneed his seat, Ronald gritted his teeth to hold his tongue.

"Did you *really* enter the Island of Ice and Snow to slay the White Queen?" Tomo's voice rose in pitch and cracked near the end. Che side-eyed Ronald, and they exchanged playful eye rolls. "Then, you went to the Upside Isles with Master Daichi, to take on the entire Sideways Samurai clan! And now you're here, and I'm here, and you're just like driving a freakin' EV around the suburbs? Man, how wild is this? Somebody pinch me."

Ronald obliged. Tomo jabbed Ronald with his elbow, and the assassin's eyebrows all but said "Huh? Huh?" as if egging him into a fight. Ronald half-smiled in return, resisting the urge to facepalm.

When Ronald rode the bus between Normal and New Province, he felt like he was part of the song. It was a living, breathing work of art, and on the bus, he was part of that creative conversation. He was one with the melody, transported to a different state of mind, riding the rhythm of the engine, of the many little imperfections of the road, of the human sounds all around him: coughing, humming, loud and oftentimes private phone conversations. People tapping to a beat that no one else could hear but everyone everywhere was still somehow playing their part.

In the front seat of Che's Hyundai, he was just passing through, skipping all the good parts. The longest he'd ever been in a car was in Aubrey's, from his house to school and back. This was an altogether different experience. One he didn't particularly care for. Mostly, he was bored stiff, watching a thousand identical cars streak by as they wound their way around the highway.

Ronald couldn't help but notice Che knew exactly which exit to take without asking or consulting a GPS. When she passed the strip mall with Starbucks, Chipotle, a Verizon store, and one of those aqua massage places and took a hard right into his neighborhood, he chuckled to himself. All this time, his mother had known exactly where to find him. He understood why she hadn't come, or at least he was trying to understand, but that didn't ease the sting of abandonment he continued to tussle with.

By the time they pulled into his driveway, Tomo had recanted every single one of Che's past exploits, and Ronald's jaw was starting to tighten. The assassin's voice grated. If Ronald had to be confined with him much longer, his mild annoyance was certain to bloom into a full-blown anxiety attack.

RONALD, THE RONIN

He unbuckled fast, hands trembling slightly, and was first out of the car. Home felt like a foreign land, a place he was neither welcome nor accustomed to since his father was gone.

Ronald took a deep breath and gulped. His skin tingled, and his cheeks were flushed. Why did he get this way every time he was about to confront Daichi? Even in death, why couldn't he for once have the courage to face his father? Flesh or ghost, the prospect made his knees weak and his stomach churn, but he had to put their relationship to rest once and for all. It was just a matter of how, now that Daichi had gone and died on him before they could really sit down and talk.

"Wait here," he said.

Che and Tomo hung back without complaint. Ronald could feel their expectant gazes on him as he approached the house, hot like high noon sun rays. Sweat trickled down his neck, and he itched at it while he psyched himself up to open the door. He took a deep breath, fumbled for his keys. When he dropped them, Che got out of the car to help, but Tomo barred her path. Ronald waved to them before finally entering the house. *His* house now. His home.

The smell was awful: a combination of Chinese food left to spoil, body odor, and the ever-present Hashimoto household staple of beer and booze. Flies buzzed around the kitchen trash can, and Ronald wondered why no one in the Order had thought to clean up a little while they were intruding. Daichi was, of course, not passed out in his chair this time, the remote wedged between his thigh and the armrest. Daichi was nowhere and everywhere. There was a heavy, ever-present emptiness that Ronald waded through as he moved from room to room.

Like a ritual, Ronald made his way around the living room and kitchen, picking up beer cans, righting spilled bottles, and tying off two full bags of trash. He rummaged underneath the sink for a bottle of Febreze and sprayed it until he could practically swim in its clean linen mist. He even picked up the messy pile of political advertisements, useless coupons, and credit card offers that had gathered beneath the mail slot, leaving them in a stack on a nearby end table. Then, he admitted he couldn't stall with mundane chores any longer.

He sat cross-legged on the floor directly in front of Daichi's empty armchair, feeling like he was seriously going to throw up. "Dad?" he asked. Even though he knew better, when no response came from Daichi, he sniffled. "Dad, it's me, Ronald. We need to talk. If you can hear me, I need to tell you some things."

He laughed at the ridiculousness of the whole situation. Jiro may or may not have spoken to him before, but had he really expected his father to do the same? It was a joke that he thought reconciliation would be easy.

"Daichi," he all but hissed, "wake the hell up, old man. Wherever you are... Talk to me!"

Ronald fought hot tears, but once the dam finally broke, he was powerless against the flood of emotions that assaulted him. He stormed away, hoping for a safe place to hide in his world of violence.

"I tried to go back. I failed, Dad. I need your help... I can't make things right on my own."

As in life, in death... Ronald mused. Rage surfaced. His hands trembled, but he couldn't let it get the best of him. Instead of lashing out, Ronald took one deep cleansing breath and slammed his fists on the kitchen counter. There, he rested his elbows, buried his face between his arms, and broke down into loud, violent sobs.

A true warrior does not quit every time he faces adversity. Jiro's voice again. So, his brother could answer him, but not Daichi himself? Typical. *He takes a step back, assesses his enemy's weaknesses, and examines his own flaws. Then, with a greater understanding of the whole picture, he attacks from a different angle, one planned for maximum efficiency.*

"What if your enemy happens to be your own father? What if you never had a chance to confront him, to make things right?"

Then, you execute your attack with the dull side of your blade instead. Or, you channel that regret into some other confrontation rather than letting it get the best of you.

Ronald squared his shoulders and crossed back into the living room in a few strides. Then, standing in front of Daichi's chair, he froze up. Again.

Not this time, he told himself. This time, he was in control.

"Answer me, you lazy old bastard!"

Still, there was no response from the other side. Was his father truly lost to him forever?

"Fine. Whatever. I'll tell you, anyway. And I hope you listen, even if you don't have anything useful to say.

"There's a psycho samurai warlord amassing an army, wearing your son's swords on her hip like trophies. Your other son is facing banishment by the very Order you raised him to join, and he's nearly died twice now trying to perpetuate your legacy or whatever the hell it is you expect. I fought a freaking assassin while you were passed out"—for simplicity's sake, Ronald skipped the part where Daichi had also been poisoned—"and where were you while I was recovering? Nowhere! Here, drowning in another bottle, no doubt. You left me with my long-lost mother, and you always tell me what a failure I am?"

Behind him, Ronald heard the door click open, but he continued regardless of his uninvited audience. Che and Tomo might benefit from hearing what he had to say, too, and he'd left them in the car a long time, so he couldn't blame them for not waiting any longer.

"So, you restored your honor? Cool. Cool, cool, cool. That's what it's all about, isn't it? You went out on your own terms, and I'm sooooo happy for you. Sorry, I get it now. All of this was too much for you, the great and powerful Daichi Hashimoto...

"She was right there, Dad. I had a chance to make things right with Jiro, and I failed again. I need your help. But, of course, you're nowhere to be found!"

As Ronald's tirade met its crescendo, Tomo intervened, grabbing Ronald by the shoulders and pulling him to his chest in a tight hug.

The assassin pressed his chin to the top of Ronald's forehead, grabbed him firmly yet lovingly by the back of his neck. "Shh, shh, shh. It's okay, man. Let it out, but everything's going to be okay. I've got you."

Slowly, reluctantly, Ronald cooled off. At first, he struggled against the embrace, but then he fell into it and buried his face in Tomo's chest.

"I'm so sorry," Che said, but she didn't clarify for what. She just stood to the side, staring past the two hugging men. "I'm so, so terribly sorry."

Ronald pulled away to wipe his eyes and noticed a single piece of crumpled mail on the coffee table. From the sake stains and smudged ink, it was clear Daichi had read the letter over and over again. It was faded, and some words were hard to read, but its purpose was clear.

Ronald's lips moved as he read what he could make out in his head. His gut ached as he handed it to Che and ghost-walked to the couch.

"What's up?" Tomo asked.

"They're expelling me. And Daichi was facing a court summons, for allowing me to miss so much school."

"Ah, shit." Tomo squatted low and swiped at empty air. "Sorry kid. For all of this. No one should have to endure so much pain in such a short span of time."

Tomo snapped his fingers and rushed out of the house. He came back carrying a long, unadorned wooden box, which he handed to Ronald.

"I'm supposed to give these to Che, but they belong to you."

Ronald's swords. He shrugged. They were the least of his concerns, but it was nice to know he still had something familiar to hold onto.

Che sat beside Ronald, her added weight on the cushion a small, desperately needed comfort. She wrapped her arms around him, and he fell into her embrace. Tomorrow was Monday, and he could face his school problems then. Today, he needed to let it all out. And for once, he had someone to help him through the pain. Two someones, he realized, almost as if he finally had the family he so desperately needed...

Almost...

CHAPTER TWENTY

Ronald found his friends—or who he hoped were still his friends, at least—at DJ's locker. On his way to school, he'd rehearsed everything he was going to say in painstaking detail. His script was mostly a continuation of their conversations before he went back to Shima Gōdatsusha, but as soon as he saw them together, talking and laughing as if he never even existed, his lines slid right out of his brain through his open mouth.

"Hey, guys." He half-expected them to ignore him completely. He felt like a ghost at that moment, and he knew he deserved it. He wouldn't blame them, either. He'd been a real jerk before disappearing.

Instead, Aubrey stopped mid-sentence and threw her arms around him. "Ronald! Oh my God, you're okay."

"Sup, man?" With a wink, DJ snuck a fist bump behind Aubrey's back. "Good to have you back."

After a tight squeeze and a quick peck on the cheek, Aubrey

let him go. She was beaming, her eyes glistening under the school's fluorescent lights. She was practically glowing, and all of his feelings for her came rushing back, making him lightheaded and hopeful for one divine moment.

Ronald's presence even managed to pull Robert from his game. "Great to see ya. Work out at all over the last few days?" Then, his head dipped, and his eyes returned to his screen, a slight grin threatening his usually serious face. "Nah. You didn't, did ya? What a bum."

Ronald ignored the quizzical looks from Aubrey and DJ. He shook his head. "Something like it, though."

"Did you..." Aubrey left the question hanging. "Did you finish what you needed to finish?"

"Not quite." He didn't have time to expand, though. Mrs. Johnson, Normal Community's assistant principal, was stomping down the hallway towards them, a stern look on her face. "Not yet, at least. Hey, I'm in trouble here, guys. I wanted to see you all before it goes down, but I'm pretty sure I'm getting expelled right now."

Aubrey tilted her head and scrunched her perfect little nose. "Expelled!?"

"For what, man?" DJ asked.

Ronald raised to his tiptoes and bit his lip. Mrs. Johnson was close, and he didn't have much time to explain. "Daichi—my dad—got a court order. For me missing so much school."

Robert snorted. "Yeah, makes sense."

"It's not funny!" Aubrey gently slapped Robert's shoulder, and he acted as if he'd just been punched by Derrick Lewis. "Can you explain to them what's been going on?" Ronald was about to point out the many flaws in that plan when Aubrey sighed. "Ope, never mind. That was a stupid question."

"What *has* been going on?" DJ asked. "You didn't really tell me shit."

"Mr. Hashimoto!" Mrs. Johnson's shrill voice cut through the wall of sound around them. Ronald cringed. "My office. Now." Ronald looked to his friends for sympathy. "Immediately, young man."

"Talk soon, guys." He stopped halfway to the Vice Principal's side, grimaced over his shoulder, and mouthed, "I hope."

Mrs. Johnson stormed towards the main office, Ronald close in toe. Students parted to let them pass undeterred, and he heard their whispers, but he couldn't worry about that now. Nothing else mattered besides getting through this one inconvenience so he could face all his other real problems.

Skylar poked his head out from the crowd and cupped his hands over his mouth. "Uh oh! Dead man walking."

Chad and Eli, always quick to bootlick their leader, laughed on cue, and Ronald almost reacted. He didn't find it funny in the least. In truth, he barely gave the jab a second thought. At the beginning of the year, before Tomo, before Akuma Araki, before... his father, the bullying may have gotten under his skin. Now, it seemed pathetic and played out. What were words to blood and steel? What were a few juvenile insults to death and the threat of banishment? Recent events really put it all into perspective for him, and Skylar was the least of his concerns.

Mrs. Johnson's office was little more than a utility closet tucked behind the unorganized area where the school secretaries worked. The room's single window was covered by stained vinyl blinds, their slats bent and broken. She made her way around a small, L-shaped wooden desk cluttered with knick-knacks and a framed photograph—her family probably, a significant other, maybe even kids if they had been part of the plan for her. Normal faces, living normal lives. She glanced at the photo as she sat gingerly in an oversized leather chair, reorienting it ever so slightly, and a hint of a smile crossed her face.

She steepled her fingers. "I guess you know why you're here." Her foot tapped rapidly beneath her desk as she spoke. "We've had a hard time reaching your father regarding your truancy."

"No kidding? I've been trying to reach him for years."

Mrs. Johnson raised a thin drawn eyebrow. "Are you telling me he's left you all alone?"

She produced a binder from beneath a pile of papers and waved to the window at Ronald's back. Officer Pact, the school's resource officer, appeared.

"I'm sorry to hear that. Really, I am. It's a shame when parents aren't there for their children."

Ronald laughed nervously. "Only kidding. He's usually just in the other room." He wanted to tell them Daichi was usually drunk, so he might as well have been long gone, but instead he sniffled. *Daichi's dead. He's... he's really gone, isn't he?* He cleared his throat. "I... uh... my dad actually died yesterday. Before that, he was fine. My being absent so much wasn't his fault, though."

"Ah, I see. Well, I'm sorry to hear that." She glanced at the floor, and by the way her lips twitched, Ronald could tell she wanted to say something else. He couldn't blame her when she didn't. What else was there to say? "It's almost winter break, and you've been in school for a total of, what, ten days?"

Ronald took a quick mental count, ticking each day off on his fingers. "Sounds about right."

"You don't seem to be taking this very seriously." She reached into her bottom drawer and produced a clear plastic cup with an orange twist-off lid. She slid it towards him. "We're going to need you to take a drug test. Then, Officer Pact is going to search your locker." *My swords!* Ronald's guts twisted. "Before these things happen, and they are going to happen, is there anything you'd like to tell us up front? Honesty is always the best policy in situations like yours."

Ronald weighed the pros and cons of telling her everything.

Pro: She'd be one less person he had to hide the truth from. Two, counting Officer Pact.

Con: She'd *definitely* think he was on drugs after he told her about Shima Gōdatsusha, its insect swarms, and his kitsune friends.

Pro: There was an off-chance Mrs. Johnson would actually believe his story and excuse all of his absences. Maybe she would allow him a few more days' leave to finish what he started.

Con: She wouldn't. She would just think he was insane.

Pro: His swords *were* pretty cool.

Con: They were definitely *not* school sanctioned cultural or religious relics and possessing them on grounds would likely land him in juvie.

In the end, Ronald pleaded the fifth in the most common ways teenagers plead the fifth when being interrogated by school admins. He crossed his arms over his chest, leaned back as disrespectfully as he could manage, and blew a raspberry through his cheeks.

"I don't have anything to hide," he lied.

Mrs. Johnson glared at him over her thick-framed glasses and sighed. "Fine, then. We'll do this the hard way."

She snapped, and Officer Pact entered, allowing the door to slam behind her.

"Yes, ma'am?"

"Please escort Mr. Hashimoto to the boys' room. He'll be providing you a sample before you search his belongings."

Officer Pact nodded dutifully and grabbed Ronald's wrist. Instinct nearly took over, but he managed to refrain from resisting. The last thing he needed was to add an assault of a police officer to his already mounting rap sheet of truancy and possession of a deadly weapon, two counts.

"Sorry, kid," the officer said, and she almost sounded sincere.

"Meh. It is what it is."

By then, he should have known nothing in his life was as it seemed. Nothing went according to plan. His, or otherwise. A scream echoed from outside the office. Dozens of students stampeded past the doorway, away from whatever had elicited the scream. They were yelling, pushing each other out of the way, oblivious to their own safety and well-being, just desperately trying to get somewhere else as fast as humanly possible.

Ronald caught a familiar foul stench in the air. Sulfur and bleach, something he hadn't smelled since Jiro and him fought the oni together in Shima Gōdatsusha. But that was impossible.

Officer Pact was frozen like a deer in traffic, lower lip quivering, and free hand resting on her holster. He wrenched his arm free from her tightening grip. She didn't even attempt to restrain him.

"I need to get to my locker." The officer trembled, her eyes wide. "Officer!" At the sound of his raised voice, she snapped back to reality. "I need to get to my locker. Now."

She nodded and groaned, but no words came out. He took that as all the permission he needed and left her standing there, dumbstruck. Ronald didn't plan to sit idly by while other people were in danger.

CHAPTER TWENTY-ONE

Ronald's instinct told him the oni was close before he ever saw it coming. It wasn't the reek of farts and Clorox cleaning spray that tipped him off, either. It was the way the entire hallway seemed to shake to the beat of something *very* large's footsteps.

He was alone at his locker. The three simple numbers that made up his combination might as well have been three parts of a calculus equation. His hand trembled as he spun the black knob one way then the other, only to pass the last variable for the fourth time.

"Shit." He wiped his sweaty palm on his pants and started over. A growl that rattled his teeth boomed through the hallway. "Come on, come on, come on..."

The locker finally clicked open, and just in time too. He could see a massive shadow forming from around the corner.

There they were: his swords. His trusted companions, friends he'd spent more time with through his short years of consciousness than almost everyone else combined. Everyone besides Jiro, that is. And maybe Daichi, as the old man pushed his boys harder and harder into young adulthood, as he honed them into killers.

As soon as the oni's first massive, veiny leg appeared, Ronald's side where the insect creature from Shima Gōdatsusha had left its stinger started to burn. He winced as he applied pressure to the spot, feeling more than a little as if he were the main character in a bad Harry Potter spoof. Soon, if the oni got its way, he would be the Boy Who Died.

The demon carried a club the size of a small human and an axe with a head twice the size of Normal Community's mascot's. One in each hand, like they were nothing more than hockey sticks. The oni itself was twice the size of the oni Ronald had slain—and that one had been large enough for him to easily slide between its legs—and three times as ugly. It hunched slightly to fit through the hall. Even so, the oni's head struck the overhead lights as it passed beneath them, causing them to *pop* and *crack,* untethered electricity and sparks showering to the floor. But it didn't seem to notice the destruction it was causing and minded even less the sparks tickling its thick, red skin.

As it got closer, and he finally noticed the oni's face for the first time, Ronald gripped the hilt of his katana tighter. It was elongated, as red as blood, with a single horn jutting out from the top of its head, coiling around it like a crown. *Or a boa,* he thought, his nerves constricting. Its forehead bulged beneath the horn, a wet, oozing cluster of eyeballs darting in every direction at once. It unhinged its jaw to growl once more, revealing several rows of sharp, jagged teeth, the two most prominent on the top and bottom bent at awkward angles, more tusks than fangs. Every inch of its exposed skin, of which there was more than Ronald would have liked, was covered in intricate, black tattoos.

Ronald raised his swords. The oni slammed its club into the nearest wall, caving in four lockers like they were made of cardboard. Ronald gulped, his feet sliding involuntarily back, away from the monster.

He held his free hand out, palm up. With his best *Kill Bill* impression—or *the Matrix*, or *Rush Hour*, or just about any other martial arts inspired movie of the Twentieth Century—he beckoned to the monster with an open palm. It roared, close enough now that acidic saliva burned Ronald's face and neck.

Shots rang out. *Pop, pop. Pop, pop, pop.* Officer Pact, from an intersecting hallway. She was crouched, feet facing the oni, clearly over her initial state of shock. In the perfect cop stance, she emptied all fifteen shots of her Glock's magazine. She expelled the spent magazine, and as she reached for a replacement, the oni slapped her aside. Like a rag doll, she flew across the hall, bones crunching, falling onto the floor in a motionless heap.

Seeing the dead resource officer, Ronald sprang into action. He charged the oni with short, quick steps, his sword angled behind him, waiting for just the right moment to strike. He side-stepped to avoid a lazy axe swing and was surprised by how fast the hulking monster could move. When he was close enough to feel the oni's breath, he brought his katana around in a quick slash, expecting to feel the satisfying splitting of skin. Instead, the sword bounced off as if he had struck a thick wall of stone, the force of which sent tendrils of numbness through his wrist and up his shoulder.

Behind the oni, he spun hard and stabbed into its calf. The sharp tip of his katana poked into the flesh as if it were a giant thumbtack before it once again bounced off in the opposite direction. This time, with his arm already tingling, Ronald couldn't hold on. His sword went flying, skittering across the floor and out of sight.

The oni reached back and caught Ronald in the ribs with a clenched backhand. The club gripped in that fist brushed him, and that was the closest he'd ever come to meeting Death. It felt as if he'd been struck by a bus, and he reeled, lungs gasping for air. Before he could recover, the oni's club came swinging toward him, followed by the sharp, many-notched head of the axe. He jumped back, the club narrowly missing his stomach, and then rolled forward, underneath the axe. It came close to taking a layer of Ronald off, but he managed to come through mostly unscathed, positioned once again behind the monster.

He chuckled. So far, this was easier than he'd hoped. Could he actually pull this off?

Then, the oni kicked back like a horse and sent Ronald sprawling. He slid down the hallway, the skin on the back of his arms squeaking as it rubbed off onto the polished tile flooring. By the time he was on his feet, disoriented and throbbing all over, the oni was already charging down the hallway towards him, swinging its weapons like a maniac.

There was his katana, on the floor three strides away. Ronald dove for his sword, but the oni beat him to it. With the stomp of a foot, it sent the katana sliding further out of reach.

Ronald drew his wakizashi. Gripped tight in both hands, he plunged the blade into the monster's foot with all his strength, between its lateral and intermediate cuneiforms. *Anatomy, finally paying off,* he mused as the oni hobbled on one foot and growled in pain. He used the brief moment of distraction to retrieve his other sword and catch his breath, but it was a short moment.

If the oni was mad before, it was *pissed* now. It slammed both club and axe into the walls as it charged. Pieces of plaster and drywall fell from the ceiling, and if Ronald had a chance to think about anything beyond his own bodily well-being, he would have worried about the literal ceiling falling on top of him. As it was, he had no choice but to stand his ground. He was running out of room to retreat, and it was clear the oni wasn't stopping its assault until one of them was dead. But how to penetrate the veritable whirlwind of club and axe flailing towards him? Ronald followed each weapon's sporadic circles, calculated any possible weakness in their motion, and found nada, zilch, nothing. He was about to be beat to a pulp by the world's largest blender, and even if he could get past its weapons, he wasn't strong enough to cut through its skin.

A hail of shurikens spun over his head. Seven in total, each plunging into a separate eyeball. The oni dropped its axe, the weapon clanging on the ground with enough force to nearly knock Ronald off his feet, and reached for the oozing wounds. It screamed and recoiled, pawed at the tiny projectiles, and slammed into lockers as it struggled to dislodge them.

Before it could make any significant progress, however, three arrows in a tight cluster whistled towards it. They struck home, pinning its grasping hand to its face. They were thin, elegant shafts, tipped by dazzling purple feathers, and they seemed to dig further into the oni's flesh as it struggled to tear itself free from itself.

At first, Ronald couldn't process what he was seeing. It made no sense. He should be dead, crushed or ripped to pieces. Instead, something—or someone—had saved him at the last moment.

Now, his killer was reeling, gurgling cries of pain and flailing about like a helpless turtle on its back. In a flash, it was reduced to a sad, pathetic thing, fighting desperately in agony. But who? Certainly no one at Normal Community High School was capable of such a tremendous feat of combat. They had all run in panic at the first sight of danger.

"Get back, Ronald."

Che—his mother, come to the rescue of her baby boy—pushed him behind her protective wing. She was clad in pristine purple armor, wielding a yumi almost her same height. It wasn't a wicked, twisted thing like Akuma Araki's. Che's bow was a work of art, but its craftsmanship couldn't compare to her skill with it. She let another arrow fly, then another. The first ricocheted off the oni's tough skin. The other caught its opposite wrist, causing it to fumble its grip on the club. Another hail of shurikens finished the job.

"Sup, kid?" Tomo patted Ronald on the back and winked. "Didn't think we'd let you have all the fun, did you?"

Ronald was too awestruck to respond. He simply gawked as they went to work on the monster.

Disarmed, it was only a matter of a few well-placed arrows before they had the oni on its knees. From there, Tomo rushed forward, drawing his sais. He leaped, arcing the two blades over his head, and stabbed them directly into the oni's eye cluster. It cried out once more before it slumped, its prone body wedged between destroyed lockers, taking up the entire width of the hallway. Ronald wondered how they were going to dislodge the carcass, and the image of Mrs. Johnson and the custodian struggling with the task nearly made him snort with laughter.

Che grabbed him by his shoulders, frantic. "Are you okay? Where are you hurt?"

While he appreciated his mother's concern, it was uncharted territory for him. Suddenly, he found himself overwhelmed by embarrassment.

"Mom, I'm fine. It's okay." He wriggled free in a huff. "Nothing that won't heal."

"Hot damn, I've never seen one this big before." Tomo flipped Ronald his wakizashi. "Between the toes, eh? Nice touch. Bet that hurt like a *B*."

Still baffled, and stuck in something resembling shock, Ronald stared at the dead demon. Now that the fight was over, his brain started processing a million questions at once. Where did it come from? What was it doing in his school? Why did it seem like it knew who he was, like it had a personal vendetta against him? Was anyone hurt before it found him?

Ronald remembered Officer Pact and panicked. He sheathed his swords and climbed the dead creature, using whatever limbs he could find to manage the sizable climb. On the other side, he rushed to the fallen resource officer's side. He didn't have to check to know she was dead, and the unnecessary loss of life broke his heart. She had just been doing her job. If only she hadn't intervened…

"A true hero," he said out loud, crossing her arms over her lap. "I'm so, so sorry this happened to you. You didn't deserve—"

But he didn't have a chance to finish the thought. A loud, disembodied, mocking laughter echoed from all ends of the hallway. He recognized the voice immediately, but it took him a minute to put a name to it: *Akuma Araki.*

Ronald winced and doubled over. His side throbbed. *The sting,* he thought. Where that damn insect in Shima Gōdatsusha had jabbed him. Could the mark have been how the oni found him?

Black steam wafted off the oni's carcass. Even from a distance, Ronald could feel the heat. Its skin bubbled and popped as it began to melt away, the body deflating. The vile smell of decay filled the hall, choking Ronald. Over the warlord's continuous laughter, he could hear Che and Tomo gagging too and saw them covering their mouths in revulsion. Liquefied, the remains melted holes through the floor, leaving only bones in place of flesh and muscle.

Ronald drew his sword. He swiveled back and forth, frantically trying to find the evil samurai, but she was nowhere to be seen. Her laughter echoed and pierced his senses, dredging up memories of the time he and Jiro had first laid eyes on her. It was all he could do not to curl up into a ball as it went on and on, louder and louder, mocking him, tormenting him.

Suddenly, the laughter stopped. Then, the oni's bones began to crack and twist. They split apart, growing in length and in girth, and rattled free from their original confines. They stretched and curved, joining in some places and diverging in others. New configurations rose and undulated as they morphed into familiar forms. As the first risen figure began to grow a chitinous shell, Ronald understood exactly what was happening and what the bones were transforming into.

"Uh... Guys!" he called over the din. "It's not over yet. Get ready!"

The first insect darted for Ronald, its still-forming pincers clicking and clacking, its open mandibles biting for him. He narrowly avoided losing a hand as he slashed wildly. The insect exploded in a pile of bone fragments only for three more to instantly rise in its place. Ronald cut and slashed, backed away, slashed some more. They fell in their dozens to his sword, to Tomo's sais, to Che's bow. They rose in their hundreds, swarming, hopping along the walls and ceiling, fluttering sheer, newly formed wings. Soon, the sound of their hissing was overwhelming and omnipresent, almost too loud to bear.

Ronald jumped away from one and slammed into another. He flicked his wrist, and the slightest touch of his blade broke his attacker to pieces. But it didn't matter. More just rose to replace it.

A barbed appendage slashed across his neck and cheek, sending a shooting, tingling pain down his spine. An explosion of bone fragments sent him staggering to his knees, and a body Tomo had pushed back slammed into him. On the ground, fumbling for footing, struggling to keep hold of his sword, Ronald was quickly overtaken by stomping, twitching, razor-sharp legs. He dodged this way and that, wiggling free from the mass of insects. There were too many to count now, and more every second they kept fighting.

As the insect-things continued to multiply, they somehow managed to grow in size with each new iteration. It contradicted everything Ronald thought he knew about physics. His logic circuits fried, he watched in horror as he completely lost control of the situation. It was as if he'd left his own body. He was a hovering void of exhausted energy, simply existing as everything fell apart around him.

There: Tomo.

Backing away from an attacker, blood and bug guts covering him from head to toe. He stabbed desperately with his sais, contacting one of the insect's bulbous eyes which popped like a disgusting Double-Bubble bubble. In return, it latched its barbed forelimbs onto his calf and pulled him towards its busy mandibles. Tomo swore and thrashed, managing to break loose, but others joined the fray. He circled them, chest heaving, blades slick with viscous, other-islandy blood.

Then, there: Che.

Tossing her bow aside, arrows spent and scattered beyond her reach, for what little good they had done against the swarm. When she drew her long sword, the intimidating purple-handled nagamaki of legend, Ronald felt a sliver of hope. Surely, Murasaki no Doragon could stave off the swarm. At first, it indeed looked as if she could. She cut and slashed so fast her sword became a blur, slicing and dicing dozens of insects into tiny pieces. She moved so quickly through them that she managed to cut down the fully-formed and still-rising at the same time. One of the massive amalgamations struck her hard from the side with both its great forelimbs. It skittered on top of her, semi-pearlescent wings flicking wildly, yet she managed to toss it aside. Three more piled on, and Che squirmed to find purchase beneath the writhing mass.

She popped free from the pile, legs kicking, sword slashing off limbs and chunks of chitin. Ronald slid to her side on one knee, grabbed her hand. She squeezed tight, and he yanked as hard as he could, sliding with her on all fours to put space between them and the twitching pile.

"There's sorcery here, and the perpetrator is close."

"I won't leave you."

"Ronald, you have to. Find whoever, or whatever's behind this swarm."

"I... I can't..."

Che gave him a sad smile. "You must."

All around him, the insects chittered and hopped. There were so many now he couldn't possibly count them. A few wandered off, disappearing around corners to other hallways, and he spared a fleeting thought for the safety of his fellow students and teachers, but most of the insects concentrated on him.

Bodies bumped into him. Legs stepped on him and prodded him. Mandibles pinched and snipped at him. But Ronald did absolutely nothing to fight back. He was beyond powerless, and what was the point anyway?

You know what you have to do, Jiro's voice ensured. *Get up, Ronald. Get up and go get it done. I don't want to have to tell you again.*

In his mind's eye, he could see exactly where the sorceress was. He could practically feel the wretch's hot breath as she continued chanting her spell, lips moving independent of any conscious thought, eyes rolled to their whites. She wore a black cloak, similar to the awful figure who stood beside Akuma Araki upon the lift, and oozed the same evil aura.

He launched to his feet, dodged a reaching arm to his right, and sprinted down the hallway. He cut one turn, then another, nearly toppling over a tall student with blood trickling from her hairline.

"Wrong way." He redirected her, pointed her towards one of the school's emergency exits by where the gearheads had Auto Body. At first, she didn't seem to comprehend, but when he spun her around and yelled "That way. Go!" she mumbled her thanks and was gone.

Ronald looked over his shoulder to see another swarm rounding the corner. Some barreled towards him, while others split off in opposite directions. His inner dialogue begged him to go back, to cut them down and save whomever they might be after. But he couldn't be in multiple places at a time, could he? His only option was to keep on his chosen course, to slay the wicked devil behind their existence. That was the only way he could save his fellow classmates. That was how he could end this new nightmare once and for all.

He found the sorceress exactly where he'd seen her in his mind, tucked in the back corner of a dark science classroom. It wasn't *the* sorceress, Minata, but by the way her aura glowed an eerie green, it was clear this woman was part of Minata's retinue. She was so entranced she didn't even notice when he threw open the door. He made quick work of the violent business, cutting her down without remorse. The moment she fell to the ground, he felt a weight lift from inside the school, a quiet and calm only possible through the peace of safety and security.

Ignoring everything around him, he rushed back to where he had fought the oni. To his relief, he found two bodies moving ever so slightly among the mass of shells and limbs. Tomo, spread eagle in the middle of the hallway, groaned and rolled his head from side to side. Che, leaning against a locker, her sword on her lap, was breathing heavily. They were both barely conscious, but they were still alive.

Thank Hachiman, they were still alive!

CHAPTER TWENTY-TWO

Ronald hardly noticed the gold-hooded monks moving among the students and teachers and tending the wounded. He glanced right past the Order samurai, standing to the side, clad in full armor. He even missed Master Oda himself, chatting in a hushed tone with Mrs. Johnson and the school's principal, Mr. Vane.

Just like at his house the day he found Daichi dead, the Order and everything surrounding them was invisible. All he saw was the gurney being wheeled out the front door, the zipped white bag resting on top of it—one of over a dozen—but he barely spared the others a passing thought.

He hadn't known Officer Pact. She was reputed to be a fair and reasonable resource officer who took the time to get to know "trouble" students. On more than one occasion, she was even caught playing soccer or throwing a football around during home games. She'd been a Normal Community High School staple since her graduation from the police academy, and Ronald took her death personally. If it wasn't for him, the oni never would have been there in the first place. And like with his brother, Ronald had simply let her die.

Ronald felt a hand on his shoulder. Che's. "It's not your fault."

He sniffled. "I could have—"

"It's. Not. Your. Fault." She gave him that stern look mothers give their sons when they're being stubborn. "We can't save everyone, Ronald. Besides, she died doing her job, protecting her students. There's honor in that."

"Pssh." He waved her off. "What's honor? I'm sure her family doesn't give two shits about honor." He didn't realize it right away, but he was practically quoting Tomo from when he first encountered the assassin. If he wasn't so distraught, it might have been funny.

"Should I, like, scold you for bad language or something?"

Ronald rolled his eyes. "Probably."

His mother put on her best serious face, but it looked more like she was constipated than anything. They both laughed, and she playfully shoved Ronald before he fell into her arms.

"Guess we're not there yet, huh?"

"Nah," he answered. "Guess not."

"You did so good. I'm so proud of you."

"Who was the woman? The one I killed..." he asked suddenly. "I've never seen anything like her, before my last trip to Shima Gōdatsusha. Are they seriously like for real-life wizards? Or sorceresses, or whatever."

Che's gaze drew to her feet. Sullen, she cleared her throat. "Oh, sweet child. The old powers are stronger on some of the other islands. The lines between people and gods, mundane and supernatural are much less clear. They aren't supposed to be in our world, but sometimes they slip through. But they need a conduit of sorts, or someone to let them in."

Ronald felt a sudden, stabbing pain between his ribs. He lifted his shirt, and Che gasped at the spiderweb of throbbing, purple veins. At its epicenter, the end of a thick, black barb was just visible, like a splinter having worked its way into the skin. He pinched it between his fingernails, gritted his teeth, and pulled the barb out. A trickle of blood-like pus ran down his side, and the pain seemed to throb and radiate across his whole torso.

"What the hell..." Che's eyes went wide as Ronald flicked it away.

"When Tomo and I went to confront Akuma Araki, one of those insect monster things must have left that behind."

"That'd do it," she said, pursing her lips and nodding.

"Do what?" he asked, feeling more than a little left out of a world life seemed to keep trying to force him back into.

"Something like that, a piece from another island, would be enough for a powerful enough sorcerer—"

"Or sorceress." Minata's cruel, green eyes came to mind, and a tickle shivered its way down his back.

"Right, *sorceress* to breach the gaps between."

Shouting from the crowd stole Ronald's attention before he had a chance to contemplate what he'd just learned. However the conversation between Master Oda and the school admins ended, they must have been less than satisfied. Mrs. Johnson stormed off, and Mr. Vane clasped his hands behind his back, head down. He walked away too, stopping occasionally to check on injured students or give a quick word of encouragement to one of the monks.

When Oda made eye contact with Ronald, the old master waved. He began to approach, but Ronald saw someone else he needed to talk to first.

"Head him off for me?"

Puzzled, Che asked, "Say what now? Me?"

"Please. It's important."

She drew her forehead back, as if unconvinced she of all people could stall Master Oda, then shrugged. "Aight, then. I'll do my best, I guess. But no promises."

"Thank you. I owe you one."

She snorted. "Nah, I'm way down on the box score list if we're really keeping track. It's the least I can do."

Skylar was sitting beneath the school's trophy case—an impressive collection Ronald had to admit—legs outstretched, face buried in his hands. Even from a distance, Ronald could tell he was crying. He made his way over to his one-time bully, ignoring several classmates and Order members vying for his attention.

Not wanting to startle Skylar, Ronald cleared his throat. "Can I sit?"

Skylar wiped his face in an obvious attempt to cover up the fact that he had been crying. Ronald couldn't imagine what could possibly make someone like Skylar cry, but he wasn't one to judge. The boy was clearly injured. Blood soaked his shirt beneath his ribs, and he winced at every little movement, but somehow Ronald knew that wasn't the reason. Skylar's pain went much deeper than physical harm.

After a few awkward moments, Skylar nodded, and Ronald slid

down beside him, pulling his knees to his chest. He remembered what Mr. Mendez had asked him. "Do you want to talk about it, or do you need a minute?"

"They're both dead," Skylar said. "One of those... things got Chad. It... it... grabbed him, and... He was trying to get away, but he's just always been so damn slow. When it started biting, he was already gone." Skylar sniffled. "Then... then when Eli tried to help him... Oh my God!"

"I'm sorry, man. I should have stayed to help instead of..." But even then, Ronald understood he couldn't have saved either boy. He'd done the right thing. If he hadn't found the sorceress when he had, there was no telling how many others would be dead, too.

"Not your fault. Nothing anyone could have done." He smacked his own head a few times. "What the hell even was that? That shit can't have been real, right? This is all just a bad dream. I'm having a nightmare, aren't I? I'm sleeping, and I just need to wake up."

But, at the same time, it *was* Ronald's fault. Same with Officer Pact. Had Ronald stayed in his lane, had he not insisted on going back to Shima Gōdatsusha, none of this would have happened. Chad and Eli were complete douche bags, but neither boy deserved to die. None of those people did...

Ronald didn't know what else to say, so he patted Skylar's back and said, "Sorry, man. Really, I am. If you ever need anything..."

Skylar forced a half-smile. "I appreciate that. Hey, so, you're like a real samurai, huh? Had me fooled."

He choked and coughed blood into his hands. Ronald moved Skylar's shirt aside, and saw the wound was still bleeding. He glanced around for help, but all the Order monks were busy tending to others. Not knowing what to do other than what he had seen on TV, he placed either hand against Skylar's torso, above and below the wound, and applied pressure.

A sudden warmth radiated from his fingertips, and Skylar clenched his teeth. But soon he relaxed, and the blood stopped flowing. Ronald couldn't believe his eyes at first, but the wound even seemed to be closing, a thin scab forming around its edges. Skylar's eyes went wide, and his lips parted as if to say something, but what was there to say?

"Hmpf," came a passing voice. Sakiko's, Ronald realized, surprised to see her standing beside him, trench coat tied loosely around her sightly figure, hands on her hips. She shook her head. "Well, I've seen everything, now. The boy has healing powers, too." She face-palmed, and walked away, muttering something about how unfair life was and how she'd never hear the end of it from Hikari. "These freakin' Hashimoto kids..."

While Ronald wasn't able to completely heal Skylar's wound with... whatever strange power had just seeped out of him, it had closed enough to where he knew his classmate was going to survive without long-term repercussions. No problem. Everything was fine and normal, as always.

Ronald remembered he was still wearing his swords, and he could only imagine how rough and beat up he looked after the fight. It hadn't dawned on him that his big secret was officially out in an even bigger way.

"Not sure I'd call myself a real samurai. Not a very good one, at least."

"But you fought those things." Skylar said. "Huh. Bad ass, Ronny. For real. And you have magic powers, too? So, so dope. Hey, DJ played your beat for me."

"Oh yeah?"

"Fire. I have some bars I think would be a good fit, for when things get back to normal."

"*If* things get back to normal," both boys said at the same time. They laughed awkwardly, and Ronald looked away in case they were accidentally becoming friends.

Suddenly, Skylar slapped his knee and pointed, a sly look on his face. "Hey, ain't that your girl comin' this way?"

Ronald didn't think twice when he said, "Yeah. It is."

Aubrey waved with her good arm and winced. Her other arm was in a sling. There was an angry red gash on the same shoulder.

Ronald leaped to his feet way too fast. Blood rushed to his head, and he was still dizzy when she moved in for a kiss. It was long and passionate. Despite the slight iron taste, it was one of the best experiences of Ronald's life. When she drew back, he stammered, his lips still moving, and very nearly fell forward. He barely had the faculties to snap and say, "Ah-hah, I gotchya," before placing his hands on her shoulder. There came that warmth again, and the gash began to fade ever-so slightly, and more importantly, Aubrey seemed to be able to move her arm a little easier.

She frowned and narrowed her eyes at him, clearly weirded out about everything going on, but didn't bother to comment on this recent turn of events. He couldn't blame her. It was a lot to take in.

"They were saying you were dead. Eaten up by some giant monster. D Hall is a total mess. Lockers all torn to shit, ceiling collapsing, floor cracked wide open. They said... you were with Officer Pact..."

"I'm okay. Look." He indicated to his intact body, spun a slow circle so she could see. "I'm okay, really."

"You're an asshole, is what you are." She produced his medallion from beneath her shirt and ran a finger along its curves. "So, you weren't bullshitting me, huh?"

"I wasn't bullshitting you. I'd never bullshit you."

She stared over his shoulder for a moment before squeezing the medallion and dropping it back beneath her shirt. She patted it, and said, "You really could have died, you know?"

"Yup." He nodded. "Several times, actually."

"I... I have so many questions."

"Same."

Ronald glanced around at the monks, still tending to the wounded, at Che and Master Oda chit-chatting animatedly like old friends, at Tomo flirting with a sophomore English teacher whose name he couldn't remember. Nothing made sense anymore. Every time he thought he was doing the right thing, everything else seemed to get harder, weirder. But life just kept going on, didn't it? Life didn't care who got hurt along the way, and if you were one of the lucky ones who made it through something as tragic and horrific as what had happened today at Normal Community High School, you just had to keep going on too.

Yeah, he had a lot of questions alright. Eventually, he'd have to admit he might never get any of the answers he was looking for.

"I have to end this," he said. When he saw the betrayal on Aubrey's face, he rose his arms to everything around him. "I mean, all of this. It happened because of me. It will happen again if I don't—"

She grabbed him by his collar and pulled him in. Really pulled him in. After his initial shock wore off, he leaned into this latest kiss and forgot about everything else for a few moments.

When they stopped for air, Aubrey sighed. "You can't do, uh, whatever it is you think you need to do. It's too dangerous, and you're the first person I've..." She stopped, blushing, and picked at her chin. "I don't hate you, is all. And I'd be pissed if you left me alone with DJ and Robert forever. Like, seriously. Livid, Ronny Boy."

"But I have to—"

"You don't have to do anything! Look at all these warriors and stuff around us. Whatever you think you need to do, let them handle it. You're a kid, for crying out loud. Not some samurai warlord."

No, but Akuma Araki was a samurai warlord, and she clearly wanted Ronald dead, among other things. How could he explain that? To someone outside the Order, a place like Shima Gōdatsusha would just sound like a fairy tale or the setting of some cheesy, over-the-top anime.

But Akuma Araki needed to be stopped. She wouldn't quit until her and her horde found a way into their world. Now, for some reason Ronald didn't quite understand, they were linked. Through him, she could exist here—if not physically, spiritually—and bring with her all kinds of unpleasant troubles upon the people closest to him.

He wanted to tell Aubrey about Jiro too. Make her see how important it was to restore his brother's honor, to bring home the only pieces left of him. He wanted to tell her that he needed to make things right for his brother, to prove that his life was worth living after he'd left Jiro there to die, that Ronald Hashimoto was more than the wrong son to survive.

"Please. Promise me. You can't put yourself in danger like this again. I don't know if I could stand to lose you."

Ronald held Aubrey's hand in his and looked her straight in the eyes...

She was so beautiful, so sincere. He could get lost in those deep, wide, dark eyes...

It was a strange feeling, having someone sincerely care about him. Jiro always had, in his own way. The way older brothers did. He never would have admitted it out loud, of course, but before Ronald found out who Che Perkins really was, he had been more or less alone. And here was this girl who he'd chosen as his person who had also chosen him. It was wild, really. Absolutely bat shit crazy.

So, Ronald held Aubrey's hand, looked her straight in those deep, dark eyes, and lied to her face for what he hoped would be the last time.

CHAPTER TWENTY-THREE

Over the last few weeks, Ronald had had too many reasons to be afraid to count. Oddly, none of them compared to the gut-wrenching, heart-skipping sensation that came over him as he walked into his own house after his fight with the oni.

He'd left Normal Community after a brief, semi-reassuring conversation with Master Oda, but it hadn't eased his troubled mind. For most of the afternoon, Ronald walked the suburbs aimlessly, hands in his hoodie pocket, music loud enough for his phone to warn him about hearing loss. He had to laugh about that. He listened to his music so loud because he *already* had hearing loss. It was pretty simple, really.

Not knowing what song came next was one thing. He'd set his YouTube playlist to shuffle, and anything could come on after a fade-out. Joyner Lucas's *ADHD* followed Kudi's *Pursuit of Happiness*, Aesop Rock's *None Shall Pass* followed Bizzy Bone's *Warriors*, and so on and so forth until his phone battery died. This kind of unknown was sacred to Ronald. He relished the thrill of the aural ride it took him on.

The unknown of what came next in his own life, how he was meant to carry on in an empty home without a father, hurt his soul and left him physically ill to the point he thought he might throw up in someone's mailbox.

The last thing he expected was a sparkling clean house. A new TV hung on the wall. New furniture. A new chair for Daichi's spirit, lingering or otherwise, with the tags still on it.

"What in the *Don't Worry Darling* is going on here?" he mumbled.

There wasn't a can or bottle or plate of stinky leftovers in sight. In fact, the living room looked like a picture off Realtor.com: perfectly arranged in every way. It gave Ronald the creeps, and he reached for his wakizashi, hovering his hand over its hilt just in case as he made his way through the house.

"Hello?" It came out as little more than a whisper. Silence responded. "Anybody here?"

As he moved into the kitchen, the back doorknob began to twist. His years of vigorous training took over, and he drew his short sword and crouched, ready for a fight, muscles tensed for action. But when the door opened, he relaxed. A little.

"Hey, man! What's up?" Che came in, half a dozen grocery bags hanging precariously on her arms. "I hope you're hungry."

Tomo followed close behind, puppy-dog eyes open wide. "I know I am."

Ronald slid his wakizashi back into its sheath, hiding its potentially deadly presence behind his back. He stared at them, dumbstruck, and watched as they unpacked groceries. They chitchatted the whole time, small talk about the weather, about the neighborhood. Gossip about their bagger. Random opinions about a news segment they heard on the radio, or the merits of some podcaster's ridiculous stance on the dichotomy of *blah, blah, blah*. When they started laughing together, all but flirting across the island, Ronald couldn't stand it anymore.

"What the *hell* is going on here?"

"Language, young man." Che snorted as she reprimanded him, and she and Tomo started laughing even harder, as if they'd been best friends forever.

It was like a bad episode of *Black Mirror*. A renowned ex-samurai and a deadly assassin, united and replaced by suburbanite robots. Perfectly domesticated, despite the combined decades of blood on their hands, pretending as if everything was normal, as if Ronald's life wasn't getting stranger and stranger by the day.

"Seriously," he said, growing more than a little impatient. "Just what!?"

Che slapped a bundle of green onions on the counter. "We're making ramen." She stuck out her tongue as she pulled out a sleeve of narutomaki, fish cake paste. "Wanna help?"

Tomo was standing at the sink, filling a fancy ceramic kettle with water. He was whistling. Actually. Freaking. Whistling.

Ronald felt lightheaded all of a sudden. "I think I need to go lay down."

"Eh, you'll be fine after a cup of tea." Tomo swiveled to the stovetop—a device Ronald was convinced the assassin had never even touched—and ignited a back burner. He jumped back, then grinned at his own overreaction. "Sit down, kid. Sit down. You've been through a lot today. Relax. We'll get dinner ready, then we can all talk."

Confusion swam around in Ronald's head like a bowl of sticky rice noodles. Tomo was right about one thing, though: he *did* need to sit down.

Ronald watched in utter fascination as his mom and the assassin worked around each other. Their motions were well-coordinated, flawless in their execution, but cold in their calculation. Was this the natural outcome of Order training? Was this going to be him, years down the line? A smooth, honed killing machine, even as a cook in a kitchen?

Che slid a colorful bowl of noodles, sliced narutomaki, over-medium eggs, pork slices, and a variety of vegetables in front of him. Steam wafted off the soup, and the salty, slightly fishy aroma made Ronald's stomach grumble. He had to admit, it looked damn good. Better than anything he'd had outside of Ling's restaurant in a long time. It beat yesterday's cold pizza and Pop-Tarts.

Around the kitchen island, they ate their first meal together. It should have been more momentous, this unexpected gathering of legends, but it was just another meal, filled with slurping and sighs of satisfaction. It was a meal shared in silence, with only an occasional smile shared between them.

When everyone was finished, Tomo gathered their bowls, dumped them in the kitchen sink, and sighed heavily. He sat back down, his foot tapping nervously on the leg of his chair. On several occasions, he acted as if he were about to say something, but then he'd look away or clear his throat or scratch his head, and they'd all fall back into uncomfortable silence. Ronald's mother and the assassin had at least one thing in common that he could tell: they were both terrible at *real* communication and proficient at BS and small talk.

So, Ronald decided to break the ice, wasting no time getting straight to the point.

"Why are you being so nice to me? Acting like nothing happened? All those people, Officer Pact. They died, and it was my fault."

"Ronald, it wasn't—"

"Stop it." He held a hand in Che's face. "I left the portal open. I let that nasty demon through. If it wasn't my fault, whose was it?"

"Forgiving the fact that your hand is in my face right now, you did an amazing job back there."

"One hundred percent." Tomo leaned forward, and Ronald could tell he was trying his hardest to be serious. "You knew exactly what needed to be done and when to do it. Before we got there, you had that oni under control, which gave countless people enough time to get to safety. Then, when those insects started sprouting out of nowhere, you dealt with them without hesitation." The assassin indicated himself and Che. "You saved our sorry asses, too."

"It wasn't enough. People still died."

"People die all the time, kid. We cannot stop Death; we can only embrace her when she comes."

Ronald slammed the table. "You sound just like my dad, reciting rote Order *wisdom*. I don't need that, man. I never did. I need someone to understand where I'm coming from."

"Ronald..." Che reached for his arm, but he snapped it back. "Please, listen to what Tomo has to say. He's no poet, but this is important. Please, just consider what he said, okay? For me."

He wanted to ask why he'd do it for her, a mother who'd

abandoned him for his entire childhood, but he kept his mouth shut. Instead, he leaned back, folded his arms across his chest, and sucked his teeth.

"Jiro talks to you?" she said, but it was more of a question than a statement. Ronald nodded slightly, a sharp pain shooting through his gut at the thought of his brother. "He talked to me, too. At first. At the shop, when I closed up for the night. Then, one day, he stopped talking to me as often. I knew he was dead before anyone told me, knew he was watching over you. He always cared so much about you, Ronald."

She closed her eyes, tears forming beneath them, and exhaled a raspy, labored sigh. "Eventually, he stopped coming all together. I loved your brother. I loved you. I... I love you."

Ronald's face flushed. A lightness of heart overtook him, and despite himself, he smiled. He wished he could have heard these words from Daichi before the old man took his own life, but coming from Che, he felt as if he might happy-laugh himself into hysterics.

"You were such a good son to Daichi. He told me everything you did for him while he drowned himself in bottle after bottle. Before he left that first night, after bringing you to me, he was a broken man. Shamed beyond repair, in his mind."

"What did you talk about, before Jiro stopped talking?"

At this point, Tomo gave Ronald a weak smile and ducked away, leaving them to their conversation.

Che ground her teeth together, glanced once again at the fridge. She craned her neck and scratched the top of her hand, anything to not have to answer the question.

"Mostly about you. Jiro was always so jealous of you. We talked about how proud of you I was. And, occasionally, we talked about your father. All Jiro understood was combat. You? You were nearly his equal, yet the training and the Order were hardly an afterthought for you. From a young age, you were destined for greatness in things beyond the sword. You walked your own path and still managed to keep up with Order demands."

Ronald realized he was still wearing his swords. He lifted them and noticed no difference in weight. Despite how hard he'd tried to deny his heritage, his katana and wakizashi were part of him, an extension of his own flesh and bones.

"I... I don't expect you to forgive Daichi," Che continued. "I wouldn't forgive him. All I ask is that you forgive yourself. In time, maybe you'll start to understand that Daichi only ever wanted what he thought was best for you boys. He was a good man, once. A loving man. But the Order broke him. All that death... all that violence. From his perspective, he had to make you strong, to prepare you to face the nightmares he once endured. If you were weak, he was afraid life as he knew it from his perspective would break you, too."

Ronald didn't miss a beat. "I'm going to get Jiro's swords back. I'm going to slay Akuma Araki." Che's eyes opened wide in shock. "I spoke to Master Oda. We're going to end this, come the next full moon. Akuma Araki fears the moon, or so I'm told, and we're going to strike before she's grown too strong to defeat."

A grim frown came across Che's face. "She does not fear the moon." Ronald began to interject, but she held up her hand. "Akuma Araki only fears one thing."

Frustration set in. "What does she fear, then?"

"She fears Ronald Hashimoto." Che gently flicked his nose. "Because he is Fated."

CURTIS A. DEETER

INTERLUDE FIVE: BEFORE

Akuma Araki ducked through the cave's shadowy entrance. She ordered her samurai to remain outside, to let no one besides her leave the cave alive. Reluctantly, they obeyed and disappeared among the foliage and crags surrounding the mountain's base. To a casual onlooker, it would appear as if her and her handmaiden were alone. The casual onlooker would have been very, very mistaken.

A winding passage narrowed and widened, its slick stone ground uneven and treacherous, and all of her concentration was spent on keeping careful footing. She never noticed the light's shift to pitch or when the far-off flickering of torchlight began to seep into the blackness. She never noticed the onyx and diamonds lodged into the walls, blinking and watching her as she made her way deeper, deeper, and deeper. She never even noticed the way her shadow bent and twitched under no light's influence, independent of her corporeal body's movements.

This was an old and once-sacred place. A dead place, filled with an eerie, tangible eldritch intelligence.

She came to the passage's abrupt end, nearly stumbling onto her hands and knees in the cramped, ovular chamber. Torches that seemed to float under their own volition cast dancing clarity on the chamber's meager contents: a roughly-hewn sleep sack; a rickety wooden table with a single place setting, a cluster of odd alchemical tools, and a slab of what she could only hope was meat; a cauldron over a cold hearth; and a gnarly, haggard old woman hovering cross-legged at its center.

"Finally, you have come."

Akuma cleared her throat. "I seek Tsukuyomi-no-Mikoto. This is their final refuge."

The crone cackled and coughed before saying, "There are no gods left here. They left this place a long, long time ago."

"Then my journey has been a waste, and your life is of no use to me."

"Are you so certain, great warlord?" The crone's body began a slow rotation towards her, revealing matted, black hair, pallid, gray skin, and eyes like deep wells. "Are you so vain, Kangei sa Renai, that you can learn nothing from the World's Eye?"

The torches flashed and flickered, their light suddenly blinding for a time. The hearth ignited with a *whoompf*, and Akuma flinched. Her heart raced, as she had not felt fear like this—true fear—in quite some time. But how could a mere old woman instill such a fear in her? What pain could she possibly inflict upon Akuma that she had yet to endure? She was not afraid of magic or gods. She had never been concerned over the Earth's old, weakened powers. Why this one of all Shima Gōdatsusha's wretched creatures?

"And what can you teach me," Akuma asked, her voice cracking as she did her best to maintain eye contact, losing herself to the void of space and time within the crone's, "that I do not already know?"

"There is a boy. A child"

"Impossible."

Again, the crone cackled. "Not that kind of child, dear." Akuma clenched her fists at the sudden shift from honorific to endearment. "The kind who could bring ruin to you and your campaign against this island. Would you wish to know of him, if I was possessed of such knowledge?"

Despite herself, Akuma bowed her head. "I would."

"Then I ask, what can you offer me in return?"

Akuma Araki took a knee, clasped a closed fist in the palm of her opposite hand. "Loyalty." She looked at the crone. "The strength and security of my army to live here in this cave undisturbed, should that be your desire. Whatever you would like, great one, I can provide."

The crone's cackling came again, this time from all around the chamber. It reverberated off the walls. It rattled Akuma's bones and filled her with dread and doubt.

"Hmm, not much. Enough, perhaps, for me to repeat the words to you that you've likely already heard. Listen, child, for the truth cannot be denied. As the prophecy goes, so shall it be.

Behold, a child born of Struggle and Strife. Beware, a child born of Shima Gōdatsusha, tempered by the fires of Her trials. Sower of Chaos where there was once Order. Uprooter of the ancient Bonsai, awash in golden waves of destruction, reborn anew under a crimson dawn."

"You are correct: I have heard it before. But what does it mean?

What can I give you to help me better understand this so-called truth?"

"You have nothing I want."

"Then, you must die."

Akuma was not certain if she had voiced the threat out loud, but the moment she thought it, the flames in the hearth and from the torches flared. The old woman erupted in black fire, growing to four or five times her original size. She spoke the beginnings of an enchantment, a great black eye forming behind her, but Akuma did not wait to give the crone enough time to complete her spell.

She lunged forward, her blade sliding loose from its sheath and slicing in one singular motion. It cut clean through the front of the old woman's torso, and she let out a horrible screech, her incantation interrupted by blood. She fell like a sack of turnips, slammed bodily into the stone ground below her, undulating as she shrunk back to her normal size. Akuma cut again, this time opening her throat.

The dying crone gargled as she attempted to speak one last spell, her words competing against blood and lack of breath. Still, it was enough. As Akuma's samurai barged into the chamber, an explosion of black fire blew them all back, away from the dying World's Eye. Akuma received the brunt of it, and the searing pain on her neck, face, and arms only lasted a second before she went numb and cold.

Minata, one of her first followers, and now a strong woman of great resolve and courageous heart, was the first at her side. No longer a girl, and now one of the most powerful sorceresses in Akuma's army, she had more than proven her worth.

"Master," she cradled Akuma in her arms, resting the warlord's head against her chest, "you are wounded. We must leave and find—"

"No," Akuma managed, her voice less than a whisper. "I must claim what I came for."

She strained and groaned as she rose, leaning most of her weight onto Minata. After collecting her scorched sword from the shadows beneath the charred table, she found a cup among splintered wood. Akuma limped towards the dark lump that used to be the ancient god, the World's Eye. Ice spread through her body with every step, but she needed to finish the ritual. She needed the crone's power.

"My knife." She indicated to her side, and Minata gingerly drew a sleek tanto from a hidden sheath. "Hold this."

The sorceress held the cup steady in both hands. Akuma Araki lifted the body without ceremony, slit a gash across the old woman's cheek. Blood dripped into the cup from the fresh wound. Then, Akuma drew the knife across an exposed, and badly burned, section of her forearm. There was no pain, and she knew that was not a good sign. Still, she added her own blood into the cup, stirred it with the tip of the knife, and offered the cup to Minata.

"Now, drink." When Minata hesitated, Akuma pushed the cup towards her. "I said *drink*. To the last drop."

Minata nodded and reluctantly brought the cup to her lips. Always the dutiful servant, she tipped the cup back, gagging upon first taste, and did as she was ordered without another peep of complaint.

At first, nothing happened. Akuma Araki slumped on the cave floor, body spent and mind in ruins. She had been so hopeful to harness the World's Eye's power. The ritual was supposed to work, to show her how to fully dominate Shima Gōdatsusha. It was supposed to bring an end to the bloodshed, to all her doubts and worries, but even the island's last living god could not bring her the satisfaction she sought. She had come so far and been so close to realizing her ambitions.

Minata knelt beside her warlord. "We need to get you out of here, take you to a healer. You're badly burned, and I'm afraid…"

Her head jerked, neck cracking as her shoulders spasmed. Minata staggered backward, away from the wounded warlord, and her limbs popped and twisted at impossible angles. She tripped over the crone's cauldron, spilling a nasty, viscous substance. On her back, she began to writhe, her muscles seizing and bulging, until finally she let out a horrible wheeze. The cave fell silent, and Minata fell still, the cauldron's unknowable contents leaking all over her limp body.

Her samurai were busy now. They tended to Akuma Araki, first helping her to her feet and then sliding her towards the exit passage. She ordered two of them to help Minata, to bring her out of the cave. Everything was blurry as that awful chamber drew further and further away. The last thing she remembered seeing before her vision went black was Minata, rising from the floor, arms and legs splayed. Ignited in black flame, the same cackle she had first heard from the World's Eye boomed throughout the cave, and the sorceress's eyes shot open, fixated directly on Akuma. A cruel smile spread across Minata's face, and Akuma Araki returned her servant's grin. Everything she had always dreamed of and more *was* within her grasp. She never should have doubted herself or her plans.

CHAPTER TWENTY-FOUR

There was no raised dais, no gavel. There were no ritual hymns or rote decrees. And the lighting was actually passable: hipster dim, not the anticipated darkness with only a single, overly bright spotlight shining on him. Nothing cliché about this particular tribunal. Nothing that fit any of the tropes Ronald had seen on TV.

Ronald sat at a coffee shop, in a secluded backroom, with Master Oda—drinking an iced coffee rimmed with cinnamon sugar of all things—and his two counterparts, Master Fuma from the west and Master Jin from the east. They talked among each other as if Ronald wasn't even there. They laughed as they reminisced, and after a while, once he realized he'd learn nothing juicy or useful from the excitable trio, Ronald began to tune them out. There was too much at stake for him to waste so much time listening to idle chit-chat of lost relics and old glories. He wished they'd shut up and get the whole thing over with already.

Master Oda slurped the remainder of his coffee and pushed the cup aside. He wiped his fingers dry and clapped, causing Ronald to jump nearly out of his seat.

"Shall we begin, then?"

"Aye," Master Fuma said. He was much younger than Master Oda, and his beard nearly fell to his knees when he stood up. He had a funny little way of wiggling his upper lip when he talked, and while he listened, he stroked his beard from chin to tip, a polite grin on his face.

Master Jin was the exact opposite. He had to have been ancient, older than anyone Ronald had ever met. His hair was full and white, his skin loose and wrinkled like a Minskin cat. Master Jin was a stern, serious man, with a lifetime of battle scars to his credit. When he laughed with the others, it was a deep, rumbling laughter, almost a growl. He said little, and only nodded slightly to communicate his readiness.

Master Oda addressed Ronald. "I needn't remind you why you are here. This is a tribunal, to determine a fitting punishment for your crimes against the Order of the Golden Bonsai. Before we proceed, do you have anything to say on your behalf?" Ronald shook his head. What could he say that they didn't already know? "Very well. Master Fuma, will you please remind Mr. Hashimoto of his transgressions, as is required by Order law?"

The younger master wiggled his lip with extra vim before clearing his throat. "Mr. Ronald Hashimoto, son of Daichi Hashimoto, known to the Order of the Golden Bonsai as Shinjitsu no Yaiba—"

"Yes, yes, yes. Master Fuma, we know all of that. Need I remind you that this tribunal is significantly less formal than most? Let's skip the honorifics and whatnots, yes?"

Master Jin grunted, as if he were displeased by those very circumstances, but Master Fuma smiled and continued, unfazed.

"You are here before us today for entering another island without prior sanction, trespassing, unauthorized use of an Order-owned portal, and failure to close said portal upon entering, creating a hazardous potential for catastrophic disaster, of which you are now well aware of said disaster's possibilities. Do you understand the severity of your transgressions?"

"Yes, Master," Ronald answered, humbled.

"Good." Master Fuma stroked his beard furiously. "Good, good, good. I, well, we didn't know how receptive you'd be to this inquiry, and I seem to have lost my train of thought."

Master Jin leaned towards Ronald, a quivering frown on his face. "The threshold between our island and Shima Gōdatsusha is thin and thinning further with every moment we fail to act.

"For that reason, we had abandoned the shrine you entered with plans in motion to destroy it entirely, to sever its connection to the other islands."

Ronald shivered. He couldn't fully wrap his brain around all the implications, but he'd recently experienced firsthand just a sliver of Shima Gōdatsusha having crossed over. If that threshold were indeed to dissipate, he could only imagine the hellscape that Earth would become.

"Right, very true. But you were not in a position to know this reality," Master Fuma said. "Thus, your actions could not have been entered upon with any malicious intent. We have spoken with your mother, and with a number of other *in-good-standing* members of the Order, including Master Oda's own *daughters*." He said this last with more than a hint of scorn.

"Each has spoken highly of your potential within the Order and of your masterful understanding of combat for someone of such a young age. And, more importantly, your intentions behind crossing onto a different island without first consulting Master Oda. I am truly sorry to hear about the unfortunate circumstances that befell your family, and it is of great regret that the Order hasn't been more supportive of the Hashimoto legacy up until this point. Furthermore, one Tomo Nakajima has testified that you did indeed send him to us with a request to present your plans. In that matter, he dropped the ball. Between us four, Tomo is unparalleled as an assassin, but he's a dimwit when it comes to matters of a more delicate nature."

"He's an ass," Master Jin said bluntly. "And a moron."

Master Oda sneered. "Now, now. Tomo Nakajima is an irreplaceable asset. We are truly fortunate to have him on our side." He exchanged knowing glances with the other two masters, then turned back to Ronald. "Ronald, this tribunal has weighed your crimes and the circumstances behind them. As you are well aware, the Order takes these kinds of transgressions very seriously."

He slid out a long, clasped box shaped like an oversized, elongated guitar case and placed it on the table between them. Despite the fact that it took up the entire table and then some, Ronald hadn't noticed the box before. It was simple, unadorned, mundane. But he knew that whatever it contained was far from mundane, and contrary to his initial impression, most certainly not a Fender.

"This was crafted for your mother, before she left the Order." Master Oda unclasped the box but left its lid closed. "She never used it, and we've kept it safe for her in the hope that she may one day return."

"Open the damn case," Master Jin barked.

"The anticipation is going to send the poor boy over the edge." Master Fuma was sitting on the edge of his seat, and Ronald couldn't help but wonder if he was actually talking about himself. He was extra wiggly as he spoke.

"Right." Master Oda flipped the lid open, knocking over his own cup. Ice skittered across the coffee shop floor, over Ronald's shoes, but he hardly noticed it. He was too busy drooling at the magnificent yumi held inside the case. "Ronald Hashimoto, we offer you this gift: Mugendai, the Infinity Bow. Your mother is quite skilled in archery, as you've witnessed firsthand, and it is my hope that you possess at least a smattering of her abilities. In your hands, this bow will work wonders."

He was speechless. It had already been a strange, confusing week, but it just seemed to get weirder and harder to understand every new day. When he woke up earlier that morning, he prepared himself for the worst. Exile, death, pain of torture. He accepted his fate, no matter what the tribunal might choose. If he had a thousand opportunities, he wouldn't have guessed they'd give him such an extraordinary gift instead.

"This bow possesses endless precision, and wielded by a worthy samurai such as yourself, shall prove a vital tool in our battle against evil."

"I don't understand," he said, dumbly, too afraid to touch the yumi.

"Your punishment is simple: return to Shima Gōdatsusha, slay the Usurping Warlord, Akuma Araki, and retrieve your brother's swords. Upon successful completion of this task, backed by the full strength of the Order of the Golden Bonsai, of course, this tribunal shall consider you absolved of all wrong-doing."

The full strength of the Order? Absolved?

Ronald's head spun, but he couldn't find the breath to ask any of the innumerable questions bouncing back and forth inside it. Instead, he reached for the bow. The second his fingers brushed its polished wood, a surge of energy like nothing he'd ever felt coursed through his body. This bow, Mugendai, as Master Oda had named it, was special beyond anything of his own island.

Mugendai was *magic,* and that meant magic was real, not only in Shima Gōdatsusha but where Ronald was at that very moment. Which in turn meant his healing magic back at school, which he had been highly skeptical about in the first place, was also real.

"We may have had to permanently close the portal you used due to its instability." Master Oda looked grim for a moment. "But we have found another to repurpose. Somewhere you are quite familiar. When you enter, I am afraid Akuma Araki's grip on our island will strengthen, and we will lose our ability to keep her and her forces from crossing over. The Order of the Golden Bonsai will fight them here, once the threshold dissipates. You will fight her there, and I will accompany you as far as circumstances allow. We've weighed the possibilities, and this is the best course of action. The only course. One skilled samurai, like yourself, might be able to enter the heart of Shima Gōdatsusha undetected, with the appropriate amount of distraction, of course. *One* might be able to make his way through the keep to confront her in her inner sanctum, where she least expects to be confronted. While her forces are distracted here, by the Order, and there, by myself, you will finally be able to finish what you and your brother started.

"Are you ready, Ronald Hashimoto, to fulfill your destiny?"

Ronald still wasn't sure he believed in destiny, and he definitely didn't believe he was bound for greatness, but what choice did he have? If the Order said his punishment was Akuma Araki, someone he already had unfinished business with, he wasn't about to question it. "Fated" or not, it was time to set things right.

CHAPTER TWENTY-FIVE

"There you are." Tomo stopped pacing and snapped to attention. "What took you so long?"

Ronald squeezed through the mass of bodies. He'd never seen so many armored people in one place. If he were honest, he didn't know the Order had so many members. Monks and Samurai. Ordinary-looking folks and kitsune. Ninja, all dressed similarly to Tomo, watching him from the shadows. Che Perkins. And, of course, the three masters. There were enough people waiting on him to make his stomach churn. Since the moment he stepped into Ling's restaurant, he was fighting the urge to run and hide.

Did they know? Had all these... people heard his story, about how he failed the Order? And his brother...

They must have, the way they all turned to watch him pass. He could feel their eyes on him, judging the young samurai chosen by the Order's leaders to face off against Akuma Araki. In mid-conversation, there would be a brief, almost imperceptible pause

RONALD, THE RONIN

followed by an even briefer side-eye. They thought they were slick, these people, but Ronald knew better. He understood a blunder like his wasn't exempt from petty gossip. He just wished they weren't so obvious in their judgments of him.

Ling was there, too. At least when he caught her watching, she had the decency to smile and wave. But there was also a sadness to her. It was the forced smile of someone being made to be a stranger in their own home. Ronald waved back, truly empathizing with how she must be feeling, and then even Mrs. Ling's familiar face disappeared among the crowd of strangers.

The usual comforting smells of her restaurant were gone, replaced by too-many-people smells. Sweat, pungent body odor, freshly lacquered armor and polished steel. It was surreal, the lack of dumpling and tempura, and out of everything else, that particular change slash absence unnerved Ronald the most. If Akuma Araki could have this profound an effect on Ling's restaurant, nowhere was safe.

Then, he saw the shrine. A hodge-podge collection of tokens and mementos, flickering candles, and a single bust of Hachiman, sitting upon a scattering of dried cherry blossom petals. There was the same tanto from his family shrine, placed unceremoniously beside this new statue. If he didn't focus on it, he could still see the blood from his own palm trickling from its sharp point. Jiro's, too.

The hushed conversations around the restaurant grew into a roar, assaulting Ronald's eardrums. He could feel their voices, undoubtedly talking about him, in his temples, behind his eyes. It was too much pressure. If he didn't get away now, he was going to explode.

Ronald turned abruptly, pushed through a pair of kitsune

he didn't recognize, and all but ran out, through the restaurant's dining room, past the street-clothed Order guards sitting in booths, pretending to casually eat dinner. By the time he was out in the streets, the brisk air refreshing against his hot skin, he could hardly breathe.

He was hunched over, hands on his knees, basically hyperventilating when he heard a far-off voice. "Hey, handsome." Hikari, actually right next to him on the sidewalk. "Running away again?"

"Here to stop me if I am?"

"Nah." Her tail swished, and Ronald was honestly shocked to see it. Part of him had to have known she had one. He knew what she was, after all, but he'd never actually seen it before. "I never had a choice to run. One master or another has always held my leash. When they tug, I follow."

"Not much of a life of your own, I imagine."

Hikari shrugged, arms raised. "It's all I've ever known." She indicated her piercings and wiggled her nose. "Might explain all these, huh? Anyway, I don't know what I'd do in your position, but I'd be real tempted."

"What do you think I should do?"

"Ask yourself why you're here. What made you go back into Shima Gōdatsusha to begin with?"

"Jiro."

Hikari shook her head. "Wrong answer."

"Then it has to be Daichi."

"Bzzt." She made a sound like a game show wrong answer buzzer. "Try again."

Ronald thought long and hard. The answer seemed so simple

when he finally found it. "Me." He shuffled his feet, hands in his pockets, and sighed. "If I'm honest, I did it for me."

"*Ding, ding, ding.*" She booped him on his nose. Her finger was cold and sent shivers down his spine. "Ask yourself, if you run away now, will you be able to live with yourself? If you give up, will you ever find inner peace? Will you ever stop seeing Jiro's face when you dream? Or Daichi's ghost waving its disappointed finger at you every time you close your eyes?"

She was right. Ronald had a hard time admitting as much, but if it wasn't for how Jiro's death affected him, he wouldn't be here, would he? If it wasn't for the guilt, for the shame, Ronald would be able to live a semi-normal life. His own internal struggles pulled his leash. Like Hikari, he was a slave to a master: his own wants and desires. It was time to break that leash.

"Thanks," he said. "I'll be inside in a minute."

Hikari leaned towards him and kissed him on the cheek. He blushed, and she winked. "See you soon, handsome. We'll be ready when you're ready."

Ronald blew air between his lips and zombie-walked to the curb. Despite the cold, despite the small Order army waiting on him, he flopped down and buried his face in his hands. He knew he had to do this, but he didn't know if he could. Was he the right one for the task? He'd failed twice already, and they expected him to try a third time?

With all his other doubts, Ronald hadn't thought much about whether he could even beat Akuma Araki in a one-on-one fight. When it came down to it, he knew very little about the warlord. He knew what the Order taught him, what Daichi reiterated to Jiro and him over and over, and what he'd seen in Shima Gōdatsusha, both the real island and the island of his frequent nightmares. She had her bow, and her army, but what else? He was charging headfirst into the hardest battle of his life all but blind. What advantage could he use to seize the upper hand? What were her weaknesses? What did she fear—really fear? Because he didn't believe for a second it was him.

Eyes closed tight, he tried to imagine a route to her, through the volcano. If the rock bridge was still there, if Shima Gōdatsusha wasn't completely unrecognizable as it had been on his last visit, he could probably get back into the forge. Then what? Strongarm the smiths to allow him to take the lift to… where? Akuma's inner fortress?

The more he mentally plotted, the more insane the plan sounded. With the added pressure of those who would remain here, to fight whatever might cross the threshold, Ronald managed to bring himself back to the brink of another panic attack. But someone sat next to him, their sudden presence grounding him in the moment, their weight against his anchoring him back to earth, to stability.

"I know, I know. I'm coming," he said as he rubbed his eyes until the stars came out.

"I thought you weren't going to put yourself in danger anymore." Aubrey nudged him, and he opened his eyes to a sad, adorable smile. "Yet here you are."

"I… I don't really know what to say."

She put her arm around him, the one not in a sling at least, and rested her head on his shoulder. "It's okay. Che came and talked to me. Your mom is too cool, I almost don't believe you two are related."

"Ha! You're so funny."

She scrunched her nose. "And don't you forget it."

Once again, confronted with the unexpected, Ronald wasn't quite sure how to react. Aubrey was the last person he'd think to see here, in a place swarming with Order samurai. It was an unsettling instance of when worlds collide. His mundane life and his other-islander life crashing against each other to create a potentially beautiful—but more likely horrific—disaster.

But he was glad to see her, especially since it might be the last time.

"What are you doing here, anyway?"

She pulled away and gave him the look. "Excuse me?"

"Sorry. That didn't come out right. I'm glad you're here. I just don't understand anything anymore."

She handed him the Hashimoto heirloom he'd given her and kissed him. "You can give it back to me when you come back. I came to tell you that I think you're pretty cool. And that this bitch, this Akumani whatever her name is—"

"Akuma Araki."

"Right. Like I said, whatever her name is, she doesn't stand a chance against my Ronny Boy. You've got this."

"Thanks. Your confidence means the world." He heard his own monotone response and added, "Really. It does."

Out of the blue, she kissed him again. It was a kiss right out of a Hallmark movie, and it left him lightheaded.

"If you don't come back, I'll kick your ass."

She'd said it once before, and the second time wasn't any less convincing. He took a deep breath and steeled himself for the hardest challenge of his life. Believe it or not, it didn't feel like

Shima Gōdatsusha was even it.

Ronald excused himself, struggled not to look back as he left Aubrey on the sidewalk, and made his way through the ever-expectant onlookers inside Ling's store.

"Ah, I see you've decided to join us, Mr. Hashimoto," Master Oda said as the crowd split for him. "Hikari assured me you were coming right behind her, but an old man worries."

Ronald slipped his armor on, thanked the monks who had brought it for him without bothering to question their oddly intrusive efficiency, and secured his swords. The last thing he wanted was to hand Akuma his in addition to Jiro's. Unstrung, he slung Mugendai over his shoulder. The bow already felt comfortable, too, another extension of his body like his swords. Its magic seeped and swirled and surged within him. He embraced it for what it was and took one last deep breath to clear the doubts from his mind.

"No worries," he said. "I'm ready." *Or as ready as I'll ever be.*

"Good, good." Master Oda struck an impressive figure in his full armor. He certainly looked the part of a legend. "We sent scouts into Shima Gōdatsusha before shutting down the other shrine. Akuma Araki's forces are on the move. They've gathered en masse in the foothills and forests around her stronghold, with more pouring through the front gates as we speak."

The forests? "Are we going to enter right on top of them?"

"We've spread cherry blossom petals within the cave you and Tomo discovered. From the very same tree these petals came from." Master Oda scooped a handful of dry petals and allowed them to fall through his fingers. "If all goes according to plan, they won't know we're there until it's too late."

Ronald always assumed the cherry blossoms were more symbolic than anything. He knew how important symbols were to ritual, but he'd never bothered to ask if they played a more significant role in traversing between islands. The fact so much hinged on an object as fickle as flower petals went a long way towards further stripping his confidence. What if the cave collapsed or the petals blew into the lava or something? Would he appear in Shima Gōdatsusha buried to his neck in ash or burning to a crisp below the molten surface?

Focus. He had to focus...

"Hikari and Sakiko, along with the rest of their kind," Oda continued, with no effort to disguise the hint of disdain behind his tone, "will follow us through the shrine. They are only partially of this world, so they can move about and withstand the Out Beyond unlike any of us. They will act as our first line of defense against Akuma Araki's assault."

They are your daughters, Ronald thought. *Supposedly.*

He couldn't believe how little regard Master Oda had for their lives. He acted as if they were fodder, and his blatant disregard for Hikari and Sakiko made Ronald clench his fists. But what could he say? He had his role to play, and they did too. It wasn't his place to question a master.

"Let's get it over with," he said. *Before I completely lose my nerve.*

It was time to enter Shima Gōdatsusha and kill Akuma Araki. Not for Jiro, not for Daichi, not for the Order. It was time to end this, for Ronald and Ronald alone.

His fingers rose to his lips, and he could still feel where Aubrey had kissed him. *Well, maybe not entirely for me alone*, he thought, a giddy smile rising until his cheeks hurt.

CHAPTER TWENTY-SIX

Ronald moved through the Out Beyond with purpose. He could hear the metallic clanking of Master Oda's armor as the older man tried to keep up, but he paid him no mind. The kitsune took to the stars, becoming blurs of space dust all around him as they fell into their places, but he hardly noticed the spectacle. He was focused, determined. Up ahead, through the star burning brightest, Akuma Araki awaited.

Flares of light dripped and sputtered from the star. Reality distorted around it, faces appeared, elongated bodies, newly formed in this astral space. One took shape right beside Ronald. An oni, breaching the threshold now that they had opened it from the other side. Ronald resisted the sudden urge to draw his katana and strike the monster down. The kitsune would handle that. If not them, the Order waiting on the other side of the shrine.

Stay focused, he told himself. *You have a greater target, just ahead. You'll have your chance...*

For once in his life, Ronald wasn't anxious. His path was clear. There weren't a thousand different possibilities for every decision he made. Staring into Shima Gōdatsusha's star, his life boiled down to two simple realities.

Either Akuma Araki was going to die. Or Ronald Hashimoto.

One way or another, this part of his story would be over.

His insides twisted and throbbed as he dematerialized into the star. His vision became a tunnel of twinkling light, followed by blackness, then the gray of that familiar cave. The rocky ground came fast, and he touched down with enough force to buckle his legs. He rolled forward with an *oof* and sprang up, katana ready. Remembering what Tomo had said, he sheathed it for his wakizashi. There was no telling what, or who, he might encounter in the tunnels leading to the forge.

Master Oda appeared shortly thereafter, as disoriented and confused as Tomo had been. It made Ronald wonder if he was the Order's official unofficial expert of Out Beyond travel. He dismissed the notion as ridiculous and helped Master Oda steady himself.

"Thank you, son," the old master said. "It's been a long, long time since I left our island. This is not a sensation I have missed."

Son. Until recently, it was a word he hardly ever heard used in reference to himself. Now, he was everyone's son it seemed, and more and more people were vying for his affections. Was this what being famous entailed? Was he *actually* famous? He dismissed the notion as ridiculous. Clout was the last thing he needed to worry about.

"I'm starting to like it," he joked.

"You must be a glutton for misery, then." Master Oda fiddled with his seam and straightened his helmet. "Are you ready to do what must be done?"

"I am, Master."

"When the time is right, you must not hesitate."

"How will I know?"

Master Oda lifted his faceplate and gave Ronald an exaggerated, almost silly wink. "Oh, you'll know. Or you aren't paying attention."

At that, the old master swirled into a golden ball of light before winking out of existence. There was no other way to describe it, and his sudden disappearance threw Ronald completely off guard. A wave of hot energy struck him from the epicenter of where Master Oda once stood, striking Ronald like a hammer, knocking him back a step. A gust of wind passed near his feet and ended in a brief tornado of dust. Then, the cave fell completely silent, still.

"Uh, Master Oda?" Ronald peeked around, knowing full well the old master wasn't hiding behind a rock. "Hello?"

He was answered by a sudden rumbling and cascade of debris from the ceiling. Beyond the cave, muffled by layers of sediment, came a loud screech, like that of a falcon. Ronald staggered to the cave's entrance and ducked out to face whatever had made that awful sound. What he saw took his breath away.

Akuma Araki's troops were swarming from the depths of her fortress. They were everywhere: scaling the cliffs, crossing the massive land bridge from the fortress's entrance to the edge of the nearby forest, packed into tight formations along the ledge. Whatever made that sound had their undivided attention, and they were moving more like one massive organism than hundreds of thousands of individual bodies.

A long shadow flashed across the lava, expanding and

transforming to fill crags as it climbed the cliff. There came that horrible screech again, louder this time. Loud enough Ronald had to cover his ears.

Then, he saw the lithe, streaking body, an arrow screaming through the sky, and the plume of gray, crown-like horns upon the dragon's head appeared as it dipped towards the oozing mass of Akuma Araki's army. It was a wingless, twisting creature with thick, overlapping golden scales, much like the plates of a samurai's armor, and it shimmered with tendrils of magical energy that dissipated in its wake. It took him a moment to process what he was seeing, but when he finally realized the dragon's true nature, he chuckled to himself.

"Master Oda, you are full of surprises, aren't you?"

When the master let out a third screech, fire erupted from his toothy beak, scorching the ledge and inciting panic among those gathered alongside the forest's edge.

"Woo, baby!" Ronald yelled, elated.

He clapped and cheered as Master Oda circled back to unleash another deadly volley of fireballs. Even from down in the ravine, Ronald could hear the panicked, pained skittering of dying insects. They scattered, swarmed, and one thing was very clear: all of Akuma Araki's eyes were on the golden dragon.

There was no doubt in his mind. It was his time to shine.

He slithered through the tunnel in silence, ready around every corner for whatever he might meet. But the way to the forge was clear, exactly as it had been when he'd trekked the tunnels with Tomo. He hadn't needed his short sword after all, but he felt a little more secure as he navigated ever closer towards his destination. For that, Ronald supposed, he had Tomo to thank. If any stalagmites had jumped out at him, he would have been ready.

The forge itself was another story. Despite Akuma Araki's army being on the move, her smiths were as busy as ever. They worked around each other in choreographed chaos, building new arms and armor, repairing broken swords and axes, pounding out dented armor plates. Beyond the caldera, four bipedal, elephant-like beasts of burden stood idle.

He considered stealth, but he didn't know how much time he had. He also didn't think it would matter at this point with the very foundations of the fortress trembling beneath Master Oda's assault.

The moment he dropped from the ledge, the smiths stopped to inspect the intruder. A tense moment passed, then most of them returned to their work, uninterested. But a dozen or so took up arms, one even wielding a sword hot off the forge, its jagged blade glowing red. Ronald raised his sword, reluctantly readying himself for a fight.

The first to attack was a brute of a creature, half its face covered in scarred, gray scales. Whatever the chitinous skin was, it continued along its side, leading to several thick spines on its back. It moved sluggishly yet with purpose, a crescent-tipped sword as thick as Ronald's torso held high over its lulling head.

Ronald blocked its initial clumsy blow and struck it across its chest with the flat side of his katana. The smith stumbled, nearly stepping on Ronald's foot which would have surely flattened his bones. While it was off balance, he slammed into it with his shoulder, knocking it back into a couple of others.

How long, he wondered, would he be able to continue delaying the inevitable? Bloodshed was only a matter of when. Yet, these poor creatures were almost too pathetic to kill. For a while, he drove them back with nonlethal attacks, but he was tiring fast and wasting a lot of time. Too much time. He turned his blade inward, sharp edge poised to strike, as the scaly smith approached again. It swung its sword over its head like a helicopter as it trampled towards him.

A deep, guttural, almost snorting bark echoed throughout the forge. All at once, the attacking smiths stopped, including Scales. Ronald lowered his katana, breath ragged, but he didn't fully drop his guard.

The familiar, pig-like creature he'd saved from the insects stepped to the forefront of the defenders, holding a large hammer in one hand. It was the same creature, there was no doubt in his mind, and it had a vestige of recognition on its face as it approached without fear. It vocalized a series of snorts and barks while waving its stubby arms all over the place, and then the smith bowed and held up its hands to Ronald.

"I'm sorry, I don't understand what you're saying." He shook his head, and the smith barked with renewed vigor. Slowly, enunciating with what he hoped were the right hand motions, Ronald continued, "I didn't come to hurt you. Akuma Araki? Can you help me get to Akuma Araki?" He pointed up into the shadow-shrouded upper levels of the fortress.

The smith tilted its head one way, then the other, grunting, its wide, wet nostrils flaring. Finally, it looked to the lift sitting dormant a few hundred feet above the platform. It wheezed as it produced a small horn from its side. The sudden and surprisingly deep blast startled Ronald. A loud *pop* responded, followed by sliding chains and a trumpeting from the four beasts of burden.

They eased into circular motion, and the lift began its descent, much, much larger and sturdier than the one Ronald had seen before.

Before he could refuse its help, the smith grabbed Ronald by his arm and herded him towards the platform. As they passed its scaly counterpart, which was still struggling to its feet, Ronald shrugged a half-hearted apology. Despite the language barrier, he could tell the fallen creature didn't accept his apology. His escort all but shoved him onto the lift the moment it stopped descending, pointed upward, and made excited stabbing gestures with its hammer.

"That's the plan," Ronald said, but any elaboration was cut off by another blow of the smith's horn.

The lift lurched as the beasts changed direction, setting Ronald's final ascent towards the unknown in motion. Somewhere high above him, Akuma Araki awaited. Did she know he was coming for her? Would she be ready for him if... *when* he found her? Or would he be able to catch her off guard and end this quickly? Only time could tell, and time seemed to stop completely as he rose higher and higher until the volcano's boiling caldera was nothing but an orange blip far, far below.

Ronald's grip tightened on his sword, and he counted the seconds as his heart raced.

You got this, Ronald. Ain't nothin' to it... It's kill or be killed now. That's all that's left...

CHAPTER TWENTY-SEVEN

The lift lurched to a stop. Ronald couldn't help but look over the edge, fully expecting to succumb to vertigo before he could even step into Akuma Araki's fortress proper, but what he saw was too dark and too deep to fathom. It was hard to believe he came from somewhere down there—*far* down there—and an impossible reach of comprehension to assume he'd ever return to the forge. Or home, for that matter. But the unknown ahead seemed even more daunting, even further away.

He followed a rocky, inclined path towards the fortress's apex. At first, the walls were smooth and plain. Then, they began to give way to hive-like structures—honeycombed alcoves that stretched as far as the eye could see. Inside the hives, he could hear skittering and scratching. On his tiptoes, he peered into one. Back there, beyond where he could reach, there came a perpetual, squelching movement. A set of eyes, maybe. Antennae probing, chitinous legs prodding.

In another hole, he found a cluster of blue-green eggs clinging to the walls and ceiling. They pulsed, veins throbbing inside their semi-transparent shells. He'd learned the hard way what hatched from those eggs, and he had no desire to face any more insects. Still, Ronald clung tighter to his sword and thanked his luck trypophobia wasn't one of his many mental health issues.

The circular path went on forever. Gradually, the incline became steeper, the plain, flat walls less numerous. He passed large corridors, likely sleeping quarters for Akuma Araki's troops by the stone slabs patterned throughout, and ducked beneath a pair of low arches that gave way to a massive chamber. Inside, there were natural vents, repurposed as cooking stoves. Embers burned in hearths. A pair of cooks, similar creatures to the smiths far below, moved about the room. By the looks of it, they were clearing away one feast in preparation for the next. It was hard to imagine two cooks could keep an entire army fed, and Ronald briefly wondered how many other kitchens there were like this one, how many innumerable slabs for weary warriors.

As he continued upward, he wished he had some idea of the fortress's layout. His best guess was up, and that wasn't much to go off. But weren't all final showdowns at the top of castles? Didn't rulers watch from those high places as their plans unfurled, out of harm's way? Trope: it was all he had, and he supposed it was better than nothing. Thanks, sophomore English class and countless deep-dives into fantasy and science fiction pop-culture.

A series of stalagmites and stalactites like broken teeth lined the edge of an outcropping along the outer wall. Natural windows, the rock formations gave Ronald a bird's eye view of the great bridge that spanned the lava moat around the fortress, and an even better view of Master Oda's slender body as he glided past. The dragon was riddled with arrows and broken spears. Countless scales were either shattered or peeling, and the master's flight was sluggish, strained.

From the bridge, a cluster of faceless warriors were busy firing a hail of arrows the master's way. Ronald slipped Mugendai from his back, strung the bow, and nocked an arrow, one of eight resting in the quiver at his side. He was no brilliant marksman, but he had to do something. Even a dragon could only take so much damage before it could no longer fly. He pulled the arrow back, let loose, and watched as it whistled downward, straight for an archer in the middle of nocking its own arrow.

Ronald reached for a second and a third, and both arced downward with precise trajectory, finding their marks just as their victims were about to fire. He loosed the remaining arrows in his quiver, each finding its mark, and managed to kill five more soldiers. From such a height, it was almost unthinkable that any found their mark, yet alone every single shot. The bow was magic, he reminded himself. In hindsight, he just wished he'd brought more arrows.

Subconsciously, he reached for his hip only to find his quiver was full again. One by one, he felt eight new, pristine feathers. His heart fluttered, and the sheer brilliance of Mugendai's magic overwhelmed him. From his high vantage point, he released arrow after arrow upon the bridge until it was fully cleared of attackers. Then, he unstrung the incredible bow and hoped he had at least bought Master Oda—and himself—enough time.

Near the threshold of the forest, small, circular portals like stars were beginning to appear. Those troops near the front lines not dealing with their sudden dragon problem were approaching the stars, blinking away—through the Out Beyond. There, they'd face Hikari and Sakiko, but how long could a small group of kitsune fend off an entire army? How long until Akuma Araki cleared the way to her ultimate goal?

To my world, he realized with mounting horror. To everything and everyone he'd ever loved. Che. DJ and Robert. Aubrey. Even Tomo, who he'd never officially thought of as a friend until that moment. His computer. His music. His entire pantheon of heroes. There was more at stake here than just his life or Akuma's.

Ronald took one last look at the chaos below before taking off at a dead sprint. He'd wasted too much time gawping, and he could be of no more help from atop the fortress.

Besides a number of servants, who either scampered away from him or ignored him completely, the fortress was all but deserted. The warlord's forces were all out, it seemed. Maybe this would be easier than he had initially thought.

Then, he came to a wide corridor that ended with a large archway barred by massive, ornamental wooden doors. They were four or five times his height, stretched from floor to ceiling. Two torches at either end of the corridor flickered brightly, casting sinister shadows on the polished stone around them. Even from a distance, he could feel their immense heat. Sweat trickled down his back from his neck.

Along either wall, all-too-familiar red-armored samurai stood at attention. At first, they pretended not to notice him and remained statue-still, but when he stepped out from the entrance, they turned as one, their demon facemasks twisted into menacing, fanged smiles. Ten in total. Ten katanas reflecting torch light as they were drawn in unison. Ten warriors between him and what was undoubtedly Akuma Araki's chambers. Ten before Ronald Hashimoto embraced Death: Akuma Araki's or otherwise.

He held his katana out before him, slid one foot slightly back. *Ten warriors... One Ronald.* He wasn't a brilliant mathematician or anything, but those odds weren't stacked in his favor.

What would Daichi say? *When the odds are stacked against you, embrace Death. Know that you are already dead, and then use that knowledge to your advantage.*

Ronald practically snorted. His made-up Daichi-esque proverb honestly wasn't too far-fetched from the nonsense he'd heard growing up.

He tried to picture what Jiro would have done. The answer came easily: Jiro would have trusted his instincts. He would have thrown himself into battle, undeterred by the dozens of different scenarios running through Ronald's mind, and he would have fought to his last breath, knowing who was waiting for him on the other side of that great door.

Ronald inhaled sharply and closed his eyes. Even sightless, he could see the hazy silhouettes of the samurai as they approached, where their next steps were going to be, who would come at him first. They were shadows, distilled in his mind's eye by their subtle movements—the beating of their hearts, the exhalations of their breath, the minute twitching of their muscles. He could hear their muffled footsteps, their ragged breaths through their face masks, his own heartbeat in his chest, a drum heralding the beginning of his final showdown.

The first came suddenly, but Ronald was prepared. Eyes still closed, he stepped aside and blocked the samurai's slash with the flat side of his katana. Momentum carried his attacker past Ronald.

As the samurai struggled to recover his balance, Ronald's sword flashed. Blood splattered on the wall, and the odds became one better in Ronald's favor.

Two came at once now, and Ronald wove between them, barely avoiding a blade across the back of his shoulders. He rolled out of reach, springing up beside a fourth, blade slicing in an upward motion.

Ronald charged, just aware enough of the two samurai approaching from behind to keep ahead of them, and cut one way, then the other. His first cut found flesh. The second rebounded off metal, the clanging of steel on steel ringing in his ears. He ignored the numbness in his hands to finish off the wounded samurai before him.

He didn't stay in place long enough for a follow up. Instead, he leapt forward, nearly to Akuma Araki's door, and spun on his heels. He whipped around just in time to slap away one slash, another, a third. Despite the samurai's onslaught, Ronald gave no ground. He held firm, anticipated every new attack, and ignored the throbbing soreness developing in his shoulders, triceps, and forearms. If he could only find the right moment... There! The samurai hesitated, and Ronald drove his katana forward in a smooth, lightning-fast stab. His opponent's weapon clanged on the stone floor as he staggered back, clutching the wound in his stomach.

Ronald flicked his sword to the side, splattering blood on the floor. At his back, torches flickered. It felt as if they might singe the hair on his neck, but the warmth eased the growing tension in his shoulders.

Two rushed him, swords at the ready behind them. Ronald waited until the last moment before dodging one way then the other. They didn't fall for his feint this time. He managed to avoid a low slash from one, but the other caught Ronald across the side with the tip of his katana. He winced in pain, resisted reaching for the wound. Warm blood was already beginning to spread down his leg, but there wasn't anything he could do about it, yet.

Kill or be killed. Then, you can worry about your wounds.

A muffled screech exploded through the corridor. The keep rumbled, Master Oda having his fun with Akuma's remaining troops, no doubt. While the samurai were distracted by the sudden quake, Ronald struck fast. Two more fell, but the battle was far from won.

When he moved for his next opponent, a shooting pain exploded up his torso. He staggered, nearly losing his footing and his sword at the same time. The samurai took advantage of his vulnerability and sent him sliding back with a boot to his forehead. A rim of red pulsed across Ronald's vision, and he fought hard for consciousness. He was woozy, disoriented, and far from sure-footed as his vision ebbed.

Instinct told him to raise his sword. He listened. Metal clanged, and he temporarily lost feeling from his wrist to his elbow. He raised his sword again and somehow managed to block another attack. And another. But he couldn't grip his katana any longer. It flew out of his hand, disappearing in the blackness beyond his waning peripheral vision.

He drew his short sword and all but fell forward into his attacker. The blade plunged into flesh, and the two warriors toppled together. Ronald stabbed again and again until he finally felt the samurai go limp. He wrenched the dead man's katana from his fingers. It felt awkward and unwieldy, nothing like Ronald's own. It was heavier, longer, but it was better than nothing.

The fortress rocked again, and Ronald grabbed for the wall to remain upright. He'd lost track of the remaining guards, and now that his vision was returning and the nausea was beginning to subside, he frantically scanned his surroundings to find them. Two were approaching from the side. The last was holding back, as if he were watching to see what happened next before joining the fray, keeping himself between Ronald and the exit.

Three left, Ronald thought.

And then there was Akuma Araki herself. He wasn't sure he could take on three more samurai, yet alone their shogun. He was gassed, in pain, and likely bleeding out as the battle dragged on. How much more wear and tear could his body handle before he could no longer fight?

Ronald dug deep, though he wasn't sure what he was digging for. He didn't have anything left. But whatever it was, he needed to bring it out. And fast.

"I need you, Jiro. Now more than ever."

At first, no answer came. He realized the only times his brother had come to speak with him, Jiro had initiated the conversation. Could he call upon him now, in this time of his greatest need?

"Please..." His chest heaved, lungs hurting from exertion as he tried to bring oxygen into them. The pain in his side was excruciating, and he could feel the blood trickling down the back of his leg. "Jiro, where are you?"

Then, his brother's voice came. It sounded like a gently plucked koto.

The thing is you don't. You don't need me at all, and you never did.

"But you pushed me to be better. I would be nothing without you."

That's not even slightly true. You kept me human, from becoming our father. You were always his favorite, you know? That's why he was so hard on me. Because he knew that you would turn out okay, in the end, that you would be better than both of us one day. You didn't need his guidance nearly as much as I did.

Ronald laughed out loud. Two parts manic, one part hysterical. The approaching samurai stopped in their tracks. He didn't know if he bought it, but it was a nice thought. Daichi, believing in him? That was the funniest joke he'd ever heard.

"What are you waiting for?" Ronald asked, still stifling laughter. He threw his borrowed katana to the floor, knelt to replace it with his own. *Hello, old friend.* "Don't you have a tyrant to defend?" he yelled.

They hesitated, looking to each other to make the first move. Then, they both came at him, shouting warriors' eulogies, and he struck them down without pleasure.

Ronald glared at the last samurai, chest heaving. He waited, expecting his foe to come at him recklessly like the rest of them, but the samurai held back, content to stare at Ronald through his black mask—lifeless, lacking emotion. The exact opposite of how Ronald felt in that moment.

"Even if you strike me down," the samurai said, his voice deep and seeming to come from everywhere all at once, "do you think you stand a chance against my master?"

Ronald didn't respond. He rolled his wrist, adjusted his grip on his sword.

"We are too great in number. We've invaded your island. It's too late, young samurai. No matter what happens here today, you have failed once more. Akuma Araki's revenge is in motion." *Revenge?* What could he possibly mean by her *revenge?* "I was there, you know?"

Ronald growled. He had a feeling he knew where this was leading, but he took the bait anyway. "And where's that?"

"You'll die just like your brother. If not by my blade, by the Shogun's."

At that, the tenth was done talking. He moved faster than the rest, zigzagging down the hallway towards Ronald. When Ronald struck out, the samurai faded from existence, only to reappear directly behind him. Ronald twisted to one side, narrowly avoiding what surely would have been a deadly blow and spun to face the samurai. But he was gone again, coming once more from behind at a blinding pace, moving like a whisper through the breeze.

Ronald feinted, showing a forward slash with his katana. The samurai blinked away again as Ronald bent at the knees and stabbed backwards, the blunt side of his blade guided along the armor protecting his torso. He met resistance. A thin metal plate. Leather straps. Flesh. And then bone.

Ten, Ronald thought.

It was only a number, right? But he'd just taken ten lives. He had ten fingers stained with blood. He'd faced ten skilled samurai alone and came out the victor. He was ten steps closer to Destiny.

CHAPTER TWENTY-EIGHT

An arrow split the massive doors, showering Ronald with splinters. The shaft passed close enough he could feel a slight breeze and stuck to its feathers in the far wall. In thick, skillfully masoned stone, no less. If he hadn't been so terrified, his jaw might have dropped.

A million images flashed back into Ronald's mind. Jiro's face as he drifted away. Ronald's mad scramble up the hillside. Tomo glaring at him after he put both their lives at risk.

Then, a second arrow followed the first, but it wasn't nearly as close this time. On the other side of the doors, he could hear Akuma Araki laughing, mocking him.

Ronald pushed through the splintered entryway and stepped into the large, circular room that was Akuma's chamber. It was lined with torches and sets of red and black samurai armor. A large oak table sat in the middle, a rolled parchment half spread across its surface. On the other side of the table, there was a sunken space containing several weapon racks and training dummies. It was as sparse a war room as he'd ever seen.

Akuma Araki, herself, stood tall beside the table, a smug almost playful cock to her stance. She unstrung her yumi as Ronald approached, unfazed and unrushed. Despite its mass, she was able to bend it with ease as if it were nothing more than a twig.

"I knew they'd send somebody," she said. "But I didn't think it would be a child."

Ronald swished his katana side to side in front of him, rage swelling. He glanced down at Jiro's swords, still strapped to her belt, and bared his teeth.

"Don't you remember me?"

"A whelp? No, I can't say that I do. Are you the best the Order has to challenge me? I know it's not what it once was, but I have to say, I'm a little offended. All these years, and the devils send you to finish what they started?"

"It was always going to be me." Underneath all her blustering, he sensed something. Hesitancy? Forced bravado? Whatever it was, she hid it well. "And I think you've known it, too." Ronald held his katana out to one side. Torchlight flickered off its shiny, blood-slicked blade. "Whatever's between you and the Order is between you and the Order. I'm here for my brother."

A glint of recognition showed in her eyes. Though he couldn't see most of her face behind her mask, he could tell she was smiling a wicked, self-satisfied smile.

"I do remember you." She gently laid her bow across the table, hand moving to Jiro's swords. "You came with that other child all those years ago. My, but you've barely aged a day, and here I am, an old warrior with such little time left to leave her legacy."

Akuma Araki began to draw Jiro's katana but stopped halfway, allowing the blade to drop back into its sheath. She wagged her finger at Ronald and clicked her teeth.

"No, no, no. That won't do. I couldn't kill you with your own brother's sword. That would make me *evil,* wouldn't it? And in time, you would see, Ronald Hashimoto"—she *did* know who he was!—"that I am not the bad guy in this story. It's a shame you won't be alive to see how it ends, to find out who the real villains are."

She shrugged off her cloak and revealed a naginata even longer than her yumi. She brought it around in a flourish and dropped the end of its haft hard onto the stone floor as her cloak fluttered into a messy pile beside her. Its thick blade looked sharp enough to cut diamond, and she had maneuvered it as if it weighed less than a feather.

Ronald gulped. He'd never faced anyone skilled with a naginata before, and it was clear Akuma Araki had skill to spare. Daichi ran both him and his brother through their paces and taught them the best counters to defend against the long-reaching weapon, but a wooden replica was much different than the real deal. With her naginata, the warlord could strike him dead before he could get anywhere near her. If only he had Tomo's shuriken or Mugendai still strung, but it was far too late for what-ifs. Besides, he wasn't thrilled about the proposal of going up against her yumi in a close-quarters shootout.

He had to move quickly or he was in for a long fight, so in a few swift steps he closed the gap between them. To Ronald, it was the fastest he'd ever pressed an attack. To Akuma Araki, he might as well have been slogging through thick tar.

She brought her spear in an upward arc, knocking Ronald's katana aside. She jabbed once, twice, three times, crying out as she executed each new attack. She jabbed so fast that the sharp blade became a silver blur. Ronald wove from side to side to narrowly avoid decapitation, but she was relentless. A short sweep came from the left. A flurry of smaller, wobbly cuts from the right. More jabs. Ronald darted from foot to foot, flashed his katana in desperation to send aside each new potential death blow. She worked him back, away from the table, towards the door, and it required all his strength and focus to simply stay alive.

Akuma swung her naginata around her waist, bringing its blade around her body, and leaned back, well out of reach of Ronald's sword. She was calm, collected, barely even breathing hard despite the bulk of her weapon and the furious onslaught of her attacks.

Ronald, on the other hand, was gassed and beginning to weaken from blood loss. He glanced down at his side and winced. Blood continued to run down his leg and the entire side of his armor along his ribs was stained a reddish brown.

"You're not done already, are you?" Akuma Araki mocked. "I was just starting to have fun. It's been so long since I've faced another samurai one on one like this, even if you are just a *whelp*."

You need to get in close. Jiro's voice. *Do you remember when I dueled Father? Naginata versus katana.*

Ronald shook his head. He couldn't remember anything right now. He could barely keep his eyes open.

When I moved in close, inside the reach of its bladed end, I pulled my short sword. He called it dishonorable, slapped me around for not following the Way, or whatever. But I won. That's all that really mattered.

An image came to mind: Jiro on the ground, lip bloody, arms raised against an enraged Daichi. He could see Jiro's practice wakizashi on the other side of the room, broken in half, could see the sheer fear on Jiro's face. Ronald had missed the incident, but it all made sense now. Daichi hadn't been furious with Jiro because of honor or the samurai way. He'd been mad because Jiro had beaten him, the legendary samurai Shinjitsu no Yaiba, the Blade of Truth.

Go ahead, son. It's not cheating if it leads to victory. Daichi's voice? It was actually Daichi's voice, and Ronald suddenly felt light and giddy. *Stick that blade between her ribs, and feel no remorse for the ruse. I was only mad because I knew my sons were surpassing me.*

I love you, son. You can do this... You were born to face her.

At that, Daichi's voice faded away, and Ronald knew he would never hear it again. Nor Jiro's, once the deed was done. One way or another. Blood or blood.

Ronald resisted the urge to check his wakizashi. Instead, he feigned exhaustion, which wasn't too difficult considering he could hardly lift his sword, and limped towards Akuma Araki. Still as undisturbed water, she let him come. In her mind, she was confident that she already had him beat—exactly what Ronald wanted her to think.

The moment he got within her reach, the naginata flashed towards him. He darted forward, between its bladed end and the shogun. She slapped at him with the weapon's shaft, but he managed to slow its momentum with the edge of his katana just enough that the blow didn't knock him off his feet. Even so, he grunted under the impact, his ribs screaming. She'd hit him directly above his wound, and it was the worst pain he'd ever felt, but he had to push through. *Just a little longer...*

He feinted a killing slash with his katana. Akuma Araki anticipated it, brought her naginata down with the intent to block it and send him tumbling. The moment its handle touched his sword, he let go, reached for his sash, and thrust with all the energy he had left.

The shogun let out a raspy, wet exhalation and stumbled backwards into the table, her weapon clattering on the ground. She looked down at the wound in disbelief. Blood seeped through her armor. She grasped at it in a pathetic attempt to staunch the fatal wound, before falling to her knees. Her helmet tumbled off her head, that grim faceplate smacking stone beside her, revealing a face haunted by burn scars and years of untempered hatred.

Ronald approached, scooping up his katana and sheathing it in one fluid motion. She gazed at him, eyes wide and wet. Her face was pallid, scars covering almost every inch of exposed skin. He pushed her back with a boot to her shoulder, and she flopped like a ragdoll. She gurgled something to him as he untied Jiro's swords with shaky hands, but he refused to listen to whatever it was she had to say.

She forced the issue, reaching up and grabbing him by one of his chest plates. Even in death, her strength was immense as she pulled him down to face her.

"You... must..." She choked and began coughing. When she composed herself enough to speak again, she was pale, eyes running with tears. "Understand, Hashimoto, that not everything is as it seems. The Order... You must not..."

Ronald strained to hear what she had to say. The deed was done, and there was no harm in hearing her dying words, was there?

"Prophecy is a funny thing, is it not? Look at you, a child of

Shima Gōdatsusha. I was right to fear you, and they were so, so wrong. It's going to be you, Ronald Hashimoto. You—not me—that brings chaos to..."

"No..." Ronald said. She was wrong. He couldn't be the one... could he? "Why do you hate the Order so much?"

Akuma smiled a sad smile, a thin line of blood trickling from the corner of her lips. She slumped, scooting back until she rested against one of the table's legs.

"They came for me. For us. They burned our villages, slaughtered my friends and family." At this, she choked, and Ronald helped her sit upright until the coughing stopped. "All because of your little prophecy."

"I... I'm sorry. But I don't believe you."

Akuma chuckled until her coughing returned, and then she grabbed Ronald by one of his armor's straps and brought him close. Face to face, he could see the pain in her infinitely deep eyes. The truth.

"Believe or do not believe, I think you know it's true. But it's over now. You've got what you came for, and the Order of the Golden Bonsai will burn. Go, take what you've earned, and let me rest."

At that, she forced Ronald's short sword into his hand. He struggled against her, but despite life draining from her veins, there was still a preternatural strength to the fallen warlord. She clasped his wrist, smiled one last time, and forced him to plunge the blade into her chest, right into her heart.

As her body went slack, Ronald couldn't help but think back to his time with Che Perkins in the Shogunate, their brief conversation about the story of Princess Takiyasha. Was Akuma

Araki the princess? Had she been driven to do the awful things she did, to raise a literal skeletal army, under the twisted guise of revenge against some perceived slight against her?

No, she was evil. Plain and simple. He had been justified in slaying her, in reclaiming what rightfully belonged to his family. The warlord had killed his brother, after all. She deserved what she got... didn't she?

He shook the second-guessing out of his mind. It was finally over. Ronald Hashimoto had slayed the usurper of Shima Gōdatsusha. He had avenged his brother, brought honor back to his family. More importantly, he had proven to himself he could do it, for himself. His way, without a master breathing down his neck, without being constrained by their rules and regulations.

Ronald was officially freed from all his bonds, and in that moment, with the dead samurai warlord lying in his lap, he was too overwhelmed by emotions to even begin to process what that freedom truly entailed.

Now, he just needed to figure out how to get back home, how to deal with all those other simple, real-world problems. Even after defeating one of the greatest warlords of his time, the prospect of going back to being a normal teenager scared the hell out of him.

CHAPTER TWENTY-NINE

Ronald's ears were starting to ring. He was too close, this was too personal, and he had stayed quiet for far too long. With a deep breath, he cleared his mind and closed his eyes to collect his thoughts. He had to tread lightly here. His next move might be the most important move of his entire life.

"You can't be serious," he said, his eyes blinking slowly, condescendingly open. "Lil Wayne? The GOAT? Man, you must be drinkin' some kind of Kool-Aid."

Skylar shrugged. "Name a rapper more iconic, who spits like Weezy spits. My man doesn't even write out his songs. He's just lyrically blessed."

"His lyrics don't even make sense!" Ronald clenched his fists. This was too much. "More iconic, you say? How about, I don't know, Nas, KRS-One, Tupac, Biggie, Kool G Rap, the whole of Wu-Tang. Man, I'm just scratching the surface here."

"*You know I'm on the grass,*" Aubrey recited, "*don't cut on the sprinklers*. Yeah, lyrically blessed, alright." Ronald could almost taste the sarcasm on her tongue as she chided Skylar's taste in music.

"Haters gon' hate," Skylar said. "A tale as old as time."

"Fine, I'll admit, if I want to listen to a Smurf sing about private parts and cash money, there's worse choices out there."

"Talkin' newer-ish school, though," DJ chimed in, "what about Kendrick, Cole, Yeezy?"

Skylar clicked his tongue. "A dozen albums, all certified gold or better? And then some. Nearly three hundred singles, featured with *countless*, I mean countless, big shots. GOAT. I'm tellin' you."

Ronald pinched the bridge of his nose and shook his head. He couldn't believe what he was hearing. The school year was nearly over, and this was his official first meeting with Normal Community's Hip-Hop club. He agreed to sit out from a leadership role this year—the least he could do after blowing up at his friends earlier—but he never promised to keep his mouth shut. Especially to defend the integrity of the music he loved so much.

"Freakin'. Lil. Wayne," he said to himself. He'd leave it at that. For now.

Mr. Mendez cracked his knuckles, and his chair squeaked as he stood up. For most of the meeting, he'd been patiently soaking it all in. It was apparent he could also no longer sit idly by while Skylar sullied the genre's good name.

"You're both nuts," he said. "I could name about a dozen West Coast heavy hitters more talented than any of the fools and pretenders you've mentioned."

"Psh." DJ rolled his eyes. "Only millennials like West Coast rap anymore. Sit down with that, Mr. M."

RONALD, THE RONIN

"Hey, now, no need to make this generational. I could have said Run DMC or Sugarhill Gang, you know?"

"Ew," Aubrey said. "You're so *old*."

That elicited a round of giggling, and Mr. Mendez took his seat again, humbled but grinning ear to ear.

In the back, Robert set his headphones on his desk and cleared his throat. "I think what we're learning here is that music is subjective and this conversation is pointless."

"Oh yeah?" Mr. Mendez said. "And who, might I ask, is *your* favorite, Mr. Polson?"

Robert looked from Ronald to DJ, Aubrey to Skylar, then back to their staff sponsor. A rare smile stretched across his face, part devious, part giddy sincerity.

"Gojira, right now. Tomorrow? I don't know. Maybe Deftones or Godsmack. T-Swift on a Tuesday, depending on how I'm feeling."

The room went silent for several uncomfortable moments before everyone, Robert included, started cracking up. Ronald laughed until tears came, and then the small chosen group enjoyed the last half hour of the club meeting swapping favorite songs and playfully picking on each other's taste in music. To Ronald, it was perfect. He couldn't think of any better way to spend a Wednesday afternoon than analyzing Del the Funky Homosapien lyrics, breaking down the differences between good ole American hip-hop and British grime, and comparing the careers of T.I., Rick Ross, and Nelly, among other early-2000s giants. If the sheer number of names dropped that day didn't put respect on the genre's name, nothing would. He'd just have to get comfortable with the fact he would never discover every single artist, but he would certainly try.

"Speaking of lyrical geniuses," DJ said, "next week's meeting will focus on the lyrics of one of my personal votes for GOAT: Aesop Rock. Specifically, we'll be taking a look at *The Impossible Kid*."

"Pssh." Skylar waved DJ off. "Rock is great and all, but his lyrics just aren't accessible. How can you be the Greatest of All Time if most people can't understand a word you're saying?"

Aubrey snorted. "*Most* people named Skylar, maybe."

"Hey, now." Mr. Mendez perked up from behind his desk. "Remember, this is supposed to be a safe space for us to discuss what we all love. Let's call it a day here, before things get out of hand."

"Great!" Aubrey said in a huff. She glared at Skylar as he packed his stuff. "Sounds fine to me."

Ronald dapped DJ, Robert, and Skylar up, the three other boys going their own separate ways. Then, he put his arm around Aubrey's waist and they walked towards the classroom's door together.

"Ahem." Mr. Mendez was side-eyeing them, one eyebrow raised to his hairline. "Need I remind you young lovebirds of the school's PDA policy?"

Aubrey planted a kiss on Ronald's cheek, grabbed his hand, and ushered him out of the classroom as fast as she could, ignoring Mr. Mendez's reproach from the doorway. Ronald's heart fluttered as they ran down the hallway, and he realized that everything was finally going to be okay.

RONALD, THE RONIN

"Pass me another slice of cheese, would ya?"

Ronald flipped the Dominos box open and peeled another slice free from what little was left. He tossed it across the table, and it landed half on and half off Che's plate. She rolled her eyes before digging in.

Tomo polished off his second non-alcoholic beverage of the night, a good ole Sprite, and let out a belch that immediately filled the room with the stench of tomato sauce. Since the fall of Daichi, Ronald just couldn't stomach booze in his house—and it was *his* house now, wasn't it?—and luckily neither his mother nor the assassin had any problem with that decision.

"Gross, man." Ronald plugged his nose and glared at Tomo. "Seriously?"

Aubrey giggled as Che kicked Tomo underneath the table. He jolted, knees banging the bottom and nearly spilling Ronald's drink. He cleared his throat. "Erm, I'm sorry. I mean, excuse me."

They all laughed as the assassin stumbled for the right words. It was almost like they were a real family, and Ronald couldn't help but smile. A weird family, maybe, but a family nonetheless.

Across the table, Aubrey winked and blew him a kiss.

Che made a gagging sound. "Get a room, you two."

Aubrey's eyes got big and her eyebrows raised almost to the center of her forehead in mock shock. "Can we really?"

"Absolutely. Not," Tomo barked.

They were a family, alright. The only family he ever had. With them, he might be able to do this whole teenager thing after all. He didn't even question Tomo giving him orders, but he couldn't help but jab at the assassin a little. Like any normal teenager would.

"I'm not going to call you Dad, ya know?"

Tomo nearly sprayed Sprite out of his nose. "Excuse me?"

"You heard me. Don't think I haven't noticed you and Che... er, Mom getting close. Whatever you two are, I ain't calling you Dad anytime soon."

"No worries, kid. You're far too much to handle anyway."

Then, the doorbell rang, followed by a loud, pseudo-rhythmic knock.

"I'll get it," Aubrey said.

"Psh." Che leaned back in her chair, dropped her boots on the table. "You don't even live here."

Aubrey just shrugged as she left the kitchen. "I basically do at this point."

"Hashtag adopted," Che said in her best fake cheerleader voice.

"Now that's gross." Ronald scrunched his nose and shook his head. "What is this, one of *those* videos?"

"I'm going to pretend you didn't say that, mkay?" Che glared at him, horribly unimpressed and disappointed.

Ronald blinked and sighed. "And I'm going to pretend you didn't know what I was talking about. Because you're my mom, and that's just weird."

Aubrey came back into the kitchen looking slightly concerned. Shortly after, an old friend appeared in the doorway, one Aubrey looked less than pleased to see again.

"Hikari!" Ronald hopped up and hugged the kitsune. Her tail swished, and Aubrey folded her arms across her chest. Ronald let go, scratched the back of his neck. "Erm, great to see you."

"Sup, handsome? Hey, y'all. Sorry to interrupt your gourmet meal, but we found another one of Akuma Araki's escaped ronin. Holed up in an abandoned warehouse with some pretty nasty yokai."

"Hmm," Ronald said. "Order-sanctioned raid?"

Hikari shook her head. "Of course not. After bringing so much attention to themselves when we took out Akuma, the Order is lying low. Master Oda has no idea I'm here, but someone has to eliminate this threat. I can't directly confront the samurai without risking my own standing, but a little bird tells me one Hashimoto is now a freelancer."

Tomo pushed Ronald forward, towards the center of the room. "Ronny Boy here"—he smirked at Aubrey, who blushed—"and I can handle it. You already know. Grab your stuff, kid. And your best pair of jammies. Sounds like we've got quite the job ahead of us."

Che clicked her tongue. "And who's going to drive you?"

Tomo scratched the back of his neck and looked everywhere but towards the kitchen table as he spoke. "I sorta hoped maybe you would."

"Oh yeah?"

"If it's not an imposition, of course."

Che sat silent for a moment. Then, she grinned. "I'll grab my keys."

"Can I, uh, stay here while you guys are out?" Aubrey asked.

"Of course, sweetheart." Che kissed her forehead and tousled her hair. "Make yourself at home."

"Just like you already do," Tomo added beneath his breath.

Ronald skipped off towards his bedroom. He hadn't seen any action all summer, and senior year was just around the corner. They may have given him grace after saving the school, but the admins at Normal Community High School wouldn't be thrilled if he kept running off to fight monsters. It was now or never, and he was worried he might be getting a little rusty. Making out with Aubrey and mixing new music was fun and all, but he longed to wield his katana once more.

As he pulled his swords from the plaque over his bed, he stopped to admire the second set above his computer. Jiro's. Not exactly where they belonged, but the second-best place as far as he was concerned.

By the time he got into the car, Tomo was already doting over Che, asking her a million questions.

"Nuh uh," Ronald said. "Back seat, buddy."

Tomo squeezed over the console and flopped into the middle seat, an exaggerated frown on his face. He wriggled into comfort, as far away from the kitsune as possible. Hikari winked and purred at him, causing Tomo to blush. He was clearly miserable, and Ronald soaked in every second of that misery.

"I think this will make you feel better," Ronald said as he thought about connecting his phone via an aux cord. Che's car was relatively new, and Ronald was newer yet at figuring out technology beyond ancient samurai crap.

"Dude," Hikari said, rolling her eyes. "Just connect the damn thing."

"Uh…" Ronald floundered.

The kitsune grabbed his phone from him and after a few moments, details from SoundCloud showed up on Che's dashboard.

"Did you finally finish your collab?" she asked.

"Skylar sent me his part late last night. I might tweak it a bit more when we get home, but I dig how this turned out."

The beat came in slow at first. Then, it began to pick up with the koto, a traditional Japanese harp, in the forefront.

"Dope," Tomo said.

To Ronald's utter surprise, Hikari started tapping her fingers on the headrest and bobbing her head, an expression of approval on her face. "I didn't know you were an engineer."

Then, the bars started and played them on their way to fight another Ronin samurai from Shima Gōdatsusha and his minions. Life was good, Ronald had to admit as he stared out the window, watching this free new world of his pass by and losing himself in the music. *His* music.

And after a scratchy, static intro with a faint koto playing in sporadic rhythms and a sample of some samurai's creed—from one of the old movies, no doubt—it went a little something like this:

> [intro]
> *They who meet,*
> *Must part.*
> *He who is born,*
> *Must die.*
> *Those who have fallen,*
> *Must rise.*
> *She who has suffered,*
> *Must prevail.*
>
> *As a child, stolen from his mother's breast,*
> *As a swift, soaring the clouds, adrift,*
> *Upon Shima Gōdatsusha's mountains below*
> *Her emerald forests and crystal waves, behold,*
> *A child of prophecy surfaces*
> *Forged by the fires of the Island of Usurpers*

[hook]
Ronald, the Ronin,
Slayer of Oni,
Healer of the Broken,
Hashimoto's last son,
Warrior by birth,
The Usurper Warlord's scourge.

[verse 1]
One visit to Shima Gōdatsusha,
His brother, Jiro, by his side.
Two visits to Shima Gōdatsusha,
Through lava and Akuma's army he flies.
Three visits to Shima Gōdatsusha,
Fights to the death to restore his honor.

[hook]
Ronald, the Ronin,
Slayer of Oni,
Healer of the Broken,
Hashimoto's last son,
Warrior by birth,
The Usurper Warlord's scourge.

[verse 2]
On silent feet, two brothers snuck past lines
To uncover Akuma's vision.
A mission failed, a life taken too soon.

RONALD, THE RONIN

When, finally, the chosen one returned
Through a portal on a great dragon's wings
To drive a blade through the Usurper's heart.

[hook]
Ronald, the Ronin,
Slayer of Oni,
Healer of the Broken,
Hashimoto's last son,
Warrior by birth,
The Usurper Warlord's scourge.

[verse 3]
With a skulk of Kitsune guarding his back,
And the great golden in the skies,
Ronald delved into the Usurper's spire,
His blades sharp, his vow for revenge a-fire.
Ten samurai fell to his fated blade,
Akuma's head, his journey's last end.

[hook]
Ronald, the Ronin,
Slayer of Oni,
Healer of the Broken,
Hashimoto's last son,
Warrior by birth,
The Usurper Warlord's scourge

[outro]

Ronald, the Ronin.
Yes, Ronald, the Ronin.
The Chosen One,
Ronald, the Ronin.
His chains unbroken,
It's Ronald, the Ronin.
Healer of wounds,
Bringer of peace,
Avenger of wrongs,
And master of beats,
Yes, uh-huh, you heard,
It's Ronald, the Ronin.

As his song faded, a serene calmness fell over the car's occupants. A comfortable silence, which Ronald embraced. Before facing Akuma Araki, the silences were always the loudest. Now, it seemed, he could enjoy them for what they were: restful, worthy breaks in between the hard days of life.

He still hadn't defeated his own demons. There was still the lingering anxiety, the vivid flashes of violence done unto Jiro, his father, and Officer Pact, the times where for no reason whatsoever he wanted to scream at the world at the top of his lungs. These moments of struggle, he realized, would probably never fully go away, but they were growing more and more seldom, and he was starting to learn how to face down the enemies within just as he had faced those without.

Sure, trouble *would* keep on finding him, but from now on, he'd charge headfirst, knowing there was no challenge too great for him and his swords and his family to overcome. It helped a

RONALD, THE RONIN

whole hell of a lot that he had an amazing family, now. A misfit family, sure, but the best a kid like Ronald Hashimoto could ever hope for, and more.

EPILOGUE: AFTER

She floated past the fallen samurai like a shadow possessed, her slender fingers tracing wavy lines across the stone walls. The light around her bent and broke to allow her passage through places inaccessible to others.

She crossed through the splintered doors, silent as a knife, and stabbed her way through the darkness towards her target.

She approached Akuma Araki, spat black spittle from deep within her chest onto the warlord's exposed face, and kicked her kabuto across the room, its clatter the only sound left within the fallen keep.

"This too was fated, you know? There was nothing you could have done to alter your circumstances." She knelt, tilting Akuma's stiff neck one way then the other, examining all the burn scars from when the warlord attempted to usurp the World's Eye. "Never attempt to deny prophecy, child. Never, ever, ever."

Behold, a child born of Struggle and Strife. Beware, a child born of Shima Gōdatsusha, tempered by the fires of Her trials. Sower of Chaos where there was once Order. Uprooter of the ancient Bonsai, awash in golden waves of destruction, reborn anew under a crimson dawn.

She had spoken the same words to Akuma Araki the night the World's Eye had been reborn, but no one listened to an old woman's wisdom.

"Like the Order, you never fully understood. You knew it was the boy, but you didn't realize the part you had to play—a part you played well, Kangei sa Renai."

With her foot, Minata rolled the corpse on its back. Akuma had been a benevolent master, but that was not what burned deep within her. No, it was simply that Akuma had been her master in any capacity, pulling all the strings, every day tightening the binds around Minata's wrists. She had always had a master of one ilk or another—her parents, her betrothed before he died, her own internal strife—but gods did not have masters. The World's Eye could not be bound by chain or by tongue or by whip.

Akuma Araki was wrong to try to control Minata, to have thrown her and her sisters' lives into the lion's den that was her war so haphazardly, but she had not been wrong about everything. The gold devils had brought nothing but death and destruction to Shima Gōdatsusha, and all in the name of prophecy. The people deserved justice. They deserved peace, protection, and prosperity.

They deserved revenge.

A cruel, confident smile stretched across her once-beautiful face as she closed her eyes and opened a thousand-thousand others. Black, all-seeing eyes. Watchful, knowing, obedient eyes. The scant light trapped within the room flickered and dimmed until all was void dark, but now that the veil between islands was so thin, Minata could see her way forward clearer than ever before.

A disc-shaped eye as large as the moon opened around her. It blinked and scanned, rolled in its invisible socket as it absorbed the room around it. Minata raised her arms to the ceiling, embraced the eye, and cackled as her body became a twirling, amorphous thing. Then, through the great eye's pupil, she disappeared, and it blinked and scanned one last time before it too was gone, leaving the corpse of Akuma Araki to rot alone. A swirl of cherry blossom petals blew across the dusty floor, finding stillness among the wreckage of the once-fated warlord's failed legacy.

ABOUT CURTIS

Curtis A. Deeter is an author of fantasy, science fiction, and horror. When he is not writing, he enjoys spending time with his family, discovering new music, and taste-testing craft beer at local breweries.

ACKNOWLEDGMENTS

First and foremost, a colossal thank you to Japan and Hip-Hop. *Ronald, the Ronin,* and the A Servant's Creed series, was and continues to be an ongoing education for me. Any acts of appropriation are entirely unintentional, and my appreciation for the impact both cultures have had on today's world is vast and unending.

As I delve deeper into Japanese culture, weaving my way through stories of samurai and yokai, while simultaneously attempting to learn their language (no easy feat—if you know, you know), I realize more and more what they say is true: to be truly wise is to know you know absolutely nothing. All I can do is try, and as I unravel more and more of the mysteries of folklore in Japan, so too will this series broaden its authenticity and story-telling depth.

To Hip-Hop, I am but a tertiary beneficiary of a cultural movement that has endured despite ceaseless criticism, internal strife, and the powers that be doing everything they can to "burn it all down." I am no DJ or MC. I cannot dance (even though I try sometimes), and my artistic skills beyond the written word are lacking. I did not grow up in the culture, and so for my three-plus decades of living, I have experienced it as an outsider and loved every single minute of my barely-below-surface level exposure to everything the movement has created thus far.

There are too many artists to name them all, but here is a short list of rappers and musicians whose music directly contributed to the shaping of this book:

50 Cent. "Many Men (Wish Death)" *Get Rich or Die Tryin'*, Aftermath Entertainment, 2003.

Aesop Rock. "None Shall Pass" *None Shall Pass,* Definitive Jux, 2007.

Big Boi. "Kill Jill" *Boomiverse,* featuring Killer Mike and Jeezy, Epic Records, 2017.

Bizzy Bone and AC Killer. "Warriors" *Countdown to Armageddon,* featuring Krayze Bone, CNO Records, 2020.

Bone Thugs-N-Harmony. "I Tried" *Strength & Harmony,* featuring Akon, Interscope Records, 2007.

Deltron 3030. "Do You Remember" *Event 2,* featuring Jamie Cullum, Bulk Recordings, 2013.

Eazy-E. "Creep N Crawl" *Str8 off The Streets of Muthaphukkin' Compton,* Ruthless Records, 1996.

Homebody Sandman. "Satellite" *Still Champion,* Mello Music Group, 2023.

Joyner Lucas. "ADHD" *ADHD,* Twenty Nine Music Group, 2020.

Kid Kudi. "Pursuit of Happiness" *Man on the Moon: The End of Day,* featuring Ratatat and MGMT, Universal Records, 2009.

Lil Wayne. "Days and Days" *I Am Not a Human Being II,*

featuring 2 Chainz, Young Money Entertainment, 2013.

Nate Dogg. "Nobody Does it Better" *G-Funk Classics, Vol. 1 & 2,* featuring Warren G, Dogg Foundation, 1998.

Pharoahe Monch. "Losing my Mind" *PTSD,* featuring Denaun Porter, W.A.R. Media and INgrooves, 2014.

Rob $tone "Chill Bill" *Urban Power Beats,* featuring J. Davi$ and Spooks, Sony Music Entertainment, 2019.

RZA "Trouble Shooting" *Bobby Digital and the Pit of Snakes,* featuring Shot, MNRK Records, 2022.

Tech N9ne "Face Off" *Asin9ne,* featuring Joey Cool, King Iso, and Dwayne Johnson, Strange Music, 2021.

Yasiin Bey formerly known as Mos Def. "Mathematics" *Black on Both Sides,* Rawkus Records, 1999.

I want to give a special shout-out to two indomitable female artists, whom one of my favorite characters, Che Perkins, is named after and based off of: Ché Aimee Dorval and Sa-Roc (Assata Perkins). While wildly different genre-wise, these two women kept me energized creatively and mentally while writing this book. Thank you, from the bottom of my soul, for your music.

I would be remiss if I did not use at least a little white space here to thank the team at Riverfolk Books. You took a chance on Ronald and his story, and that is a beautiful thing. What started with my horror short story, "NHesi, Unlock the Door," being picked up by their imprint, Rabid Otter, has taken me to a place I have dreamed about since I was writing StarCraft fan-fiction in elementary school. My gratitude goes out to Weaver, Alexa Lee, Freya, Maxine, Zaq, and Sebastian for their trust and hard work. Next, we just have to sell a million copies!

Before the book made its way to Riverfolk, it passed through the hands of two insightful readers: my wife, Danielle, and longtime writerly friend, Teresa. Thank you for telling me you liked my story, but thank you more for pointing out the broken parts.

And a special thank you to Emily McCosh, who brought the story to life through cherry blossoms, magic wisps, and the shadow of Akuma Araki's fortress. Your visual interpretation of my world far surpassed my expectations. Every time I look at the cover, I am reminded to actually start drawing one of these days.

Last, but not least, thank you Theo. Your encouragement and enthusiasm in all things is a constant reminder not to get too wrapped up in life's dips and dives.

Follow us:

riverfolkbooks.com

Facebook /riverfolkp

Bluesky /riverfolkbooks.bsky.social

Instagram /riverfolkp

If you want to discuss our books with other readers and maybe even the author, join our discord server using the link on our website.

www.ingramcontent.com/pod-product-compliance
Lightning Source LLC
LaVergne TN
LVHW040133080526
838202LV00042B/2891